Praise for Simon Le

'The adventure proves gripping and always surprising, and uses its historical background to perfection. A most rewarding read' *Guardian*

'The tale makes for a neat twist on the historical detective story and is packed full with details of an Aztec world at its height. A formidable debut' *Good Book Guide*

'Fascinatingly complex and unusual, providing intriguing insights into a coherent and brutal society; the language, food, customs and family. I loved the black humour' Conn Iggulden

'An exciting murder mystery mixed with a mordant sense of humour . . . one of the few novels to vividly recreate and clearly describe the glorious but bloodsoaked culture of the Aztec empire. A marvellous read' Paul Doherty

'The storyline is intriguing, with sufficient wit and humour to balance the bloodthirsty descriptions of torture and brutality that were the norm in Aztec society . . . The writing is excellent, and given the unusual setting and the intriguspect the v   Cadfael and I   sleuth' Bern

By the same author
Demon of the Air
Shadow of the Lords

About the author

Simon Levack trained as a solicitor and still works in the legal profession. *City of Spies* is his third novel. His first, *Demon of the Air*, won the Crime Writers' Association's prestigious Debut Dagger Award.

Visit <u>www.simonlevack.co.uk</u>

CITY OF
SPIES

SIMON LEVACK

POCKET
BOOKS

LONDON • SYDNEY • NEW YORK • TORONTO

First published in Great Britain by Simon & Schuster UK Ltd, 2006
This edition first published by Pocket Books, 2007
An imprint of Simon & Schuster UK
A CBS COMPANY

Extracts from 'Nezahualpilli's lament', taken from *Flower and Song: Poems
of the Aztec Peoples*, translated by Eduard Kissam & Michael Schmidt are
reproduced by kind permission of the publishers, Anvil Press Poetry.

1 3 5 7 9 10 8 6 4 2

Simon & Schuster UK Ltd
Africa House
64–78 Kingsway
London WC2B 6AH

www.simonsays.co.uk

Simon & Schuster Australia
Sydney

A CIP catalogue record for this book
is available from the British Library

ISBN-10: 1-4165-0254-8
ISBN-13: 978-1-4165-0254-8

This book is a work of fiction. Names, characters, places and incidents are
either a product of the author's imagination or are used fictitiously.
Any resemblance to actual people living or dead, is purely coincidental.

Typeset in Bembo by M Rules
Printed and bound in Great Britain
by Cox & Wyman Ltd, Reading, Berks

For Sarah and Isaac, with love

Acknowledgements

I doubt whether anybody who hasn't written a book for publication can appreciate how much authors rely on agents and editors. My name wouldn't be on the cover without the help and advice (and salesmanship!) of Jane Gregory and the rest of her team at Gregory & Co, especially Anna, for her very detailed notes. Thanks likewise to Kate Lyall Grant at Simon & Schuster for her continued encouragement and support.

And thanks, as ever, to Sarah, for her trenchant remarks and for providing me with inspiration on demand.

Author's Note

City of Spies is the third novel featuring Cemiquiztli Yaotl and set in the Mexico of the early sixteenth century, in the final years before the coming of the Conquistadors. It picks up the story of Yaotl and his friends and enemies at the point where my previous book, *Shadow of the Lords*, left them, and transports them across the waters of Lake Tetzcoco to the town of Tetzcoco, the second power in the Aztec world.

Tetzcoco was a separate kingdom linked to the Aztec city of Mexico-Tenochtitlan in an arrangement sometimes known as the Triple Alliance (the third member of the alliance was the small state of Tlacopan).

Tetzcoco was regarded as the centre of Aztec culture, renowned for its artists, its poets, its elevated form of the Aztec language Nahuatl, and its courts. However, in its last hundred years or so of independent existence, the city had a chequered history: first humbled by a rival state, Azcapotzalco, then resurgent under its great Kings Nezahualcoyotl ('Hungry Coyote') and Nezahualpilli ('Hungry Child'), but finally eclipsed by the all-powerful Aztec Emperors. After Nezahualpilli's death, the Aztecs sought to impose their own candidate on the throne, Montezuma's nephew Cacama ('Maize Ear'). This triggered a civil war, which, by the time this novel opens in the beginning of 1518 (the end of the Aztec year Twelve House), had subsided into an uneasy truce, with half the kingdom ruled, in defiance of Montezuma, by Maize Ear's half-brother, Ixtlilxochitl ('Black Flower').

This novel, then, is set against a background of political turbulence. I have imagined Tetzcoco as a place where suspicion and intrigue rule, and spies are everywhere . . .

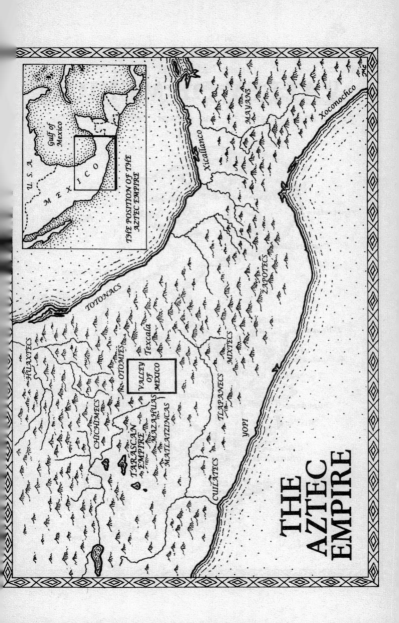

VALLEY OF MEXICO

- Citlaltepec
- Zompanco
- LAKE ZOMPANCO
- Xaltocan
- LAKE XALTOCAN
- Tepotzotlan
- Teotihuacan
- Cuauhtitlan
- Tepexpan
- Papalotla
- Tenayuca
- Tlalnepantla
- LAKE TETZCOCO
- Tetzcoco
- Tetzcotzinco
- Azcapotzalco
- Huexotla
- Tlacopan
- Tlatelolco
- Tenochtitlan
- Coatlichan
- Chapultepec
- Coatepec
- Mixóac
- Chimalhuacan
- Iztapalapan
- Coyoacan
- Tepepolco
- Mexicaltzinco
- Huitzilopchco
- Iztahuacan
- Colhuacan
- LAKE XOCHIMILCO
- LAKE CHALCO
- Chalco
- Xochimilco
- CHALCO
- Cuitlahuac
- Mixquic
- Ayotzinco

N
W E
S

0 miles 5

A Note on Nahuatl

The Aztec language, Nahuatl, is not difficult to pronounce, but is burdened with spellings based on sixteenth-century Castilian. The following note should help:

Spelling	Pronunciation
c	c as in 'Cecil' before e or i; k before a or o
ch	sh
x	sh
hu, uh	w
qu	k as in 'kettle' before e or i; qu as in 'quack' before a
tl	as in English, but where '-tl' occurs at the end of a word the 'l' is hardly sounded.

The stress always falls on the penultimate syllable.

I have used as few Nahuatl words as possible and favoured clarity at the expense of strict accuracy in choosing English equivalents. Hence, for example, I have rendered *Cihuacoatl* as 'Chief Minister', *calpolli* as 'parish', *octli* as 'sacred wine' and *maquahuitl* as 'sword', and have been similarly cavalier in choosing English replacements for most of the frequently recurring personal names. In referring to the Aztec Emperor at the time when this story is set I have used the most familiar form of his name, Montezuma, although Motecuhzoma would be more accurate.

I have used two different English words to translate the title *Huey Tlatoani*. This literally means 'Revered Speaker' and was applied to rulers, including Montezuma. I have referred to Montezuma as the 'Emperor' of Mexico, but to avoid confusion I have used 'King' for the ruler of Tetzcoco, although he was a *Huey Tlatoani* as well.

Finally, I have called the people of Mexico-Tenochtitlan 'Aztecs', although their own name for themselves was *Mexica*, 'Mexicans'.

The name of the principal character in the novel, Yaotl, is pronounced 'YAH-ot'.

The Aztec Calendar

The Aztecs lived in a world governed by religion and magic, and their rituals and auguries were in turn ordered by the calendar.

The solar year, which began in our February, was divided into eighteen twenty-day periods (often called 'months'). Each month had its own religious observances associated with it; often these involved sacrifices, some of them human, to one or more of the many Aztec gods. At the end of the year were five 'Useless Days' that were considered profoundly unlucky.

Parallel to this ran a divinatory calendar of 260 days divided into twenty groups of thirteen days (sometimes called 'weeks'). The first day in the 'week' would bear the number 1 and one of twenty names – Reed, Jaguar, Eagle, Vulture, and so on. The second day would bear the number 2 and the next name in the sequence. On the fourteenth day the number would revert to 1 but the sequence of names continued seamlessly, with each combination of names and numbers repeating itself every 260 days.

A year was named after the day in the divinatory calendar on which it began. For mathematical reasons these days could bear only one of four names – Reed, Flint Knife, House and Rabbit – combined with a number from 1 to 13. This produced a cycle of fifty-two years at the beginning and end of which the solar and divinatory calendars coincided. The Aztecs called this period a 'Bundle of Years'.

Every day in a Bundle of Years was the product of a unique combination of year, month and date in the divinatory calendar, and so had, for the Aztecs, its own individual character and religious and magical significance.

1

In my first few days in the slave-dealers' warehouse, I sought to escape my tormentors. I cowered, with my back pressed hard against the stout bars at the back of my wooden cage, and tried to ward off their blows by putting my hands over my face, shielding my eyes by making fists over them like a sobbing child. It never worked. The cage was too small for me to stand up in, let alone dodge the long canes they prodded me with, and if I managed to shield my face for a moment they would only aim for some other delicate, fleshy part of me. Besides, they did not have to use sticks. On one occasion a whole bag of ground-up maguey thorns was tipped over me, and then all they had to do was stand back and laugh as I writhed, wept and scratched myself bloody in the midst of a blinding, itching cloud. And I was spat at and had excrement thrown over me through the bars, although soon I was so badly soiled with my own ordure that I barely noticed.

After a while I stopped cowering. I crouched, naked, in the middle of my tiny space, neither inviting the blows nor flinching from them, neither watching nor ignoring the faces leering at me, neither marking the passage of the days nor trying to escape them by falling asleep. Sleeping was not much better than being conscious, anyway. Being asleep just meant waking up again, discovering afresh my wounds and bruises and the agony of limbs I never had room to straighten. Worst of all, it meant dreams: nightmares about the fate that awaited me.

'The fire sacrifice,' my master's steward crowed, standing in front of my cage just after the top had been shut over me and weighted down with a rock. 'Did you ever see anyone die that way? Horrible, wasn't it?'

'Yes,' I said shortly, in answer to both questions. The victims, bound hand and foot, would be dragged up the steps of the pyramid of Teccalco to where a huge brazier had been set up on its summit. They must have felt its heat as they were carried around it, and their terrified faces, whitened with chalk to give them a deathly cast, used to glow pink in its red light. They rarely made a sound, and in the moment when each one was about to die a strange silence would descend on the whole scene, disturbed only by the crackling of the brazier. Then, after four unhurried, much-practised swings, the priests holding the trussed captive would toss him alive on to the coals.

While he twisted and shrieked and his skin blackened and split, there would be music and dancing. A young man dressed as a squirrel would prance around the fire, whistling through his fingers, while another, got up as a bat, shook a pair of gourd rattles as gaily as an entertainer at a feast.

I remembered especially how one brave man had died. He had not screamed when the priests threw him on to the fire and made no sound even when they hooked him out again, still alive, and let him tumble on to the ground, scattering white-hot coals around him. He had made a noise only when they tried to pick him up and a long strip of burned skin peeled away from his back. Then, through what was left of his throat, he had forced a strange, keening cry, like a sick animal's whimpering, that had ended only when he was stretched over the sacrificial stone and the priest was tearing the heart out of his chest for an offering to the god of fire.

'I bet that'll be it,' the steward said. 'Which festival is it? Come on, Yaotl, you used to be a priest. You must know.'

'They kill some that way at the Festival of the Fall of the Fruit,' I mumbled automatically, 'and some others at the Arrival of the Gods.'

'Lots of time to look forward to it, then!' I had been shut in my cage in the middle of winter, and both the festivals I had mentioned took place in late summer.

'You know that won't happen to me. The fire sacrifice is reserved for captured enemy warriors. I'm not a warrior; I'm a slave.'

'Oh, I'm sure the priests will make an exception. What if there hasn't been a war lately and captives are hard to get? They could throw you in as a makeweight. It's like the way a woman ekes out a stew sometimes, hiding dog meat under a layer of turkey. I don't suppose the god will notice the difference.'

I said nothing. I knew what he was telling me was probably true, but I preferred not to think about it, far less discuss it.

'Of course, you're assuming you're going to be bought by civilized people like Aztecs. Maybe it'll be some horrible barbarians. Some of those savages are capable of anything: the Matlatzinca, for instance. They've got this way of crushing their victims slowly in a net. Very messy!'

'Maybe I won't be bought as a sacrifice. Someone might want to put me to work. Lord Tlilpotonqui did, after all.'

The steward's only answer to that was to walk away, laughing.

My master, Lord Tlilpotonqui, whose name meant Feathered in Black, was being careful.

He was the second most powerful man in the World. He was the *Cihuacoatl*, priest of the goddess of that name, and also

Chief Priest, Chief Justice and Chief Minister of the Aztecs. Within the Aztec capital, Mexico, only the Emperor Montezuma's voice carried greater weight. All the same, he was not all-powerful. Montezuma did not trust him, with good reason. He was not beyond the reach of the law. And he could not, any more than could the most miserable serf stirring shit into a muddy field with his digging stick, afford to ignore the will of the gods.

I was his lordship's slave. Aztec law looked remarkably kindly upon slaves, because we were the creatures of Tezcatlipoca, the Smoking Mirror, the most powerful and dangerous god of them all.

Tezcatlipoca was the lord of chance, of unlooked-for good fortune and unforeseen calamity. He was known as the Mocker for his capriciousness, as Him Whose Slaves We Are for his arbitrary toying with human lives, as the Enemy on both hands. Gamblers at the *Patolli*-mat and the Ball-court feared and courted him, and he was naturally the foe of the rich and the friend of those with nothing to lose – and who had less to lose than a slave, another man's possession?

In a perverse way, it was the Smoking Mirror's patronage of slaves that explained my present predicament.

I had done more than enough to exhaust Lord Feathered in Black's patience. I had run away more than once, disobeyed him, connived with those he saw as his enemies, even assaulted members of his household. If ever a master had reason to ill-treat a slave, he had, but neither human nor divine law allowed anything beyond a beating. The very worst thing he could do to me, and then only after having three occasions to admonish me formally, before witnesses, was to sell me. And that, I had foolishly hoped when we finally confronted each other after my last escapade, might just be enough to save me.

He had been sitting in the middle of a courtyard, on a high-backed cane chair placed there for him by his servants: an ancient man, whose sunken cheeks and swollen, liver-spotted hands belied the bright, feral gleam in his eyes as he surveyed me. He was dressed in a long cotton cloak, embroidered with butterflies, in a design repeated on the dangling tassels of his breechcloth and echoed in the little jewelled ornaments on his earplugs, labret and sandals, every item chosen to mark him out as a great lord. Around him stood a squad of warriors, huge men, every one of them clad from head to toe in green cotton and with his hair piled high on top of his head and cascading down his back in the style of Otomies, the fiercest and most pitiless of Aztec warriors. Between two of the Otomies, not held by them physically but plainly having no more chance of escape than a mouse caught between the paws of a jaguar, stood the courtyard's owner, a rich merchant, and his daughter. Their names were Icnoyo – 'Kindly' – and Oceloxochitl, or 'Tiger Lily'. The woman and I had been lovers once, for a very short while. As I looked at her now, seeming very small and far away across her father's courtyard, my feelings were a strange blend of pity and resentment at the hold she still had over me. My master had known taking her hostage would bring me to him.

'You have to let them go,' I said. I had decided, when I walked through the entrance to the courtyard, that I was not going to prostrate myself before him, as I normally would. If I were to survive this meeting it could only be as his equal, not as his possession.

The old man regarded me steadily, his eyes unblinking and betraying no hint of surprise at my insolence. 'Let them go, Yaotl? What do you mean?'

'They are merchants. Even if they had done anything wrong, it would be for their own courts to try them. You have no authority here . . .'

The old man said nothing. The thinnest of smiles barely touched the corners of his mouth before one of his henchmen delivered his answer for him, and I was on my knees with my hands in the dust in front of me, choking and gasping for breath as I fought to recover from the blow between my shoulder blades that had felled me.

I half turned to look at my assailant. A single eye glared back at me. I felt sick at the sight of it, and of the face it nestled in: a wreck of a face, half of it reduced by a sword cut years before to a featureless glistening slab of scar tissue.

The captain of the Otomies grinned mirthlessly back at me.

'That's where you belong in the presence of your betters, you scum – on your knees! My lord, why don't I cut his legs off so we don't have to remind him again?'

I twisted my head anxiously around to look at my master again. He was stroking his chin thoughtfully, as though considering the captain's idea.

'I'm sure that won't be necessary,' he murmured. 'As for the merchant and his daughter – really, Yaotl, you surprise me. Let them go? From their own house, where they were kind enough to receive me and my friends as their guests? What an idea! Of course, if Kindly here were to tell me I was no longer welcome . . .'

He did not deign to look around. If he had he would have seen the woman start forward, as if to protest, only to be halted by her father kicking her ankle. Already hunched over with age, he had his eyes so downcast that he seemed on the verge of toppling over. No doubt he would have kneeled, if only he had been able to bend his knees far enough. 'Of course, my lord, whatever meagre hospitality my pitiful household can extend to you is yours . . .'

'Shut up,' said Lord Feathered in Black.

'Thank you, my lord.'

'So much for the merchant, slave,' my master said to me. 'What do you suggest I do with you?'

'Sell me.'

'Sell you?' He sounded surprised or even disappointed. I dared not try to stand for fear of the violent presence at my back, and from my position on the ground I had to crane my neck awkwardly to see my master's face. There was no expression on it whatever.

'Sell you?' he repeated. 'How unimaginative!'

I shuddered at the thought of the kinds of torment his imagination might run to. 'What else? I've given you cause. You've had to admonish me three times. You can be rid of me . . .'

Suddenly the Chief Minister laughed. It was a harsh explosion that burst from his lips in a cloud of spittle, followed by a fit of dry, painful coughing.

'I can be rid of you any time I want to, slave!' he gasped when he had his breath back. 'Never forget it! But as for selling you . . . Oh, I know what you've got in mind. You think there's a risk you'll be bought for sacrifice, but there's always the chance someone might have a use for slave with a brain, a bit of initiative, who can read and write, and so what if he needs keeping an eye on, he's still cheap at twice the price — that's it, isn't it? That's what you think!'

'B–but you've no choice!' I spluttered. 'You can't do anything else to me. That's what the law says. I know my rights!'

Lord Feathered in Black was capable of rages that could make Mount Popacatepetl in full eruption seem tame, but he was never more dangerous than when he lowered his voice, and when he spoke next he was barely audible.

'Don't tell me about the law or your rights, Yaotl. I happen to be the Chief Justice of Mexico. I know the law better than anybody. I know exactly what you are entitled to and what you aren't.' He gestured to the warrior standing behind me with the merest nod of his head. 'Captain, perhaps you'd care to take this slave away now?'

Suddenly two massive hands were under my shoulders, almost yanking my arms from their sockets as they hauled me to my feet.

'Wait!' I cried. 'You can't do this! It's against the law! There are witnesses!' In desperation I looked imploringly towards the old man and his daughter; but the warriors flanking them were watching them too, and they kept their eyes fixed on the ground in front of them.

Then I was being dragged backwards towards the courtyard entrance, with my heels scraping along the ground and my eyes fixed on my master's face as he leaned contentedly back in his chair.

'You'll be confined, of course,' he called after me. 'No court would refuse me that after you've run away three times. But I won't ill-treat you. As if I would!'

The moment we had turned the corner and were out of the Chief Minister's sight I was face down on the ground, my head in the captain's hands, my nose streaming blood from where he had ground it into the dirt.

'He said he wouldn't ill-treat you,' the voice in my ear rasped. 'Couldn't promise nobody else would, though, could he?'

Lord Feathered in Black was true to his word. He never came to peer into my cage and prod its inmate with a stick, and nor did any member of his household. Even his steward did nothing more than gloat. It was the Otomies, who did my master's bidding but were not his men, whose faces peered at me through the wooden bars so often that I saw their grins and heard their laughter in my sleep. As their captain had pointed out, his lordship was not answerable for what they did to me.

And they needed no inducement from him to torture and humiliate me. I had once made a fool of the captain, duping him and leading him into the midst of a hostile crowd of foreigners, people he saw as his inferiors, from whom he had only just managed to get away with his life. He was not a man to pass up a chance of revenge.

Once, while the monstrous one-eyed warrior was standing in front of my cage, smoking a tube full of coarse tobacco and blowing the fumes into my face while he fiddled with the knot in his breechclout, I wondered aloud why nobody had posed an obvious question.

'I know this is all on account of my son. How come none of you has asked me where he is?'

'Why would we bother?'

'Why? Because he stole from my master, and he knows things about him that old Black Feathers can't afford to have anyone know. And he got away from you, when my master sent you after him. And now you've got me locked in this cage, but you don't seem to want to know about him any more.'

'All right,' the Captain grunted. 'Where is he, then?'

'I don't know.'

'Thought not. You're not that stupid, are you? You gave yourself up so he had time to get away. Any fool could see that much. Not much point doing that only to let us torture the boy's whereabouts out of you, was there? No, I know you don't know where he is. Don't give a toss, either. We can make you suffer enough for both of you . . . Aah, at last!'

The knot had finally come undone. I shut my eyes and held my breath as a hot, stinking jet of urine soused my face. But I smiled, because at least I knew my son was safe.

The lad's name was Quimatini, which meant 'Nimble', and it suited him. He was young – about fifteen – but smart beyond his years and agile, and I was confident that, while the Chief Minister and his tame warriors were congratulating themselves on my capture, he was running as fast and as far as he could. He would survive, I told myself. He was used to living on his wits. His mother, a prostitute named Miahuaxihuitl, had borne him – unknown to me – far away from Mexico, and he had grown up among the Tarascan barbarians beyond the mountains in the West. He still had a marked Tarascan accent. After enduring the gods knew what privations, he had come back to Mexico, alone, mainly to look for me. There, like so many youngsters before him, he had fallen victim to the procurers and perverts who haunted the marketplaces, and to one brutal predator in particular, a young merchant named Ocotl. But he had survived that too.

During the days and nights I spent huddled in a remote corner of a slave-dealer's dingy kennel near the great marketplace of Tlatelolco, I kept Nimble in my head and the thought of him kept me sane. Whatever happened to me, I told myself, he would carry on, and now there was nothing else that mattered.

It was hard to care that much even about Lily. My master might bluster and threaten her and her father, but in the end there was little even he could do in the face of the immense power and wealth of the merchant class. She should be all right, I knew, and when I thought about her that pleased me, but what had happened between us was too complicated for a man being slowly tormented to death to hold it all in his head. We had shared a sleeping mat once, but I could never forget how it had been her own child – that same Ocotl, her Shining Light – who had dragged my son into his dangerous scheme to cheat my master, and so imperilled all our lives. Nor, I supposed, could she ever forget that it had been my brother and I who had killed her boy.

So all the while, as I squatted in the middle of my cage, I kept my son's face behind my closed eyes, and if the half-smile that the sight of him brought to my lips only made the jeering warriors outside hit me harder, I was past caring.

2

'Here.'

I looked up wearily at the sound of the slave-dealer's voice.

After dragging me away from the old merchant's courtyard, the Otomies had taken me to a dingy warehouse near the great market of Tlatelolco. The dealers who owned the place seemed to have fallen on hard times, judging by the state of their filthy, frayed cloaks and breechcloths and their constant bickering with one another. Their names were Itzcuintli and Cuetzpallin: Dog and Lizard. My first sight of this surly, snarling pair had seemed to confirm my worst fears. Nobody who bought from them would be overly particular about what he got. The chances were the buyer would not expect his purchase to live long enough for it to matter.

The man standing in front of my cage now was Dog. His tone was the one he used at feeding-time, to warn me that he was about to throw a mouldy tortilla in my direction. Because of the smell coming from my cage, however, he normally stood so far away that as often as not he missed, or else the stale, stiff bread bounced off the bars and landed out of my reach, so that I could only watch hungrily as the rats dragged it away.

This morning, however, he stood directly in front of me, although his nose wrinkled in disgust, and the bread he pushed towards me was soft and still warm from the griddle.

'But this is fresh!' I croaked, before tearing off a lump and cramming it into my mouth.

'Yes,' he confirmed, backing away.

'What's going on?'

'It's a big day for you. Lord Feathered in Black obviously thinks you've been here long enough that there's no chance of anyone buying you for your looks. You're going on sale!'

I stared at him stupidly, dribbling crumbs.

'That's so you can at least stand up,' he added, indicating the remains of the tortilla in my hand. 'Otherwise you'll probably choke when we put the collar on you. Get on with it. We haven't much time.'

I had barely finished my meal when the stones were lifted from the roof of my cage and I was hauled out and dropped on the floor. When I tried to stand, my legs buckled and my head spun, and I promptly toppled over.

That earned me a sharp kick in the side. 'Come on, get up! We're all waiting for you!'

Somehow I got to my knees and then unsteadily to my feet. I looked wonderingly around me, until I caught sight of my fellow slaves and understood the slave-dealer's comment about the collar.

I had been kept well away from the rest of the merchandise, presumably for fear that they might catch something from me, and so I had not seen my companions before. There were two of them, both tall men, probably captured warriors. It was easy to see how they had come to be sold off cheaply, because they both had dreadful wounds. One had lost an arm, almost certainly hacked off in battle, and judging by its blood-soaked wrappings the stump had not healed well. The other had gaping, ragged holes in his earlobes and lower lip. I guessed he had been wearing a labret and earplugs when he was taken and some looter had torn them out without taking the trouble to unclasp them first. I wondered what had become of the warrior who had captured him. Perhaps he had died himself. I would have expected him to have guarded his captive jealously, for there was not much prestige to be earned presenting the gods with a badly disfigured offering.

They were attached to each end of a wooden slave-collar, a long pole to which they were fastened by ropes bound tightly around their necks. A third, as yet unused, length of rope dangled from the middle of the pole. I was meant to go between them, but there was one obvious problem.

'They're both a head taller than me,' I protested, while a relatively clean breechcloth was put around my loins for decency's sake. 'I'll throttle!'

'I'd have thought that was the least of your worries,' growled the slave-dealer as he tied me up. 'If you stand on tiptoe and they stoop, you'll be all right. Comfy, everybody?'

What do you say to two strangers with whom you have nothing in common except that you have all been lashed to the same piece of wood and are likely to suffer the same unpleasant death? 'My name's Yaotl,' I ventured.

The man on my left with the missing arm said: 'So what?' The man on my right said nothing. It must have been hard to get words past that shredded lip.

'Where are you from?' I tried again.

'Where do you think, you piece of Aztec shit?'

I looked at both men again and understood. They were from Texcala. They wore their hair thickly braided in the style favoured by warriors from that benighted province. I sighed in resignation as I realized that I had been roped together with two of my people's sworn enemies. Texcala was an impoverished place that the Aztecs had never bothered to subdue. Instead we made war on them continually, to provide the gods with sacrifices and our own warriors with much-needed practice.

Texcalans hated all Aztecs, naturally. These two were not going to make an exception for me just because we were all tied together.

'So, er, what happened to you, then?' I asked nervously.

'Mind your own business!'

As if that were a signal, both Texcalans straightened up and suddenly I was hanging by my neck, with my mouth open like a hungry chick's and my legs kicking desperately in midair.

A cane cracked across the Texcalan warrior's back. 'Behave yourselves!' Dog shouted, and then my feet were back on the ground again and I was stumbling towards the doorway, much of the time, as I had been advised, on tiptoe.

I decided against trying to start any more conversations.

I emerged from the gloom of the slave-dealers' warehouse into brilliant sunshine. The sky was clear of clouds and was the pure, bottomless blue that only people who, like the Aztecs, live high up in the mountains ever truly get to know.

After all the time I had spent in the dark, I found myself surrounded by so much light and colour that my eyes had to squint. I had forgotten how brightly the whitewashed walls of the buildings gleamed and how deep was the indigo of the canals. I watched a duck paddling idly by and wondered why it was going so fast. It was the first animal I had seen, besides the rats, since my capture.

A canoe took us to the marketplace, where we somehow stumbled through the early-morning crowds to Dog's and Lizard's pitch. Lurching uncertainly from side to side as we were, it was surprising that none of us bumped into anybody, but people got smartly out of our way. Either the sight or the smell of me must have been enough to ward them off.

Trading had begun by the time we arrived. We were shoved

into a corner and told to squat and keep quiet. 'We'll sell these last,' Dog told his partner. 'In the meantime, I don't want them putting customers off the rest of the stock!'

Lizard glanced sideways at the three of us. 'I never understood what was up with that one in the middle. He was a bit scrawny when you got him, and he'd been roughed up a bit, but you might have made something of him. Didn't I hear you say he could read and write?'

'More trouble than he was worth, though, I gather. But old Black Feathers was pretty clear about what he wanted. Starvation rations and not to bat an eyelid if he got some funny visitors. Not to go on sale until he looks like something a dog's sicked up.' He seemed oblivious to the pun on his own name. 'Who are we to question the Chief Minister? Anyway, he was practically giving him to us. We keep what we get for him, remember? In the meantime, like I said, just keep the three of them out of sight . . .'

As I looked around me, at my fellow slaves and at the customers looking at them, feeling their muscles and peering into their mouths, sometimes haggling with the slave-dealers but more often walking away, I suddenly felt more despondent than I had in my cage. At least when the Otomies had mocked and abused me they had been treating me as an individual, albeit one they loathed and despised. For all Dog and Lizard and their customers cared, we might as well have been planks of wood or strips of cooked meat. 'It's not supposed to be like this,' I muttered to myself.

'What are you talking about?' growled the one-armed Texcalan, to my surprise: for a moment I had forgotten we were still tied together.

'The market. Being sold as a slave. It should be a formal affair. That's what it was like for me the first time, anyway. When I sold myself to Lord Feathered in Black, I had four witnesses and the money counted out in front of me. Twenty large cloaks, enough to live on for a year. All very solemn.'

The Texcalan replied with a non-committal grunt. His companion spoke, or tried to. I could not understand the words his ruined mouth was struggling to form, but the one-armed man interpreted them for me. 'He wants to know how you got to be a slave in the first place.'

'To keep myself in drink.'

He laughed. It was an ugly, hollow sound.

'No, you don't understand,' I protested, stung into justifying myself. 'I used to be a priest, you see, and . . .'

'You Aztecs must be a slacker lot than we thought, then. Since when did you let your priests drink sacred wine?'

'We don't. It's a capital crime for a priest to be drunk unless there's a good reason. But I'd already been thrown out of the priesthood, and the judges . . .' I hesitated as the memory reared up behind my eyes, and once again I saw, for an instant, the crowded square in front of the palace and heard the sickening crunch of cudgels hitting the heads of my fellow prisoners. 'The judges decided to be merciful, in my case,' I concluded in a low voice.

The laughter came again. 'Oh, this is priceless!' the one-armed warrior cried, slapping his thigh. 'Did you hear that?' he called across to his companion. 'Did you hear what we're roped to? A failed priest, a failed drunk and failed slave! We're in good company here, aren't we?'

'And you two are doing so much better for yourselves, of course!' I spat back at him resentfully.

'That's war,' the Texcalan replied indifferently. 'One day you meet a man who's bigger or luckier than you. So what? We'll get a flowery death, we'll dance around the Sun as he rises every morning and then we'll come back as hummingbirds or butterflies. That suits me. What have you got coming to you?'

I hung my head. He was right. What was going to happen to him and his comrade was only what all warriors anticipated: death in battle or under a sacrificial knife. If they had not been so badly disfigured they might have been able to look forward to a last fight, too, against hand-picked Aztec warriors at the Festival of the Flaying of Men. Even with their wounds, it was hard to see what they were doing among such a crowd of weary, broken wretches.

And what a crowd we were! There were many forms of slavery, and Aztecs submitted to it for many different reasons. A field hand or labourer might find himself short of work and food, for example, while a family with too many mouths to feed might sell a child's services on the understanding that they would redeem him or replace him with a younger brother or sister when he grew up. In every case a fair bargain was struck and the slave or his parents got something out of it, such as the twenty large cloaks I had received. Discerning customers were prepared to pay well for a sturdy, healthy, intelligent worker.

The briefest glance at their stock-in-trade was enough to confirm to me that Dog and Lizard were not in that sort of market. I was surrounded by a miscellaneous collection of failed gamblers being disposed of by their creditors, thieves being sold to recover the value of what they had stolen, and foreigners, captives, like the two I was roped to, too clumsy or ugly to be of much use even as sacrifices.

There were some, especially merchants, who would pay as much as forty or sixty large cloaks merely for the privilege and prestige of having a fine-looking slave dance and die for them at an important festival. I doubted the lot of us would fetch more than thirty at most.

I was watching a young girl trying to show off her skills with a spindle. She was trying to balance it on end in a little clay bowl while she wound the coarse fibre on to it, but it kept toppling over. Every time this happened, one of the dealers would lean over and clout her ear, eliciting a little sob of pain and frustration. The customer, an elderly woman, decided there were no bargains here after all and walked away.

'Now look what you've done!' Dog snapped, hitting the unfortunate girl again. Her borrowed skirt and blouse – put on her for show, and to be stripped off her again the moment she was sold – were too large and made her look smaller and more wretched than ever as she huddled inside them, shrinking in silence from the blows and rebukes. 'At this rate we'll never get rid of any of you! What is it? Do you like your cage so much you want to be put back in it? I can . . .Oh, what do you want?'

The last words were addressed to someone standing in front of the slave-dealers' pitch, looking curiously at their wares. I could just about see him between the backs of two of the men on sale in front of me. I caught a glimpse of a nondescript face, shoulder-length, unornamented hair and a short, plain cloak before I saw the stranger's eyes and noticed with a start that they seemed to be staring straight into my own.

The man had the look of a commoner, or perhaps a well-treated slave. There was something familiar about him, but I could not remember where I might have seen him before.

Lizard elbowed his partner aside. 'Idiot,' he muttered. 'Is that any way to talk to a customer? Sir, what can I interest you in? I've got spinners, embroiderers, labourers. You want someone cheap to help manure your fields, I've got just what you need here . . .'

'How much for that one at the back?'

'Dancers? I've got dancers . . . My drummer's gone off to buy himself a bowl of snails, but as soon as he's back I'll put them through their paces . . . Which one?'

'Over there, tied to the collar, between the one-armed man and one with all the scars. How much?'

I caught my breath as I realized what was happening. The transaction that was going to seal my fate was about to take place.

Lizard gave an embarrassed cough. 'For him? Um . . . He's not for sale, he's . . . er, the three of them, they come as a set. Special purchase.'

I stared at him. What was he talking about? I could not understand what the Texcalans and I could possibly have to do with one another.

The customer was undeterred. 'Well, all right. What do you want for the three of them, then?'

Dog butted in. 'No, you don't understand. We can't let them go to just anybody, because – well – because . . .'

His voice tailed off, but I could have completed the sentence for him. I had just worked out what was going on. I was supposed to be bought by some stooge of my master's. Lord Feathered in Black could not have me killed himself, but I realized there was nothing to stop him encouraging someone else to have me sacrificed in the nastiest fashion possible.

Regardless of the way the movement tightened the rope around my neck, I slumped forward in despair, not unlike the girl with the spindle. A small part of me had been clinging to the remote hope that I might be bought for something other than a hideous death at the top of a pyramid, but now I saw how illusory that was.

'I'll give you twenty capes.'

Lizard gasped. He stared at the man before recollecting himself just in time to respond in a weak voice: 'Each?'

The man said nothing.

Dog plucked urgently at his colleague's cloak. 'Careful!' he hissed. 'Remember what his lordship said . . .'

'I know, I know, but twenty capes . . .'

'Thirty.'

Now it was the stranger's turn to start and stare.

The new offer had come from someone standing behind him. I could just make out a tall figure with his hair piled up over his head in the fashion we called 'pillar of stone'. It was the style of a seasoned warrior.

My stomach lurched as I thought of the Otomies. Was this one of the captain's men? The hair was not quite right for an Otomi, though, and the voice was not one of those I had heard taunting me every day for as long as I could remember.

The commoner scowled at the newcomer. 'All right. Thirty each!'

'A hundred for the lot, then.' The big man shouldered his way forward to stand next to his rival. His bright red netted cape, long blue labret and eagle feather headband showed that he had taken at least five captives in war and was reckoned a great fighter. And I suddenly realized that there was something vaguely familiar about him as well, although again I could not place it.

The two slave-dealers looked at each other, slack-jawed. They plainly had no idea what to do and were not helped by the fact that a small crowd of curious spectators was beginning to gather, drawn by this impromptu auction. After a morning spent desperately trying to attract customers, suddenly they had more than they knew what to do with.

Eventually Lizard turned to the bidders. He sighed regretfully. 'Look, I'm sorry, but it's not that simple. I can't let these men go to just anybody, I told you. I've strict instructions about what they can be sold for, you see . . .'

'These wouldn't be any use for anything other than a cheap sacrifice,' snapped the warrior.

'Well, that's it, you see. They have to be sold for sacrifice.

And besides, I've already got a buyer.' So my suspicion about what Lord Feathered in Black was up to had been right.

'Will he pay a hundred?'

'Well, no.'

'I'll match that,' the commoner cried suddenly. 'And I promise you, they'll all die. Slowly.'

'How?' Lizard asked suspiciously.

The man hesitated. 'How? Er . . . arrows. You know, when the priests string them up and shoot them full of holes as an offering to the rain-god.'

Beside me, my Texcalan friend muttered: 'You Aztec bastard.'

I was not sure whether he meant me, the slave-dealer or the commoner, but he had cause. The arrow sacrifice was perhaps even more unpleasant than the fire sacrifice, because there was no quick, clean kill with a flint knife at the end. The idea was to make the victim's blood spurt violently on the ground from as many wounds as possible, to resemble the rain the priests were trying to encourage. They would keep us alive for as long as they could, shooting small bird arrows into our arms and legs, until we stopped wriggling and bled to death.

'Why these three?'

'They're ideal. The big ones are for the novices, for practice. The runt in the middle will be harder to hit, a challenge, better sport for the more experienced archer.'

'Hang on,' the warrior growled. 'I can do better than that. And I bid a hundred first, remember.'

The slave-dealers were speechless. It was left to a small boy at the front of the rapidly growing crowd, a lad too young even to be wearing a breechcloth under his short brown cape, to call out: 'Go on, then, what are you going to do to them?'

My fellow slave with the ragged lip and ears uttered a dangerous noise in the back of his throat. I wondered nervously if the two Texcalans were about to launch themselves at the crowd, dragging me with them into the middle of a one-sided fight, but neither moved.

'Cut their hearts out, of course.'

'Why is that better?' Lizard asked. 'That happens to nearly all sacrifices.'

'Because the people I represent are Mayans, that's why. They don't slice cleanly through the breastbone like Aztecs; they go in under the ribcage. So they'll have to pull their guts out of the way first! Only it takes practice, see. Very particular, their gods are, and their priests don't do nearly as many as ours, so they need some live bodies to hone their skills on before trying the real thing.'

'All the same, Lizard,' Dog murmured, 'one hundred cloaks . . .'

'Look, do you want the money or not?'

'I'll go to a hundred and five!'

The big man's eyes widened as if in shock. The slave-dealers looked at him expectantly, but he said nothing. For a distinguished warrior he looked strangely unsure of himself. He stared at the ground, then shot a look of hatred at his rival, and finally turned his back, wrapping his cloak around him.

At last he said softly: 'I can't go that high.'

'They're mine, then!' the successful bidder crowed.

The other looked over his shoulder, straight at me. He seemed about to say something but then, apparently thinking better of it, pushed his way through the crowd and left.

The slave-dealers looked at each other. 'What do you think?' said Lizard.

'A hundred and five,' Dog repeated dreamily. He must have been thinking that this was far more than he had expected to make all day.

'Yes, but what about old Black Feathers?'

'He won't mind, will he? Look, the arrow sacrifice is pretty nasty. And think of the money! We could restock! We could clear out all this rubbish and start again!'

His colleague looked at their customer, who was waiting patiently for them to finish their wrangling. I looked at him too. I was still wondering where I might have seen him before, and trying to guess what he could possibly be up to.

Would anyone really pay a hundred and five large cloaks just to have me and my companions perforated with arrows?

Eventually Lizard said: 'You've got the money?'

3

The cloaks must have come from another stall in the marketplace, because they arrived in no time. They were formally counted out into five lots of twenty and one of five, and then we were released into our new owner's custody. The men who had brought the cloaks escorted us as we followed our mysterious buyer through the marketplace, with the crowds parting and swirling around us as we staggered forward.

'Hurry up! We've no time to waste!'

I could barely keep up. Most of the time my legs were paddling uselessly in the air as the slave-collar, hoisted on the necks of my two huge companions, dragged me clear of the ground. I could not breathe except on the rare occasions when my feet hit the earth, and then I was too busy taking gulps of air to speak. Just once I managed to blurt out: 'Where are we going?'

'The canal,' the man in front of us told me shortly. 'There's a canoe waiting.' A broad waterway enabled merchants to bring their boats right into the marketplace.

'A canoe?' I echoed.

'Just shut up and move, won't you?' he snapped. His head kept moving sharply from side to side, as if he were afraid someone would spring out from one of the market stalls as we passed and attack us. Nobody did, but the moment he looked straight ahead he gave a cry of alarm and froze in his tracks.

There was no way I and my two fellow slaves, dragged forward under our own weight, could stop fast enough to avoid running him down. I hit him square in the back, and he sprawled in the dust, giving me a momentary glimpse of what had brought him up short before the wooden collar cracked into the nape of my neck and the three of us who were lashed to it tumbled on top of him.

While my head rang from the blow and I struggled to get up, what I had just seen hung in front of my eyes, as vivid as a feather mosaic suspended on a wall. It might as well have been a picture, I told myself, because it could not be real.

We were almost at one of the entrances to the marketplace, a wide gap in its long, colonnaded wall carefully guarded by the market police. Several of these men were engaged in what looked like a heated argument with a group of warriors, and one of the warriors was the man whose bid had just failed to secure me and my companions. But it was the man at the centre of the group who had attracted my attention: the man wearing a distinctive long yellow cloak with a red border, with his hair bound with white cotton ribbons, his face stained black like a priest's and fine leather sandals on his feet.

'It can't be,' I muttered thickly as I forced myself up on to my elbows and once again took the weight of the slave-collar on my neck. 'Mamiztli?' Aloud I swore at the two men who had been threatening to hang me by the neck before and whose weight was now holding me down. 'Come on, get up! What's the matter with you?'

'Can't,' growled the one on my left. 'Only got one arm, remember? Why should I, anyway? Might as well die here. You filthy Aztec . . .'

'Oh, shut up.'

Just then the man in the yellow cloak caught sight of me.

His jaw dropped, and then he was moving, shoving aside two policemen as he strode through the gateway towards me.

'Yaotl! It is you! Look, I'm sorry. I told that idiot Ollin I'd pay a hundred large cloaks to get you out of this and the fool thought that meant he wasn't allowed to go any higher. I'm really sorry. There's nothing I can do . . .'

For a moment I thought I must have been mistaken. The man standing over me, babbling almost incoherently about how sorry he was, looked exactly like my elder brother: Mamiztli, the Mountain Lion, the fearless warrior, the man who had fought his way up from nothing, whose prowess had been rewarded with one of the highest ranks a commoner could aspire to: *Atenpanecatl*, Guardian of the Waterfront. He even had the harsh, barking voice, so suitable for shouting orders. However, he did not talk like him. I had never known Lion apologize to anybody, least of all his younger brother, whom he normally belittled every chance he got.

That explained why the warrior who had been bidding for me had looked familiar. He was one of my brother's bodyguards.

'I wish I could help . . .'

'You can,' I said.

'How?' he asked eagerly.

'Get your men to lift this pole up that we're all tied to before it breaks my neck!'

Two warriors rushed to our aid, brushing aside the feeble protests of the policemen, much as my brother had. It occurred to me that Lion was going to have to get this resolved quickly: neither he nor any other official from Tenochtitlan had any jurisdiction in the marketplace, which was controlled by merchants and had its own police force and its own courts. If anybody suspected him of trying to steal anyone else's property here – even if the property was his own brother – the consequences would be severe.

As I stood up before him, he took a step backwards, as if I had threatened to hit him.

'What have they been doing with you? You look worse than you did when you were in prison!'

'Just lost a bit of weight, that's all. I'd feel better if someone could untie me from this thing.'

Lion looked at the ground. 'I wish I could. It would just get us both into more trouble, though. Look, I'm sorry . . .'

'You keep saying that. It's starting to sound boring.'

His head snapped up and his eyes flared. I saw his hands make fists as he fought to control his sudden burst of temper. 'Now, listen, you little . . .'

That was better. That was the Lion I knew. Suddenly I felt almost cheerful, as if I had not just been bought by someone intent on using me for ritual target practice.

'All right,' I said soothingly. 'Calm down.' I prodded the man who had bought me with my foot. He was still lying face down in front of me, groaning. No doubt he was feeling sorry for himself, having just been pressed into the dirt by the weight of three slaves. 'That's the man who bought me, but he was acting as someone's agent. Why don't you pick him up and ask him what was so special about us that he was prepared to pay so much?'

He did as I suggested. 'It's a good question,' he said as he dragged the wretched man to his feet. 'It beats me why anyone would have given a cocoa bean for you, even if you didn't look as if a house had fallen on you! And what's that smell?'

I ignored his question and concentrated on the man trying to stand in front of me. With his cloak ripped, his palms raw from trying to break his fall and his eyes rolling dazedly, it was easy to forget that the man in front of me was, if not my owner, then very obviously someone whose standing was a good deal higher than my own. Even though I was the one still lashed to a pole with two enemy captives, all of us doomed to a ghastly fate, I found myself interrogating him.

'Who are you working for? Who's my new owner?'

The man blinked stupidly at me. I frowned at him, suddenly struck once again by the feeling that I had seen him somewhere before.

My brother seized his shoulder and shook him roughly. 'Come on, answer the question! I want to know who put up all that money!'

'Put him down and move away,' said a stern voice from behind me. I could not turn around to look at the speaker, but I could guess what was happening. The men guarding the gateway, finding themselves outnumbered by Lion's bodyguards, had gone for reinforcements.

My brother was unmoved. 'Who are you?' he asked coolly, looking past me.

'Market police. Let that man go, or you'll answer to the judges for it. The court is sitting over there.' I could not see, but I assumed the man was gesturing towards the large, low building where the marketplace's court was permanently in session. I hoped my brother would control himself: justice here tended to be swift and brutal. 'And I want you to tell me what you're doing with these slaves. They're not your property.'

'Whose are they, then?'

And then, before the policeman could reply to my brother's insolent question, I saw the answer, sweeping through the entrance to Tlatelolco marketplace in a cloud of filth: obscenities pouring from the mouth of a middle-aged woman, plainly although smartly dressed in a blouse and skirt of finely woven maguey fibre. Her long, silver-streaked hair was conservatively styled, divided and bound at the nape of the neck with both ends sticking up in front. In her agitation these bobbed about like an ant's feelers.

I could have told she was of the merchant class by her dress – too fine for a commoner, but not made of the cotton that was reserved for the families of lords and mighty warriors. I did not need the clue, however.

'Lily?' I said wonderingly.

Her handsome face was distorted in fury. 'One hundred and five large cloaks! When I get my hands on that bonehead, he'll wish he'd been eaten alive by rats! I'm going to skin him for this! One hundred and five!'

My brother turned and, along with the rest of us, gazed at her in amazement as he followed her progress through the gateway. Then he looked at the man he and I had just been questioning and did what, for him, was a rare thing: he smiled.

'I suppose she must mean you,' he said drily.

The man moaned and sagged and would have fallen had Lion not grabbed him. I knew now who he was and where I had seen him before: he was Chihuicoyo, a household slave belonging to Lily and Kindly, whose name meant 'Partridge'.

But now I could not see Partridge, my brother, Lily or anything else, because my eyes had misted over. A strange, bubbling noise was coming from the back of my throat, without my willing it, and then it burst out of my mouth in great, whooping cries, and I was laughing and weeping at the same time.

It took Lily a few moments to notice us. At first she merely stared, abruptly speechless, with her hands on her hips, before compressing her lips into a thin line and striding determinedly towards us.

'Lily,' I croaked.

She seemed surprisingly unenthusiastic to see me, considering what I had cost her. Ignoring me, she turned to her slave.

'What's the meaning of this? What did you think you were doing? Are you completely insane? I'll make you eat your own breechcloth for this, you halfwitted excuse for a flea on a coyote's backside, you!'

'But . . . you said you'd pay any price . . .'

'I didn't mean that much!' she shrieked illogically.

'What could I do?' wailed Partridge. 'There was this warrior bidding against me! He said he was going to have them all disembowelled!'

'Warrior? What warrior?'

That was when she noticed my brother for the first time. She took a step backward, away from him, and hissed: 'What are you doing here?'

The last time Lily had met Lion, my brother's sword had been sticking out of her son's skull. They were not the best of friends.

The fleeting smile was gone from his face, but I could see it threatening to break out again as he murmured: 'I was the other bidder. My man didn't realize . . .'

'You!' she screamed. For a moment I thought she was going to fly at him, tear him with her fingernails or bite his nose off, but instead she stamped her bare foot on the ground in frustration and turned on her slave again. 'You moron! You had me bidding against Yaotl's own brother!'

Partridge's wail of protest was cut off by the stern voice of the man in charge of the police. 'All right, that's enough. Are you saying you own this, madam?' By 'this' he plainly meant the three of us still lashed to the pole.

'Yes,' she sighed wearily.

'Then move it along. It's causing a disturbance! Come on, break it up!' he called out aloud, and I realized he was addressing the second small crowd to have gathered around me that day. 'Go on, all of you. We've all got business to attend to!'

'We'd better get to that canoe,' Lily told her servant, her voice calmer now but still tense. 'Cut them loose and bring Yaotl with you. And hurry up! We've wasted enough time. Cihtli isn't going to hang around in Tetzcoco for ever.'

'Cihtli' meant 'Hare'. Who was Hare, I wondered, and did this mean we were going to Tetzcoco? But then I saw something that drove the questions from my mind and wiped out all sense of relief at my deliverance.

The crowd around us was scattering, as the bailiff had ordered. Only one man remained in his place, with his eyes fixed on me. He was a tall man with muscles that bulged so far they seemed about to split the seams in his green uniform, and he wore his hair piled up on top of his head and flowing over his shoulders in a style I was unlikely ever to forget.

The Otomi did nothing and said nothing. He just grinned at me, and that was enough. His meaning would not have been plainer if he had said the words aloud: 'We'll get you yet. Just you wait and see.'

Partridge's nervous fingers were not up to untying us. Every time Lily shouted at him his hands jerked convulsively, and at one point I was afraid he was going to strangle me by mistake. Eventually my brother pushed him aside and, using a sword borrowed from one of his men, began sawing at the rope with its obsidian blade.

'Yaotl,' he muttered, 'you know what I was saying earlier . . .'

'I suppose you're not sorry any more,' I said, rubbing my neck.

'I don't know.' He glanced at Lily, who glared back at both

of us. 'I'm not sure I wouldn't sooner be sacrificed than have her as my mistress!' He raised his voice. 'Now, what about these two?'

'Let them go,' the woman said shortly. 'They're no use to me.'

The two men still lashed to the slave-collar watched sullenly while their bonds were cut. 'You two had better bugger off back to Texcala, or wherever you come from,' Lion advised them.

As soon as they were free, the one with the torn lip did a strange thing. He sat down, put his disfigured face in his hands and began to weep quietly.

'What's up with him?'

The one-armed warrior stared at my brother as though he thought the question stupid. 'What do you think?' he sneered. 'He wanted to be sacrificed! He was looking forward to a flowery death and his spirit joining the Sun in the sky every morning. What do you think he's got waiting for him at home, in that state?'

Lion looked from one of them to the other, took a step towards the weeping warrior, and then thought better of whatever he was going to say. 'Well, maybe I'll see you on some battlefield somewhere,' he mumbled.

'Not if we see you first, Aztec!'

Lion turned to me. 'You'd better get out of here before old Black Feathers finds out what's happened!'

'You saw the Otomi, then?' The green-clad warrior had vanished, presumably gone to tell my master what had happened. I could imagine the old man's rage when he learned about it. It would not be long before he started plotting his revenge.

'Where's my son?' I asked suddenly.

'Don't worry about Nimble. He's long gone. He didn't

want to leave you – I practically had to drive him out of the city with the flat of a sword – but he's as safe as can be now.' He clapped me on the shoulder. 'Just look out for yourself! It's what you're good at, after all!'

As the exhilaration of being alive and out of my cage wore off, the pain of my bruises and the weakness of my atrophied limbs started to make themselves felt again. Even without the collar – especially without the collar, and two tall men dragging me upright by the throat – it was an effort to stand, let alone walk. Somehow I made it as far as the canal. I stumbled over the side of Lily's boat and fell, groaning, into the bottom.

Lily was less than sympathetic. 'I suppose you can't pole the canoe?'

'Doesn't look like it,' a gruff voice responded. 'He'd fall in the water if he tried. If you insist on sending Partridge home then it's going to be up to you.'

I looked up, surprised to recognize the speaker as Lily's father. The old man was slumped in the bow of the boat. He was snugly wrapped in an ancient, patched leather cloak. It had the same colour and texture as his skin. He looked like someone about to embark on a long journey. His staff, a pole the height of a man, wrapped in strips of paper spotted with rubber and blood, was propped between his knees.

'What are you doing here?' I asked.

'We're all going,' Lily said crisply. 'You, my father and me.' The boat rocked alarmingly as she stepped into the stern and picked up a long pole, which she used to push us away from the wooden pilings at the water's edge. She handled the canoe naturally, driving the pole into the bottom of the canal and letting it trail in our wake. It reminded me how much of a breed apart the *Pochteca*, the long-distance merchants, were. All Aztec girls went to school, but after that most women concerned themselves with cooking, cleaning, weaving and raising children. Among the merchants, whose menfolk were often away for years at a time, other skills were often needed. Lily had obviously found it useful to be able to manoeuvre her own canoe, presumably when she was short-handed and merchandise had to be got to the market. The only surviving adult male in her household, apart from slaves, was her father, who was obviously too decrepit to be of much use. He was usually, in my experience of him, too drunk as well. Drinking sacred wine was a privilege allowed men and women over seventy who had grandchildren, and Kindly exploited it to the full.

'Where?'

'Tetzcoco. Mexico's too dangerous for you now. And we've got some business there, so you'll have to come with us.'

I frowned. 'I'm not sure I want to go to Tetzcoco. That's on the eastern shore of the lake. I thought I might try to look for Nimble, but he'd most likely have gone West, towards Tarascan country, where he grew up . . .'

Lily stopped poling the canoe for a moment to lean over me. She held her face so close to mine that I could smell her: she had the fresh, earthy scent of the soap-tree root she washed with, overlaid by the yellow *axin* she used to protect her skin from the cold.

'Let's get one thing clear, Yaotl. I may have bought you – at a grossly extravagant price, I must say – because I thought it was the least I could do after you came back to save us from Lord Feathered in Black. That doesn't alter the fact that you are now my slave and will bloody well go where I tell you!'

'But . . .'

She took no notice of my protest. 'We're going to be out on the open lake for a while. It'll get cold. There's a clean cloak in front of you. Put it on before you freeze to death.'

4

While her father dozed in the bow, Lily threaded her way through the network of crowded canals that crisscrossed Tlatelolco, often changing direction but generally taking us to the North. She seemed to be going out of her way to avoid the area around her home parish, Pochtlan. I wondered if she was afraid my former master might come looking for her once he had heard what she had done. It seemed likely.

'If the weather holds, we should make it by nightfall. Otherwise we'll have to stop in Tepeyac. Of course, it would help if everyone got out of my way! Who taught you to handle a paddle?' The last words were hurled at a young man trying to put his canoe about in a waterway about as broad as his vessel was long. He appeared harassed even before Lily shouted at him. He had the plain breechcloth and tonsured hair of one who had never taken an enemy warrior captive and never would, the lowliest of commoners, and his look as he saw the ferocious woman bearing down on him was one of pure terror.

'Go on, move that thing!' she cried. Obediently he began churning the water with his paddle, and his canoe shot forward so fast that its bow ground into the side of the canal with enough force to split the wood. Lily's boat coasted past his with barely a finger's breadth between them.

'Serve him right if he sinks.'

'Why Tetzcoco?' I asked over the sounding of frantic bailing behind us.

'I told you, we've business there.'

'Funny business, though.' Kindly had not been asleep after all. His filmy eyes regarded me briefly before closing once more. 'Mysterious, even. Might appeal to you, Yaotl.'

'You're not getting me looking for any more of your stolen property, not after what happened last time,' I said, before looking nervously around at Lily and adding: 'That's not what you had in mind, is it?'

'Nothing like that,' the woman said, adding after a brief hesitation: 'It's just a message. A fellow merchant named Hare wants it given to someone at the royal palace in Tetzcoco. All I have to do is put him in touch with the recipient.'

'You're a go-between,' I said. 'Why do they need you, though?'

'Hare doesn't know anyone in Tetzcoco. He's been living and trading with the Mayans and spent most of the last thirty years at the coast, near Cozumel.' Cozumel was a large island just off the shore of the great Divine Sea, far to the East.

'Not surprising if he needs help finding his way around after all that time among barbarians,' Kindly remarked. 'He's probably forgotten how to behave in polite society, and society doesn't come more polite than in Tetzcoco!'

'What's the message?' I asked.

'I don't know. I gather it's in Mayan – only someone who speaks Mayan can make sense of it, I was told. But apparently the woman it's intended for doesn't have a problem with that.'

'Who's the woman?'

'Her name's Tonalna.' The name meant 'Mother of Light', but by itself that told me nothing about the person who bore it. 'I don't know much about her. My contacts in Tetzcoco put us in touch with each other. I've only met her once, when she gave me Hare's fee for handing over the message. She was a royal concubine, back in the time of the last King, and that's about all I know. As for what she wants with some piece of barbarian nonsense, and how she's going to make sense of it when she's got it, I've no idea.'

'They're a brainy lot in Tetzcoco.' Kindly showed his respect for learning by spitting over the side. 'But it'll be interesting to see what this message says. I know a little Mayan myself, since I used to do business with them in my days as a merchant.'

'What it says is nothing to do with us,' Lily warned. 'Tetzcoco isn't a very safe place to be caught running around with secret messages at the moment, with two rival kings at war with each other. I wouldn't have got involved in this if you hadn't owed Hare a favour from years back.'

I groaned, and it was not from the pain of my wounds. Kindly had an eccentric sense of honour. I would not have put it past him to steal a small bag of cocoa beans from a poor widow, but favours he felt obliged to do for his old friends had nearly cost me my life before now.

The weather held, but Lily decided against trying to paddle us all the way across the lake herself. She took us as far as Tepeyac and hired a canoe and a boatman to take us on to Tetzcoco.

The Sun was just setting as we set out on the last leg of our journey. However, twilight lasts a long time in the mountains, and by the time we reached the eastern shore of the lake the sky above the peaks to the West was still pale, with a strange glow crowning some of the very tallest, as though their shapes were outlined in gold thread, the last of the sunshine reflecting off their snowy caps. Far below them, the great city in the middle of the lake was in shadow, a vague dark mass, harbouring here and there a spark where a temple fire burned day and night.

When I looked back at it, the nearest shore of Mexico's island looked as if it had been sheared off in a straight line. This was the edge of the open water to the East of the city, where a great dyke kept Mexico safe from the floods that had once engulfed it periodically. On this eastern side of the dyke the water was noticeably choppier, although it was still not rough enough to produce more than a gentle rocking motion, which even I could bear without being seasick. Boats surrounded us, their gaily painted hulls only dimly visible among the dark waters but their short bow-waves startlingly pale. There were no fishing boats, because nothing lived in the salty waters on this side of the dyke, but there were many canoes. They carried men, women or freight, and most were headed in the same direction as we were: towards Tetzcoco, on the eastern edge of the lake.

From where we were, the city's whitewashed houses, palaces and temples were pale shapes like pieces of chalk scattered along the shadowed shoreline and studded into the sides of its hills. They were far fewer in number and generally larger than the countless tiny boxes most Aztecs lived in. Tetzcoco looked to have been laid out on a more generous scale than Mexico: from what I could see beyond the masses of reeds right in front of us, the whole eastern edge of the lake was built up, although many houses were surrounded by orchards and gardens.

A band of pale orange light crept up the sides of the hills above and beyond the city. Watching its progress put me in mind of the passage of time and a question that had been troubling me.

'Lily, what day is it?'

'You mean you don't know?'

'I kind of lost track. You know how it gets when one day is just the same as the last.'

'Twelve House, in the month of Rebirth.'

I frowned while I tried to work out from that how long I must have been in my cage. I had told Lily the truth: for all I could remember it might have been years or days. I had given myself up to Lord Feathered in Black on Seven Grass, during the month of the Coming Down of Water. The entire month of the Stretching – twenty days – had passed since then, but I lost count when I tried to work out how much of the year's final month I had missed.

'You were in there twenty-nine days, if that's what you were wondering.'

I stared at her. She was sitting just across from me in the boat, and her eyes glittered as she returned my look, although in the near darkness it was impossible to read her expression.

'I had to hire a man to keep an eye on the slave-dealers' pitch,' she explained quietly. 'I paid him by the day, and I know exactly what his wages came to! We'd no way of knowing when you were going to go on sale, you see.' Her face took on a rueful grimace. 'Of course, your brother must have done the same. If only I'd known!'

'Couldn't you just have gone along to the slave-dealers' warehouse and made them an offer?'

'It's illegal to buy and sell merchandise outside the market-place. It may be all very well for the likes of your master – your former master, I mean – to play fast and loose with the law, but my father and I have already had enough trouble from the authorities in Tlatelolco to last a lifetime. Anyway, it doesn't matter, does it? You're here now.'

'Why, though?' Hearing a little indrawn breath from her, I added hastily: 'Don't think I'm not grateful, Lily, but this is the second time, maybe the third, that you've saved my life.' On one occasion she had had me dragged from a crowd intent on beating me to death. On another she had rescued me from a highly physical interrogation by the chief of her own parish of

Pochtlan. Both times she had wanted something from me, but what could I possibly have for her now?

The glitter vanished from her eyes as she shut them. There was a long pause, broken only by the splashing of our boatman's oars as he took us among the reeds fringing Tetzcoco's shoreline and by a loud snoring from Kindly, who had at long last fallen truly asleep in the bow. His daughter shot him a nervous glance before she answered me.

'Yaotl, I honestly don't know. Do you think I ought to hate you for what happened to my son?'

I could think of nothing to say.

'Maybe I do hate you. Maybe I didn't want you to be sacrificed so that I could go on hating you, rather than just hating what I remembered about you. Do you think that's it? Sort of a way of punishing myself, because deep down I blame myself for what Shining Light turned into? Or did I want to see you again, just to find out whether I really hated you or not?'

I was not sure whether I was supposed to answer that or not. 'I don't understand,' I said truthfully.

She sighed. 'I don't either. It just seemed wrong to do nothing, that's all.' Suddenly I saw her teeth flash white in a grin. 'Just don't get any ideas, slave! You're not exactly an object of desire at the moment!'

It hurt to laugh, but I could not help it. Lily was a fine-looking woman, for all that she was about my age and far from being a girl, but just then the only things my wasted, bruised body craved were a meal, sleep and a bath.

Lily had taken two rooms in a guesthouse reserved for merchants. It was a short walk there from the dock. The road took us past the landing stages and merchants' warehouses by the lakeside and up a gentle slope among bare maize fields, towards where the centre of the town sprawled in its careless fashion around the King's palace and the temples of the gods in the sacred plaza. Ordinarily I could have run all the way, but by the time we arrived I needed both Lily and her father to hold me up. The old man was not out of breath. He was less frail than he looked.

'You'll be able to get some rest here,' he said, showing me, by the flickering light of a pine torch, a sleeping mat in the corner of the room we were to share. To my amazement, a clean rabbit's fur blanket lay on top of the mat. 'Nice and quiet, with Huexotzincatl's palace just behind us.'

'They go in for palaces here, don't they? This room alone is about half as big as my parents' entire house, including the courtyard.'

'They can afford to spread themselves out: they've got the land. They're not all squashed together on a little island like us. But we're right by the palace district anyway. The present King's grandfather, Lord Nezahualcoyotl, had his children's houses built so they abutted on to his own. No doubt he wanted to keep an eye on them! His son, Nezahualpilli, did the same. Hence this place next door – Huexotzincatl was the last King's eldest son.'

Nezahualcoyotl and Nezahualpilli: Hungry Coyote and his son, Hungry Child. I knew their names well, as every Aztec did. The father had been one of our leading allies in the wars to overthrow the tyranny of the King of Azcapotzalco, long before I was born, and he and his son had both been renowned builders, law-makers and poets. It was Hungry Coyote who had suggested building a dyke across the lake, separating the salt water from the fresh, and sparing Mexico from the floods that had regularly ravaged it.

Much more than that, I did not know. Huexotzincatl was a name that was vaguely familiar to me, although all I could remember about him, apart from the fact that Hungry Child had been his father, was that he had come to a bad end. His name simply meant 'Man from Huexotzinco', although, of course, he had not come from any such place. Since 'Huexotzinco' in turn meant 'By the Place of the Willows', I thought of him as Prince of Willows.

The present King, Cacamatzin, Lord Maize Ear, a young man of about twenty, had been on the throne less than three years, having ascended it shortly after Hungry Child died. I gathered that he had neither his father's nor his grandfather's stature. He was, however, a nephew of our Emperor, Montezuma, which presumably counted for more than his personal qualities.

'If you're up to it, we'll take a look around tomorrow. I haven't been here in years, but there's plenty worth seeing. Did you know the great pyramid here is taller than our war-god Huitzilopochtli's in Tenochtitlan? It's dedicated to your old patron, Tezcatlipoca. Or rather the Lord of the Near and the Nigh, as they call him in Tetzcoco.'

I looked at him a little sharply. I was not sure whether the mention of the Smoking Mirror was meant to recall my status as a slave or the fact that I had served him as a priest. He ignored me, though, instead looking hopefully out into the guesthouse's courtyard. 'I wonder whether Lily's found us any food. I could do with a drink as well.'

Lily appeared then, as if summoned, bearing two drinking-gourds. Almost before she was through the doorway her father had seized one, pulled out the maize cob stopper and taken a swig. Then he spat, with an expression of disgust.

'This is water!'

'Of course it is. Straight from the spring. I managed to get some filled tortillas as well. Amaranth greens or shrimp?' she asked me as she offered me the other gourd. 'First thing tomorrow, I hope we can go and look for Hare and get this business over with.'

'First thing tomorrow,' the old man grumbled, 'I hope I can get a real drink.'

I did not have a quiet night, even though, as Kindly had anticipated, there was not a sound from the nearby palace.

Exhausted as I was, I still found it strange to lie on a sleeping mat. It required an effort of will not to draw my knees up to my chest, and when I made the effort, expecting to luxuriate in my ability to stretch my legs out to their full length, the pain in my calves and thighs made me wince. I found I had sores on my buttocks and hips from crouching in the same position all day, and they hurt every time I tried to roll over. Finally, the palace behind the house may have been quiet, but my fellow lodger was not. Whether it was from a lifetime's smoking tobacco, years of drinking sacred wine in seemingly suicidal quantities or sheer cussedness, I could not have said, but Lily's father had the loudest and most persistent snore I have ever heard.

I doubt that any of that would have kept me awake, however. The thing that made me toss and turn before, eventually, giving up and going to lean against the doorway and look morosely out into the dark, empty courtyard was in my head.

I ought to have been elated to be where I was: freed from my cage and the certainty of a gruesome death, and for once in my life among people who, whether or not they saw themselves as my friends, were surely not my enemies. Over and over again I told myself that I had had more good fortune than I deserved, certainly far more than I would ever have dared ask the gods to grant. Not so long before, I would have resigned myself to being for ever subject to the whim of a capricious, spiteful, callous old man and his nightmarish henchmen. Temporarily, at least, I had swapped my old quarters, a cramped, noisy, stinking space beside the kitchen of Lord

Feathered in Black's palace, for the spacious apartment I found myself in now, and what did it matter if I had to share it with an old man who snored?

I was still a slave, but that, I knew, ought not to matter. I had never expected my former master to grant me my freedom. In fact, I had sold myself to him thinking that I would never again be my own man, and welcoming the thought: it was a comfort to know that no one would ever again ask anything of me except obedience. And remembering that, I began to see what was wrong and why I was less than overjoyed now.

I had no idea what Lily intended to do with me. Judging by what she had told me that evening, she had very little notion herself. However, I could not see her bullying me the way she did Partridge. Too much had happened to both of us for that, and for all her talk of hating me I knew that she saw, as clearly as I did, what a tangle of feelings we were caught up in. We might end up hating each other, but for us to be nothing more than mistress and servant was inconceivable.

What, then, was my status? A slave was the meanest of persons, but he knew how much his master could lawfully ask of him, and was free of all tribute obligations so long as he obeyed. A commoner might be forced to go to war or join a labour gang working on some monumental building project, if the Emperor or his parish required it, but otherwise he was free to follow his own occupation and take his own chances with the gods, and what he said counted for something, somewhere, even if it was just in his own household.

Status was almost everything to the Aztecs. We had laws that told us what clothes we might wear – cotton for a lord, maguey fibre for a commoner – whether we might wear sandals or must go barefoot, even how we wore our hair, because these things represented a man's position in society to everyone who saw him. To look at my brother, for example, was to know precisely what his rank was and what he had done to earn it. There were many in Mexico who cherished their status more than their lives.

It seemed that night as if I had no standing among my people at all. It felt as if I was not quite a slave, not quite a commoner, not quite a former priest. It was as if I had forgotten my own name, and for one mad moment I found myself thinking I had been less unhappy in my cage, when, with the benefit of continual reminders from the Otomies, I had been in no doubt about exactly what and where I was.

In the end I shook myself from my reverie by reminding myself that there was one thing I did have, one thing that was worth more than name or rank. It was something I might never experience again, but which nobody had managed to take away from me, the one thing that I could hope to have even after my body had been burned or buried and my soul departed for the Place of the Fleshless.

As I rolled over on my sleeping mat, with sleep approaching at last, I remembered I had a son.

5

In the event, I had to disappoint Kindly. By the next morning I was not up to touring the city or to anything else beyond lying on my sleeping mat, moaning pathetically and shivering as though I were freezing to death in spite of my blanket.

'It's not surprising,' Kindly observed, in reply to Lily's impatient demand to know what was the matter with me now. 'He's been penned up like a turkey on sale in the market for a month and a half and worked over pretty thoroughly too, if I'm any judge. He had a pretty strenuous day yesterday. You're probably lucky to find him still alive at all.'

'I'm not sure how lucky that is,' the woman responded sourly. 'Now I suppose I've got to nurse him, when we ought to be looking for that bloody merchant. Oh, well. I suppose I should see it as protecting my investment!'

Lily did nurse me, though, however grudgingly. She changed my bedding, treated my sores with poultices of pine resin and squashed black beetles, and every day forced me to my feet and drove me into the guesthouse's dome-shaped sweat bath. After my bath she would feed me, at first with bowls of thin gruel, later with tortillas and dishes of pinole.

I saw little of Kindly, except at night. I gathered he spent his days in the marketplace, looking for old acquaintances and, knowing him, indulging in sacred wine. As a result, Lily and I spent a lot of time alone together, but we talked little, and most of what we said was strictly to the point: how my recovery was coming along, and Lily's plans for dealing with Hare.

'I know he has a house in Huexotla,' she told me. 'It's not his own, of course. He rented it when he came to Tetzcoco. I've not been there. I don't want to go alone. I need you better so that you can come with me.'

'Does he know you're looking for him? Why can't he come to you? If he's got something he wants to sell, wouldn't it be worth his while?'

Lily hesitated. 'I'd have thought so,' she conceded eventually. 'But he's a strange man – a bit of a recluse. It probably comes of living in the jungle for a few years.' Suddenly she sighed. 'Hurry up and get well, can't you? I need to have this over and done with!'

Over the next few days I found myself getting stronger, while Lily became more and more anxious. Once I could eat unaided, or potter about in the courtyard by myself, she took to spending time on her own, staring absently out of the doorway leading to the street and plucking nervously at a loose thread hanging from the hem of her blouse.

'I don't know,' Kindly said when I asked him what he thought was the matter. 'She looks as if she's waiting for something, as though she's expecting a messenger to come through that gateway with bad news. I suppose it's sitting here all day when there are things to do. You'd better make fast work of your recovery!'

On our fourth morning in Tetzcoco, I awoke to find Lily's urgent, anxious face peering down at me.

It took me some moments to work out where I was. I was still so unused to being able to move that, on first waking, it did not occur to me to try getting up, or even to straighten myself out from my huddled posture. Eventually the woman grasped my shoulder and shook it roughly.

'Come on! Wake up! If this is the sort of service I can expect from you, you'll find yourself back on the market!'

I managed to haul myself into a sitting position. It hurt, but my groan got no reaction from my new mistress. This was only to be expected: through the doorway, I could see that half the courtyard was bathed in sunlight. I had slept disgracefully late. Aztecs prided themselves on being up and about before dawn, but day and night had had no meaning for me for so long that I still found myself lying awake until well after midnight and then missing the sunrise.

'Sorry,' I muttered, throwing off my blanket and reaching for my new cloak. 'I thought your father would wake me. Where is he?' The other sleeping mat in the room was empty, except for a rumpled blanket on one corner.

'Off buying sacred wine, as usual.'

I got painfully to my feet, swaying a little as I stood upright. My calves and thighs still felt as if they were about to turn into water, but I knew they would only stiffen up further if I did not exercise them. A few aches were nothing. I could put up with a good deal of pain and discomfort: as a priest, I had fasted nearly to the point of starvation and taken ritual baths in freezing lake water in the name of one or other of our gods, and lacerated myself all over in order to give them my own blood for nourishment. I knew I was in much better condition than I had been, and that thought by itself cheered me.

'What's the matter?' I asked.

'Nothing. But I'm tired of waiting. You're well enough to walk now. You can come to Hare's house with me.'

'But . . .' I began to protest, but she had already turned to lead the way out of the house. Over her shoulder, she snapped back: 'I've fed you like a baby long enough. Now it's time for

you to earn your keep. Anyway, walking will feel easier than
standing still, I should think.'

I might have added that lying down was even easier, but
then I remembered that I was still, after all, a slave. With a sigh,
I limped out into the daylight.

Huexotla was a suburb of Tetzcoco, a village that had long ago
been absorbed into the city's sprawl. It was not a great distance
away, but Lily set a brisk pace and my legs were out of practice.
I gritted my teeth, stumbled along behind her and distracted
myself from the pain in my thighs by looking at the people and
buildings around me.

The people were a varied lot. Most looked just like Aztecs,
the men with their loins wrapped in breechcloths and their
cloaks knotted at the throat or over the right shoulder, just as
they were worn in Mexico, and the women in blouses worn
loose over long skirts, and their hairstyles were familiar: long
and tangled for the black-cloaked priests, short and sometimes
tonsured for commoners, bound up and tied over the forehead
for respectable women. There were many obvious foreigners as
well. I recognized several Huaxtecs in tall, conical caps, who
would keep adjusting their breechcloths, a garment they rarely
bothered with when at home. And I saw many Otomies: not
the fierce warriors I dreaded so much, but members of the race
of savages they were named after, tribesmen from the mountains in the North-East, distinguished by the blue dye that
decorated their faces and bodies. Watching this varied crowd
flowing through the wide streets, mainly converging on the
marketplace like several streams emptying into a valley, I
recalled that Tetzcoco was, at least in theory, at the centre of an
empire of its own, and practically everyone I saw, however
exotic, was a subject of its King.

The people who lived here were not, strictly speaking,

Aztecs, although they shared our ancestry and spoke our language and we considered them our allies. They were Acolhuans, whose ancestors had emerged from the Seven Caves before ours had, and had come South into the valley to found their city at a time when Mexico was nothing more than a couple of boggy islands in the middle of a salt lake. Over the years much of the eastern side of the valley, as well as large tracts of land outside it, as far as the Texcalan frontier beyond the mountains, had fallen under Tetzcoco's sway. At length the Acolhuans had come to blows with another nation from the western side of the lake, the Tepanecs; the struggle had brought both contenders low, allowing us Aztecs, safe in the fortress-city my forefathers had built on those two boggy islands, to triumph over both of them. Since then, Tetzcoco had been Mexico's ally, but it was an unequal relationship. It said much for Tetzcoco's standing with its mighty neighbour that King Maize Ear was the nephew of our Emperor, Montezuma. Just before he had died, Maize Ear's father, Hungry Child, was said to have given up all thought of war or conquest, contenting himself to be the ruler of a people who thought themselves the most cultivated and refined in the World.

Looking over the heads of the people, I saw the long, low wall of the palace at the back of our lodgings, the one Kindly had described as having belonged to Lord Prince of Willows.

'Your father said it was a quiet place. It looks more than that. It's all overgrown, and those trees don't look as if they've been pruned in years.' A few boughs even bore wizened fruit, long since destroyed by frost.

'I don't suppose they have,' Lily answered. 'The place has been deserted for ten years at least. Don't you know the story?'

'No.'

'It's typically Tetzcocan. Prince of Willows was the son of

Hungry Child, his favourite. He'd probably have succeeded him if he'd lived. He made the mistake of getting too friendly with one of his father's concubines.'

'Ah, I see. Why is that typically Tetzcocan, though? That sort of thing could happen anywhere – son making eyes at father's mistress, the old man getting suspicious . . .'

'Because you don't see at all! It's not as if anyone ever caught the two of them sharing the same sleeping mat. From what I've heard, they really were just swapping poems. The girl was talented that way, apparently, so much so they called her "the Lady of Tollan".' Tollan was the legendary home of the Toltecs, the ancient god-like race we credited with inventing and perfecting every art form from poetry to architecture, a people so clever that not only could they cultivate cotton up in the mountains but they made it grow in different colours so as to be spared the effort of dyeing it.

'Maybe the young man touched a raw nerve,' I suggested. 'They do pride themselves on their poetry here, don't they?'

'I'm sure there was more to it than that,' Lily asserted. 'A raw nerve, yes – but considering what happened, this girl obviously meant a lot more to the King than most of his other wives and concubines did. After all, he had thousands to choose from any time he wanted, so whatever it was that made her so important, it can't have been just sex!' Her frankness surprised me, but she followed the remark with what may have been a wistful sigh. 'Maybe he really wanted her for her mind!'

A thoughtful pause followed while I tried to think of an answer to that. However, Lily beat me to it: 'But I was telling you what the really stupid – I mean the really Tetzcocan – thing about it was. When the King wanted to try his son for treason, he wouldn't preside over the trial himself. He claimed he wanted the court to be impartial. That's what they do

around here, you see: everybody has to get a fair trial, even the
son of a king. They can't see that rich and powerful men can't
be tried fairly, because too many people stand to gain from
either letting them go or disposing of them once and for all.
And when the judges found the lad guilty, on what sort of evidence I don't know, Hungry Child wouldn't intervene to
pardon him, because he wouldn't have it thought that his son
was above the law.

'I heard the King had had it in mind to exile Prince of
Willows, but they garrotted him instead. His father was so
grief-stricken that he had his house walled up and forbade
anyone from going in there ever again on pain of death.'

'Oh.' I was beginning to get the idea that Tetzcoco was a
strange place. 'What happened to the lady?'

She frowned in puzzlement for a moment, as though the
question had never occurred to her. Then she gave a bitter
laugh. 'Do you know, I've no idea? Come to that, I can't even
tell you her name! But what do you think? What always happens to the woman in these cases? She was strangled, I expect,
or maybe her head was crushed between two stones. I'm sure
Hungry Child had no trouble taking that decision for himself!'

As Lily and I respectively walked and limped towards
Huexotla, I began to notice something curious about the
demeanour of many of the people around me. The foreigners
seemed normal, acting as foreigners always do, craning their
necks and staring open-mouthed every time they saw a lord
being carried in a litter or any building taller than a single-
storey house. However, the locals, the ones who looked and
dressed like Aztecs, often had a nervous, furtive air about
them. They seemed prone to glancing frequently over their
shoulders, taking quick, nervous steps and bowing their heads
as if they did not want to be noticed.

I was about to draw Lily's attention to this when she announced that we had arrived.

I stopped, collapsing with relief in the shade of a stout larch growing by the roadside. 'That was a long walk. Are you sure this is the place?' It was not prepossessing. The road was lined on both sides with small dwellings, none of them substantial. I could not see any stone houses: the favoured materials in this part of the town seemed to be mud bricks or wattle and daub, faced with cracked, hastily whitewashed adobe. The houses mostly stood apart from one another, rather than being crammed together like the houses in Mexico, but that was not necessarily a good thing. Some of them looked as if they would benefit from having something to lean against, and the spaces between them were mostly filled with foul slops and trash: gnawed bones, maize husks, broken pots, cracked and worn obsidian flakes. Elsewhere, trees mingled haphazardly with the houses, and here and there were patches of tall grass and nettles and overgrown bushes. There seemed to be nobody about.

'He can't be a very prosperous merchant,' I observed.

'He will be when he's got what I've brought for him,' Lily said drily. 'Let's get this over with. You stay here.'

I stared at her in astonishment. 'I thought you needed me. That's why I've walked all this way. What do you want me to do out here, anyway?'

'Keep watch,' she replied mysteriously. She walked up to the entrance to one of the houses, a dark doorway with no screen or cloth covering it. Lumps of brick hung from a rope attached to the lintel. She rattled them with a swift tug.

Nothing happened.

'Not at home, then,' I said, after she had tried again. 'Are you sure this is the right house?'

'Quite sure. I had someone describe it to me.'

I could not see much difference between this hovel and its neighbours, but before I could say so the woman said abruptly: 'Well, I haven't come all this way for nothing. I'm going inside.'

She walked through the doorway. 'Hare! Where are you?'

Nobody answered.

I hesitated, unsure whether to get up from my seat under the tree and follow her, when suddenly the silence inside the house was split by a shriek.

I was on my feet and running across the street before the sound had died away.

I burst through the doorway, stumbling to a halt just in time to avoid falling over a large object on the floor. I barely spared it a glance as I looked quickly at the people around me.

There were too many people in the room.

A man stood behind Lily, holding her firmly by her upper arms. A second stood in front of her. He was holding something, which he had been examining at the moment when I made my entrance. It looked like a knife. They both had the look of warriors, with thickset bodies, pillar-of-stone hairstyles and grim, purposeful expressions.

The third man was the thing I had almost tripped over. When I looked down at it again, I saw that his body lay sprawled in the centre of the room, and the floor around it was black with his blood. The inside of the house reeked of gore, a smell that recalled many a human sacrifice and countless offerings of my own Precious Water of Life. I knew it well enough to be able to judge that the blood had been shed a few days before. There was a long, gaping gash in the side of the dead man's neck.

My first thought was that this must be Hare, but then I looked at the corpse's face and the shock of recognition almost had me turning and bolting through the doorway in terror.

When I had last seen this man, he and I had just been untied from the same collar in Tlatelolco. He was the Texcalan with the torn lip and earlobes.

'Look, Amimitl! Here's another one. What are you doing here?'

The speaker was the warrior standing in front of Lily. He had taken his eyes off the object in his fingers and was watching me keenly.

'I . . .' I stopped myself just in time. What if I told the truth and admitted to being Lily's slave? She had walked into what looked very much like a trap. Instead of Hare and his message she had found a corpse and two warriors, both of whom, I realized with a growing sense of foreboding, had the air of policemen. If they were going to accuse Lily of being responsible for killing the Texcalan, then it would do neither of us any good for me to be taken up for the crime as well, as her accomplice.

I could only hope that Lily would reach the same conclusion as I had, and as quickly. She was staring at me, silent and open-mouthed. She trembled slightly, and her breathing was quick and shallow.

'I was just having a nap out there when I heard the scream. I'm sorry, do you want me to go?'

The man holding Lily – the one called Amimitl, which meant 'Hunter' – said: 'He sounds like an Aztec, Chief.'

'She does too,' his comrade remarked.

'I'm not an Aztec,' I said hastily. 'I'm from Oztoma. It's an Aztec colony. So I may sound as if I come from Mexico, but I've never even been there.' I had never been to Oztoma either, for that matter, but I thought it was safe to assume that Hunter was unacquainted with it. It was a long way off to the West, a town near the Tarascan border. I knew one of

Montezuma's predecessors had planted settlers there in an effort to civilize the place.

'What are you doing here, then?' He held Lily as firmly as ever. I forced myself not to look at her.

'Looking for work, seeing the world. You want to try living in a frontier town surrounded by soldiers and savages. It's no fun at all. I heard Tetzcoco was the centre of civilization, so I came here. Beginning to wish I hadn't bothered,' I added sincerely. 'I feel as if I've been on the road for ever, and I'm tired and hungry.' Then I said, as if it were an afterthought: 'Was it the woman doing all the screaming? Who's she?'

'Mind your own business,' Hunter snapped.

The other warrior frowned at me. 'What's your name, then?'

'Yaotl.' There seemed no reason to lie: it was a common enough name and there was, I thought, no likelihood that anyone in Tetzcoco knew me. Then I remembered the Texcalan lying dead on the floor, and wondered how true that was.

He turned to Lily. 'Do you know this man?' he demanded.

I held my breath while the woman looked at me. She stared, as if she had been unaware of my presence until it was pointed out to her. Then, at last, she said quietly: 'I've never seen him before.'

'Just like you've never seen this before, either, I suppose?' He prodded the corpse with his foot.

'No! I don't even know who he is. Where's the man who lives in this house? What have you done with him?'

The man ignored the question. He grinned at her and waved the thing he was holding in front of her face. It was not a knife, I realized, but a wooden spike, its blunt end splintered as if it had been snapped off something else. It was black with dried blood.

'And what about this, then?'

'You tell me,' Lily snapped defiantly. 'I've never seen that before, either.'

'What are you doing here?'

'Visiting a friend.'

He laughed. 'He can't be a very close friend. I heard you were in the marketplace a few days ago, asking directions to his house.'

That drew a faint gasp from Lily, and I wondered how he had known about it. Were Lily's enquiries what had drawn the men here? With a thrill of fear I remembered what she had said a few days before: Tetzcoco was not a safe place in which to be caught carrying secret messages, or even associating with their bearers. I began to reappraise the two men, realizing that they might not be policemen after all, but something more sinister.

To divert them from questioning Lily further, I said: 'It stinks in here. Do you mind if I go outside?'

'Stay there! I'll deal with you in a moment.'

'We could all go out, then. Why don't you drag the body out into the courtyard? Then we – I mean you – can get a proper look at it.'

The man holding the spike scowled at me. 'What's it to do with you?' he asked pointedly.

'Nothing. But you can't stumble over a corpse in the middle of a room full of blood and not be a bit curious, can you?' Or, in my case, extremely curious. I stared at the Texcalan's ruined face, silently wondering how he could possibly have come to be here.

Unexpectedly, Hunter supported me. 'He's got a point, Tecuancoatl. It does stink in here.' So now I knew his chief's name: 'Rattlesnake.'

Rattlesnake scowled. 'All right, we'll go into the courtyard.

But we're not moving the body. We don't need to look at it any more. He was stabbed with this—' he made a violent gesture with the spike '—and that's that! Bring the woman.'

As we all stepped outside I looked quickly around, taking in as much of my surroundings as I could at a glance.

The house had only one room, whose furnishings consisted of nothing but a sleeping mat and a large wicker chest. The chest lay open and empty. The whole place spoke of an occupant who had left in a hurry, emptying out the contents of his chest but for some reason forgetting to take his sleeping mat. There was a second doorway at the back of the room, leading to a small, bare yard surrounded by a low wall. The courtyard proved to be as bare of ornament as the interior. There were not even the customary images of the gods that no home in Mexico, or for that matter Tetzcoco, would be without. I assumed from this that the house had never been anything more than a temporary lodging. That would make sense if it was used mainly by merchants, because a merchant's god, Yacatecuhtli, Lord of the Vanguard, was represented by his travelling staff, and while on their travels they needed no other idols. The low wall was made of the same flimsy stuff as the building, and one corner was broken down.

Once outside, Rattlesnake turned to look at Lily and me. 'Now, let's try again, shall we? Why don't you try telling me what happened to our friend in there?'

'You do realize,' I replied, keeping my tone as casual as I could, 'that there's no way the woman could have had anything to do with this?'

Rattlesnake glared at me. 'Why's that, then?'

'Well – look, I'm sorry to butt in like this. I know it's none of my business – for one thing, that man's been dead for days.'

'About two or three, I'd say,' Hunter said.

'Well, there you are. So she didn't just come along and

somehow murder him this morning, did she? I mean, apart from anything else, he looked like a big, beefy warrior. Does she look as if she'd have the build to take him on?' I gave her an appraising glance.

'Why are you so keen to protect her?' Rattlesnake asked.

'I'm not. I'm just pointing out the obvious.'

'We know she didn't kill him this morning. She did it a few days ago, and now she's come back to the scene of the crime. Wanted to dispose of the murder weapon.'

'What murder weapon?' Lily asked suddenly. 'You mean that wooden spike? There's no way that could have made that cut in his neck. That was done with a blade, obsidian or tortoiseshell or something like that.'

'How do you know?' Rattlesnake challenged her.

'Ever try slicing meat with a piece of wood?'

'So you did manage to throw the weapon away!' he cried triumphantly.

'What?' Lily cried hoarsely, probably as shocked by the man's twisted logic as she was by his accusation. 'Don't be ridiculous! I've never set eyes on it! All I said was that it couldn't be that spike!'

'What about those, then?' I asked. My eye had been drawn to the marks that ran from the doorway across the courtyard, ending at the point where the wall had broken down. 'They look like footprints to me.'

'You were told to mind your own business,' Rattlesnake said sourly. Nonetheless he turned away from Lily for a moment to inspect the marks. 'Well, it looks as if you're right,' he admitted grudgingly. 'But so what?' He stepped over to the wall and peered over it. For a moment he seemed lost in thought. Then he turned, and I was dismayed to see an unmistakable smirk on his lips. 'That settles it,' he told Lily coldly. 'You're under arrest!'

'But . . .' Nobody tried to stop me from going up to the wall and looking over it myself.

On the other side, the ground sloped away steeply towards a narrow stream. It was thickly strewn with plants, mostly weeds, although scattered among them were a few cultivated varieties, dead or dying maize and amaranth plants, frostbitten or choked by the growth around them. I guessed that some seeds had tumbled down the hillside from the middens next to the houses, along, presumably, with a fair amount of manure. Plenty of other things had ended up on the slope as well, and looking at them I began to understand what Rattlesnake had been getting at. His explanation sounded like a commentary on what I was seeing.

'There's any amount of rubbish on the hillside back there. I bet it's covered in cast-off obsidian flakes, along with all the other stuff. Some of them probably have dried blood on them from skinning rabbits or whatever. That's what you were doing, wasn't it? You walked over to the wall and threw the weapon over it, knowing that even if we found it we'd never be able to prove it was the one you used!'

'I haven't been near that back wall,' Lily snapped.

'Oh, no? How are you going to prove that?'

I turned quickly. 'Now wait a moment . . .' I began, but to my amazement it was Lily who interrupted me.

'Forget it,' she said. 'Look, I don't know who you are, but you're not helping!'

I stared at her in unfeigned shock. Then, for a moment, our eyes met, and I understood what she was about.

She had, after all, had the same thought as I had: it was better for both of us if I remained free. To do that, we had to convince Rattlesnake and Hunter that we had nothing to do with each other.

I held out my hands in a gesture of submission. 'All right,' I said. 'If you say so, I'll shut up.'

'Come along,' Rattlesnake said crisply. To Hunter, he said: 'You'd better stay here with the body. And keep an eye on him.' It seemed that Rattlesnake was not about to take my story at face value, after all.

As she was led away, Lily demanded to know where they were going.

'The palace, of course.'

'And what's the charge?'

'Murder. What else?'

She laughed harshly. 'Don't be absurd! You know you won't be able to make that stick! Why don't you tell me what this is really about?'

It was Rattlesnake's turn to laugh, but as with Lily, there was no mirth in it. 'Tiger Lily, you'll find out soon enough!'

Hunter and I were left alone with the body.

For a long time neither of us said anything. This was less out of hostility than a feeling of awkwardness. Rattlesnake had not arrested me or accused me of anything, and so his colleague had no idea what to do with me. On the other hand, there was no point in trying to run away: he stood between me and the doorway, and if I started to clamber over the wall he would be behind me, pulling me back down, in an instant.

I found myself staring at the ground instead of meeting Hunter's eyes, and I suspected he was doing the same.

The whole situation put me in mind of a custom at Aztec weddings. After the ceremony, which might well be their first meeting, the bride and groom would be led to their room and expected to stay there for four days, during which time they were required not to touch each other. I very much doubted that any couple really obeyed this rule, but, if they did, I could imagine them experiencing the same sort of baffled indecision

as Hunter and I had at that moment, having no idea what to
say or do next. The thought made me chuckle.

'What are you laughing at?'

'Oh, just a thought I had. Sorry.' Feeling able to speak at
last, I looked up at the other man. 'Look, I know you're going
to say it's none of my business, but you do realize this is all
nonsense, don't you?'

His only answer was to stare silently towards the interior of
the house.

'I mean, look at these footprints, for example. Not ours, the
ones that were here before.'

'Rattlesnake said . . .'

'Rattlesnake knew perfectly well what I'm talking about!
Look for yourself, man – there's only one set of these prints
leading to the wall. There isn't another set coming back!
There's no way Lily – this woman, Tiger Lily, whatever her
name is – could have made them taking something over there
to throw away. Not unless she flew back to the house.' He said
nothing, so I added: 'And another thing. I didn't notice it at
first, but each of these prints is about half the size of my foot.
They're too small to be the woman's.'

I looked at his face, which was now wearing a troubled
frown. 'Even so . . .'

'Even so, nothing! Look, I don't care what happens to the
woman, but I seem to have got caught up in this thing just by
being here. And in case it's escaped your notice, whoever did
kill that man in there is still at large. He could be right next
door, listening to us through the wall.' That had the desired
effect, as Hunter cast a quick, nervous glance towards the
nearest neighbouring house. 'Maybe it would be an idea if you
told me what all this is really about.'

The warrior hesitated before replying: 'All I can tell you is,
we knew she'd been asking after this man Hare. Don't know

anything about him, except that he's some kind of merchant, from the hot lands on the coast. We know the woman's up to something, though. So we thought we'd pay Hare a visit before she did. Pity we were too late.'

'It looks as if you were, one way or another. What had the woman done to get you so suspicious, though?'

He sighed. 'She'd been keeping bad company. That's enough. We watch people, and they talk to other people, and we end up watching them too.'

'Keeping bad company?' I put a sulky expression on my face. 'That's hardly fair, is it? I mean, look at it my from my point of view. I'm a stranger here. How am I supposed to know who I can talk to, and who I've got to avoid? I could get arrested just for asking the wrong person the way to the marketplace.'

'Not unless their name was Mother of Light,' replied Hunter sardonically.

'"Mother of—"' I checked myself, remembering that my interest in Lily's doings was supposed to be casual. After a short pause, I added: 'You and Rattlesnake aren't parish police-men, are you?'

He smiled, as if he found that amusing. 'No.'

'And you aren't constables.' I meant high-ranking officers such as my brother, who might well be involved in investigat-ing what they thought of as crimes against the state. My brother, though, would never dream of going anywhere on official business and not wearing his full regalia, and I was sure the same would be true here.

'No.'

'Then . . .'

'You ask too many questions. Look, I still don't know what I'm supposed to be doing with you. You've got to stay here, but that's all I'm saying, for now, all right? Just don't push your luck.'

I made the same submissive gesture as I had when Lily had told me to mind my own business earlier. Then I turned away, staring at the broken section of the wall while I thought about what to do next.

Eventually I said: 'Mind if I take another look over the wall?'

'Why?'

'I just had an idea about what might have happened. After all, how else are we supposed to pass the time?'

'I'll come with you. I don't want you getting ideas about climbing over it!'

Together we peered down the slope towards the stream.

'It's easy to see what happened,' I said. 'Our killer does the deed, runs into the courtyard, jumps over the wall and legs it down the hill. I bet if we checked the slope for footprints, we'd find some. Of course, he'd have gone straight for the stream to wash the blood off his feet, unless he was a complete idiot, so there wouldn't be much of a trail to follow.'

'Sounds reasonable. All right, what if it wasn't the woman. Who was it, then?'

'I don't know. Who'd kill a . . . a merchant?' I had remembered just in time that I was not supposed to know who the dead Texcalan was; for all I was meant to know, it was most likely Hare's body lying inside the house. 'A thief, I suppose. I noticed that chest in there was empty. And he'd had his labret and earplugs ripped off. Did you notice that?'

The other man glanced over his shoulder into the house and sighed. 'It's beyond me.'

'Well,' I said cheerfully, 'never mind. Look, there's your murder weapon.'

He whipped his head around and stared over the wall again. 'Where? What are you looking at?'

There was a fair amount of rubble around our feet: mostly

mud bricks and chips of plaster. I might have wished for something more substantial, but I was not in a position to be
choosy. Quietly picking up the heaviest thing I could reach, I
replied: 'Just beneath us. No, a bit to the right – it's a big piece
of obsidian, hardly chipped at all, so it can't have been thrown
away because it was rubbish . . . Can't you see it?'

'No,' he said. Since I was making it up, this was hardly surprising, but as he stooped and craned his neck in an effort to
follow my directions, he left the back of his head exposed and
at just the right angle for me to knock him out with a brick.

Summoning all the force I could muster, I struck him hard
enough to shatter the block of dried mud in my hands.

Nothing happened. He just stood where he was, bending
over the wall, neither moving nor making a sound.

I gulped fearfully. It had not worked. The big warrior was
going to turn around in a moment, his face dark and his eyes
blazing with rage, and in my weakened state I would not stand
a chance. I wondered whether he would be able to restrain
himself from killing me, to save me for a more painful punish-
ment later.

A sound like a low sigh escaped from him, and he slid slowly
to the ground at my feet.

I found myself gasping for breath, suddenly realizing I had
not dared to breathe since picking up the brick.

Quickly, I checked Hunter's pulse, and then lifted one of his
eyelids to make sure. He was unconscious but still very much
alive. I had to decide what to do next in a hurry. It would not
be long before he woke up, and I did not want to be around
when that happened.

I contemplated going back into the house, to search it, but
I decided against it. There was no time, and if I left through
the street doorway, the trail of bloody footprints I would leave
would be as plain as a glyph saying: 'Yaotl went this way.'

I decided to copy the killer. I scrambled over the wall, muttering 'Sorry' as I planted a foot on Hunter's back to boost myself up, and dropped down on to the hillside. I scrambled and slithered through the bushes as fast as I could while taking care not to cut myself on any of the rubbish strewn among them. Then I splashed along the stream-bed until the house with the broken courtyard wall was well out of sight.

By the time I had regained the road back into Tetzcoco, I was exhausted. Still, I forced myself to carry on. I told myself I had to get help.

There was only one man in Tetzcoco I could think of turning to. I only hoped he was sober enough to be of any use.

6

'What we need,' Kindly said, a few moments before exhaustion and pain finally overcame me and I fell asleep, 'is a lawyer.'

The old man had certainly been drinking, but as usual with him it barely showed. As I had babbled my way through the story of what had happened to his daughter and me, he took occasional nips at a drinking-gourd, but his head nodded only to acknowledge what I was telling him. He had offered me the gourd the moment I staggered into our room and he saw what state I was in, but I was so weak and thirsty by then that all I wanted was water.

'I wonder if Itznenepilli is still practising?' he mused. He took one more swig before hauling himself reluctantly to his feet. 'I suppose it's no use telling you to go and look for him, is it? Thought not.' He managed to make it sound as if it were my fault. 'This won't be cheap, either. Let me warn you, Yaotl: no matter how grown up your children think they are, you never stop paying for them!'

I managed a grunt in reply, but by the time he was out of the door I was unconscious. When I awoke, there were two other men in the room.

One was Kindly. The other was a stranger, a tall, fleshy man whom I took to be the lawyer, Itznenepilli. It was an appropriate name: it meant 'Obsidian Tongue'.

It took me a little while to take in his appearance and work out what I found incongruous about it. His cloak and breech-cloth were not made of cotton, and that marked him out as a commoner. However, they looked more expensive than any commoner's garb I had ever seen. They were finely woven of something like sisal; the cloak and the trailing ends of the breechcloth were almost long enough to amount to an offence, and the flowers embroidered on them were exquisite, their colour so rich they looked better than real. As a com-moner within the city limits, he wore no sandals, but his toenails had been neatly trimmed, the backs of his heels had a fresh, pink tinge, as if their calluses had been carefully rubbed away, and his short, immaculate hair had the unnatural black-ness of the indigo dye used by some women. Everything about this man's extraordinary appearance spoke of somebody deter-mined to do everything the law allowed to rise above his status.

He was holding Kindly's drinking-gourd. I might have expected him to take a decorous sip and swirl the liquid appre-ciatively around his mouth, savouring it before swallowing it, but instead he downed an enormous draught, sighing in satis-faction when he had finished. He did not offer the gourd back to its owner.

'Not bad. Now, as I was saying . . .'

I sat up with a groan. Much of the stiffness in my joints, which had showed signs of easing during the long walk to Hare's house, was coming back. 'You must be the lawyer,' I said.

He ignored me. 'In a case of this kind, I have to ask for my fees in advance. I require twenty large cloaks a day. The case will be concluded in four days – it has to be, since the Useless Days are nearly upon us – and so that comes to eighty large cloaks.'

I gasped. That was enough for an ordinary person to live on for four years.

'I suppose it does,' Kindly conceded grudgingly. 'I thought the usual arrangement was that if you won, you took a percentage of whatever was being fought over. Can't we come to some agreement like that?'

The lawyer sighed. 'I'd like to, but, frankly, in a criminal case . . . well, people about to be executed are sometimes less than punctilious about settling their debts. I'm sure you know how it is. I'm really sorry.' He gave a thin smile that told me exactly how sorry he felt.

'Lily isn't going to be executed!' I protested. 'She didn't have anything to do with the murder. She wasn't even arrested for that, not really. It was a pretext. Look, let me tell you what Hunter told me . . .'

Obsidian Tongue stared at me as if I had just appeared out of nowhere. Then he turned to Kindly. 'Who is this?'

Kindly said: 'His name's Yaotl. He's Lily's, er, slave.'

'Ah, good! You can replenish this gourd for us, then,' he said, waving the vessel in my direction. From the lack of any sloshing noises from inside it, I gathered he had drained it.

I stood up, feeling at something of a disadvantage addressing Obsidian Tongue from a sitting position, and was surprised to find that he was in reality no taller than I. 'Surely you want to know what I saw today?'

'No,' he replied shortly.

'How come?'

He heaved a sigh, as though talking to me were an unpleasant task that he had to resign himself to. 'Assuming your mistress's father agrees to my terms, then I may, at some point, be interested in what you've got to say. But there would be procedural matters to undertake first. Anyway, if I've understood correctly, what you saw at Hare's house is likely to be peripheral to the main charge, at best.'

'Peripheral?' I squawked. I was so astonished I could barely speak coherently enough to pronounce the word. 'But . . .'

He was already talking to Kindly again, although the gourd remained hanging in the air between us. 'Now, the first thing we need to do is make an application to transfer Lily's trial to the Merchants' Court in Tlatelolco.'

'She'd get a fairer hearing from her own people,' Kindly said eagerly. 'Will it work?'

'No. The Tlatelolco merchants have no jurisdiction here. But we should make the application anyway.'

I began to feel giddy. I was convinced that this had nothing to do with pain and tiredness but everything to do with the fact that I could not believe my own ears. 'If it won't work, why do it?'

Obsidian Tongue was ignoring me again. 'My fee for that application . . .'

'Which won't work . . .'

'. . . will be a further ten large cloaks. Kindly, we haven't agreed that I'm going to take this case, and I regret to say that if this slave interrupts me again . . .'

'All right,' the merchant growled. 'Yaotl, for my sake, shut up, will you? I'll pay what you ask. It's not as if I have any choice. Will you take gold quills in lieu? It would save me the trouble of exchanging them. Oh,' he added as an afterthought, 'that is your fee for representing Lily on both charges, isn't it?'

'Both charges?' I asked.

'Of course, both charges,' the lawyer said reproachfully. 'What sort of greedy person do you take me for?'

Under other circumstances I might have laughed, but I had something else to think of now. 'Both charges?' I asked again.

Now that his fee was settled, Obsidian Tongue seemed to

become a little more affable, even deigning to reply to me. 'Why, yes. Both charges. You see, you may be right about the murder being a pretext. But there's a much more serious accusation: conspiring against the King.'

'The murder is straightforward enough. Hare is found . . .'

'No, he isn't,' I said. 'I told you, he was a Texcalan warrior. Lily bought him at the same time as me, but she let him go.'

Obsidian Tongue scowled in annoyance before taking another swig at the fresh gourd I had been sent out to buy. While carrying the sacred wine back to the guesthouse, I had been tempted to try a sip, just to see whether it still tasted as good as it had all those years ago, but I had refrained. I knew that one sip would lead to another, and I had to keep a clear head now. Somebody had to find a way of getting Lily out of prison and away from the threat of death hanging over her. Her father may have been less infirm than he pretended, but he clearly could not do it on his own, and Obsidian Tongue struck me as the sort who could be trusted up to the point at which he received his fee and no further.

Inevitably, I found myself wondering why I should care. Of course, I was Lily's slave and could not expect to be treated very kindly if she were convicted of a crime against the state. But I was not known in Tetzcoco, and there was little to stop me from running away and pursuing the goal I had mentioned to Lily on the lake – heading West, in the direction I presumed my son had taken. It was a forlorn hope, but it seemed to represent the only chance I had of seeing him again. I asked myself why I did not seize it and why, instead, I was frantically turning over one daft scheme after another to rescue the woman from wherever in the heart of Lord Maize Ear's palace she was being held.

It was that tangle of feelings between us once again, made only more tortuous by her having saved me from the grisly fate

Lord Feathered in Black and his associates had planned for me. I was indebted to her for that, and for other things, and to run away now would be somehow to repudiate it all, and deny that anything had ever passed between us beyond a few sweaty moments on a sleeping mat. I felt that I owed myself more than that, besides whatever was due to Lily.

Besides, I reminded myself, Lily had once saved my son's life too, and if I were ever to see him again how could I look him in the eye and tell him I had deserted her?

And so I had returned faithfully to Kindly and the lawyer with the gourd still full and the stopper firmly jammed into its hole.

Obsidian Tongue put the drink down and said: 'It doesn't really matter who the dead man was. The court will be told she was arrested at the scene of the crime. The simplest explanation is that she did it, and even the fairest of judges find simple explanations hard to resist. Still, we can make the most of what you saw, and she may get the benefit of the doubt.'

He had grudgingly agreed to pretend he found me worth speaking to directly, since Kindly had told him to and the old man was, after all, his client.

'What you can't help with is the charge of plotting against the King.'

'What is all that about?' Kindly asked, watching the gourd the way a weasel watches a rabbit. 'It makes no sense to me.'

'It's not intended to make sense,' Obsidian Tongue replied loftily. 'Lily was overheard talking to a lady from the palace named Mother of Light. I gather merely talking to this woman was enough to cast suspicion on Lily, but you tell me she was making arrangements for some sort of secret message to be passed to her. If this is what the judges are told, and they are satisfied that it is true, that's all they will need to know. In fact, they will be very eager *not* to know any more than that.'

'This is a peculiar place,' Kindly rumbled. He made a sudden move to snatch the gourd but was too late: the lawyer had it halfway to his lips already.

'I'd have to agree,' Obsidian Tongue said sadly. It was the first hint of real emotion, other than irritation, that he had betrayed. 'But you have to understand, Tetzcoco isn't what it was, just a few years ago, in the time of Hungry Coyote and Hungry Child, when not even the King was above the law, and a judge who let himself be swayed by fear or greed could expect to be strangled. Those were the days!' he cried, and I suspected the sacred wine was beginning to do its work as he went on: 'I don't really remember Hungry Coyote, of course, but my father told me stories about him. He told me the King once overheard a poor boy calling him harsh for not allowing the poor to take sticks and branches from the ground in the royal forest to use as firewood. Hungry Coyote promptly changed the law so that they could, provided they did not damage any growing tree or plant. And, of course, I remember Hungry Child's reign. That was when to practise law! The truth was all we had to concern ourselves with, and it was a thing worth fighting for. Sometimes, when I was a young man, I would take a case for nothing, because I believed in it.'

'Imagine,' I said under my breath.

'Not now. What's the point, when the truth is manipulated by powerful men and the judges are for ever looking over their shoulders at their masters, seeking to fulfil their wishes?'

He was weeping by now, silent tears starting from his eyes. I found it hard to believe that any of this was real, and that it was not merely the sacred wine talking. On the other hand, I had to admit that I had never had that much regard for the truth.

'Does any of this have anything to do with why Lily's on trial or how we get her off?' Kindly asked.

The lawyer sniffed loudly. 'In a sense, it does. Do you understand what's going on in Tetzcoco at the moment?'

Lily had said it was not a safe place to be carrying secret messages. Hunter had talked of watching people, and then watching the people they talked to. And I remembered the demeanour of the people I had noticed on the way to Hare's house: furtive, almost frightened.

'You'll appreciate, I have to be careful what I say,' he said, although I was unsure what the word 'careful' might mean to someone who had drunk as much sacred wine as he had. 'But what everybody knows is this. Before the old King, Hungry Child, died, he shut himself away in his retreat in Tetzcotzinco and pined away, supposedly from grief at what happened to his son.'

'Prince of Willows?' I asked.

'Yes. He would have succeeded his father, no doubt, if it hadn't been for that wretched girl, but instead there was a dispute. Four of Hungry Child's sons contended for the throne; in the end, it went to Lord Maize Ear.'

'Our beloved Emperor's nephew,' Kindly observed. 'But his brother, Black Flower, didn't take it lying down, did he?'

The lawyer looked annoyed, like a man trying to tell a joke when someone else steals the punch line. 'He did not. He roused his supporters in the North of the valley, and beyond the mountains, and the next thing Maize Ear knew, he had a civil war on his hands. Black Flower was very popular, you see – his mother was one of Hungry Child's lawful wives, not a concubine like Maize Ear's mother, and in Tetzcoco it's normally the King's eldest lawful son who succeeds his father.' Obsidian Tongue looked significantly at Kindly and me when he said this. I took the point: among the Aztecs, Emperors were elected by a small clique of nobles. The Tetzcocans clearly resented Maize Ear, not just because he was

Montezuma's nephew but because the manner of his accession was essentially alien to their way of doing things – an Aztec imposition.

'So, even with his uncle backing him, Maize Ear hasn't been able to get rid of his half-brother to this day. Now there's a truce between them, with Black Flower still in power up in the North and his half-brother sitting on the throne here. But neither man is exactly happy with the state of things. The city is – I should say, is rumoured to be – full of spies for both sides.'

'And anyone, like Lily, who gets caught in the middle of all this is in trouble,' Kindly said grimly.

'But she wasn't spying for anyone!' I protested. 'All she did was put Hare in touch with someone at the palace . . . Ah.'

'You see?' the lawyer said. 'That in itself may have amounted to a crime against the state, depending on who Lily's contact at the palace was and what the message was that Hare was trying to get to her.'

I frowned. 'We know her contact was a concubine called Mother of Light. What else do we know?'

Kindly replied: 'No one I've asked seems to know her. I gathered she was one of Hungry Child's women, but that doesn't tell us much. He had a couple of thousand of them, I believe. I suppose if she was one of his favourites, that might explain why she hasn't been arrested herself.'

'Probably,' Obsidian Tongue agreed. 'She'd be too important, or at least too well known, to proceed against without some evidence. Lily, of course, very helpfully provided the police with all the evidence they needed against herself by stumbling on a freshly killed corpse.'

'It wasn't that fresh,' I said. 'And they weren't the police. From what Hunter told me, they must be working for Maize Ear himself.' I thought for a moment. 'What if we could prove the message was entirely innocent? That it was — I don't know — the current prices for obsidian spear-points down in the jungle or something.'

'How would you do that?' the lawyer asked sceptically. 'Even Lily doesn't know what the message was about.'

'Would it help, though?' I persisted.

'Well, I suppose it might. It would have to be very convincing, though. As I said, the judges will want to know as little as possible about the message itself, and they certainly won't assume it was something harmless unless you give them a good reason to.'

'Right,' I declared. 'Then this is what we do. I find Hare and get him to give this thing to me. Since it's in Mayan, Kindly, you'll then have to interpret it. Hopefully that'll give your lawyer something he can use at the trial.'

Obsidian Tongue's sudden explosive laugh showered me in a fine spray of sacred wine. 'Is that all?' he cried.

'Why, have I left something out?'

'Yes. How are you going to find Hare? Assuming he's still in Tetzcoco, which he probably isn't. This may be a small town compared with Mexico, but it's not some little village. Are you really going to track down one man in a city of thirty thousand people? Remember the trial has to be up in four days.'

'He's still in Tetzcoco. He hasn't been paid yet, remember? And from what Lily told me, it's definitely worth his while sticking around until he is. And that's where you come in. I've got to see Lily.'

'You can't.' There was a hint of smugness in his voice as he explained what he thought was the fatal flaw in my scheme. 'I'm the only person who's allowed to see her.'

'Because you're a lawyer. I thought so. That's fine. I can be her lawyer too. You go and see her, and I'll come with you.'

I had to talk to Lily, to find out as much as she could tell me about Hare, and in particular to get my hands on whatever she had been intending to pay him with. Besides, I wanted to see for myself where she was being held, just in case I had to put any of those daft plans to rescue her into practice. More than that, I wanted to see her, and I wanted her to see me, to know that I had not deserted her and was doing what I could to get her out of her cage. It was not as if I did not know what being in prison felt like.

Obsidian Tongue stared at me while sacred wine dribbled, unregarded, out of his wide-open mouth. 'You?' he gasped. 'Out of the question! You're a slave and you look like one. In fact, you look as if you've been rolled down a mountain. It would get me disbarred. I . . .'

'Will do what you're told, if you want my money,' growled Kindly. 'Yaotl's right. Our best chance of getting my daughter out of this is to find that merchant. And this slave can pass for one of you if he has to. He used to be a priest, so he can read and write and knows enough law to get by. He can be Lily's regular lawyer, hotfoot from Mexico to help with her defence.'

Obsidian Tongue scowled, and for a moment I thought he was going to get up and walk out, but in the end the thought of all the goose quills filled with gold dust that Kindly was about to give him overcame his pride. 'It's not really necessary,' he sulked. 'I can put together a pretty good defence with what I have . . .'

'This is a game to you, isn't it?' I said, exasperated. 'It's all very well for you to get up on your feet and make a few fine speeches, knowing you'll be paid whatever happens, but to the rest of us it's a matter of life and death! Besides,' I added maliciously, 'wouldn't you like to know the truth about this message? I thought the truth mattered to you – or is that all over now?'

That stung him. He frowned at me, looked at the floor and

finally took a quick pull at the gourd. 'All right,' he sighed. 'If you get caught, though, I'll say you blackmailed me into it.'

The royal palace in Tetzcoco was, like its counterparts in Mexico, far more than just the place where the ruler rested his head. It served as the seat of government, the military headquarters and armoury, the courts of justice, the zoo and the jail, among other things. At its heart was as large a building as I had ever seen: an immense, two-storey structure whose colonnaded façade stretched so far in each direction that I made myself dizzy trying to see both ends of it.

The palace occupied half of an immense space, enclosed by walls that must have been a thousand paces on each side. The other half was Tetzcoco's main marketplace. Even in the chilly pre-dawn twilight, this space heaved with buyers, sellers, spectators and others, such as Obsidian Tongue and I, who were just passing through. As we threaded our way among stalls selling everything from turquoise labrets to edible dogs, the lawyer attempted to give me a crash course in his nation's laws.

'Our system is a lot more sophisticated than yours in Mexico,' he bragged, as if he really were talking to a visiting Aztec colleague. 'We have over eighty offences and four courts. Which court hears a case depends on the offence and the status of the offender. The Council of Music, for example, tries anyone charged with practising witchcraft without a licence, as well as overseeing the priests. The War Council tries military crimes – beheading deserters and so on – and adjudicates disputes over captured enemy warriors. The Treasury Council deals with arguments about the collection of tribute. The one we're concerned with, though, is the Supreme Court. That has jurisdiction over most things – including crimes against the King and murder.'

'What if things go badly?' I asked. 'Can we appeal to anyone?'

'There's a Court of Appeal, yes, with two judges. But I hope it won't come to that. They have to decide every case in consultation with the King, you see . . .'

'And it was the King's men who brought Lily in in the first place,' I acknowledged. I shivered. The task I had set myself was looking harder and harder. I had lain awake much of the night wondering what I would do if we located Hare and obtained and deciphered his message only to find that it was, in fact, something that might threaten the realm. I dismissed the thought now. There was no point in worrying about it when my chances of finding the missing merchant to begin with were so slim.

'The other thing we have to bear in mind,' the lawyer went on, 'is that the Useless Days are coming up, and the trial has to be concluded by then. As I said yesterday, that gives us four days at most.'

A year was three hundred and sixty days. Because, however, the passage of the seasons takes a little longer than that, there were, at the end of each year, five days that belonged to no month, had no names and over which no god presided. This was a frightening time when any sensible person would stay indoors, and not even sacred work such as sweeping and washing the faces of the idols was done. Naturally, no court would sit during the Useless Days.

'It's a pity all this had to happen so near the end of the session,' Obsidian Tongue mused, 'but we'll just have to make the best of it. Now, we go in here. You'll be taken to see your, er, client. I have an application to make,' he concluded with relish, no doubt thinking of the extra fee he had induced Kindly to part with.

'You're a bit scruffy for a lawyer,' the guard at the palace gate told me. 'You look like you've been rolled down a mountain.'

'Accidents happen, even to lawyers,' I said. 'I fell out of a canoe and got caught between it and the bank. And all my clothes were ruined by the water, so I had to borrow these rags.' Obsidian Tongue was attired as splendidly as he had been the day before. I still wore what Lily had given me when she rescued me.

The man grunted. 'Well, Obsidian Tongue, if you'll vouch for him . . .'

The lawyer pulled a face but said he would, and so we were let in.

A steward conducted me through corridors and courtyards, across immense, echoing hallways and around so many corners that, by the time we reached our destination, I had no idea which way I was facing or how far I had come. So much, I thought, for my plan to find out just where Lily was being held. Without a guard I could conceivably wander, lost, inside this vast building until I starved to death.

I was too preoccupied with what I was trying to do to pay much attention to what was going on around me, but I could not fail to notice how opulent my surroundings were. Walls were framed and panelled in oak and cypress that had been planed and polished until they shone, even in the poor light of early morning. The gaps between the smooth slabs under-foot, against which my guide's and my soles slapped as we walked, were almost invisible. Feather mosaics decorated the walls in every room – roseate spoonbill, the brilliant green of quetzal, the blue of cotinga, every plume priceless even before they had been made into a work of art. Statues glowered down at me wherever I went: some of granite, others of greenstone, a few small, delicate ones of gold. Many of them portrayed the same man: it seemed that Hungry Coyote was still watching over his domain, even in death.

Eventually we left the brilliant wall-hangings and exquisite statuary behind. The wooden panelling became bare stone, looking rough and unfinished in places, and the passageways became narrower, stuffier and darker. I became aware of an unmistakable odour: a combination of piss, ordure, stale sweat and the faint, sharp scent of fear.

When I became aware of it, I stopped and had to will myself to go on. I had been in such places before, but seldom had I gone into one expecting to get out alive.

'We're near the prison, aren't we?'

'It's right here,' my guide confirmed, leading the way into a long, low, dingy hall lined on both sides with wooden cages. 'Your client is over there – that one on its own.'

I looked keenly at the cages and their occupants, and was surprised. The men and women huddling behind their bars looked as dejected as prisoners anywhere, but their conditions were better than the ones I had endured. They had more space than I ever had, enough even to lie down in, and they had pots to relieve themselves in which were not overflowing. In Mexico, prisoners were often slowly starved to death. None of the inmates here was fat, but they did not look like skeletons either.

Lily's cage was at the far end of one of the rows. As my guide had indicated, it stood a little apart from its nearest neighbour, and it had its own guard, a young one-captive warrior who looked as surprised to be here as I was to find him.

'Lawyer,' my guide announced before stepping quickly out of the hall. From where I stood I could hear him letting out a long, low exhalation as soon as he got outside. He must have been holding his breath.

Lily lay at the rear of her cage with her face turned away. She was wearing the skirt and blouse she had had on when she was arrested. They were still relatively clean.

'I didn't know she had her own guard,' I muttered to the warrior.

He started, as if I had woken him from a deep sleep. His hands tightened their grip on his sword, and for an instant I was afraid he was going to mistake me for an enemy, an intruder bent on relieving him of his charge, but then he relaxed.

'I said, I didn't know she had her own guard.'

'Who? Oh, my prisoner,' he mumbled. 'Yes, I was just told to stand here and – well, I'm not quite sure what else I'm supposed to be doing, to be honest. Just stand here, that's what I was told. Whoever she is, she must be pretty important.'

I found that depressing. It could only mean that whatever Lily was supposed to have done was viewed as being particularly heinous.

'You look after your prisoners well here, don't you?' I said, pretending to eye the lines of cages while searching the walls for non-existent exits. There was only one way in and out, as far as I could tell.

'You're an Aztec. I can tell by your voice. Well, we don't just shut people away and leave them to rot in Tetzcoco. No, we treat them properly, until they're sentenced. Then we kill them.'

'What if they're acquitted?'

He pursed his lips thoughtfully. 'Well, it happens,' he conceded. 'I suppose then we have to let them go.'

Out of the corner of my eye I saw the cage's occupant stirring.

'Exactly where were you told to stand?' I asked the guard.

'In front of the cage. Why?'

'How close to the cage? I mean, if you stood a little further away – say, over there – you wouldn't be disobeying orders, would you?' I was pointing to a spot halfway down the hall, in the hope that we could compromise on a distance that would not allow the guard to overhear what passed between Lily and me. We were, after all, supposed to be lawyer and client.

He frowned. 'I don't know about that. What if you passed her a weapon or something and I couldn't see?'

'You can search me,' I said. 'Besides, what good would it do her if I did? Tell you what, if you move away a bit, the next time I come I'll give you a present.'

The man was outraged. Trust me, I thought, to run into a squaddie with a sense of duty. 'A bribe, you mean? How dare you! What do you take me for?' he cried in a voice that echoed off the hall's low ceiling.

'Well, not exactly a bribe, you know . . .'

'I've a good mind to take this sword to you, or . . . or . . .' He spluttered into silence while he tried to think of what might be worse than carving slices off me with the obsidian blades set into the weapon's shaft. Before he could come up with anything, Lily interrupted him.

'What's all that noise?' she said sleepily as she got up into a kneeling position, sweeping her skirt under her knees. 'Is that you, Calquimichin? What are you shouting for? You woke me up!'

I had to smile. The warrior's name meant 'House Mouse', and I would have guessed that he had never been happy with it.

However, his reaction to Lily's words was extraordinary. He stopped shouting. He took a step away from the cage, as though it contained a dangerous animal that might lash out at him at any moment, and looked at the floor. 'I'm sorry,' he mumbled, 'but this man . . .'

'What man? Is that my lawyer? About bloody time! Now, listen, I want . . . Yaotl?'

Her eyes widened in shock as she took in my appearance. I

grinned encouragingly at her through the bars. 'Yes, that's right. Yaotl the lawyer.'

'Yaotl the lawyer. Yaotl-the-lawyer.' It was as if repeating the phrase would help her get used to the idea. Then she said: 'Have you gone raving mad?'

'No. Look, we've got a plan . . .'

'Mouse!'

The guard jumped when she called his name.

'I need this pot emptied.'

'Um . . . I'll go and fetch the slave,' he said. 'Stay there, won't you?' He shot me a nervous glance before hurrying away. I squatted in front of the cage.

'Where does he think I'm likely to go?' the woman muttered under her breath.

'You've got him well trained,' I observed.

She laughed. 'He's convinced himself I'm someone of consequence, a queen or a princess or at least a royal concubine. Besides, I think I remind him of his mother. His grandmother even!' The laughter subsided as she looked at me seriously. I noticed that, for all her seeming ebullience, the lines around her mouth and across her forehead seemed deeper than they had just a day before.

'How are you?' I asked awkwardly.

'Pretty good, considering I've got to spend the rest of my life in this cage, before they take me out and kill me. Yaotl, about Hare . . .'

'Hare, yes,' I said eagerly. 'He's what I wanted to talk about. We've got a plan . . .'

She interrupted me, bending her head towards the bars and hissing urgently: 'Never mind that now! Did you find the ring?'

I stared at her. 'What ring?'

She gave an exasperated sigh, as if I ought to have known

what she was talking about. 'The ring I was supposed to pay Hare with. A very special gold ring with a greenstone skull mounted on it. I hid it in Hare's house.'

'Oh, terrific!' I said bitterly. 'Maize Ear's men will have been all over the place by now. They'll have found it for sure. What did you want to go and do that for?'

'Calm down, and don't talk so loudly! I couldn't keep it on me – someone would have been bound to find it by now. Look, if Rattlesnake and Hunter are anything to go by, Maize Ear's men may not have found it. I jammed it into the wall, in a gap by one of the doorposts. You've got to find it.'

'Well, yes, all right, but as I was saying . . .'

Lily looked up again, her manner suddenly brisk. 'No. Listen to me, Yaotl. Nobody must know about this ring. Nobody! Mother of Light told me when she gave it to me – if it falls into the wrong hands or if word of it gets out, it means death to everyone who's had anything to do with it. And don't expect to get a trial first!'

'But . . .'

'Careful. Here comes the guard again.'

I swore under my breath as Mouse came lumbering towards us, with a slave trotting at his heels. The slave peered critically through the bars at the almost empty pot. 'Hardly anything in it,' he complained. 'Do you think I empty these things for fun?'

The guard looked reproachfully at Lily. 'I'm sorry,' she said meekly. 'I haven't got used to this yet.'

'I'll come back later.'

As the slave trotted off again, obviously keen to spend as little time in the prison as he could, Mouse said: 'I hope you two haven't been plotting anything while I was away.'

'I was just explaining something to my client,' I said stiffly, while wondering what Lily had been talking about. Obviously she wanted me to go back to the house and retrieve a ring. With Mouse standing next to me I could not ask her why, or why it was such a secret. I would just have to add it to a growing list of mysteries, of which the most pressing, from my point of view, was what in the Nine Regions of Hell had the Texcalan been doing there? Who had killed him?

'Well, carry on,' Mouse said encouragingly. 'Don't mind me!'

I hesitated, trying to find a way of outlining my plan in a way that could safely be overheard. 'The man who owned the house – assuming it wasn't him who was found dead on the floor there – we have to find him, don't we? Any ideas about where I can look for him, or someone who knows him?'

Lily held my gaze for a moment and opened her mouth as if there were something she wanted to say, but then, after a quick, nervous glance at her jailer, she lowered her eyes. 'I don't think it will work,' she said softly.

'Well, maybe not, but we have to try. I heard he was a merchant, from the hot lands on the coast. Is it worth asking the people who trade in the stuff they produce there? What would that be?'

'Chocolate, seashells, fish,' she mumbled automatically. 'Yaotl, please, don't waste your time on him. It won't help.'

'Well, it's all I can think of,' I said sharply. I was a little hurt to have my scheme dismissed so hastily. 'Do you have a better idea?'

'No. I'm sorry, it's just that . . . Well, I don't know how to say it . . .'

She plucked a few times at the hem of her blouse, which I recognised as an old nervous habit. As she looked at the floor of her cell, her dark, silver-streaked hair, unbound now, fell over her forehead. I had a sudden impulse to reach into the cage and touch it with my fingers, the way you might stroke a pet dog to reassure it during a thunderstorm.

'We're doing everything we can, you know,' I told her.

'I know,' she whispered. When she looked up, I was surprised to see tears in her eyes. 'And I know you shouldn't really be here. Thank you.'

I wondered whether she meant that I should not have come to the prison in the guise of her lawyer or was echoing my own thoughts of the day before, when I had toyed with the idea of running away from the city altogether. Either way, I could not think of a reply. We both fell silent, until, concerned that her guard might start to become suspicious, I got to my feet and mumbled a gruff goodbye.

'Conch shells, scallops, crab meat, turtle, stuff like that? Try any stall in this row.'

After leaving Lily I had decided that, whatever she might say, I had to follow my original scheme and find Hare. I would try to find the ring she had told me about as well, but it made sense to begin with the merchant. The obvious place to look for a merchant was in the marketplace, and that was right in front of the palace.

Now I looked in dismay at a line of pitches, most of them nothing more than reed mats strewn with merchandise, which seemed to stretch the entire length of the marketplace. It was going to take a long time to search this part of the market alone, and then I had to look for the chocolate sellers and anybody else trading in goods from the hot lands: dealers in exotic feathers, amber, tobacco, cotton and so many other things. Every type of merchandise had its own space, with dealers specializing in it grouped together. It made it easier for customers and traders alike, as well as for men like my informant, one of the policemen who patrolled the aisles between the stalls, keeping an eye out for thieves and short measures. I supposed, I admitted to myself, that it made it easier for me too: at least I knew to ignore the traders in slaves or obsidian spear-points or cochineal, for instance.

'What were you looking for, exactly?'

'Hare,' I said absently.

The policeman frowned. 'No, no. You're in the wrong place entirely. You want dealers in game, don't you? Mind you, it'll be a bit stringy at this time of year. You want to wait until summer, get one young and plump . . .'

'Not *a* hare,' I said impatiently. 'A man named Hare. A merchant.'

'You should have said.'

'Do you know him?'

'No,' the policeman replied, before suddenly remembering that he had urgent duties to perform elsewhere and leaving me to it.

I swore once, and then started to work my way along the row of stalls.

'Never heard of him.'

'Do you mean Rabbit? There are lots of people called Rabbit . . .'

'We sell seafood here. If you want a hare . . .'

As the morning wore on and I neared the end of the row, I found myself becoming more and more dispirited. This had seemed one of the most promising places to look for a merchant who specialized in goods from near the coast, but nobody seemed to have heard of him.

I was also getting hungry. I had never spent much time in this part of any market, assuming that it would be a revolting, malodorous quarter full of slimy things that no self-respecting Aztec would even want to look at, let alone eat. As my eyes wandered over the goods on display, however, I realized it was not like that. In front of me were sea creatures of every shape, from strange flat things to the long, narrow, silvery forms that

I thought of as fish, crabs and lobsters, piles of scallops and clams in their shells and even a few turtles, some still alive, judging by the heavy, forlorn waving of their flippers. The dead creatures were mostly packed in ice scraped from the mountains so that they did not smell too much, and the air around them had a sharp, salty tang that was not unpleasant.

Kindly had given me some money before I came out that morning, and I handed over a small bag of cocoa beans in return for a tortilla stuffed with chillies and crab meat.

'How do you keep it so fresh?' I asked wonderingly. 'It must take ages to get fish here from the coast.'

'About two days, at most,' the vendor told me proudly. 'There are chains of runners, you see. They operate day and night, just like royal messengers. The moment the fish is landed, it gets taken up by the first man in the chain and it goes from hand to hand all the way here.'

All the way from the jungle, I reflected, up into the mountains, taking the long way around to skirt enemy territory around Texcala and Huexotzinco, and then down into the valley. 'Impressive system. I don't suppose you know anything about a merchant called Hare, who used to trade with the Mayans on the coast?'

The man frowned. 'Never met him.'

'Never mind,' I said, turning away. 'Thanks anyway. Good food!'

'Wait a moment.'

I stopped with my jaws poised around my tortilla.

'I don't know anything about Hare, but I think I may have something of his.'

I looked around at once. The stallholder was facing away from me, bending over as he rummaged for something at the rear of his pitch. When he stood up and turned around, he had a heavy cloak, lined with rabbit's fur, draped over one arm. It looked like the sort of garment a merchant might well take with him to keep him warm on his travels.

'I was given this, this morning,' he said. 'There was a man hawking these along this row. I took this in exchange for a measure of clams.'

I stared at the cloak. 'What makes you think it's Hare's?'

'The man who gave it to me said he was acting on Hare's behalf. I had the feeling Hare himself doesn't want to show his face around here for some reason.'

'Did he say anything else, this man? What was he like, anyway?'

'Big bloke, built like a warrior, with enough scars too, but without the haircut. I thought maybe he was a labourer, a quarryman, something like that. All he told me was that Hare had given him this to sell, and there was more stuff if I was interested. Why do you want to know?'

I took a thoughtful bite at my tortilla before answering. 'I may be interested too. What sort of stuff?'

'Clothes, mostly. A few pots and plates, obsidian knives, that sort of thing. Oh, and a merchant's travelling staff. Sounds as if it may be everything the man owns, as though he's trying to raise money in a hurry.'

'Do you think he'll be back, the man who gave you the cloak? Only, I'd like to meet Hare anyway, and if he's got things to sell . . .'

The trader grinned as he turned aside to put the cloak away again. 'You're thinking you'd like to get your hands on some of them to cover what he owes you, right? Well, I'll keep a look-out. If the big man comes back, I'll ask him. I suppose I don't mention your name?'

'Better not.'

I wandered back along the row of stalls, munching thought-

fully on my tortilla and trying to decide what to make of what
I had just been told.

Hare might have been disposing of his property, as the man
had said, perhaps with a view to converting it into something
portable and taking it out of Tetzcoco as quickly as possible. I
could well see why he would have done that, considering
what we had found at his house, but there was something
about it that did not ring true. I was sure that no merchant, no
matter how desperate he was, would ever willingly part with
his travelling staff. It was sacred to the merchants' god,
Yacatecuhtli, Lord of the Vanguard, and was supposed to
remain with its owner until they were buried or cremated
together.

If whoever was selling Hare's property was not Hare himself,
then who was he? I wondered about the man who had sold
the market trader his cape. A man built like a warrior. The
body we had found at Hare's house had been a warrior's.
Perhaps two warriors had pillaged the house, one of them had
been killed, and the other was now trying to sell off the pro-
ceeds. I immediately thought of the other man I had been
roped to, the other Texcalan, but the fish seller had not
described a one-armed man to me. Did that mean there had
been yet another man at the house?

The effort of trying to work out what might have come
about made me groan. Who had cut the dead man's throat?
Who was now claiming to represent the merchant? And where
was Hare?

I finished my tortilla and looked around, trying to find
something on which to wipe away the grease, other than my
cloak. I was still looking for a suitable piece of cloth or a large,
flat leaf when I noticed someone looking at me.

He was not the sort of man who would normally have merited a second glance. He wore a plain maguey fibre cloak and

wore his hair loose like any commoner. His face was equally undistinguished, his weak nose, shallow cheekbones and fleshy mouth somehow seeming to melt into the flesh around them so as to be immediately forgettable. His eyes alone commanded attention, and when I first looked around they were fixed on me as intently as a toad's upon the fly it is about to eat.

As I turned fully towards this man, he dropped his gaze, abandoned whatever business he had been pretending to contract, and stepped swiftly away. A moment later he was lost in the crowd.

I took a couple of steps after him but stopped myself. If he had been watching me, I thought, then there was no need for me to pursue him. He would come and find me.

I wiped my hands on my cloak and sauntered away deliberately, at a pace that anybody following me would find easy to match.

I wandered vaguely around the marketplace for a while, casting occasional nonchalant glances over my shoulder. It was difficult to tell whether my tail was still with me or not. The moment he had vanished the first time, I realized that I could not remember quite what he looked like, and although from time to time I caught sight of someone I thought might be him, I was never sure. It was an unnerving sensation, believing I was being followed by someone who was effectively invisible.

I walked over to where the sellers of cocoa beans had their pitches. It occurred to me that anybody planning to covert his assets into money might well have started here, since cocoa beans were an easy form of currency to use: not too valuable to be exchanged for small, essential items such as food and much less trouble to carry around than large pieces of cloth. As with the fish sellers, I made my discreetly casual enquiries while pretending to admire the wares.

Chocolate was the drink of lords, a luxury I had rarely had

the opportunity to indulge in. Hence I knew little about it, and was immediately struck by the sheer variety of forms it came in. A bean is a bean, is what I had always imagined, a small, oval, white thing. Here, I was presented with beans of every size and colour: tiny ones like chilli seeds, green ones, brown ones, even some that were variegated, and separate piles of beans from different sources – Tochtepec, Coatolco, Xolteca, Zacatollan, even as far south as Guatemala. There were piles of cracked and broken beans, and heaps of others ground into various grades of powder. Every stall sold a selection of flavourings as well – vanilla or honey or pimentos – and bowls, jugs and wooden whisks for mixing the drink and beating it into the perfect frothy consistency.

'This is as good a selection as you'll find anywhere in the valley,' I was told. 'Whatever your master wants, I can supply it. If you don't see what you want here, I can probably get it for you.'

'Thanks,' I said dubiously. I looked quickly up and down the row of pitches, most of which had at least as great a variety of beans on display as this one.

The vendor intercepted my glance. 'Well, please yourself,' he said huffily, 'but just do me one favour: don't buy anything from him over there. He's a shyster. Toasts his beans in hot ashes to make them swell up and turn white.'

I turned to look at the stall he indicated. As I did so, my eyes passed over a nondescript man in a plain cloak slipping quietly across the aisle. I decided to ignore him. There was little I could do about him for the moment in any case.

I began asking about Hare again. It was not long before I found what I was looking for: a bundle of smoking tubes, bought very cheaply that morning, from a large man who said their owner was in a hurry to raise cash.

I left the same message here as I had with the seafood seller, to ask whoever was trying to get rid of the merchant's property to meet me, and then started walking back to the guesthouse.

I felt pleased with myself. The plan I had come up with was still not much of a plan, but so far it was working.

I wondered whether I ought to make an effort to get rid of my tail. I stepped up my pace, heading briskly and purposefully towards the wide entrance to the marketplace and the palace precinct. The stalls and crowded aisles around me resembled a maze, but it was easy enough to get my bearings simply by glancing up at the great bulk of Tezcatlipoca's pyramid, which towered over the walls and the sacred precinct beyond them. As I got closer to its base, the top of the pyramid vanished from sight, hidden by the lower slope of its great stairway, and all I could see up there was a thin wisp of smoke from the temple fire, a faint dark smudge against the clear sky.

At moments such as this I remembered that the Lord of the Here and Now was my divine patron. 'Well, O Giver of Life,' I murmured, 'this is your city, and I'm one of your own. If you can't look after me here, where can you?'

When I looked down again, I found that an extraordinary fracas had broken out just in front of me.

I had reached the entrance to the marketplace, and at first I thought I was seeing a repeat of the scene I had watched on the day of my sale, when my brother had forced his way past the police, but I soon saw that this was different. In particular, everything was happening on the far side of the gateway, and all the police on this side of it were doing was standing and watching with amused expressions, in between scrutinizing people going in and out.

A tall woman and a little wizened man were being harassed by what I took to be two unusually persistent beggars.

She was well dressed in a blouse and skirt embroidered with popcorn flowers and wore her hair elegantly braided. He wore a tattered cloak, and his head was bent so far over that all I could see of it was the very top, which was the colour of a heavy frost. His arms and legs were mostly hidden by the cloak, although the fingers of one hand were visible, their sinews standing out as they gripped the material, bunching it together to hold the garment closed around him. He must be feeling the cold, I thought, although it was a mild day.

As I drew closer I realized that their antagonists were a couple of itinerant pedlars, trying, somewhat over-enthusiastically, to sell the white-haired man cures for the diseases of old age.

'What's the trouble, old man? Cataracts? We've just the thing for cataracts. Lizard-shit and soot. Provided you rub it in just the way I tell you, it's a guaranteed cure.'

'I think it's haemorrhoids,' the other one said. 'Now, have I got the enema for you! You just boil up these herbs . . .'

'Just go away and leave him alone, won't you?' the woman cried suddenly. 'Otherwise I'll call the police!'

Her voice was striking: surprisingly deep, not loud, but clear and well modulated, as though she had been coached, in the way the children of lords and youngsters in the House of Tears were taught to speak. It drew my attention to her appearance. She had been a beauty, and although she was no longer young – I guessed she was a little younger than I, a few years short of forty – still she looked striking. Her eyes were so dark as to be black, or nearly so, and her skin was unusually pale, with none of the yellowish tinge that would have suggested its colour came out of a jar, unless it was a very expensive one.

Her goal, and that of her ancient companion, was clearly the marketplace, but one of the pedlars was standing between them and the entrance. 'Look, let me show you. Having trouble passing water? You just take an extract of some roots I've got and squirt it up through a tube into your member . . .'

'I said go away!' the woman snapped, flapping at the man with her hands.

'It's a pity,' said one of the policemen to nobody in particular. 'If those two tried that in here we'd nick them for trading without a licence. As it is, she'll have to wait for the parish police to come along. Or for them to get fed up and move on to their next victim.'

'What if somebody sent them on their way?' I asked.

'Nothing to do with us.' The policeman eyed my scrawny frame, with all its signs of recent ill-treatment, with interest. 'If you want to have a go, we could do with a laugh!'

'I . . .' I swallowed. Something about the woman had stirred up an impulse to intervene, but I had no idea how. I had never been much of a fighter, even though, like all priests, I had learned something of soldiering as a youth and had served in the army. And these two pedlars were substantial specimens, each of them bigger than I was and neither, I could safely assume, suffering the after-effects of being made to live in a cage.

Unfortunately the idea of my tackling them was rapidly growing in popularity. The policeman had told his mates, and several passers-by had stopped to watch. I heard bets being placed on the outcome.

'Go on, then,' said a voice behind me. I looked around to see a burly man hefting a bag of cocoa beans, presumably his stake, in his hand. 'What are you waiting for?' A broad hand shoved me between the shoulder blades, hard.

Wishing my elder brother were with me, I reluctantly stepped through the gateway and up to the nearest pedlar, the one blocking the woman's way into the marketplace. He had his back to me.

'Excuse me,' I said, interrupting his sales talk. 'Do you have anything for bruises? A salve or a poultice or anything like that?'

The man half turned but kept his eye on the woman and the old man in front of him, as if unwilling to abandon them in favour of a fresh potential customer. Probably a victim who volunteered himself was too good to be true, in his eyes.

'I have,' he said gruffly. That was not surprising: I imagined he would claim to have a cure for death without blushing. 'Why?'

'Because you may need it,' I said in my lowest, most menacing voice. 'Now get away from these two and leave them alone!'

That got his attention, at least. He turned fully towards me and looked down, taking in my appearance at a glance. 'What?'

'I told you . . .' I managed to say, before he hit me in the stomach.

At first I did not feel the pain. I just found myself on my back, but doubled over so that my legs were waving in the air like a beetle's when it cannot get itself upright. Then it caught me, a fiery anguish in my gut that made me want to cry out, except that I had had the breath knocked out of me and could barely manage a wheeze. Then he kicked me between the legs, and a jolt of agony shot up through my whole body, making my stomach heave and everything in front of my eyes turn dark red.

I may have passed out for a moment. There may have been other blows, but if there were I did not feel them.

The next thing I knew, a hand was pulling on mine, in an effort to tug me to my feet, and a fine-sounding female voice was urging me to get up.

I smelled blood.

'Come on, you idiot! If you don't move you'll be in as much trouble as we will!'

Somehow I managed it. I stood, blinking stupidly at the

beautiful woman, while I waited for my surroundings to stop spinning long enough for me to look at them.

'What . . . what happened?' I mumbled thickly.

'You nearly got yourself killed over nothing!'

I shook my head, wincing at the blinding pain at the back of my skull. I realized I must have hit it hard on the ground when I was knocked over. 'Hope that man won his bet,' I muttered inconsequentially.

'What?'

I tried looking down. I seemed to be in one piece and was not, to my surprise, covered in blood, although I could still smell the stuff. Then I looked to one side and saw the man who had hit me.

He was on his knees, with his head bowed. One hand was on the ground, propping him up. The other was clamped to his side, trying to stanch the flow that was feeding a growing dark pool underneath him.

There was no sign of his partner in crime, or of the old man. I looked up at the woman again. 'What . . .?'

'My father stabbed him,' she said matter-of-factly.

I gaped at her.

'Look, he's an old man. He's vulnerable, especially when I'm not around to protect him. What would he do if he came across a couple of young warriors with their bellies full of sacred wine and spoiling for a fight? So he carries this obsidian knife under his cloak. Of course, he wouldn't have had to use it if it hadn't been for your stupid stunt!'

'Sorry,' I said. 'It seemed like a good idea at the time.' I looked at the injured pedlar again. He had not moved, but had started moaning softly to himself. 'Will he be all right?'

'Oh, fine. Father won't have hurt him that much.'

'I suppose I ought to thank him,' I said, remembering my manners. 'Where's he gone?'

She sighed. 'After the other one, of course. He gets carried away. I'll tell him you said thank you.' She turned towards the marketplace and started walking.

'Wait a moment!' I hobbled after her as best I could, considering how difficult it was to stand up straight. 'I don't even know who you are! And who's your father?' I was loath to let this fine-looking woman go without at least finding out her name.

'My father?' She laughed, without turning her head. 'He's only a serf, don't mind him!'

With that she strode through the entrance to the marketplace, leaving me staring speechlessly at her back.

Just before she vanished from my sight, she brushed past an insignificant-looking man in a plain cloak. He turned and stared after her for a long time and then glanced at me. For a moment our eyes met, and for once I was sure: he was the man who had been following me all morning.

Then I blinked, and both he and the woman were gone.

7

Kindly did not seem much interested in my encounter with the woman and her aged father, but he paid close attention to my account of my nondescript shadow.

'You're still being followed?'

'I should think so,' I admitted. 'But I reckon I can lose him, come nightfall.'

'Really?' he said sceptically. 'Well, I hope you can. Sounds as if your tail knows what he's about, though. It's a funny town, this, isn't it? Spies everywhere. And it seems there's no way of telling which lot you're up against. I mean, is this one working for Maize Ear, like the two who picked Lily up, or for his half-brother?'

I had no answer to that. Instead, with a sigh, I got up.

'Where are you going now?'

'Back to Hare's house. I want to look for . . . to see if I can find any clues. To where he's gone or what happened to him.' I recalled what Lily had told me, how nobody must know about the ring she had left there. I knew from experience that the last person Lily would trust with any secret was her own father, so I thought it best to say nothing about it.

Kindly rolled his filmed-over eyes and groaned loudly. Then, to my astonishment, he began to get up. 'I suppose I'd better come too, then. Just in case you find that message and need me to tell you what it says.'

'You?' I had never known the old man exert himself for any reason other than to pick up a drinking-gourd that had rolled out of his reach.

'Who else do you know who knows any Mayan? Just let me get my staff and then let's get a move on. It would be good to be there before nightfall.'

He stumped towards our room, leaving me staring after him and thinking that his daughter really ought to see this.

The afternoon was already well advanced when we set out on the road to Huexotla.

The old man could not move as fast as I would have liked, and so to begin with, as we made our way through the busy streets of central Tetzcoco, I had to be content to assume we were being followed. It would have been an easy matter for anybody to keep an eye on us without being seen, slipping in and out of the crowds pouring out of the palace and the marketplace. When we got into the quieter suburbs it would be a different matter. I would know just where to look for my uninvited companion then: in the lengthening shadows of the buildings around us.

On the way, I asked Kindly how Obsidian Tongue had got on in court that morning.

'Oh, his application failed,' he said lightly. 'As he said it would.'

'How could you let him do it? And charge you for it?'

Kindly laughed. 'Oh, his fees? Don't worry, Yaotl. I'll swindle the money back out of him in no time! After the case is over I'll get him drunk and persuade him to invest it in some trading venture. A cocoa plantation somewhere in the hot lands to the South, or something like that. He won't expect a return for a few years, and by the time he starts getting suspicious I'll probably be dead!'

I laughed. 'You're joking, aren't you? He can't be much of a lawyer if he's that gullible!'

'Oh, yes, he can. In spite of what you may think, he's actually very good. And let's face it, he'd better be – right now he's the only thing that stands between Lily and being strangled.' He fell silent for a moment, and I looked at him anxiously, but his expression was unreadable.

A moment later he gave a thin smile. 'But as for gullible – well, you know these clever lawyers. They may know every rule and precedent there is, but outside a courtroom they're as helpless as babies! Now, are we still being followed?'

I had started taking frequent glances over my shoulder, looking at shady places, the gaps between houses, low walls, trees and bushes, and listening for the sound of a footfall or the rustle of foliage being pulled aside for a pair of prying eyes to peer through. 'I'm pretty sure we are. What we'll do is, we'll split up. He'll probably follow me, since that's what he's been doing all day. So why don't you go straight on to the house, and I'll try to lose him?' I quickly gave Kindly directions, assuring him that it was no great distance, even groping blindly as he would have to, and he would certainly get there before the Sun went down.

'What if he follows me?' he asked.

Lacking any satisfactory answer to that, I merely said brusquely: 'You'll just have to make sure he doesn't! Go on. You don't want to be stuck out here in the chill of the evening, do you?'

Muttering, he gripped his staff and walked off.

I stood in the middle of the road, feeling suddenly lonely and very much out in the open. I was tempted to dash into the shadows and hide, but I told myself that this was what I had planned to do: to make sure my follower saw me and would stick to me and leave the old man to go on alone. I peered into the shadows, trying to catch a glimpse of him, but saw nothing.

'Well, off we go, then,' I muttered under my breath, as I turned and headed off after the old merchant.

I remembered a steep track I had taken the day before, when I had climbed out of the stream behind Hare's house to rejoin the road. I thought I might as well retrace my steps now, in the opposite direction, leading my follower into the tangle of undergrowth and rubbish that covered the hillside. If I moved quickly enough, he would have to reveal himself, and I stood a good chance of being able to hide simply by lying flat on the uneven, overgrown slope. Once it got dark I would be almost impossible to find.

I broke into a trot, knowing that in my current condition I would not be able to keep up the pace for long, but not expecting to have to run very far.

I kept glancing back, but there was still nothing to see. I stopped abruptly a couple of times and listened in vain for footsteps.

By the time I reached my steep path, I was beginning to feel uneasy. I had not thought whoever was following me was so good that I would be unable to spot him even in this quiet, empty road. I wondered whether my plan had, after all, not come off, and he was after Kindly instead. But in that case, I told myself, he would have had to pass me while I was standing in the open.

I darted down the slope.

The hillside was really little more than a high bank with a tiny stream at the bottom that would probably have been dry but for the recent short winter rains. Beyond the stream the ground rose a little, naturally, before levelling out and then dropping again towards the lake. The Sun was almost fully in my eyes as he prepared to set over the mountains, and this made it hard to see much detail in the houses, temples and bare maize fields between me and the lake shore, but what I could not miss was the dazzling expanse of the lake itself, looking like a vast sheet of polished copper, or the shadowed expanse of the great island in the middle of it. From here, Mexico looked a long way off, and, dangerous though the place was for me at the moment, I could not look at it without yearning.

I turned aside from the vision of my home and, crouching low in the hope that any watcher would be unable to see me against the dark background of the houses beyond the stream, I ran along the side of the slope until I found what I was looking for. Then I dropped into a shallow hollow behind a stunted choysia bush, lay as flat as I could and waited.

The Sun went down and the sky darkened. The stars came out. It began to get extremely cold.

I thought I had chosen a good hiding place, but I had positioned myself in it badly. I could see nothing but a few bedraggled amaranth leaves just in front of me. I should have been facing the other way, so that I could see whether anyone was picking their way along the slope in my footsteps. I realized, with a pang of self-reproach, that I would be easy prey for anyone with even a modicum of skill as a tracker, since I must have left a clear trail of trampled and broken foliage behind me. But there was nothing to do now except listen and get ready to run if I heard anything.

There was no sound except, after a while, my own teeth chattering. I tugged my cloak around me for warmth, but it made no difference.

What was happening to Kindly, I wondered? Had he got to the house, and what had he found there?

A violent shivering began to overcome me. I willed myself to stop, fearful that I was going to give my position away, but it did no good. I realized that if I did not get up and start moving soon, I might never be able to move at all. Already my hands and feet were getting numb.

I started to rise, and that was the exact moment when I first heard someone moving stealthily through the undergrowth.

Terrified, I pressed myself flat against the ground. I jammed a finger between my teeth to silence them and held my breath.

Nothing happened for so long that I began to wonder whether I had imagined the sound. I took my finger out of my mouth and was once more on the point of getting up when it came again, and this time it was unmistakable: a soft footfall accompanied by a crackle of crushed grass.

I froze, pressing my face into the dirt. I tried to think, to decide whether I ought to carry on trying to lie perfectly still or to leap up and run away, but my mind refused to work, and then it was too late anyway, as my pursuer was on top of me.

I had one hand splayed out in front of me. I felt a sudden impulse to snatch it out of harm's way just at the moment when somebody stepped silently out of the darkness and trod on my fingers.

I winced and gritted my teeth. Luckily he was not wearing sandals and seemed not to weigh much, but as his heel rocked back and forth uncertainly, the pain made me dig holes in the palm of my other hand with my nails and brought tears to my eyes.

He seemed to stand where he was, wavering, for an age before finally lifting his foot and taking a step forward.

I could stand it no longer and let out a sob of relief.

The footsteps halted. I heard the foliage in front of me rustling as someone turned slowly around.

A voice whispered something urgently. But what it said was so unexpected that I heard myself gasping in reply: 'What?'

'I said, "Father? Is that you?"'

Now my tears were of relief, and they soon turned into

paroxysms of sobbing that kept me on the ground even while
my son was bending over me, trying to lift me up.

'I can't believe it's you!'

'You keep saying that,' the young man said a little testily.

'You're not even supposed to be in the valley. You're meant
to be beyond the mountains – in Tarascan country.'

'Why would I want to go over there? The Tarascans are a
bunch of savages. Come on, you must be even colder than I
am.'

Nimble and I crawled and stumbled uphill towards Hare's
house, feeling our way through the darkness, which for my
frozen, nerveless fingers was no easy matter. I merely followed
the young man blindly, assuming that if I climbed in his footsteps I would be all right. I was too bewildered and
disorientated to take any decisions of my own. I could not get
over my amazement at hearing my son's voice, here in
Tetzcoco of all places.

Nimble told me he had gathered some wood with a view to
kindling a fire in the courtyard but had not dared to light it yet.
'I couldn't be sure the place wasn't still being watched. I think
they've gone now, though. No one tried to stop Kindly going
in, anyway.'

As we scrambled over the broken wall into the corner of the
courtyard, I heard an old man's voice coming from somewhere within the tiny house. 'Oh, it's you at last. What did
you do, fall asleep out there?'

I bristled at this dismissal of my night of acute discomfort,
tension and terror. 'I was trying to keep our tail off your back,
you ungrateful old . . .'

'And nearly led me into a trap in the process!' I heard a faint
sound as of liquid sloshing about in a gourd, and Kindly's
voice had a slight slur, which was unusual for him in spite of

the amount he drank. Evidently he had had a stressful evening as well.

Slightly chastened, I said: 'I wasn't to know about that.'

What had happened, it seemed, was that Kindly's and my follower, instead of shadowing either me or the old man, had somehow got ahead of us and gone direct to the house.

'I don't suppose Kindly was going very fast,' Nimble pointed out. 'As soon as he was sure he knew where you were going, your tail could have overtaken both of you easily enough, without you seeing him, just by slipping past you along side roads. That's the best way to follow someone, you know – get in front of them. I bet you were looking over your shoulders all the way, weren't you?'

I looked curiously at my son, wondering, not for the first time, just what he might have had to do as a boy to have learned such things. One day, I thought, I might ask him, provided I was sure I wanted to know the answer.

'So the man who'd been following us went on ahead, to Hare's house, and ran straight into an ambush?'

'Well, let's just say that he walked into the house, and he was carried out. I don't suppose the two warriors who took him away had been left there just to offer guided tours.'

They were probably Rattlesnake and Hunter, I realized, or colleagues of theirs, and they were almost certainly looking for me. Remembering the bump on the head I had given Hunter, I suspected they would find the man they caught something of a disappointment.

'Are you going to light this fire or what?' Kindly demanded. 'It's all right for you youngsters, but I'd like to be able to feel my feet at least once more before I die!'

'It should be safe enough now,' I agreed. 'If there's anyone out there they'll probably be too frozen to notice the smoke.'

Nimble obliged, and again I was struck by how much my

son had learned in the years when he had been lost to me. Much of that time he had spent wandering, alone, in the mountains, and sparking life into a loose heap of kindling was something he must have had to do often. We were soon gathered around a healthy blaze. This cheered Kindly so much that he even offered his sacred wine around, although I preferred to share Nimble's gourd full of water instead.

'What beats me,' the old man said, 'is how our tail knew where to come.'

'The same way I did,' my son told him. 'This house is probably the worst-kept secret in Tetzcoco now. I was only in the marketplace half the morning before two people told me exactly where it was.'

'But why were you looking for Hare?' I asked. 'What are you doing in Tetzcoco at all?'

'I came after you, of course.'

'But . . .'

'Look, I still know plenty of people in Tlatelolco marketplace. I heard what happened to you. I wished I could . . . well, I wanted to do something, but Lily did it for me, didn't she?'

I grinned at the memory. 'Just as well. I don't suppose you have a hundred and five large cloaks to your name!'

'I guessed Lily might bring you here. I managed to see Partridge and he told me where you were staying. Of course, when I got there, you were all out and Lily had been arrested.'

'So you started making your own enquiries.' I could understand why. Lily had nursed my son back to health after he had been badly injured at her house. He owed her as much as I did.

'I thought I'd have a look at the place. But when I got here . . .'

'Someone was here ahead of you.'

'Yes, and I thought there was something strange about them,

so I decided to keep an eye on the place, just to see what would happen.'

'And then we turned up,' mused Kindly.

As I began to thaw out, I remembered what I had originally come for. Plucking a burning log out of the fire to use as a light, I said: 'Since we seem to have the place to ourselves, I'm going to take a look inside. You needn't get up,' I assured Kindly hastily, remembering Lily's warning. I wanted to look for the ring without being observed.

'I won't,' the old man answered gruffly. 'Just mind you don't fall into that bloody great pit, won't you?'

I looked at him, mystified. 'Pit? What pit?'

'There's a big hole in the floor. What, you mean you didn't notice it?'

'It must have been covered up.'

'Oh, yes, with an empty wicker chest. Nearly walked right into it, I did, and then I thought, why would somebody leave this in the middle of the floor instead of standing it over by the wall, out of the way? So I started shoving it to one side. I thought that was a bit curious, because you wouldn't put something like that where you can trip over it, would you? And that's when I saw the hole.'

'I'll show you,' Nimble offered. 'It's pretty deep. You could get hurt if you stumbled into it.'

'Is there anything in it?'

Kindly said: 'I know what you're thinking. The first thing you do when you go into a merchant's house is check for places where the owner may have hidden things. But I only saw a few old clothes at the bottom. That, and a nasty smell, which rather put me off poking around in there.'

I hesitated to let Nimble follow me into the house, in case he came across Lily's ring, but I could not think of a good excuse for keeping him out. Then I reasoned that if the ring was still there then it must be too well hidden for anyone to pick it up unless he was looking for it. Besides, I was curious to see what Kindly had found.

The smell of blood that had hung over the place the day before had largely dispersed outside the house, but inside was a different matter: the floor was still black with the stuff, and the place reeked like a temple after a particularly intense round of sacrifices. However, there was something else besides dried blood in the air: something still more unpleasant that should have left the room when the Texcalan's body was taken out.

Something made me talk in whispers. 'I think we'd better take a look in that hole.'

In the poor light cast by my improvised torch, the pit Lily's father had found was a featureless black square in the middle of the floor, almost as large as the chest that had covered it.

'I suppose he'd have hidden his valuables in there,' Nimble offered.

'Well, it hasn't done him much good. If there was anything worth taking in there, it's gone by now.' I held up the torch, so that we could both see what lay in the bottom: just a small pile of plain clothes. I thought I recognized a woman's blouse and skirt, and a mantle, presumably worn against the cold. There was something curious about the way they were heaped up. I was trying to work out exactly what it was that I found odd about this when the smell hit me, this time so strongly that it made me gag.

'Father?' asked Nimble anxiously. 'Are you all right? What is it?'

In answer I thrust the torch towards him. 'Hold this, son,' I gasped. 'I'm going to have to go down there.'

The hole was about half as deep as I was tall. If I were to squat in it, I would just about fit, without my head coming up above ground level. As I lowered myself gingerly into it, taking care not to tread on the little pile of clothes, I thought wryly that it was about the same size as the cage the slave-dealers had kept me in.

Inside the hole the smell was overpowering. Holding my breath, and crouching awkwardly so as not to come between what I was reluctantly looking at and the torchlight, I began to pick at the clothes. They resisted being pulled about, as though they were stuck to something. I had to tug at them before they began to come up with a faint tearing sound.

I held up the blouse, sniffed it once, and then tossed it out of the hole without speaking.

With the torchlight fully upon it, it was easy to see the bloodstains.

The skirt and mantle were in the same state, and once I had thrown them out it was easy to see why. They had been art-fully arranged so as to cover what lay at the bottom of the hole, almost filling it: a bundle, wrapped in what looked like an old, rough maguey fibre blanket. The blanket's material was thin and its edges were ragged. I could not tell what colour it had been dyed, or whether it had been dyed at all, because it was stained almost black with blood.

'Wake Kindly up and get him in here,' I croaked. 'I'll need help with this, and he'll have to hold the torch.'

It was no easy matter getting the shrouded corpse out of the hole, particularly because the old man's unsteady hands made the light gyrate wildly above us and set shadows whirling in a confusing dance around our heads. Eventually, however, Nimble and I managed to heave the body on to the floor of the house. Then we took it outside, for the sake of clearer air.

'I suppose you have to unwrap it,' Kindly said as he followed with the torch. 'Can it wait until morning?' He yawned loudly.

Instead of answering, I bent over the body. The blanket had

not been sewn or tied, so far as I could see, but it was so thickly encrusted with dried blood that its sides might as well have been glued together with pine resin or turkey fat. Nimble and I had to tug at it so fiercely that the cloth tore in our hands, but eventually the ghastly contents were laid bare.

The torchlight suddenly disappeared, leaving us with only the feeble glow of Nimble's fire, which had started to die down. Behind me, I heard the piece of wood the old man had been holding clattering to the ground, accompanied by the sound of violent retching.

'I'll put some more wood on the fire,' Nimble said quietly. I said nothing. I swallowed hard, to force down the gorge that was rising in my own throat, and made myself look at the remains again.

The body lay on its side, with its arms folded across its chest and its legs drawn up, as if it were huddling against the cold. As the last of the wrappings came off, it seemed to relax, the legs splaying grotesquely and the torso rolling over on to its back, and it was so horribly like someone stirring in his sleep that I took a hasty step back, as though I thought it was about to wake up. However, one look at the face, at the blank, milky whiteness of the wide-open eyes and the mouth hanging slackly open, would have been enough to dispel any such idea.

'How long were you in that pit?' I wondered aloud. 'Were you there before the man we found yesterday, or was he killed first?' I judged that the body must have lain where we had found it for a few days. It stank, but its flesh seemed intact, and the stiffness had worn off.

'I've lit another torch.' When Nimble handed it to me, I looked quickly around for Lily's father. He had withdrawn, to sit with his back against the wall of the house. I thought he looked pale, but it was hard to tell in the torchlight.

I turned back to the body, running my eyes over it briefly

from head to foot. When I reached the loins I stopped with a gasp.

'What is it, Father?'

'It's a man.'

The clothes we had found in the pit had led me to expect a woman or, rather, a girl, since they were very small. However, there was no mistaking the body's one item of clothing, a plain breechcloth, of the sort that men wore.

'I do hope this isn't Hare,' I muttered, as I looked the remains over more slowly. The more I saw, however, the greater my sense of foreboding grew. His face and body were covered with dried blood, and I had no doubt that even if it were cleaned off, the shrunken, collapsed features would be unrecognizable. However, even at night, disguised by death, this was plainly very different from the other corpse that had lain here. This was no burly warrior, but a small, wiry individual who, I conceded grimly, might well have been a merchant.

'What killed him?' Nimble asked. 'Suffocation, from being in that hole?'

'Wouldn't explain the blood. I can't see where he's wounded, though. We'd better turn him over.'

This proved surprisingly difficult. He kept trying to flop over on to his back again, as if he wanted to look at the stars. Eventually we managed to get him on to his side, but that was enough to tell me what I wanted to know. In the skin between his shoulders was a large, jagged rent.

We both stood and contemplated the wound in silence while I struggled to think of where I might have seen something like it before.

'It's ghastly,' Nimble said at last. 'Do you think it killed him straight away?'

'I don't know,' I said. I crouched next to the corpse. Steeling myself, I probed the puckered edges of the wound with my fingers, grimacing as I felt flakes of dried blood catching under my nails. I heard myself utter a faint whimpering noise that was half disgust and half self-loathing at what I was reduced to doing next, before plunging a finger into the hole to see how deep it was.

I tugged the finger out again quickly, shocked and nauseated by the sucking noise it made and the way the icy-cold, damp flesh clung to my hand. It felt as if the man's soul were in there still, trying to catch me and drag me with him to the Land of the Dead.

'Not pretty, is it?' said Kindly laconically, from where he still sat by the house.

'Father? What did you find?'

'That wound did for him, all right,' I replied. It was a relief to take my eyes off the body and look at my son instead. 'It's deep enough. And I know how it was made. A sharp wooden spike. We found it here yesterday. Rattlesnake and Hunter were trying to pretend it was a murder weapon. And so it was!'

'But who used it on him?'

'I can't begin to guess! We don't even know for sure who this is, do we?' I forced myself to look at the body again. I badly wanted to believe it was not the merchant, because if he was dead then so was my plan.

'Must be Hare, mustn't it?' said Kindly bluntly. 'If you get him cleaned up in the morning, I expect I'll be able to tell you for sure, although it's a long time since I've seen him. But who else could he be? And what are you going to do if he is?'

'Any suggestions?'

'Yes. Go to sleep! That's what I'm doing. Can't do much more until daylight, anyway.' With that the old man gathered his leather cloak around him for a blanket, crawled over to the fire and rolled on to his side, as he must have done on countless plains and bleak hillsides during his travels as a merchant. His loud snore a moment later was a reminder of how much tougher he was than he looked: I was not looking forward to a night under the stars in the courtyard, although sleeping inside the blood-drenched house was out of the question.

Nimble said: 'He's got a point, Father. What else can we do now? I'll build the fire up. It's going to be a cold night. If it goes out while we're asleep, we'll be in trouble.'

'Let me have the torch, then. One of us ought to keep awake, just in case.'

'Well, then, I'll . . .'

'No. You must be exhausted too.'

'Not as much as you.'

For some reason, that irritated me: perhaps because it was true, and the strain of the last two days, on top of everything else I had endured lately, was beginning to tell and shorten my temper. 'Nonsense!' I snapped. 'I got used to all-night vigils when I was a priest, remember?'

'That was a while ago now,' he observed mildly.

'What are you saying? I'm not up to it any more? Now you listen to me, young man. . .'

The torch shook in his hands as he recoiled from my outburst. 'I didn't mean that at all! It's only that when you were a priest, no one put you in a cage for a month or more, or . . .'

'You have no idea what happened to me when I was a priest.'

'I'm only trying to help.'

'Well . . .' I was about to say 'don't!' but stopped myself when I caught sight of his expression changing from shocked and concerned to resentful and sullen. But I felt a curious reluctance to back down, and instead went on, in a more conciliatory tone: 'Sorry, son. But really it'll do me good to stay

up now. It may give me an opportunity to make sure the gods
haven't forgotten who I am! Let me have the torch, eh?'

After a moment's hesitation he handed it over without a
word. As its light left his face his expression became unreadable, but the way he wrapped himself in his own cloak, lay
down by the fire and turned away from me, all in silence, was
revealing enough.

I sighed as I watched him, my brief flash of anger at an end.
It had been a mild enough argument, but it had been our first
and had left me feeling small and cheap. On the other hand, I
reflected, I had probably been right: Nimble probably had
been more tired than I. I doubted that he had slept since
coming to Tetzcoco.

As soon as I was sure they were both asleep, I went to look
for the ring.

It took me only a moment to satisfy myself that it was not
hidden by the doorpost. The gap where Lily must have put it
was wide, and if it had been there it would not have been difficult to find. I poked about a little, pushing my fingers into
the soft plaster and rotting wood, but although I thought it
would be possible to bury something in the wall I did not see
how Lily could have done it. I supposed she had had very little
time to stuff the ring in there before she was caught by
Rattlesnake and Hunter. In fact, the more I thought about it,
the more remarkable it seemed that she had had time to look
for a hiding place at all.

Disappointed, I went back out into the courtyard.

For a long time I merely huddled over the fire, occasionally
reaching for another of Nimble's sticks when it seemed to be
failing, but mostly just staring into the flames, as though I
were trying to catch sight of the Old, Old God in there.

I worried about the ring. Lily had clearly felt it was almost
more important than her trial, and that it would be a disaster

if it fell into the wrong hands, but I could not understand why. Perhaps Mother of Light had stolen it, but that was hard to believe. I assumed that, as a King's concubine, she would have had more than enough jewels to her name without needing to help herself to anyone else's. And what was so special about this ring that the merchant wanted it for his pay?

Then there was the separate matter of how two men had met their deaths in this house. I looked uneasily across at the body in the courtyard, having the uncomfortable feeling that, with Kindly and Nimble asleep, he was my only companion. 'Are you Hare?' I whispered. 'I suppose you ought to be. This is your house, after all. But what was that Texcalan doing here?' I sighed. 'And who killed whom?' I looked into the fire again. Hare, assuming it was he, had been stabbed with a wooden peg. The Texcalan had been killed with a knife, or at any rate something with a blade. Had they fought each other? Reluctantly I got up and looked at that hideous wound again. I realized that it had not been a straight fight: the wound was in the man's back, and the other, I recalled, had had his throat cut. From my limited knowledge of combat, that was unlikely to have happened during a tussle with the adversaries facing each other.

When the solution came to me, it was so obvious I had to groan at my own stupidity. Then, snatching one of the last pieces of wood from Nimble's pile, I lit one more torch and headed back indoors.

The clothes were still where I had left them after throwing them out of the hole, scattered over the floor. I picked them up and laid them out, the mantle at the bottom and the blouse and skirt on top of it, as if waiting for their owner to slip into them and wrap the mantle around her.

When I picked the mantle up, something that had been caught in its folds clattered to the floor. It was a small wooden object, which I glanced at through the corner of my eye before looking again at the clothes for some clue about their owner.

I saw at once that whoever had been hidden under the chest had been even smaller than I had thought: a child. If these clothes had been made or bought to fit her, I would put her age at maybe eleven or twelve: not quite old enough to go to school at a House of Youth.

Frowning, I bent down to pick up the wooden object.

Something sharp stabbed my finger when I touched it, making me yelp. I glared helplessly at the offending article, but felt my expression soften as I realized what it was.

In my hand lay a child's doll: a crudely carved toy, with its features daubed on so roughly the paint might have been applied with somebody's fingertip. Still, they were clear enough for me to see, even in torchlight, that there were some odd things about the little figure's face. Its eyes were distinctly crossed, as though it were trying to look at its own nose all the time, and the high forehead was flat and sloped sharply back-wards.

The doll had only one leg. That was why I had got a splin-ter, I could see, because the missing limb had been snapped off roughly. When I examined its surviving counterpart, all my suspicions about what had happened in the house appeared to be confirmed. It was about the same length as the piece of wood Lily had picked up the day before.

8

I shook the other two awake just as the first conch-shell trumpet began announcing the approach of dawn from the top of a temple. Once the yawning, scratching and grumbling had subsided, we stood around the body, trying to decide what to do with it.

It looked no prettier in the pre-dawn twilight than it had in the middle of the night, and it was not much easier to make out any distinguishing features.

'Needs a good wash,' Kindly said.

'How do you suggest we do that?' I demanded. 'Are we supposed to carry it all the way down to the stream?'

'It was only a suggestion. What else can we do with it?'

'Put it back where we found it,' Nimble answered.

'What for?' Kindly wanted to know. 'I should think whoever picked up our shadow yesterday will be on their way back here as soon as it's light enough to set out. We ought to just beat it.'

I thought this over. 'No, I think Nimble's right. I don't think Hunter and Rattlesnake know about this body. That's strange, I admit . . .'

'They probably thought they'd got what they came for when they grabbed my daughter,' the old man suggested.

'I expect so. And only another merchant would have had your suspicions about what might be under that box. But as I was saying, I don't think they came across the body, because I can't see why they'd have gone to so much trouble to hide it again if they had. And if they don't know it already, I don't think I want them finding it now. It would only give them something else to accuse Lily of.' Besides, I was uneasy about leaving the dead man in the open. If we could not decently cremate him, to put him back where we found him seemed the least we could do.

Nimble and I wrapped the corpse as best we could and put it back into the pit, along with the girl's clothes that had covered it.

As we pushed the chest back over the hole, Kindly observed: 'It's a bit like a funeral, isn't it? Don't you think one of us ought to say something?'

'Like what?' I asked sourly, my distaste for what we were doing plain in my voice. 'If it were a funeral, we'd be burning him in paper vestments and a proper shroud, with his possessions and a brown dog, not stuffing him into a hole.' I turned my back on the wicker chest, deliberately, not caring to think about what would await the poor man when he found himself, naked and destitute, in the Land of the Dead. He would have no staff with which to defend himself from the serpents or lean on as he crossed the deserts and mountains, no shield or basket to protect him from the obsidian-bladed winds, no dog to carry him across the river, no greenstone to offer in tribute to Mictlan Tecuhtli, the Lord of the Dead. He was destined to suffer for ever and never find rest.

I muttered: 'Maybe we can come back and do the thing properly once this is all over.'

We went out into the courtyard, intending to go over the back wall as I had the day before. Nimble and I would have to help Kindly along, but we thought it less risky than leaving by the front doorway.

'Before we go,' I said, 'just have a look at this.' I showed them the doll I had found in the night. Kindly took it from me and studied it, turning it over in his swollen, mottled fingers and pursing his lips thoughtfully.

'What is it?' Nimble asked, looking over the old man's shoulder.

'It's a toy, I think,' I said. 'It looks too crude and simple to be an idol. Watch out for splinters! I suppose it belonged to the girl who owned those clothes we found in the hole.'

'Maybe,' Kindly murmured. 'It would be interesting if it did, though. This is Mayan.'

'How do you know?'

'Look at the face. You or I would call it ugly, but the Mayans think crossed eyes and flat foreheads are signs of beauty. Wonder what happened to the leg, though? Did it get dropped in the hole because it was broken?'

'I can tell you what happened to the leg. Our deceased friend in there was stabbed to death with it.' I looked at the sky once more. 'Let's go. I'll tell you what I think happened on the way back to Tetzcoco.'

We managed to get down the hill, into and out of the stream, where we washed the bloodstains off our feet, and back on to the road without incident, save a good deal of cursing and complaining on the part of Kindly, who told us several times and in colourful language that he was too old and stiff to be scrabbling around in the bushes like a boy looking for birds' nests. Once we were on level ground, however, he was quiet. He wanted to hear what I had to say.

'I'm assuming Hare surprised the Texcalan warrior we saw the day before yesterday. Only the gods know what he was doing here, but Hare would have taken him for a thief.'

'Reasonable enough,' Kindly said. 'So there was a fight?'

'Yes, but not a straight one. Judging by the look of them, I think it would have been a pretty one-sided affair, even if the merchant had managed to get his hands on a knife to defend himself with. I think he must have had help.'

'The girl,' Nimble said.

'I'd guess the intruder didn't see her. While he was confronting Hare, she appeared from nowhere and distracted him. That gave Hare the opportunity to cut his throat.'

'Neat,' Kindly conceded. 'Where did she appear from, though?'

Nimble had the answer to that. 'She was in the pit, under the chest. She heard the commotion, peeked out of her hiding place and decided to join in.'

I agreed. 'I'd guess he was standing next to the hole – in a room that size he couldn't very well avoid it – and he'd have been just within her reach. She could have bitten his ankle, or something like that, or even brought him down by grabbing it and getting him off balance. I doubt if he saw her coming at all.'

'But,' Nimble pointed out, 'that means the girl must have killed Hare, surely?'

'I know. That troubles me a bit, but there's no way around it, is there? I'd guess that while he was busy dispatching the other man she crept up behind him and stuck him too. Why she'd have done that, I don't know.'

We all walked along in thoughtful silence for a few moments before Nimble suddenly announced: 'She meant to kill Hare all along.'

I glanced sideways at him. 'Why do you say that?'

'What was she doing with that sharp bit of wood to begin with? She must have spent time preparing it for something, or rather someone. I don't know how she sharpened it like that . . .'

'She used her teeth, I expect,' Kindly suggested. 'Another weird custom those savages have: they have their teeth filed.'

I looked down at the mutilated doll, which I was still carrying. I wondered if it had been a treasured possession, once, and what it could tell us about its owner. 'What made her do it?' I wondered. 'Was she planning to rob him?' If so, then she had left enough behind for her other victim's comrades to start selling it off in the marketplace, I thought.

'Maybe she just hated him,' Nimble said grimly.

'Why?'

'She must be a slave he picked up in Mayan country. He probably didn't buy her just to sweep out his courtyard every morning.'

Kindly frowned. 'But those clothes you found — if they were hers, she must be only a child!'

'So was I, when I came to Mexico.' The dry, matter-of-fact way my son reminded us what he had done, and what had been done to him, made me shudder.

'So the girl killed Hare,' I said. 'Then she shoved him in the pit. Why did she do that? It must have been difficult for her, if she's small enough for those clothes to fit her. She didn't want anyone finding the body, I suppose. That would be why she went to so much trouble to wrap it and cover it up. Do you think it was because she killed him, rather than the other man, and didn't want anyone discovering him and pinning it on her?'

'Maybe she didn't want anyone finding him and giving him a proper funeral.'

If what Nimble had suggested about her motives for killing the merchant was true, then this made sense, I realized. I could imagine the girl happily contemplating her tormentor's soul wandering for ever in the Land of the Dead.

It occurred to me that there might be another reason why

she had done it, as I thought about why she had been in the hole in the first place. Perhaps Hare had kept her confined there, when he had no immediate use for her. The chest that had covered the hole was so large that if it were filled with anything other than feathers it would be as hard to shift as the heavy stone that had weighed down the top of my cage. If she had been made to stay in that dark, stuffy pit for any length of time, I thought, it would be small wonder if she thought it an appropriate place to dump the merchant in.

I suggested this to my companions.

'What we're left with is this,' I concluded. 'The girl and Hare killed an intruder. For that to have happened, the box on top of her must have been emptied first, otherwise she could-n't have lifted it to surprise the Texcalan. If the Texcalan was ransacking the place, maybe he took everything out of the box. I think Hare must have been away somewhere while that was being done. How about this, then? The Texcalan and his one-armed friend, and maybe someone else, burgle the house. The others leave him behind while they make off with the booty. Then Hare comes back and surprises him, there's this three-cornered fight, and after that the girl kills Hare, hides the body and runs away.'

'Why do the other man's accomplices have to have taken everything before he died?' Nimble asked. 'They may have come back later.'

'No,' I said, 'because there was only one set of bloodstained footprints – the girl's – and, anyway, I don't think they'd have left his body behind. What they may have done when they discovered he was missing, though, is another matter.' It might, I realized uncomfortably, have something to do with the things of Hare's I had found on sale in the market. The Texcalan's companions would not know exactly what had happened to him: there was no way they could, because if they had been there he would surely not have died. Were they now out to trap his killer? I began to wonder whether my idea of trying to meet whoever was selling Hare's property had been such a good one.

'All of this,' Kindly reminded us, 'begs one rather vital question, doesn't it?'

'We have to find the girl,' I confirmed.

'We do. It's always possible that she has this message, or knows something about it. In any event she's just about the only chance you've got of finding it.'

'True.' We were plainly not going to get it from Hare if he was dead. On the other hand, I thought, Lily's missing ring was less important now, since we no longer had to worry about paying the merchant with it. It still troubled me, however: Lily clearly did not want it falling into the wrong hands, but somebody must have removed it from its hiding place.

'I expect I can find her,' Nimble said.

'You?' Kindly and I stared at him. I added: 'How? How are you going to find one child in a city of thirty thousand people?'

'By knowing where to look. She'd stand out a mile in most places. She's Mayan, remember, and Kindly thinks she may have had her teeth filed. So she'll go where she thinks she can blend in. That's the middle of town, the marketplace. Lots of people, including lots of foreigners. Once there . . .' He sighed. 'Well, it depends how quickly she gets picked up by someone on the lookout for a pretty young thing, something a bit exotic . . .'

'All right,' I said gruffly.

'It's just that I know what she'll have been through.'

'You need us along?' Kindly asked cautiously. 'You don't speak Mayan.'

'I don't think that matters. Besides, I'd find it easier to look for her on my own. You'd most likely scare her off.'

'Thanks,' grumbled the old man, although his relief was audible.

I protested. 'I don't like this idea at all. It isn't safe . . .'

'Safe enough for me!'

'Son, I know you think you're up to anything, but you don't know Tetzcoco.'

'I probably know it better than you!' he said defiantly. 'And who's going to be in more danger, me or Lily? Have you forgotten about her?'

'Now, just a moment . . .'

'Calm down, the two of you,' Kindly growled. 'They can probably hear you shouting on the other side of the valley!'

I took a deep, deliberate breath. 'Sorry,' I mumbled. 'I can't help worrying.'

Nimble looked away for a moment before responding quietly: 'It's all right, Father. I can do this. And I can look after myself. I've been doing it all my life.'

After parting from Nimble, Kindly and I made our way back to our lodgings, taking a short detour to buy a tortilla each and allow the old man to replenish his gourd.

'I'm getting a bit too old for living rough,' he said between mouthfuls. 'I need my own sleeping mat again! And I suppose I'd better find out what that lawyer's up to. What are you going to do?'

'Try to see Lily again. Tell her what we've been up to and find out what she makes of it all.' I paused. My tortilla had been stuffed with dried chillies, and I had just cracked a seed between my teeth. I walked on in silence for a moment, waiting for the pain to wash over and through me and for the warm, contented feeling that always came in its wake.

Kindly suddenly asked: 'Why do you suppose so many

people are interested in that house? And who are they all, anyway?'

Able to speak again, I said: 'I don't know. Maize Ear's men are looking for spies, we know that. Do you think the one who followed us yesterday was another spy? If he was the little man I saw in the marketplace, then I'd guess he was. Maybe he's working for the King's rival, Black Flower.'

'Could be. And don't forget Mother of Light – the woman he was meant to be giving the message to. Do you think she wanted it on her own account, or for someone else?'

I groaned. 'I don't know! But you're right – that's at least three lots of people, besides us, trying to get their hands on this thing. And finally there's this other group: the Texcalan, and whoever he was working with, the people selling Hare's stuff off in the marketplace. That makes four!'

The more I thought about this fourth group, the more uneasy I became. I knew I had to find them, because in spite of what Kindly had said there was every likelihood that they had taken Hare's message along with the rest of his possessions when they raided his house. There was something curious about the way they were behaving, selling the merchant's possessions piecemeal in such widely scattered places. A thief might do that, because to sell stolen goods in bulk was asking to get caught, but I could not see why he would pretend to be doing it on behalf of the man he had stolen it from. It seemed to me that was bound to attract the wrong sort of attention.

Unless, I thought, that was exactly what they wanted: to attract attention. To lure somebody who might be interested in the contents of Hare's house, and one item in particular. Somebody such as me. No, I realized, and the thought brought me up short, so that I stopped walking and for a moment could only stand and stare straight ahead of me in blind horror, not somebody such as me, but me, myself, Cemiquiztli Yaotl.

That was why the Texcalan had been at the house. The men who had burgled it were after me personally, and either he was one of them, or they had brought him along to help them identify me. Somehow they had known that I would be coming to the house and had set out to trap me there. It was no comfort at all to know that it had gone wrong for them.

And I had to confront these men.

'Kindly,' I said, 'we really need to think about what we're going to do next.'

'No, we need to sleep on it. I turned in much too late last night, and I think much better when I'm rested! Look, here are our lodgings . . . Hello, what's going on?'

Turning the last corner before our guesthouse, we found the place in uproar.

A small crowd thronged the gateway. Its members were gathered in a rough circle, with a man I recognized as our landlord in its centre. The men and women around him, who mostly seemed to be our fellow guests, were jostling each other, pushing and gesticulating and shouting as each tried to get closer to the man in the middle. Whether they wanted to harangue him or hit him was not clear.

'Don't like the look of this,' muttered Kindly.

'We'd better find out what it's all about, though.'

As it happened, the people in front of Kindly and me were all too eager to explain themselves. Someone on the edge of the crowd glanced at us over his shoulder, and a moment later there was a cry of 'There they are!' and we were being mobbed.

'This is all your fault!' someone screamed at me. A merchant's wife slapped Kindly, making him stagger, and shouted: 'Do you know what the clothes in my chest were worth? I hope you can pay for all this!' Little silver bells hung from the plugs in her earlobes and tinkled incongruously as she continued her assault. 'It's all ruined now, thanks to you! I'll have you both sold into slavery!'

'Wait a moment! Stop it!' I protested. 'What are you talking about?' Spying the landlord over the heads of some of my assailants, I called out: 'You! What's happening here?'

The man's face had turned purple with rage. 'You and that old man are buggering off out of my house, that's what's happening!' he yelled back. 'Pack up what's left of your stuff and leave, now!'

'Now hang on,' I began, but my voice was lost in the commotion. I was beginning to lose my own temper now. Being abused was not a new experience for me, but I thought the least the people screaming at me could do was tell me what they were upset about.

There was a small man in front of me. The top of his head came up to about the level of my nose, although he was hopping up and down so that with every other breath I was staring straight into his spittle-flecked mouth. I waited until he came down off his toes and then suddenly grabbed both his ears and yanked him upwards again by them.

He let out an outraged squeal. Judging I had his attention, I shouted into his face: 'What is this all about? What are we supposed to have done?'

'Let go of me!'

'Bloody well answer my question!'

'Put him down!'

I felt a pang of dread when I realized that the tall woman who had hit Kindly was trying to get between me and my victim. It looked as if she was his wife.

I went so far as to release one ear. 'You tell me what's going on, then.'

'It's your fault we all got robbed last night! And his son—' she jerked her head towards where the landlord stood, looking strangely alone, in his gateway '—was nearly killed!'

I let the other ear go. The man quickly stepped back behind his wife, whimpering in pain. 'How is it our fault? We weren't even here.'

'It's you they were after!'

'What? Look, somebody tell us this from the beginning, all right? I told you, we weren't here.'

'You'd better ask our landlord, then,' the woman spat, and, surprisingly, stepped aside.

I walked up to the lone figure in the gateway, wearing what I hoped was an open and friendly expression. He scowled back at me.

'Look, whatever happened,' I said, 'I'm sorry about – well, whatever it was! But you'll have to tell us. . .'

'Friends of yours, were they?' he snapped.

'Who?'

'The men who came and turned this place over last night. Looking for their old pal Yaotl, they said. Tore up every wicker chest in the place, threw people's belongings in the street, and when my son tried to stop them one of them hit him so hard I had to take him to a doctor this morning. And who's going to pay for that?'

'But . . .' I stared at him. 'Looking for me?'

'They seemed to know you pretty well. Gave a very good description and said they'd tear the walls down if you didn't turn up.'

The man was on the verge of tears, I noticed, although I did not know whether this was owing to rage, what had happened to his son or the impact on his business.

'Did they tell you who they were? What did they look like?'

'I told you – they said they were old friends of yours. They were Aztecs, like you, from their accents. They looked like warriors, big men – the one who hit my son only used his fist, but I thought he'd killed him! They hadn't the clothes or the haircuts for warriors, but that's what they were.'

They were the men who had robbed Hare's house, I thought, but why were they looking for me, and how did they know my name? A moment later I had the answer to both my questions. I felt my skin turn to ice as the man told me who was coming after me.

'And the man in charge of them – he was the ugliest brute I've ever seen. Half his face cut away and only one eye, and a look about him like he'd kill you just for fun. And there was another one with one arm, and he wasn't much prettier. I'm telling you, you're leaving. I'm not having the place broken up on account of the likes of you!'

'Do you realize who those men are?'

'Of course I do,' snapped Kindly. 'They were the Otomi captain and his little band. And they've got that Texcalan with them, the one you were roped to in the marketplace. Obviously they followed us here. Now don't drop any of that stuff, whatever you do!'

I stumbled after the old man, nearly collapsing under the weight of all the goods we had been able to salvage from our room. Whatever had not been broken or irreparably soiled I had bundled up into a large cape, which I had tied around my forehead in an improvised tumpline. Kindly only carried a drinking-gourd and his staff.

'But why did you have to tell everybody where we were going?'

He sighed loudly. 'Because I had to tell them something, didn't I? They'd never have let us out of the house otherwise. Anyway, I was lying. I've no idea where we're going!'

I stopped in the middle of the street and swore. 'I thought we were going to find other lodgings.'

'In the middle of Tetzcoco? You must be joking. Those bastards would find us in no time. Besides, word will have got around. I doubt if the Emperor himself could get a room here with the kind of reputation we've got now! I wish you'd choose your friends a bit more carefully, Yaotl.'

He set off on the road towards the nearest suburb, which just happened to be Huexotla, leaving me fuming behind him.

9

'I'm starting to envy you,' I told Lily morosely. 'It's a nice big cage, and it's dry, and those maniacs can't get at you in the middle of the palace – not even they would make it past all the guards.'

Lily scowled at me through the bars. 'You're forgetting that I'm likely to be executed in two days' time! And I can't see that that expensive Tetzcocan lawyer my father hired is going to do me much good. I'd be better off defending myself!'

Lily's guard had been replaced with another, who had proved impossible to shift from his post, even for a moment. I had tried distracting him by telling him about the Otomies, since I had thought he might go running to his superiors with a story of rogue Aztec warriors loose in his city. His response had been to look at me with an expression of stony indifference.

Since we could not get rid of the guard, the woman and I talked in whispers, with our heads pressed together like lovers, or as nearly so as her cage would allow. Even so, there was no way to be sure we were not being overheard. I did not dare mention our discovery of Hare's body, the message Kindly, Nimble and I had been trying to locate, or the fact that I had found no sign of the missing ring.

The first words she spoke to me when I squatted in front of the cage had been, 'Where is it?' In answer, I had told her instead about the disturbance at our lodgings the night before.

'You have to find it!' She gripped one of the bars, her knuckles whitening over it in frustration. 'What if the Otomies have got it?'

'They probably won't even recognize it,' I said, trying to sound reassuring. I was unsure whether she meant the ring or the message. 'It's obvious they weren't looking for it when they went to the house, anyway. They were looking for me.'

'Or me. They must have followed us to Tetzcoco on the day I bought you. Partridge probably told them where we were going. We didn't hire him for his courage!'

'No, it was the Texcalans who told them. They overheard you mentioning Hare, and Tetzcoco, while Lion was cutting them loose. You realize that was what old Black Feathers had in mind all along, don't you? The crafty old bastard must have insisted on the three of us being sold together just in case things went wrong and I was bought for something other than a sacrifice. They must have gone running to the Otomies the moment they were free. Then they seem to have teamed up together.'

'Why? The Otomies, I can understand, but what have the Texcalans got against us? If it wasn't for us, they'd probably both have ended up under a flint knife by now.'

'Or worse,' I confirmed. 'But that's exactly it. I think they were looking forward to being sacrificed!'

Lily groaned. 'I should have guessed. Texcalans, Aztecs, it doesn't matter – men are all the same!'

'The trouble is,' I mused, 'that even if the Otomies don't know what it is, they'll have guessed that there was something in that house that we wanted. And now they're using it as bait.'

We lapsed into thoughtful silence. I wondered whether the Otomies were still working for Lord Feathered in Black, or whether this was all being done on their own initiative – the captain's way of getting revenge on me for slipping from his grasp. I thought it might well be the latter, because I doubted that even the Chief Minister could have paid them enough to adopt their present guises, with their hard-earned clothes and haircuts cast aside. Only real hatred could have induced them to do that.

'What puzzles me,' Lily mused, 'is why the disguise? It's not as if either of us is likely to have any trouble recognizing the captain.'

'No, and it wouldn't be his style anyway. He's not one for sneaking up on people. He likes to give his victims something to look forward to. That's probably why they made so much noise at the guesthouse, just to let us know who was after us. So it's not us they're hiding from.'

'It'll be the authorities here in Tetzcoco. People are resentful enough about having Montezuma's nephew pushed on to them as King without a bunch of ferocious Aztec warriors running around scaring the populace and breaking things. With any luck, somebody will report them for what they did last night.'

'No chance. They'll have made it pretty clear what will happen to anyone going to the police. Besides, that wouldn't help us, would it? We have to find them in order to get our hands on that message. That won't be any easier if they're driven into hiding.'

We were both quiet again. I wondered what Lily's guard made of the spectacle of his inmate's lawyer squatting in front of her cage with his bowed head pressed against the bars, saying nothing. I thought I should either adopt a more professional demeanour or go away. I did not want to leave Lily, but I could think of nothing to say to her, and she seemed to have the same problem. Everything that came to mind sounded either trite or heartless, or merely recalled how hopeless the woman's situation was. We both knew that if I found the

Otomies, or rather if they found me, it was far more likely that they would kill me than part with Hare's message, and even if I did manage to get hold of it, there was no certainty that it would do Lily any good.

'Lily . . .' I mumbled, unsure what I was going to say next.

'Hush,' she said, in a voice so low I barely heard it. 'You'd better go. Haven't you got things to do outside?'

I had to go to the marketplace and get back on the track of the Otomies: an easy enough task, I thought ruefully, if they were looking for me. I plodded glumly and silently through the palace's labyrinthine corridors, following a guide who, like his predecessor the day before, had waited for me outside the prison, not wishing to breathe the tainted air around the cages.

He was a dwarf, one of the malformed creatures that kings and emperors liked to have in attendance upon them. They ran errands and entertained their masters with jokes and tricks, and were sacred, not unlike slaves, although they were fed and treated like lords. Life for a palace dwarf was pleasant enough, but subject to abrupt termination. If the King died, or the Sun was eclipsed, or some other sufficiently inauspicious event took place, they were all liable to be sacrificed at once to placate the angry gods. Of course, they knew this, and so tended to affect a determined cheerfulness, as though intent on making the most of every moment without a care for a future that might never come. As the little man stumped along ahead of me, chattering brightly, I reflected that I might have a lot to learn from his view of the World, provided it were only myself I had to worry about.

'This isn't normally my job, of course, but we're always short-handed these days.' He paused, waiting for me to break my moody silence by asking why. Since I refused to oblige, he carried on: 'So, how do you get to be a lawyer, then?'

'By talking a lot.'

'Oh, well, that wouldn't suit me! No, really, there must be more to it than that?'

Since I had no idea what men such as Obsidian Tongue did to earn their position, I changed the subject. 'Why are you always short-handed?'

He glanced about him quickly, as though afraid of eavesdroppers lurking in the shadows, and lowered his voice. 'Well, it's hardly a secret. All the warriors are away keeping an eye on Black Flower, and with no revenues from the provinces in the North the palace staff have been cut back, so when the King's away at his retreat in Tetzcotzinco, which is most of the time, he has to take practically everyone away with him. And everyone who's still here seems to spend all their time looking for spies. I tell you, it's not much fun here any more!'

I was beginning to find this interesting, in spite of myself. 'How long's it been like this?'

'I think things were better under the old king, Hungry Child. At least, I'm told they were – I wasn't here then, naturally.'

'But there wasn't a war on then.'

'That's right. He gave all that up, you know.'

'I heard.' To an Aztec, the idea of renouncing war took some getting used to. It was not just eccentric; to some, it would have seemed downright blasphemous, depriving the gods of their favourite nourishment: the hearts of captive warriors. 'What made him do that?'

'Who knows? I mean, he was supposed to have foreseen some great disaster which meant whatever our armies did would come to nothing in the end.'

'You don't believe that?'

'No, I think he just lost interest. He'd seen his son executed and lost his favourite concubine . . .'

'You mean Prince of Willows and the Lady of Tollan?'

'Yes, that's it.'

I recalled Lily's description of the affair. 'What was that all about? Were they really just swapping poems?'

'So I heard.' He leered knowingly up at me. 'But what was in the poems, eh? That's the question! And we'll never know the answer to that one. But then on top of that there was that business with Queen Chalchiuhnenetl.'

'Who's Chalchiuhnenetl?' The name was familiar, although that may have been because it was relatively common: it meant 'Jade Doll'.

'You never heard about it? Amazing! Considering it nearly got us into a war with your people, on account of her being your Emperor Axayacatl's daughter – Montezuma's sister, no less. I thought everyone knew the story. Let me tell you . . .'

'Go on, then.'

'Jade Doll wasn't much more than a child when she came here, so the King – who had plenty of concubines, but wasn't into anything kinky – had her housed in her own apartments and left her alone. Big mistake, because she grew up a lot faster than he bargained for. Amazing girl. She seems to have shared her sleeping mat with half the young men in Tetzcoco before the King found out about it.'

'I'd have thought that was difficult. Wouldn't someone have said something? It must have looked a bit suspicious, a procession of men leaving her apartments in the morning.'

He chuckled. 'Sure it would, but her trick was, they didn't leave! She usually had them for one night and then promptly had them killed. She had little statues of them made afterwards as souvenirs, though, so I guess she was quite fond of them really.'

'Oh, come on,' I said sceptically. 'Someone would have said something. What about their families, her servants, the sculptor who made the statues?'

'As I heard it, no one dared say a word. Is that surprising? Her household and the sculptor were all in on it, of course, and when Hungry Child found out they couldn't expect him to be much happier with them than with her. As for the families – well, naturally, she'd disposed of the bodies, so they had no evidence, and if they happened to know where their relations were going, that would have made them accomplices too, wouldn't it? You're the lawyer!'

'Um – I suppose so. Didn't the King start to wonder what all the statues were for, though?'

'Sure. She told him they were idols. Everybody knows you Aztecs are a bunch of religious fanatics, so he had no trouble believing it.'

'How did she get caught?'

'How does anybody get caught? She did something stupid. She sent one of her young men a ring the King had given her, her way of summoning him to her sleeping mat. It was a really distinctive thing, apparently. Of course, the stupid bastard was seen wearing it, and that was that. The King had her strangled, along with a lot of other people, naturally.'

A tall limestone statue caught my eye as we walked past it. It was of Hungry Child looking down from an alcove into a small courtyard with a pool full of water lilies. None of them was in flower now, but it looked like a pleasant place, quiet and away from the bustle of the busier parts of the palace. I wondered whether the statue showed the King as he had looked in life, staring into the water and reflecting bitterly on his misfortunes.

'He didn't have much luck with his women, did he?' I said.

'It doesn't sound like it,' my guide conceded. 'But after all, he had plenty of others to console himself with!'

He sounded envious, but what struck me then, making me break my stride while he walked on, oblivious to the fact that I was no longer following him, was not some lascivious notion of what I might do I were a King with my own harem, but the recollection that Lily's present troubles were all on account of one of Hungry Child's concubines.

Mother of Light lived in the palace, I presumed. If I could find her, then it was just possible that she could tell me enough about Hare's message herself that I would not need to meet the Otomies after all. It was a forlorn hope, but not much more forlorn than trying to deal with my sworn enemies. I thought Mother of Light must know at least what sort of message she was expecting.

My first impulse was to ask my escort about her, but I suppressed it. It was obvious that hers was not a name to be bandied about with anyone who knew my name or could connect me with Lily. I had to get rid of him and find a total stranger instead.

I swore loudly.

The dwarf stopped and looked over his shoulder. 'What is it?'

'I forgot my notes.'

'Notes?'

'The paper I was writing on while I was talking to my client.' I made a gesture like someone drawing a glyph, hoping he had forgotten that I had not been carrying anything when he led me into the prison. 'I left it next to her cell. I'd better go back and get it.'

'You must be joking! You want to go all the way back in there, just to pick up a scrap of paper?'

'I'm sorry, but it's really important.'

'Can't you just remember what your client said?'

'I need the glyphs to jog my memory.'

'It's all very well for you, but I've only got short legs, see? And I'm thirsty. It comes of holding my nose and breathing through my mouth all morning . . .'

'Look, I said I was sorry. I really need these notes. I can go on my own, if you like.'

He looked dubious. 'Don't think I can let you do that. You're not allowed to go wandering around here on your own. And what if you get lost? How would I explain that?'

'I won't be wandering. I'll go straight there and straight back. And I know the way now – I've been there before.'

'I don't know . . .'

'Why don't you go and get yourself a drink of water,' I suggested, taking a step backwards and making as if to turn away. 'I'll be back here before you are, I promise!'

He licked his lips thirstily. 'Well . . .'

I started walking. He did not call me back.

So far, so good, I told myself, but what was I going to do now?

I retraced my steps to the prison as far as the first turning, which brought me back into the courtyard with the pool and the statue.

There was a stone bench by the pool. I sat on it and stared up at the brooding basalt figure. 'You were supposed to be wise,' I said. 'What would you have done?' Not surprisingly, the dead King had nothing to say for himself. Probably, I thought, he had never found himself in this sort of predicament.

I had very little time in which to look for Mother of Light, assuming she was in the palace complex and had not gone out for any reason. It would not take the dwarf long to get himself a drink, and he would raise a hue and cry the moment he returned and found I was still missing. The best I could hope for was that he would put off sounding the alarm until he had gone back to the prison and found out that I had lied about the paper. Either way, a whole palace full of guards would soon be out looking for a missing lawyer. What was more, if they caught me they would treat me as a spy. I was not sure what would happen to a spy in Tetzcoco. In Mexico, once every useful piece of information had been wrung from them, they were dismembered and the pieces left outside the city for the vultures and coyotes. I began to wonder whether I would have been better off taking my chances with the Otomies. Then I thought about what I would have done if I had really been a lawyer. The answer was obvious: I would have disguised myself as something else.

'Wonder what old Obsidian Tongue would charge for this?' I muttered, still speaking to the statue, as I stuffed my cloak behind it. 'Here, look after this, will you? May be a while before I come back for it.' I glanced quickly at my reflection in the pool. I had not been a very convincing lawyer, I thought; it was a relief to revert to slavery again.

I set off at a brisk trot, picking a direction at random. My plan was simple: I wanted to stop the first person I saw, tell him I had been sent to find Mother of Light and ask him if he knew where she was.

This proved not to be altogether straightforward. To begin with, there seemed to be no one about: I found myself padding through one long corridor after another without seeing a soul. The moment I rounded a corner and at last set eyes on another human being – a man dressed, like me, in nothing but a breechcloth, and therefore probably a slave – I greeted him as joyfully as if he had been an old friend.

'You look lost,' he said, cordially enough.

'I'm a stranger here.'

'Aztec,' he noted.

'That's right. I'm from Mexico. My master's, um . . . Lord Feathered in Black. Sent me here with a message for someone. But I took a wrong turning somewhere and got completely confused . . . I'm looking for one of the King's concubines.'

He laughed. 'You won't find her here! Not at the moment, anyway. You're near the King's apartments, but he's away at the lodge at Tetzcotzinco. That's why there aren't many people in this part of the palace. I expect he's taken a few girls with him – sure she's not one of those?'

'Sorry, I mean the late King – Hungry Child.'

He stared. 'Oh, I see. What's her name?'

'Mother of Light.'

'Never heard of her. You sure she's still alive? Some of the prettier ones would have been sacrificed at his funeral, to keep him company in the Land of the Dead.'

'Positive.'

'Well, I don't know where you'd look for her. If she's a noble or was one of his particular favourites or bore him children, she'd probably have her own apartment somewhere, her own house, even. Otherwise, you could try the slaves' quarters.' He looked at me through narrowed eyes. 'Your master's the Aztec Chief Minister, isn't he? Why is he interested in an ex-concubine?'

'Um . . . I think they're related.'

'Oh, well, there's your answer. She's a noble, she'll have her own place.' He turned to go.

That told me nothing, since I had been lying. In truth I had no idea whether the woman was a noble or not. I thought about asking the stranger where the slaves' quarters were but decided it would just make him more suspicious.

I smelled the next person before I saw him. He had the dark robes, black-daubed skin and tangled hair of a priest, and he had the unique stench of a man who has not washed in a long time and is still covered in scabs from offering his own blood to the gods. I stepped smartly aside for him and greeted him politely. He ignored me.

'Idiot,' I muttered, scowling after him. 'You don't fool me.

Too busy communing with the gods to notice mere mortals, my arse. Think you're better than I am, do you? Why . . .'

'You!' a voice yelled. 'Stay there!'

I jumped, whirled around to confront the speaker, and then nearly fainted from terror. A small party of warriors was advancing on me. They were carrying swords, not cudgels. Their glittering obsidian blades seemed to be winking at me.

'Um . . . who, me?'

'What are you doing here?'

'D–d–d–delivering a message,' I said without thinking.

'Who to?'

'One of the, er, one of the King's concubines . . .' I fought to keep the tremor out of my voice. The men stood around me in a loose circle, eyeing me with distaste and glancing towards their leader for instructions. He was a tall man in a richly embroidered cotton cloak and matching breechcloth, with a labret and earrings of amber, leather sandals with long trailing straps and half his hair shaved off. I did not know what rank his appearance represented here in Tetzcoco, but anyone could have told that he was a senior, brave, ferocious and utterly pitiless warrior.

He looked me up and down and then rolled his eyes as if in despair. 'So I'm interrupting an assignation,' he growled. 'Too bad. We're looking for someone. A spy. Went missing around the middle of the morning.'

I said nothing.

'Well?' he snapped. His sword shook menacingly.

'I haven't seen anyone!' I wailed.

'He's a lawyer,' one of his men informed me. 'At least, he claims to be. Calls himself Yaotl. Last seen wearing a plain cloak and breechcloth, but he may have changed his disguise by now. Ugly character, apparently, weedy looking, no meat on him. Looks as if he could do with a good meal. A bit like you, I should think, but taller.'

I silently thanked my patron god for the fact that the dwarf had overestimated my height from having to look up at me all the time. 'Haven't seen anyone like that.'

The warriors' leader sighed heavily. 'Bugger. All right, you'd better get on.'

'What do I do if I see him?' I asked.

The man laughed. 'Run away and scream for help! He may not look much, but by all accounts he's extremely dangerous. He'll be well trained, desperate, ruthless, and he's armed . . .'

'Armed?'

'Threatened his escort with a concealed knife.'

As the warriors trotted away, I had to grin. Now I knew how the dwarf had explained away my disappearance. I could hardly blame him, although it did not make my position any easier.

Finally I found someone, a commoner, who had heard of Mother of Light and was able to tell me where to look for her. His suggestion surprised me.

'We rarely see her nowadays. I think she must have her own house, outside the palace, and she keeps herself to herself mostly, but somebody told me they'd seen her in one of the courtyards around where the Council of Music meets.'

'What would she be doing there?'

'Listening to someone reciting poetry, I expect. Maybe reciting some herself.' He frowned. 'Why are you looking for her, anyway?'

'I have a message to deliver.'

'What sort of message?'

'A private message,' I said with careful emphasis.

'Oh, well, please yourself. I suppose now you want me to

tell you where to find the Council of Music. Well, I'll tell you, but you'll have to hurry. She's never around for very long – a very elusive lady.'

I all but ran in the direction he indicated.

The Council of Music, when it was not trying suspected sorcerers, highway robbers or priests accused of fornication, oversaw teachers. In Mexico, anything more than rudimentary instruction in singing and other arts such as painting, writing and fine speech was a matter for the House of Tears, where priests were brought up and trained. In Tetzcoco, those who were good enough were trained in the palace itself, at least in principle under the eye of the King. Acolhuans prided themselves on speaking the finest and most polished Nahuatl to be heard anywhere in the valley, and their long-dead king, Hungry Coyote, in particular, had been renowned as a poet, as for that matter had his son, Hungry Child. Naturally both men had wanted to surround themselves with others like them, and they did everything they could to encourage them.

I had vaguely known all of this before I ever came to Tetzcoco and had long ago reached my own conclusion about why Hungry Coyote had gone to such lengths to foster his singers' and his artists' skills. No doubt he had loved these things for their own sake, but he had also known that his kingdom's prestige would never be based on prowess in war, because his warriors would never be a match for the Aztecs. All he had done, I had thought, with all an Aztec's contempt for a people we thought effete, weak and snobbish, was to make the most of the one thing they could do better than we.

None of what I had known about Tetzcoco, though, prepared me for what I found when I followed the directions I had been given.

It turned out that I only needed an approximate idea of where the Council of Music was located in order to find the place, because once I got close I only had to follow my ears. The most extraordinary noise flowed through the corridors and open spaces around it: snatches of song, fragments of unidentifiable, rhythmic speech, presumably poetry, drums, flutes, and somebody crying – probably a child being pricked with thorns for singing out of tune, if my own experiences in a House of Tears in Mexico were any guide. The sounds changed constantly as I walked, voices growing or dwindling as I crossed a corridor, or stopping suddenly when someone made a mistake or a rehearsal ended. Passing one small room, I heard a strange, high-pitched jabbering; the words were unintelligible, but I imagined the leader of a chorus shouting almost hysterically at his singers for some repeated blunder.

The Council of Music itself sat in a large, colonnaded hall, and that was easy to spot by the small crowd of people gathered outside it: black-robed priests, lords identifiable by their jewels and feathers and elaborate hairstyles, plainly dressed commoners keeping a respectful distance from their betters, and a surprising number of children. Few of them spoke, and then only in whispers, and I supposed they were all waiting their turn to be called in: the priests to deal with some business connected with a ritual or the management of a temple, perhaps, while in the case of the lords and the commoners, they might be there to hear their children audition for the palace school. I noticed a pair of miserable-looking characters, dressed in rags, squatting between two armed warriors, and suspected they were in for a less pleasant morning.

Slipping past the crowd, all of whose members were too preoccupied to notice me, and following the promising sound of a single voice chanting, I found myself at the end of a short passageway looking into a courtyard. Pillars surrounded the open space in its middle, with statues standing between some of them, looking down into it. I hid behind one of the statues while I took in the scene in front of me.

Although a few neatly trimmed azalea shrubs grew around the edge of the courtyard, it was not laid out as a garden. Instead of plants, it had a small paved space surrounded by stone seats. A handful of men sat on these, all of them dressed as nobles, their colourful cotton capes gathered over their knees and spilling over the benches around them. They listened in silence to a young man standing in the open space in the middle, and it was his voice that I had followed here, declaiming in a sorrowful tone:

> *'Sound the turquoise drum.*
> *Cactuses are drunk with fallen flowers;*
> *you with the heron headdress,*
> *you with the painted body.*
> *They hear him, go beside him,*
> *birds with flower-bright beaks*
> *accompany the strong youth*
> *With the tiger shield. He has returned to them.*
>
> *I mourn*
> *from my heart, I, Nezahualpilli . . .'*

'"Weep!"'

The woman's voice came from very close by, making me jump so violently that I almost gave myself away. I had not noticed her, because she was right in front of the statue I was hiding behind. To my amazement, I realized that I knew who she was, because I had heard her shouting at two pedlars the day before. Her voice this time was not much more gentle.

'I'm . . . I'm sorry?' the young man said, looking up at her in confusion.

'It's "weep," not "mourn,"' she snapped. Then, in an entirely different manner, superficially like the young man's but softer and more measured, with each word given its own subtly different weight and the whole having the sense that the poet's own mind was at work behind the speaker's mouth, she went on:

> *I weep*
> *from my heart, I, Nezahualpilli.*
> *I search for my comrades*
> *but the old lord is gone,*
> *that petal-green quetzal,*
> *and gone*
> *the young warrior.'*

The young man looked crestfallen, but an appreciative murmur ran through the audience. One man said: 'Well, it was a good effort, but you have to admit Mother of Light ought to know how it goes, of all people! You might have let the poor lad finish, though, Mother of Light. And remember, with you here – well, this is such a rare privilege for any student, he's probably a bit nervous.'

I had to restrain myself from leaping out from behind my pillar to jabber wildly at the owner of that fine, skilfully modulated voice. Mother of Light! I bit my tongue, willing myself to stay silent.

'I'm sorry,' the woman said mildly. 'You did recite it well, but hearing the words, I just can't help remembering how the King would have spoken them.' I noticed she did not call Hungry Child 'the late King' or 'the King's father'.

There was no more poetry after that, and the little gathering soon began to break up, with members of the audience rising and leaving in various directions. I froze, pressing myself so hard against the statue that if it had not been made of solid rock it might have fallen over. Two men walked straight past me, but they were conversing earnestly with each other and neither of them looked back before they had gone out of the courtyard. I had no chance to see where Mother of Light might have gone and was terrified that she had left too, giving me no chance to work out even which direction she had taken, but when I dared to peep around the edge of the statue she was standing in the little space in the middle, speaking earnestly to the young man. He was listening carefully, with his head bowed. I assumed she was giving him some tips on how to recite the late King's verse, with the authority of one who had shared the poet's sleeping mat.

I looked at her curiously, as best I could through one eye. She puzzled me. She clearly commanded more respect in this place than she would have merited merely by having been one of Hungry Child's countless concubines. She knew her poetry. I wondered whether she composed her own. Women poets were by no means unknown: my former master's half-sister had been a noted poet, as of course had been the unfortunate Lady of Tollan. In a city where these things were so highly prized as they were in Tetzcoco, a lady skilled with words might make herself heard among men.

It was not usual, though. Most of the women I knew were queens in their own households but as meek as mice out of doors. And how was I to reconcile the attention Mother of Light commanded here with what I had seen the day before, the woman beset by a couple of itinerant pedlars, whose father had given every appearance of being a destitute cripple?

As the young man left, she returned to her seat, to gather up some papers, and I stepped out into the open.

'Remember me?'

She let out a little cry and staggered backwards, scattering papers around her. I was afraid she was going to fall over, but she managed to regain her balance just in time. She looked up at me grimly.

'You look like that idiot from yesterday morning – the one who nearly got himself killed outside the marketplace. What are you doing here? And where's your cloak?'

'Let me help with those,' I said, brushing aside her questions as I stooped to pick up some of the papers. I noticed in passing that they were covered in delicately drawn glyphs, which may well have represented poetry. A poem had to be learned by heart – the pictures we used for writing could never convey words with the precision needed for verse – but a poet might use pictures to jog his memory.

'What do you want?'

'To talk to you. Here. I'm sorry if they're out of order. Oh, how's your father?'

'Well,' she said guardedly. 'He managed to get home, small thanks to you.'

'Look, I was trying to help . . .'

'I'm sure you were. I don't know what you expect me to say. I suppose I should welcome you formally, say something like: "You have expended breath to come here. You are weary; you are hungry." But all I'm actually going to say is goodbye!' Clutching her papers to her breast, she turned on her heel and walked away.

'I suppose you're right,' I told her departing back. 'After all, talking to you seems to be a dangerous occupation. It didn't do Tiger Lily a lot of good, did it?'

She stopped. She hesitated, the tendons in one ankle flexing as if she were making her mind up whether to take another step or not.

'What did you say?' she asked me quietly, without turning her head.

I followed her across the courtyard. 'Maybe we should sit down,' I suggested.

'Not here. You said yourself, it's too dangerous. Come with me.'

She set off in the direction the young man had taken but suddenly darted down a narrow passageway. Her manner had become furtive, and she kept glancing over her shoulder in a way that reminded me of what I had seen in the streets a couple of days before. Here, I realized, was someone else who was convinced that there were spies everywhere. We turned several corners before coming to a small room, whose entrance was sealed off by a wicker screen. I noticed that there was a tall niche on either side of the doorway, easily large enough to accommodate a man, possibly a sentry. The appearance of the room, once the woman had pulled the screen aside, seemed to confirm the idea: its walls were covered with hangings, of the richest, deepest and most opulent featherwork, and the only piece of furniture on the floor was a low wicker seat with a high, fur-covered back, the kind of seat that was used as a throne.

I stared at the seat, aghast. 'Maize Ear uses this room?'

'No, but Hungry Child used to, when he was present at the Council of Music and wanted to speak in private. The hangings stopped sound from carrying, and one of the walls is an outer wall of the palace, so there's one less side for an eavesdropper to press his ear to.'

The room was small to accommodate a King. I found it hard to imagine Mexico's Montezuma, upon whose face most were forbidden to look, in a room such as this, where others could get so close to him.

'Maize Ear isn't so concerned with the affairs of the Council of Music as his father was. It's not that he has no interest in poetry – he's not bad in that line himself, actually, though his work could be more polished . . .'

'What is it about you people and poetry?' I interrupted her rudely. I did not have time for a rambling digression on the King's poetic talents. Besides, I had had to learn a lot of verse by heart in the House of Tears, much of it bad, and had no enthusiasm for it. 'This must be the only place in the World where people can get killed over a poem!'

'What do you mean?' the woman asked sharply.

'I mean the King's son, Prince of Willows, and that concubine.'

She stiffened, as though I had said something to offend her. Then she seemed to force herself to relax before saying, as quietly as if she were speaking to herself: 'You shouldn't believe everything you hear.' Then, more briskly: 'Now, what do you want? What are you to Lily? There's no need to keep looking over your shoulder like that. We have this room to ourselves. Maize Ear is in Tetzcotzinco.'

To my horror, she sat on the seat, with her papers on her lap as if she were about to start making notes, and looked up at me levelly.

'My name's Yaotl. I'm Lily's slave,' I said. 'You heard she'd been arrested?'

'I did. What of it?'

'She was picked up because she'd been seen talking to you. Maize Ear's men started following her and found that she was trying to contact a merchant called Hare. When she went to Hare's house, they caught her.'

'And what about Hare?' she asked neutrally.

'Dead.'

I had to admire her self-possession. If the news shocked or upset her, she did not let it show, merely raising one eyebrow. 'Really? How?'

'Murdered.' I told her briefly what had happened both times I was at Hare's house. 'Look,' I ended, trying to keep the edge of desperation out of my voice as I came to the reason for my being here, 'I'm being honest, telling you everything. I don't even know if I can trust you . . .'

'Likewise!'

'But do you see the fix we're in? Lily's trial will start in a day or two, and I'm told the judges have to get it over with quickly. I'm also told it will be an open-and-shut case. They can prove she was up to something secretive, and unless we can show the court that it was all innocent she'll be executed for plotting against the King. And you could be in a lot of trouble as well.'

Mother of Light smiled thinly. 'You're assuming it *was* innocent.'

'It's the only hope we've got,' I said earnestly. Then, grasping what she had said, I added, in a subdued voice: 'It was, wasn't it?'

She ignored the question at first. She looked at me curiously. 'You took a big risk, coming here on the off chance that I could tell you what you want to hear.'

'I don't have a choice.'

'Yes, you do. Your mistress is in jail and likely to be killed. If you stay in Tetzcoco you may be implicated in whatever she's supposed to have done, but if you run away she's hardly likely to be in a position to stop you. Why don't you just make yourself scarce?'

Lily had said much the same thing to me the day before. I had had no answer to her then. Now I could only stare at Mother of Light, speechless.

'Interesting,' she said at last. 'A devoted slave! I hope your mistress paid well for your services.'

'The message?' I reminded her hopefully.

'I wish I could help you,' she sighed, 'but what I'm going to say is the truth, Yaotl or whatever your name is. I've no idea what the message was about.'

I looked at the floor, momentarily beaten. I realized that, without meaning to, I had convinced myself that a word from Mother of Light would solve all our problems, at once exonerating Lily and sparing me a potentially lethal encounter with my enemies. To learn that she apparently had nothing for me left me at something of a loss. 'Surely,' I muttered without much conviction, 'you must have some idea what it was?'

'I doubt that there was anything in it that Maize Ear ought to have worried himself about. But that's not the point, is it? I can't tell you, or the judges, any more than that. All I know is that Hare apparently turned up in Tetzcoco's marketplace with a message that he was willing to sell to the highest bidder. It apparently had something to do with something that had been seen in Mayan country, in the hot lowlands by the coast. These things fascinate me, you see. I was . . . Well, I was intrigued.'

I looked up again, studying the woman's face with renewed interest. She had her eyes on a point somewhere above my head. I wondered whether she was a magician or a soothsayer as well as a poet. It was possible; the study of the realms that lay outside the comfortable daylight world we lived in – the horrors, named and nameless, that came out at night, the thirteen layers of heaven and the nine regions of the Land of the Dead, the ways of the gods and omens and portents that revealed their will – often went hand in hand with the urge to render them into speech. Poets discovered the truth about the fragility of life here on Earth and tried to communicate it to the rest of us. And there had been plenty of material for them recently in the hot lands by the coast. Lately rumours had abounded of strange things that had been seen there: pale men with long, bushy beards, who seemed to have crossed the endless Divine Sea in boats the size of pyramids, wearing outlandish clothes, bearing powerful, exotic weapons that threw massive stones with the sound and smoke of a volcano.

The rumours had caused widespread dread, especially combined with the other portents that had been reported in recent
years: strange lights in the sky, temples catching fire for no
apparent reason, a woman – thought to be the goddess
Cihuacoatl, who always portended disaster – heard crying out
in the streets by night. I knew they had terrified Montezuma.
I supposed that was why Hare had chosen to come to
Tetzcoco and not Mexico; as soon as he found out where the
merchant came from, the Aztec Emperor would probably have
had him locked up and the contents of his message sweated
out of him. Even here, Hare had clearly felt the need to be dis-
creet – and it had not been enough to save him.

'How did you find out about Hare?' I asked.

'Through Lily. I've had dealings with her family over the
years. Mainly that devious old . . . her father. She came to me
with Hare's proposition. As it happened, I had something I
could offer him . . .'

'Ah. Funny you should mention that.'

She stiffened in alarm. 'What about it? What do you know
about it?'

Mindful of Lily's warning, I had not mentioned the ring,
but now, since I knew Mother of Light had given it to Lily in
the first place, I thought I had better tell her all about it. As I
did, I saw a change come over the woman: her hands, which
had been resting open in her lap, suddenly clenched, twisting
and creasing the paper under them, and her face seemed to age
even as I watched, darkening, eyes narrowing, furrows lengthening and growing deeper.

'You lost the ring,' she whispered.

'I didn't!' I cried defensively. 'I never had it in the first
place!'

'We have to get it back, and quickly, before it falls into the
wrong hands,' she cried, almost bouncing out of her seat in her

sudden agitation. 'Do you understand that? This is far more important than some stupid message that may or may not mean anything to anybody!'

'What? Why? No, I don't understand – why is it more important? You were prepared to give the thing to the merchant, after all! How can it be so valuable if you were willing to hand it over in exchange for a piece of information you knew nothing about?'

'Because I wasn't going to do any such thing, you fool! It was a token. It merely told the merchant who he was dealing with, assured him we had the means to pay whatever his message was worth. He was to use it to identify himself when he came to me, and give it back to me then. Then he'd get his pay – his cloaks, gold quills, copper axe heads, whatever it was. I didn't want to trust him even that far – oh, I wish I hadn't!'

I flinched: her voice had risen until it filled the room, and I was afraid it would be audible outside, despite the wall-hangings. However, there was one word in her shrill outpouring that had caught my attention and drove even the fear of discovery from my thoughts for a moment. 'Who's "we"?' I asked quietly.

'What?'

'You said "we", Mother of Light. "*We* had the means to pay." Who else is there?'

She was dumbfounded. 'Nobody. I didn't say "we", did I? I must have been confused. I meant . . .'

'I think you meant what you said.' I leaned forward, staring impolitely into her eyes, which were blinking furiously. 'It's not you this message was intended for at all, is it? You're a go-between, like Lily. Who are you working for – Black Flower, is that it?'

'No!'

'Then . . .'

For a moment I felt that I had overpowered her, that she would drop her gaze or turn aside and shamefacedly mutter that it was true, she was spying for Maize Ear's brother and his enemy, and plead with me not to give her away. Of course, then I would have promised to say nothing provided she started telling me the truth about Hare's message.

I scented victory, only to have it promptly snatched away.

She stopped blinking and returned my stare steadily. When she spoke, she had lowered her voice, but her tone was as hard as flint.

'Just listen to me. All you need to know is that that ring has to be found. If it isn't, if it's seen by the wrong people – by people who know what it represents – then it means death for all of us. For you, me, Lily and anyone else who's ever seen the thing. Do you get that, slave?'

10

You're making progress, Yaotl, I told myself bitterly as I walked back towards the hall of the Council of Music, hoping to find a way from there out of the palace. This morning you were only looking for a mysterious message. Now you've got to find a mysterious ring as well, and you don't even know why. Good work!

I had left Mother of Light in the little audience room, with the feeling that I had been dismissed from her presence. I wondered at her imperiousness. She may once have enjoyed the attentions of a King, but he was dead, and she had been only a concubine, and not, by all accounts, one of his favourites. Where, I wondered, had she got the authority and self-confidence to take charge so easily?

I was mulling this over as I found myself walking through the little courtyard where the poets had gathered. Out of the corner of my eye I saw two men lounging on one of the stone benches. I caught a brief glimpse of their hair, noticed that they both wore it piled up in the fashion of experienced warriors, and quickly looked away so as to avoid catching their eyes. I did not want to attract anybody's attention now; I just wanted to get out of the palace before anyone connected me with the missing, heavily armed and dangerous lawyer they were all looking for.

I bustled onward, getting almost to the far side of the

courtyard before a familiar voice called out after me: 'What kept you, Yaotl? We've been waiting ages. Did you find Mother of Light?'

I froze. I wanted to take to my heels but my legs suddenly refused to move. It would have done me no good anyway, as I could never have run fast enough. Instead, I turned around slowly, to see Rattlesnake unfolding himself from his seat and standing up. His companion did the same. They were both grinning.

I said nothing. I could not think of anything to say.

'Not very polite, is he, Hunter? I'd have thought at the very least he'd have asked you how your head was!'

'Um – look, I'm sorry about your head, but . . .'

'No need to apologize,' Hunter rumbled. 'Grovel and beg for mercy, yes.'

'I didn't have any choice!'

'Me neither,' remarked the warrior drily.

They both stood in front of me. Neither of them was armed, but then they did not need to be: they could easily have hammered me into the floor with their fists.

'You would not believe the fuss you've caused this morning, Yaotl,' Rattlesnake said reprovingly. 'Squads of warriors running around all over the place, all of them armed to the teeth, because they think they're after some sort of demon with the power to change how he looks, produce weapons out of thin air and vanish without trace. I bet they'll call in sorcerers this afternoon to try to make you disappear. But me, when I heard who they were all after and realized it was someone connected with Lily, I thought: That doesn't sound like the Yaotl I know. He's just a weedy little slave. Can't see him coming here disguising himself as a lawyer. Surely there must be some mistake. So I thought I ought to check. Lucky for you I did, really. If any of those nervous youngsters had seen you first, I expect they'd have killed you on sight, just to be on the safe side.'

'How . . . how did you know where to look?' I croaked through dry lips.

'You were asking for Mother of Light,' Hunter said. 'We heard she was here.'

'We take a particular interest in that lady,' his colleague explained, 'not to mention anyone we find talking to her.'

'Why?'

The two men looked at each other.

'He asks too many questions, doesn't he?' Rattlesnake said.

His colleague agreed. 'It's an unhealthy habit.'

They both stepped forward at once, one on either side of me, and without breaking stride each seized one of my arms, almost wrenching them from their sockets. I was swept up and dragged along between the two men, running frantically backwards with my heels painfully scuffing the floor.

'Where are you taking me? Put me down! I can walk – I won't try to run away. Just let me on my feet – can't you hear me?'

'Yes, more's the pity. Shut up.'

I could not see where we were going. It was as much as I could do to stay on my feet without trying to turn my head as well, and besides, I thought, if I did know what was ahead, there would be nothing I could do about it. I fell silent and gritted my teeth against the pain in my shoulders, which felt as if they were being hit with staves at every step.

'Get in here.'

The command was redundant, since Rattlesnake and Hunter promptly threw me bodily into the room. I stumbled over backwards, landing awkwardly and painfully on my shoulder blades.

'We've got to go and get the others now,' Rattlesnake said. 'What do we do with this one in the meantime?'

I scrambled to my feet, quickly noting that I was in a large, dark space. Even during the day the only illumination was from a torch in the passageway outside, and so I had no clue to my surroundings except the echo of the warrior's voice, the rough feel of a bare earth floor under my back, and a blend of nasty smells. My nose detected hints of dried blood and the air around a latrine on a hot day. I had no way of knowing what this part of the palace was used for, but it seemed unlikely to be anything pleasant.

'Others?' I asked fearfully. 'What others?'

Hunter answered his chief's question and ignored mine. 'Why don't we just do this?'

He hit me with his balled fist, just below the ribcage, and the breath exploded out of me as I fell. I rolled helplessly across the floor, coming to rest on my knees.

'That was for the bump on my scalp,' he said mildly. 'Just so we're quits. No hard feelings. This, on the other hand . . .'

I never found out what the second blow was for, because he was still speaking when his foot slammed into the side of my head, sending me into oblivion by way of a blinding pain and a shower of stars.

When I woke up, the space around me was full of people, and they all appeared to be shouting and dancing. At least, it seemed that way to me, because their voices resounded painfully in my head and their footfalls jarred my battered body like kicks. Something large made a scraping noise as it was dragged across the floor. I felt hands seize me and pull me roughly aside. My eyes opened, but the bodies milling around me were too confusing and I quickly shut them again. I tried to go back to sleep, but then somebody was shaking my shoulder and slapping my face.

'Come on, wake up! We're all ready for you now!'

The shaking became harder, jerking my head sharply back and forth until the pain made me groan aloud. I forced my eyes to open, blinking away the moisture in them until I could just about see what was in front of me.

There was more light now: someone was holding a torch aloft. Its flame flared painfully in the corner on my vision, and I turned deliberately away from it to look instead into the long, flickering shadows it made.

Most of them were cast by things all too familiar from my recent experience: the bars of a wooden cage, a small one, too small for a person to stand or lie full length in. It had been this that I had heard dragged across the floor. Before that, I presumed it had been carried into the room, perhaps on poles like a litter, although its occupant could hardly be said to have been travelling in style. From where I lay, he or she was little more than a shadow among shadows, a huddled shape squatting miserably in a space barely large enough to contain it.

Then she looked down at me, and something in the steady glint of her unblinking eyes told me who she was.

'Lily?' I croaked. I rolled over and tried to sit up. A pulse of agony hit my stomach. I doubled over and threw up, drenching my feet and those of a man standing next to me in warm vomit.

He leaped smartly out of the way. 'Filthy bastard!' he yelled, kicking me on the arm. I winced but said nothing. I could only look at the cage.

'Yaotl?' She was gripping the bars. 'What happened? What have you done?'

I blinked and shook my head. 'Done? Nothing . . . Why have they brought you here?'

'They said they were moving me. After you ran off, they couldn't keep me in the hall with the other prisoners. It wasn't safe.'

'But the cage!'

She laughed mirthlessly. 'Oh, that! Well, it's not luxurious. But let's face it – I won't be in here long!'

I groaned. 'I'm sorry, Lily. I was trying . . .'

'Don't say anything!' she hissed, just in time. I realized Rattlesnake was standing next to me.

'Trying to do what, Yaotl?' he asked.

I twisted my neck to look up at him, although his face was between me and the torch and revealed nothing. 'You know,' I told him. 'I was looking for Mother of Light.'

'Ah, yes. We heard. Did you find her?'

'No.'

'What did you want her for?'

'I'm sure Lily told you.'

'What if she did? I'm asking you.'

I licked my lips nervously and glanced at the cage. Lily said nothing. I wondered what would happen to her if she tried to prompt me.

Like any fluent liar, I was always prepared to fall back on the truth as a last resort. 'I'm just trying to find out whether Mother of Light knows anything that might help Lily in her trial. Hunter told me Lily was speaking to her – that's why you were interested in us in the first place. I just wanted to know what it was all about, what it was she really wanted from Lily.'

'Oh, wouldn't we all like to know that!' the warrior growled. 'Now that's more or less what your mistress told us.'

'It's the truth! We don't have any idea what Mother of Light's up to – I don't understand why you don't question her! She's wandering freely around in the palace, and you're . . .'

'Is she?' the man cried sharply. 'That's more than we know. I thought you said you hadn't seen her?'

'I haven't! It's what I was told!'

'Oh, so it is. I remember now. Thanks for reminding me. Of

course, Hunter and I spoke to the man who told you where to look for her.'

'There you are, you see . . .'

He bent down, not stooping but bending his legs until his face was at the same level as mine. I could feel his breath on my cheek and smell the fact that most of his teeth were rotten. 'Yes, I do see,' he hissed. 'I see that you're a bloody liar! We got this man to tell us exactly where he met you. He gave you very precise directions to the Council of Music. We made him repeat them to us, word for word. When we saw you, you weren't going from where he met you to the hall of the Council of Music. You were coming back from something. It wouldn't have been a meeting with our elusive former royal concubine, now, would it?'

'No! I told you, I didn't see her – she'd gone by the time I got there.'

'I don't believe you.' Then he reached out, grabbed me by the throat and stood up.

I was dragged to my feet, choking, instinctively hitting out with my arms and legs but striking nothing but air. When Rattlesnake let go of me I staggered forward but managed to keep my balance.

'Let me show you something,' he said in a voice that in other circumstances might have sounded friendly. 'It may give you second thoughts about telling us anything that isn't the exact whole truth.' He took my arm in a firm grip and pulled me across the room. The silent man with the torch held it up high so that it spilled its light over the thing I was being asked to look at.

It was a man, or what was left of one. I had not noticed him sitting in a corner. From the way his head was bent forward and his legs were sprawled carelessly in front of him, he looked as if he had been dumped there, and for a moment I thought he must be asleep or dead. Then, however, I noticed that he was moving, but only slightly. He was rocking back and forth, and when I listened carefully I realized I could just about detect the sound of his breathing: a faint rasping.

'Recognize this man?' Rattlesnake leaned forward, seized the man's hair and jerked it back so that I could see his face.

'I – I've never seen him before,' I whispered, in a voice hushed with shock.

I was telling the truth: I had no idea who this person was. What shocked me was his expression: utterly blank, like that of a man asleep, except that the sunken cheeks, the slack lips and the wide, unfocused eyes were more reminiscent of death. A trail of dried spittle ran down the side of his chin. He was looking straight at me but I could tell he had no idea I was there.

'Really? Well, it would be nice to introduce you then, but unfortunately he doesn't seem to be paying a lot of attention at the moment.' Rattlesnake let go of the man's hair and his head flopped forward on to his chest again. 'But this is what I wanted you to see.' He reached down again to take one of the man's limp hands. 'Now, keep this in mind when I ask you questions.'

He thrust the unresisting hand towards me.

The fingers were so heavily encrusted with glistening, black blood that at first it was hard to make out what had happened to them. But then I noticed two things about them. They were too short, ending at the second joint. And the torchlight caught slivers of something white that projected from the dark, pulpy masses around them: little jagged pieces of splintered bone. The fingertips had not been cut off, but crushed.

'Who is he?' I asked.

'You tell me.'

I stared at Rattlesnake. 'I told you. I've never seen him before.'

'You must be very unobservant then. He told us he was following you and Lily's father. That's how we caught him – he
worked out where you were going and went ahead of you to
Hare's house.'

Suddenly I remembered the nondescript man I had seen in
the marketplace. It was impossible to connect his features in
my mind with the blank face I had just seen, but I could
believe they were the same.

'All right, so we were followed,' I admitted. 'I still don't
know who he is. I can guess . . .'

'Try. If you get it right, maybe we won't start with your
thumbs!'

I closed my eyes and whispered fearfully: 'Is he working for
Black Flower?'

'Oh, well done!'

When I dared to look at him again, Rattlesnake was grinning. 'Why did you do that to him?' I demanded. 'Why not
just kill him, if you knew who he was?'

'He took some persuading before he'd answer my questions, that's why. Do you know what I'm saying? Besides, we
wanted him alive. We'll probably even let him go, after this. If
he makes it back to Black Flower, he will be a good example
to the rest of his followers. Of course, we'll tear his tongue out
first, so that he can't go back and tell his master whatever it is
he managed to find out. We've already made sure he can't
write anything down! Now, I'm going to ask you some more
questions, very politely, and I think you really ought to answer
them, because if you don't then my colleagues here will ask
you too, and they really have no manners at all.' He gestured
towards the torchbearer. The man's teeth glistened in the
torchlight as he grinned. I looked around at the other, the one
who had jumped out of my way when I was sick, who was still
standing by Lily's cage. He was grinning too.

Hunter, Rattlesnake's deputy, was still here. He stood by himself, on the far side of the cage from the grinning man. I could not see his face because he was looking at the floor.

'Now, once again,' Rattlesnake said. 'I want to know what Mother of Light said to you.'

'I told you, I didn't see her.'

A long silence followed, during which all I could hear were the sounds of breathing and the crackle of the torch. Then the man holding it spoke for the first time. 'This has gone on long enough, Rattlesnake. Which one do we do next, him or the woman?'

He took a step towards the cage.

'No!' I cried, aghast. 'Wait! You can't! This has nothing to do with Lily!'

'I should think it has everything to do with her,' Rattlesnake observed.

'All right! I did see the woman! But she couldn't tell me anything useful!'

'Well, why don't you tell us exactly what she said and then we can judge that for ourselves.'

I looked at the cage. Its occupant was staring mutely at us, but it was too far away and too dark for me to see whether her look was defiant or imploring. I was going to have to make up my own mind what to do, but then, I realized, I had done that the moment the man with the torch had opened his mouth.

Rattlesnake summoned Hunter to come and listen and drew us both away from the other two. I recounted, as accurately as I could, everything that had passed between me and Mother of Light, leaving out just one detail: the missing ring that both she and Lily had insisted must not be allowed to fall into the wrong hands. I clung to the hope that Rattlesnake and Hunter had not discovered it.

When I finished, I looked at them both as though seeking their approval, like a small boy who has just skinned his first rabbit showing off his handiwork to his father.

'Interesting,' Rattlesnake mused.

'Is he telling the truth?' muttered Hunter sceptically.

'Don't know. Well, he can tell us himself. How do we check this story of yours?'

'I don't understand you!' I cried incredulously. For all the danger I was in and the terror I felt, this latest question struck me as ludicrous. 'Why can't you just find Mother of Light and talk to her?'

'Do you think we don't want to?' Hunter replied in a slightly petulant tone. 'But we can't find her, you see. She disappears.'

'But she's in and out of the palace all the time! I saw her outside the marketplace only yesterday!' Then, realizing I had already said too much, I volunteered an account of my first meeting with the woman, before Rattlesnake or Hunter could tell me what would happen if I did not.

'We know about that old man. They've been seen together before,' Rattlesnake told me. 'But he's as slippery as she is. Don't even know for sure if he is her father.' He paused, stroking his chin thoughtfully. Then, to my astonishment and alarm, he suddenly leaned forward and slapped my arm playfully. 'You know, Yaotl, I'm beginning to like you! You're quite helpful when you want to be.'

I stared at him.

'Still don't think he's telling us everything,' Hunter rumbled unhappily.

'He probably isn't,' Rattlesnake conceded. 'But there's time yet.'

'D-does this mean . . .?' I stammered.

'That we're going to let you go? Why, yes, I think so . . .

Tell you what. You can find Mother of Light again for us, since you seem to have so much more luck than we do!'

'But you said yourself – she disappeared . . .'

'That's your problem,' he said dismissively. 'Oh, and you can take Hunter with you.'

'Chief!' his deputy protested. He was ignored.

'You two can look after each other. You'll find the woman and bring her back to the palace. I'm not having her give me the slip again! And if it helps concentrate your mind, just remember . . .'

I did not see any signal pass between them, but I was suddenly aware of quick footsteps crossing the floor. I twisted around just in time to see the man with the torch kneeling over Lily's cage. Then he thrust the burning end of it through the bars.

Lily shrieked.

'No!' I shouted, starting to run, but before I had taken a step I was on the ground with Hunter on top of me, twisting both my arms around my back and over my head. I could only stare impotently at the cage, with the torch flame poised just outside it, ready to strike again, its glow falling on a pale, tormented face inside.

'Again?' the torchbearer hissed.

'Well, Yaotl?'

I lowered my face to the floor. 'All right,' I muttered. 'You've made your point. I'll find the bloody woman!'

'So where do we start?'

Hunter threw the words at me over one shoulder. The handle of a sword, slung over his back, projected over the other, a reminder that the business he was engaged in might prove murderous.

I trudged along the passageways of the palace in his footsteps, content to let him lead me wherever he felt inclined to go and quite indifferent to my surroundings. I could not get out of my head the image of Lily's face, her eyes following me through the bars of her cage as I was led away. I realized that in all likelihood that was the last either of us would see of the other. Even if I managed to find Mother of Light, she would still have to face trial. I knew the former concubine had no information that would help with that, even assuming Rattlesnake and his comrades let her live long enough to be called as a witness.

'Did you hear me?'

I hesitated, unsure how to answer the warrior. He responded by turning on his heel and walking back towards me. He stood glowering down at me. 'Listen, you. I don't want to do this. We can always go back. I'll tell Rattlesnake you've changed your mind . . .'

'No!' I said hastily. 'Sorry, let me think . . . Why don't we try the Council of Music? There were several men – poets, sorcerers, whatever they were – with Mother of Light in the courtyard. Some of them must know where to look for her.'

'Forget it,' he said sourly. 'This has happened before, you know. She appears at one of these meetings – just drops in without warning, as far as I can tell – and disappears again before anyone knows about it. You were incredibly lucky to find her. Everyone's supposed to report to us if they see her, but we only got to hear after you did.'

'And the men I saw in the courtyard?'

He snorted. 'Waste of time! They're all nobles, palace people, not nobodies or foreigners like you. We can't lean on them in the same way. They just laugh at us. And you'll have seen how they were with her. Among that sort of people, it's the height of fashion to have her favour your little gathering with her presence. I'm told it's like having the late King among them again! All bollocks, of course, but that's how they think, and the fact that she has all this mystery about her just makes them more keen.'

So, I thought, the Council of Music was probably not the place to start. 'How about the gateways, then? If she's not in the palace . . .'

Hunter sighed. 'You take us for complete idiots, don't you? Oh, sure, we can go and ask the guards, and we can ask the guards at the entrance to the marketplace too, for that matter, since you have to go through there to get out into the city. But I can assure you it will be a waste of time. None of them will have seen her go out of the palace, or come in, for that matter. We told you before – she disappears! She's like a ghost!'

I swore. 'This is absurd! You mean Maize Ear has this little army of spies and torturers and bully-boys but can't even keep one woman out of his own palace, or find her when she is here? What's going on? I thought Tetzcocans were supposed to be clever?'

I knew as soon as I said it that that was a mistake. The big man was advancing on me again, and this time he did not stop at talking. He seized my upper arms, twisted me sideways and slammed me against the wall of the passageway so hard that my head rebounded off the hard stone with a loud crack.

As I whimpered in pain, he said softly: 'Now, listen here. You may think squashing somebody's finger ends and threatening women is something we do for fun, but you ought to take notice of what you've seen and learn from it. We don't even know what this woman's done, or whether she's done anything at all. It doesn't matter. She's found a way to get in and out of this palace without anyone knowing about it, and make fools of us in the process – especially Rattlesnake and me, who are supposed to be keeping an eye on her. If we don't find her, Maize Ear's likely to give all of us the kind of treatment that spy got. So as long as you want to be walking around like this, and not screaming your lights out in agony in some forgotten part of the palace, I suggest you watch your mouth and cooperate! Now, any more bright ideas?'

He let go, giving me a chance to rub the bump that was already rising on the back of my scalp. 'Where did you see Lily and Mother of Light together?' I asked.

'The marketplace.'

'Well, let's try there. Come to think of it, why didn't you grab her then, when you had her in your sights?'

'Should have done,' he conceded. 'But we wanted to find out where she went when she was outside. That's another mystery, you see – nobody seems to know that, either. But we had to split up, so I could follow her and Rattlesnake could follow Lily . . .'

'And you lost her.'

'Not for the first time, either! See what we're up against?'

'Maybe she is a ghost, after all. Or a sorcerer.'

'If you can catch her, we'll find out.'

Hunter eventually agreed to try the marketplace. He had no fear that I would try to take advantage of the crowds to escape, leaving Lily trapped in her cage, and he knew, from me, that Mother of Light had been at the market the day before, with the old man who appeared to be her father.

'I bet she was happy with you when you went charging into that argument with the pedlars!' he laughed.

'Not very,' I said. 'I was wondering what became of the old man.'

'He'll have vanished too. Rattlesnake told you: he's as bad as she is, and no one even knows where he came from. He may be her father – Hungry Child certainly didn't pick her for her pedigree – but as for who he is, I can't even tell you his name!'

'Isn't there a record from when she came to the palace, in Hungry Child's time?'

'Things were a bit more lax then. There isn't even a record of Mother of Light herself, let alone her father.'

By the time I walked down the steps at the palace entrance into the precinct outside, blinking and squinting against the afternoon sunlight, I was in far worse trouble than I had been in even that morning. Added to the dangers I now faced – death at the hands of the Otomies, if I could find them, torture and death at the hands of Rattlesnake and his fellows – was fear of what Lily would undergo if I failed to find both Hare's message and Mother of Light – to say nothing of the nameless but apparently dreadful consequences if I could not recover the ring. I knew all this, but it was hard, even so, to resist a feeling of exhilaration at being out in the open again. I had been in the palace only since daybreak, but it had felt like a lifetime.

The forecourt of the palace was crowded. In most cases it was easy to tell why the people were there just by looking at them: the man with his arms buried in the folds of a voluminous cotton cape was an envoy, come to deliver a message or present his credentials to the King's court. The warrior, identifiable by his piled-up hair, the red ochre smeared on his cheeks and temples, his gaily embroidered cloak and breechcloth and the jewels in his earlobes and lower lip, was surely here to claim some privilege awarded him for his success in the field, a gift or a place at a banquet. The plainly dressed man in a short cloak of maguey fibre and an unornamented breechcloth, with his hair neatly trimmed and his clothes and skin still lightly damp from being washed, was probably a party in a court case.

Less immediately obvious to me were the intentions of a few men whose clothes and hairstyles, while keeping strictly within the rules prescribing what was allowed to commoners, somehow distinguished them from those around them. Their

clothes were made of the same material as any commoners',
but it was thicker and cut better, the hems on the cloaks
straighter and their designs sharper and more vivid, while their
wearers' hairstyles, although plain, were as immaculate as any
pleasure girl's. I was puzzling over who these men might be,
and noting that they seemed to talk only to one another and to
ignore everybody else, when suddenly one of them looked
over his shoulder at me and Hunter, detached himself from the
group and all but ran in our direction.

By the time he reached us, he was so indignant that little
bubbles of spit were forming and bursting at the corners of his
mouth.

'You!' he shouted at me. 'Why, you miserable slave! You . . .
you . . .' he seemed to have difficulty expressing himself, which
was unfortunate considering his profession.

'Hello, Obsidian Tongue,' I said pleasantly.

'You know this person?' Hunter asked.

'I'll tear your liver out for what you've done!' The lawyer
was almost weeping with rage. 'You've made a fool of me –
after what you made me do, they may never let me back into
a court again! I could be ruined, you . . . you . . .'

'"Slave"?' I suggested. 'Look, I'm sorry I got found out, but
believe me it wasn't pleasant for me either, and anyway, I didn't
make you do it . . .'

That was as far as I got before the man threw himself at me.
He was no sort of a fighter, and the wild blows he flung at my
face had no force behind them and mostly swished through
empty air. As I leaped backwards out of the way, Hunter
caught him from behind and lifted him bodily off the ground.

'Oh, no, you don't!' the warrior said, grunting with the
effort of holding his captive aloft.

'Let go of me! I'm going to kill that . . . that . . .'

I grinned. 'There's a law against that, isn't there?'

'There is,' Hunter confirmed. 'You'd end up having to take his place, friend. Now, are you going to be a good boy, so I can put you down?'

'All right!' Obsidian Tongue snapped. 'But you haven't heard the last of me. I'm not the forgiving kind, I warn you!'

Hunter released him. He glared at us both, drew his cloak around himself and stalked off.

'Now, what was all that about?' the warrior asked as we watched him rejoin his colleagues. Several of them had their hands to their mouths in an unsuccessful effort to hide their mirth.

'He's upset because he vouched for me as a lawyer, and I got caught.'

'Oh, right.' Hunter uttered a short laugh. 'He's a fool, then. If he wants you dead he only has to wait a couple of days. Once your mistress is executed he can probably do what he likes to you – so long as we haven't killed you first!'

So I had made another enemy. I sighed. It was not as if they had ever been in short supply.

The marketplace beyond the palace walls was, as ever, even more crowded than the forecourt we had left, and the crowd was more varied, its members less obviously purposeful. All marketplaces attracted a great many people who seemed to have no business there except to stare at the merchandise on offer and the people haggling over it. Today there seemed to be more of this sort of person than usual, wandering aimlessly about and getting in the way as Hunter and I tried to get to the seafood stands.

'What's the matter with all these people?' I cried impatiently. 'They're not all spies, surely? Even in this city?'

'I'm going to start shoving them out of the way in a moment,' Hunter muttered. 'I still don't understand why you thought she might be in this part of the marketplace rather than any other.' He had been for starting right by the palace gateway, but I had pointed out that for the two of us to try to search every one of the narrow, bustling lanes between the traders' pitches would be hopeless: the area was so vast it would have required an army.

'I'm assuming that the reason she was trying to get in here yesterday was that she heard about Hare's property coming on to the market,' I said. 'She'd be hoping that message of his would be among it.' Not to mention the ring that was meant to pay for it, I thought. And there was yet another mystery. Rattlesnake and Hunter had said nothing about the ring, and so presumably they had not found it. But if not, then who had?

'And you think these fish sellers might have some of his stuff?'

'They did yesterday. If she figured it out the same way I did – that the best place to get news of Hare is among the people dealing in produce from his part of the World – then she'll likely look in the same places. Now – hey! It looks as if I was right! Look over there!' The last words were called out over my shoulder as I broke into a run.

A wizened old man, his hair glistening white and his back bent over with age, was standing in front of one of the pitches, and the briefest glance confirmed that the man behind it was the one who had sold me a tortilla and told me about Hare's cape.

As I raced towards him, batting people rudely out of my way with my hands, I called out: 'Hey! You! We want you! Don't move!'

The little old man started to turn towards me. At the same time a fist closed on one of my upper arms, stopping me and spinning me around as fast as one of those Totonac acrobats who jump off tall poles on the ends of ropes and pretend to be birds. Suddenly I was staring into the eyes of a grim-faced Hunter.

'Stop there, you! What's this about?'

'The old man!' I yelled into his face. 'Look at him! He's Mother of Light's father!'

'What old man?'

'The one right in front of you, you moron! White hair, bent back, trembling hands. You can't mistake him!'

'What are you talking about? There's no one there!'

I gaped at him for a moment and then whirled around.

A strange sight met my eyes. Approximately half the people I could see, traders, customers and passers-by – were staring at me and the warrior locked in what might have been either a lovers' embrace or a wrestling bout, and the rest were gazing at something else – or, rather, the absence of something. The space the old man had occupied an instant ago was empty, and the stall-holder he had been speaking to wore a bewildered frown.

'Where did he go?' I gasped. I shook Hunter off and walked up to the stallholder. 'That old man . . .'

'Weird,' the man muttered. 'He just took off. Didn't look to me as if he had the strength left in his body to go on breathing, but he didn't half move when you yelled at him!'

Hunter lumbered up after me. 'Anybody see which way he went, then?'

'Too quick for me.'

From a neighbouring pitch I heard: 'He just seemed to slip through the crowd. He could be anywhere.'

'I don't believe it!' Hunter exploded. 'The old bugger's done it again! Are these people all sorcerers, or what?'

The stallholder came out of his reverie and recognized me. 'Oh, it's you,' he said, 'the one who was asking me about Hare yesterday.'

'Let me guess,' I replied. 'The old man who was here just now, he wanted to know the same thing.'

'That's right. But I've got a message for you.'

'For me?' I repeated inanely, and then suddenly felt sick as I realized what that message must be and that a part of my original plan had fallen into place when I had been half hoping it would not.

The stallholder confirmed my fears. 'From the man who sold me that cape. Came around early this morning, wanted to know if I'd heard of anyone asking after Hare or trying to buy his stuff. I told him about you, like you asked, and he was really pleased.'

'I bet,' I said dourly.

The man lowered his voice and bent towards me like a conspirator. 'Meet him tomorrow evening,' he said, after nightfall, at Hare's house. He's got lots of things to sell – even his merchant's staff, everything. And you can have first pick at all of it!'

11

'It's a pity you scared the old man off when you did,' Hunter grumbled. 'We must have been about as close to nabbing him as we've ever got.'

'I don't know,' I said pessimistically. 'I have the impression you could be sitting on him and he'd still get away! I don't understand how he was able to move so fast. He looked as if he'd need help just getting up off his sleeping mat in the morning.'

The Sun was close to the tops of the mountains on the western side of the valley. Soon trumpets would sound to mark his setting, and the dead mothers who escorted him during the afternoon would relinquish him to the care of Mictlan Tecuhtli, the Lord of the Land of the Dead. It had been, from what little I had been able to see of it, a gloriously bright day, which at this time of year would usually mean we were in for a chilly evening, and I had left my cloak behind a statue in the palace.

'Where are we going to spend the night?' I asked dubiously.

'Hare's house, I reckon. We've got this meeting with whoever it is that has his property. That's good — there may be something in there that will help Rattlesnake get to the bottom of all this, and if Mother of Light wanted something Hare had then it won't hurt if we can get our hands on it first, will it? But I'd like to go and look the place over again before we have to deal with these people.'

I frowned, thinking that this was the last thing I wanted. What if Hunter managed to stumble across the merchant's body? 'Why not go back to the palace for now?' I suggested. 'Won't Rattlesnake be expecting some kind of report?'

'Like what?' he demanded. '"We found the old man but the arthritic old bastard managed to limp away from us?" Not likely! No, we go to Hare's place. Come on.'

Night was falling by the time we neared the house. A cold breeze had sprung up from the East, blowing towards the lake, where it would stir the surface into a froth. I was going to miss my cloak. At first I thought the goose pimples that broke out on my skin were on account of the weather. Then it occurred to me to wonder why, if that was the case, I was not shivering. Something else was making the fine, almost invisible hairs on my arms and legs stand up, a sensation that had become all too familiar in the short time I had been in Tetzcoco: the feeling that I was being followed.

I glanced over my shoulder, but there was nothing to see but the still shadows of trees and houses.

Who was it this time, I wondered – Black Flower's spies, perhaps, friends of the unfortunate man who had had his fingers crushed deep inside the palace? I suppressed the fear that it might be the Otomies. The prospect of the captain and his followers pounding the road at my heels, their lust for vengeance stoked up higher than ever by what had happened to their comrade at Hare's house, was too frightful to contemplate. But why should they come after me in the evening when they had laid a trap for me the next day, one I was bound to walk into?

I glanced at Hunter, but he merely trudged onwards, seemingly oblivious to the fears that assailed me.

I tried to ignore the pricking sensation at the back of my neck while I turned my mind to other problems.

My thoughts about meeting the Otomies had been concerned with how I was going to survive the encounter. I still had no idea how to go about doing that, but, I reflected gloomily, achieving even this seemingly impossible feat would do me no good by itself, beyond putting the final reckoning with the captain behind me. The only reason for risking my life in this venture was to get hold of whatever message Hare had borne, assuming it was among the property the brutal Aztec warriors had plundered from his house. If I could not do that – or if the Otomies did not have the message in the first place – then I might as well turn back now. Except, I told myself ruefully, that I had Hunter with me.

I found myself grinding my teeth in frustration. For all I knew, Nimble's own scheme might have succeeded, and he might have found not only the child who had escaped the carnage at Hare's house but the message itself, or some clue to where it might be. He might even now be trotting towards the palace with the thing we had been looking for, and I would have no way of knowing about it, because, unless I could escape from Hunter's side, I could not contact him. And I could not run away, not with Lily still in the hands of Rattlesnake and his silent, sadistic companions.

I might be about to get myself killed for everything or nothing and never know which.

'What's the matter with you?' the warrior asked.

'Nothing,' I said. 'Just my teeth chattering. It's the cold.'

'Not surprised. You should have worn a cloak.'

A few paces further on he suddenly stopped. 'What was that?'

I looked around, but by now it was too gloomy to see

anything further away than my outstretched hand. Even
Hunter was little more than a hulking presence beside me.

'I don't see anything.'

'Neither do I, but I heard something. Sounded like a whistle.'

I heard a faint rustle of movement, very close. I started, and
then realized that it was the warrior, unfastening the sword he
still wore slung over his back.

'Keep quiet and keep walking,' he commanded under his
breath, 'and listen, if you know what's good for you!'

We moved forward again slowly. I had not taken more than
three steps when I caught the sound myself: a low call that
could not have been made by any bird or animal I knew of.

'Someone's signalling,' Hunter whispered. 'How much further to Hare's house?'

'Not far.' I remembered what had happened when Kindly
and I had been walking along this road and I had thought we
were being followed. Then I had found my son, or rather he
had found me. Despite my tension, I managed to smile at the
memory. I dared not hope to be that fortunate this time; all the
same, it was impossible to resist trying to play the events of two
days before over again.

'Why don't we split up?' I hissed.

'What good would that do?' The words jerked out of
Hunter's mouth as he turned his head from side to side, trying
to locate the source of the sounds.

'Think about it. Whoever's out there will go for one of us.
If it's me, you can go on to Hare's house, and, let's face it,
you'll stand a better chance against the Otomies, when they
get here, than I would. If it's you, you're a skilled warrior;
you'll be able to fight them off.'

'Doesn't sound right. How do I know you won't just turn
and run?'

'Lily,' I said simply.

There was a long pause, during which I thought I heard another low whistle. This time I was able to work out where it had come from: somewhere up ahead.

'All right,' the other man said eventually. 'We'll try it. You go to the house. I'll work my way around the back, along that stream at the bottom of the slope. I think there's a path behind us that will get me down there.'

I swallowed, realizing that I was about to stroll straight into an ambush. 'Wouldn't it be better the other way around?'

'No. Get going.'

A hand reached towards me out of the night and roughly propelled me forward.

Maize Ear's henchmen were no friends of mine. All the same, when Hunter left to retrace his steps until he came to the path he had mentioned, I found myself wishing he were still with me. It was a dark night to be walking by myself into something entirely unknown.

I took a few nervous steps towards the house. Then I froze, struck suddenly by a chill deeper than that of the night air around me.

I had heard the whistling sound again, but this time it was close by.

'Who's there?' I whispered in a voice hoarse with terror.

There was no answer.

I cleared my throat and tried again, a little louder. 'Who's there?'

'Oh, so you *can* hear me. I was beginning to think you'd gone bloody deaf.'

I should have felt relieved or even joyful to hear that voice, but all I felt was shock, and it was as much as I could do to prevent my legs from buckling at the knees. The speaker was Lily's father, Kindly.

'What are you doing here?' I whispered.

'Never mind! Just get over here, quick. Where's that other fellow? Do we want him or not?'

I felt my way over towards the old man, until a hand caught my arm and dragged me off the road. 'No, we don't! He's behind me somewhere.'

'Thought not.' I could smell the old man's sour breath. At that moment it seemed as fragrant as a dahlia. 'Squat down here. I'll get Nimble.'

'He's here?' I gasped.

'Oh, yes. And not just him. Oh, do we have a surprise for you! Nimble . . .'

That was all he managed before we heard the scream.

'What was that?' I asked inanely.

'More to the point,' snarled Kindly, 'where did it come from? My ears aren't so good.'

'The road,' Nimble declared out of the gloom. 'Back there, along the way you came, Father.'

Another cry tore through the air. This was more terrifying than the first: a long wail, as of someone or something in great pain, ending in a series of diminishing sobs.

'Hunter,' I whispered. 'What's going on?'

'Where'd your pal go?' Kindly asked. 'Sounds like he may have got himself into trouble!'

'He was heading back towards where he'd seen a path branching off the road,' I explained. 'I thought someone was following us, ever since we left Tetzcoco. He must have run into them.'

'Do you think we should go and find out what happened?' my son asked.

'Balls, we should!' the old man snapped. 'We're safer here.'

'Can't stay here all night.'

I sighed. 'Nimble's right,' I said reluctantly. 'I'd better take a look.' I got up and forced my unwilling feet to step out onto the road.

'Wait!' the youth cried. 'I'll come with you.'

'No.' If Hunter was dead, I thought, I must get back to the palace and explain to Rattlesnake what had happened before his body was found. If I did not, Maize Ear's spy would assume that I was responsible for his deputy's death and Lily would bear the brunt of his rage. If Hunter was not dead, I did not want Nimble walking straight into his arms. 'You stay there.'

'But . . .'

'Stay there, I said!'

'Better do as he says, lad,' Kindly muttered.

I took Nimble's silence for assent and felt relieved. This was no time for an argument. I assumed my son would obey his father's direct command, even though we had known nothing of one another for years; he must, I thought, be enough of an Aztec for that.

I walked towards the source of the screams.

I did not have far to go. Just a few paces beyond the point where Hunter and I had parted, I began to hear somebody moaning softly. It was a fearful sound, the kind made by somebody in great pain without the strength left to cry out.

I paused, unable to decide what to do next. The noises were coming from somewhere just up ahead, but what was making them? It might be Hunter or some other person who had had the misfortune to encounter Hunter's sword, but then again, it might not. Unspeakable things were known to haunt the night, any one of which it would be death to encounter: the dead walking in their wrappings, for one, or the thing we called the Night Axe, a headless, limbless torso that rolled over the ground and groaned through its open chest cavity. If Hunter had met one of these monsters, neither his weapons nor his warrior's courage would have been of any use. On the other hand, I thought ruefully, having only my bare hands did not make me any better off than he would have been.

'Hunter?' I croaked through a mouth that had suddenly gone quite dry. I tried swirling my tongue around to stir up some spit, but my second attempt at calling out was as feeble as the first. No answer came back. The moaning had ceased.

I started moving forward again, one footstep at a time.

My bare foot landed in a puddle. As I drew it hastily back, I remembered that it had not rained lately. And the puddle was warm, and the air above it carried the unmistakable odour of fresh blood.

An unidentifiable shape lay on the road immediately in front of me. Crouching, I reached out and touched the body. It was not moving, not even breathing, but it was still warm under the thin, rough layer of cloth that covered it.

I got my hand under the cloak and slid it over the skin, feeling for the muscle and bone underneath. Although the skin was wet, covered with a slick of blood, it took me only a few moments to satisfy myself that this was not Hunter. I could feel this man's ribs, and he was plainly no muscular warrior.

'Shit,' I muttered. I looked up. 'Hunter!' I called again, managing to raise my voice this time.

Again there was no answer. I thought the moaning I had heard had been coming from a place just beyond the body I was inspecting. I picked my way towards it, dropping to my knees when I found another dark form lying on the ground.

This one was breathing, although weakly and irregularly. When I touched him, his body jerked once. The moans resumed, but as I listened they began to die away into a feeble wheezing. Then they ended altogether with a faint, throaty rattle.

I heard a soft padding of bare feet from behind me. 'Father?' Nimble whispered.

'Keep yourself hidden!' I hissed. 'And I thought I told you to stay behind?'

'Are you going to argue about that now?' he whispered.

I opened my mouth to respond and then shut it again. He had a point. 'All right,' I muttered grudgingly. Aloud, I called out once more: 'Hunter! Where are you?'

'What's . . .' my son began, but then, at last, the warrior answered me, calling out of the darkness up ahead.

'Is that you, Yaotl?'

'Where are you?' I cried again.

The reply was a bark of sardonic laughter. 'Oh, wouldn't you like to know!'

I stared blindly ahead of me, momentarily baffled.

'Nice little ambush you set up here!' the warrior shouted. 'I've got to admire you. Don't know how you managed it, with me watching you all the time!'

'What are you talking about?' I stood up. 'What ambush? Who are these men?'

'I think you can tell me that! Friends of yours, weren't they? Spying for Black Flower?'

'No!' I took a step forward, slipped on the blood and stumbled, almost falling over. I kept my eyes fixed on some imaginary point in the gloom ahead of me, from where I thought the warrior's voice was coming. 'I've no idea who they were! They must have followed us.'

'How many more of you are there? Two, three, a whole squad lying in wait for me?'

'Hunter, listen to me!' I cried in desperation. 'I swear I don't know any more about this than you do! I will eat earth!' Automatically I bent down to touch the ground with my fingertips, before putting them to my lips in the customary gesture of truthfulness.

'So what?' the disembodied voice sneered. 'You think I

trust you? I'm not standing here listening to any more of this. I'll be back, and this time I won't be alone. And just remember we've got one of you squatting in a cage! She's going to pay for this piece of work, believe me!'

'No, Hunter! Wait!' I ran forward, and then stopped, staring about me irresolutely. I heard what might have been footsteps receding quickly into the night before silence fell again.

Nimble ran to my side. 'What's he talking about?' he whispered urgently.

'Lily,' I gasped. 'If Maize Ear's men think I set this up deliberately . . .'

Nimble grasped my meaning immediately. 'We've got to get after him! If he makes it back to the palace, they'll kill her!'

'Or worse,' I confirmed. 'Come on!'

We ran, blundering through the night, staggering when we caught our feet on broken ground or had our faces whipped by low branches hanging over the road. We moved in grim silence, save for the hoarse, ragged sounds of our breathing, with our arms stretched in front of us to ward off obstacles. We had no hope at all, except that Hunter might be lying in wait for us, and the two of us together might be able to overpower him before he had time to kill us both.

We were almost back in Tetzcoco, with our way dimly lit now by the flames of temple fires and the occasional torch left crackling against the wall of a house to light its owner's way home, when I finally sank to the ground, exhausted and utterly dispirited.

Nimble collapsed next to me, his breath coming in great whooping sobs.

'I'm sorry, son,' I gasped. 'We weren't quick enough.'

'Never stood a chance, anyway,' he wheezed back. 'He'd have killed us if we had managed to catch him. What happened back there, anyway?'

'Those two obviously followed us all the way from Tetzcoco. Hunter was probably right – they must have been spying for Black Flower. Not soldiers. Once he found them the poor buggers wouldn't have stood a chance.'

'What do we do now?'

A sudden, immense weariness came over me, and I shut my eyes, as if I could have fallen asleep where I lay, in the middle of the street. It seemed to have been an age since I had lain down. Then I forced my eyes open again and began hauling myself to my feet as slowly and awkwardly as an old man. 'Come on,' I muttered. I looked towards the tallest of the pyramids I could see, a great angular shadow looming overhead with a tiny spark of flame at its peak: the old King Hungry Coyote's mighty monument to Tezcatlipoca, his Lord of the Near and the Nigh. 'Only the gods can help Lily now. We can't.' I looked back along the road to Huexotla and Hare's house. It seemed a long way to walk, but I could not see that we had any choice. 'We'd better head back. Tell Kindly what's happened. Get ready to meet the Otomies. And pray.' I looked curiously at my son. "What were you and Kindly doing at Hare's house?"

"It was the only place I could think of looking for you. I tried your lodgings but they said you'd left and they didn't know where you'd gone. Luckily Kindly had the same idea as I did."

"Good for him." It had not occurred to me that my son would have trouble finding us after we had been forced to move.

Nimble scrambled to his feet. 'There's something else,' he said. 'I didn't have a chance to tell you, but we found the girl.'

12

We picked Kindly up outside Hare's house. He still had the girl with him: a small figure, almost entirely hidden by the blanket he and Nimble had wrapped her in. She was fast asleep when my son and I returned, with the sky brightening rapidly around us. She complained childishly when we stirred her but took to the road again gamely enough once she was awake.

We went to the house Kindly had found in Huexotla. It seemed the obvious thing to do, at least for the moment. There was no point in going to Hare's place. Kindly and Nimble had planned to stop there with the girl, but after what had just happened, I assumed Hunter and his comrades would be all over it even before dawn broke. We had to leave the gruesome remains of Black Flower's spies in the roadway for them to pick up. There was no time to do anything for them.

When we returned to the house, we found a few embers still glowing in the hearth of its one room. While Nimble stirred them, Kindly went straight to the corner where his staff was propped against the wall.

The old man stood still and quiet for a few moments, as though in contemplation. Then, with difficulty and an audible creaking, he bent down to rummage through the little pile of his possessions at his feet, coming up with a tiny sliver of obsidian and a strip of paper. Straightening himself, he lanced his earlobe with the razor and held the paper up to the wound until it was soaked with blood. Finally, he wrapped the darkly stained strip around the staff, whose shape was already barely recognizable beneath the layers of wrapping it had been given in all its owner's years as a merchant.

The old man was making an offering of his own blood to Yacatecuhtli, Lord of the Vanguard, the merchants' god: his own god and Lily's.

As he turned away from the staff, his eyes caught the firelight. To my surprise, they were dry, and when he spoke his voice was steady. 'She's in the god's hands now,' he said simply.

'I understand.' I looked at my feet. There was no hint of reproach in the old man's look or in his speech; no expression of any kind that I could read. I might have preferred it if he had screamed at me or broken down and wept.

'Will you find me some incense for the fire, Nimble?' he asked.

As the room filled with the sweet, sickly scent of burning copal resin, another offering to the old man's god, I turned my attention to the girl my son had found.

She had opened the blanket to let the fire's warmth get to her. Underneath it she wore a plain blouse and skirt, both of them patched, frayed and soiled. In one hand she clutched the mutilated doll we had found at Hare's house. When I looked from the doll's face to hers, I saw confirmed what we had suspected. The girl was, I guessed, about eleven years old or so, and as unmistakably Mayan as her toy. Her forehead sloped sharply back into the line of her black hair, and her eyes were crossed, their pupils apparently fixed unwaveringly on the bridge of her nose. With her mouth closed I could not see whether her teeth were filed or not, but I saw no need to check.

She kept turning her head, looking from one of us to

another as best she could through those peculiar eyes. Her glance was disconcerting, as it was impossible to meet.

'What's your name?' I asked gently.

Nimble came and squatted next to me. 'We've tried talking to her,' he said, 'but she just looks at us blankly. I don't think she speaks any Nahuatl. The only thing I can get out of her is "Ix Men." She keeps saying that. I think it may be her name.'

'Makes sense if it is,' Kindly said. 'I think it means something like "Hen".'

Little Hen. I thought it might suit the bird-like way in which she kept moving her head. 'How did you find her?'

Nimble said: 'Like I said – just a matter of knowing where to look. I don't know Tetzcoco's markets, but I know the types; they're the same the World over. The poor kid would have gone with the first man who offered her food and shelter. That kind's easy to find. It's their business to be.'

'Talking of business,' grumbled Kindly, 'it was a pretty costly matter buying her out of there. It'll be a real shame if she can't talk to us!'

I looked at the girl keenly. 'Ix Men?' I ventured.

She whispered something in reply; a string of exotic, guttural syllables that meant nothing to me whatever.

I remembered something. Turning to Kindly, I said: 'I thought you knew Mayan? What's she saying?'

The old man sighed. 'I know the dialect they speak around Xicallanco, and I can read a few of the funny squiggles they use for writing. But this is mostly gibberish. There are lots of different sorts of Mayan, apparently.'

I groaned. 'Wonderful. Just what I wanted to hear. I don't suppose she had a message about her person, did she?'

'None that we could see.'

I turned back to the girl. 'Little Hen,' I sighed. 'I bet you could tell us everything we want to know, couldn't you? You must have seen everything Hare was up to . . . Ah.'

The girl had started, as if stung by a wasp, at the mention of the dead merchant's name. Then she unleashed a torrent of what sounded like wild abuse, her strange eyes widening, the fist with the doll in it whitening with tension while her empty hand opened and closed spasmodically.

'Not happy about something, I'd say,' Kindly observed.

I turned to Nimble. 'Sounds as if you may have had the correct idea about the merchant.'

My son came and squatted next to me. Leaning a little towards Little Hen, he reached for her doll with one hand but drew it back hastily when she clutched the toy to her chest more tightly than ever.

'Hare?' Nimble asked gently.

The girl seemed to hesitate before uttering a single, explosive syllable. She brandished the doll in a sharp, stabbing gesture. Its missing leg was plainly visible.

'Right,' I said slowly. I looked at my son again. 'Let's see if we can at least get her to tell us whether we were right about what happened at Hare's house, shall we?'

'How are you going to do that?' Kindly asked sceptically.

'We'll play a game.' I stood up. 'Nimble, you can be Hare.' I gestured towards him and spoke to the girl. 'Hare.'

She stared at me, or at least turned her head in my direction with her crossed eyes wide and her forehead creased as if in puzzlement.

'Bear with me,' I muttered. Aloud, I slapped my own chest and then stood straight upright with my shoulders back and my arms bent. I flexed my muscles and tried to look as much like a beefy warrior as my scrawny frame would allow. 'Big man.' I said it in Nahuatl, of course, but in a deep voice.

The girl frowned, as though puzzled, and looked from one

of us to the other. 'Hare,' she said haltingly, followed by a short, incomprehensible speech.

'Something she doesn't like about that,' Kindly suggested.

'I don't know,' I said thoughtfully. 'Maybe she's saying I don't look much like a Texcalan warrior with a ruined face! You can see her point.'

'Yes. You're too ugly.'

Next I gestured towards Kindly. 'Ix Men,' I announced solemnly.

'You must be joking!' spluttered the old man, but that was followed by a most unexpected sound: a sudden peal of laughter from the girl. 'Ix Men!' she giggled. 'Ix Men!'

'That's my girl!' I cried encouragingly.

'All right,' Kindly grumbled. 'Very clever. So now what?'

I hesitated. 'We need the girl to tell us that.'

'As if she was directing a play. You want us to act it all out, like in one of those awful farces they put on in front of Quetzalcoatl's temple for the Eating of Plain Water Tamales?'

'Something like that.'

Nimble said: 'If we pretend I'm Hare and this is my house, then I suppose, Father, you ought to be rummaging through my stuff, and I come home and surprise you.'

'We can try it. Why don't you step outside?' As he left I turned back to Little Hen. 'Hare,' I reminded her.

'What about me, then?' asked Kindly plaintively.

The girl told him. 'Ix Men,' she said with a grin and then slapped the ground next to her.

'Ah, of course,' I said. 'Under ground. You're hidden in the hole, aren't you?'

'Better start digging, then!' Kindly suggested.

I replied by grabbing a blanket and throwing it at him. 'Cover yourself with that.' Then I got up and walked across the room to bend over him in a dumb show of someone rummaging

through a chest. 'So here I am, rifling through Hare's possessions . . .'

A muffled voice asked: 'Do I come out and surprise you now?'

I looked over my shoulder at the girl. 'Ix Men?'

She replied at some length, gabbling in her own language
and waving her arms about. There was no point in trying to
follow what she was saying, of course, but I realized there was
a pattern in her movements as her hands reached up into her
hair, catching two strands and tugging at them so that they
stood up over her head.

'What does that mean?' I wondered aloud.

Kindly poked his head from under the blanket to watch
her. 'Perhaps she's got nits!' he suggested sourly.

'I don't think so . . . Well, never mind.' Abandoning, for the
moment, the attempt to interpret her gestures, I resumed my
pretence of rummaging through the merchant's possessions.
This time, when I looked over my shoulder and spoke her
name, she slapped the ground, as she had before Kindly had
vanished under the blanket.

'She's reminding us that you're still underneath the chest,
and you probably don't have any idea what's happening up
here. You've no way of knowing I'm not Hare . . . Right, so
what makes you come out? Hare comes in and finds me, I suppose. Nimble!'

My son came back into the room. He looked quizzically at
the blanket with Kindly under it but said nothing.

'He's – or rather she's – hiding under a wicker chest,' I
explained. 'Which is where you left her when you went out,
I presume. You've just come in to find me chucking your stuff
about.' I glanced at the girl. 'Hare?'

She started gabbling in her own language again.

'An argument or a fight,' Nimble ventured. 'After all, I've
just caught an intruder in my house, haven't I?'

'Makes sense. All right, then, so we have a fight.'

Nimble and I locked arms and began dancing around each other in a strange parody of combat.

The girl watched us intently, her head swinging back and forth in time with our mock struggle. She frowned, as though puzzled, and I had the impression that what we were doing was somehow not quite right, but she said nothing.

'She's waiting for something,' Nimble muttered.

'I agree – oh, I see. We aren't making any noise!'

Immediately we began grunting and swearing at each other. The girl continued frowning at us for a moment. Then she began gabbling and tugging her hair again.

'Maybe you should be tearing my hair out, or I should be pulling yours,' Nimble said.

'Maybe,' I said dubiously. 'Or perhaps I've got you to submit, the way warriors do it on a battlefield. I'm supposed to be a warrior, after all. So I grab my fallen opponent by the hair and shout: "This is my beloved son!"' I looked at Little Hen to see whether the ritual phrase was familiar to her.

She gave no sign of recognition.

'Still wrong,' I muttered. 'But something must have got her out of that hole.'

Nimble crouched in front of her. He spoke her name imploringly. He said it again, looking at the blanket covering Kindly. She repeated it confidently, as though she understood his meaning.

'That's something, at least,' he said. He looked at me and back at the girl again. The word that drew from her might have been birdsong for all it meant to us, but then she turned those strange eyes on Nimble himself and, for the second time, spoke Hare's name in an accent so thick it was barely intelligible.

'So we were right, then,' I said, relieved, but the girl's next words shocked me into silence. She let out a joyous shout, bouncing excitedly up and down and bawling out her own name like a war cry: 'Ix Men! Ix Men! Ix Men!'

Kindly heard her through the blanket. I felt a bony hand yank at my ankle, pulling me off balance. At the same time Nimble pulled me forward, and I went over with a yell, landing on my hands and knees.

'And then I cut your throat!' my son cried triumphantly.

'No need to sound quite so pleased about it,' I grumbled. 'I suppose you're right, though. But what about Hare?'

It was the girl who answered. Once more she plucked at her hair. This time, however, she dropped it immediately, before suddenly leaping up and racing towards Nimble and me as my son stooped to help me up.

'Look out!' Nimble cried. 'I think she's going to show us what she did for herself . . .'

None of us was prepared for what happened next. Yelling her war cry once more, she skidded across the floor to come to a halt in front of me, and before I could react she thrust her broken wooden doll towards me.

I frowned. 'Is she saying she attacked the Texcalan with the wooden spike? We didn't see any sign of that, though. His throat had been cut.' I looked down at the girl, and in response she shoved the doll in my direction again, firmly but not aggressively.

'Odd,' commented Kindly. 'Doesn't look to me as if she's trying to attack you. I think she's trying to give the thing to you.'

'Why would she do that? And what about Hare?'

Mention of the name stirred something inside the girl. Suddenly she turned on my son, leaped up at him and thumped him viciously in the small of the back with the doll.

Nimble uttered a sharp cry of alarm and pain and spun on

his heel, with his arm poised as if to strike, but when the girl stumbled backwards, her eyes widened in a show of fear, he lowered his hand.

'It's all right,' he said gently. He bent his knees to bring his face level with hers. 'It's all right. It didn't hurt really.' He twisted his mouth in a mock grimace, and Little Hen let out a giggle.

I grinned. 'Well done!'

Nimble spoke to the girl again. He pointed to the ground. 'Hare?' he said.

She responded by making a dragging motion and slapping the earth vigorously, saying something vehement in her own language.

'Thoroughly dead and buried, I guess,' I said. 'I dare say I – I mean, the Texcalan – was too heavy for her to move, not to mention too big to fit in the hole. Ix Men?' I asked.

She gestured towards the doorway.

I looked around at the other two. 'So what does all that mean?' I asked, baffled.

Nimble said slowly: 'Hare's dead and hidden in the hole. The Texcalan's dead. She killed Hare with the spike – that's what she meant by whacking me with the doll, I guess . . .'

'No, that's not it.' Kindly corrected him. 'She gave the spike to the Texcalan.'

'But we know Hare was killed with it. So it was the Texcalan who used it on him . . .'

'But then who killed the Texcalan?' I asked, capping their dialogue in a resigned tone. 'Let's face it, none of this adds up, does it? We thought we knew what had happened here, but we're as far from the truth as ever. All we know is that both men were killed and the girl ran away.' And there was no con- clusion to be drawn from that: in Little Hen's position I would not have wanted to be found near the corpses of my master and another man, even if he did turn out to have been a burglar. It would have made no difference to her whether or not she had actually had a hand in either man's death.

'Of course,' I pointed out, 'what she did was murder, you know. Technically.'

'Technically,' Nimble repeated remotely. He was not looking at me, but there was a defiant edge to his voice as he added: 'What do you want to do about it, turn her in?'

A vague scheme to trade the girl for Lily had begun to form in my mind, but even before I met Nimble's hard, determined eyes I realized it would not work. 'What do you take me for?' I replied, trying to look hurt.

Kindly said: 'So she stabbed a man to death and hid the body. Or she got someone else to do it, and that's even more impressive if you think about it. What a girl! She reminds me of my daughter.'

At the mention of Lily, I felt the grin freeze into position on my face as the muscles around my mouth tightened. I shut my eyes for a moment, while I reminded myself that what we had just done amounted to nothing more than a little play-acting, which brought us no nearer to finding what we were looking for: the message, whatever and wherever it was, whose content might exonerate Lily. Her trial, I realized, must be due to begin today or tomorrow at the latest, and it would in all likelihood end the same day as it started. As things stood, there could be little doubt about the verdict, or the sentence. The one thing I did not know now was what Rattlesnake and his cronies might be doing to their caged prisoner in the meantime.

I opened my eyes slowly, blinking a few times to get rid of the tears. Then I looked at the girl again.

'We have to find someone who speaks her dialect.'

'Don't look at me,' Kindly said sadly. 'I've no doubt there's someone among all the smartarses in this city who's fluent in it – it's the kind of place where people learn things like that just for fun - but I don't know how you'd go about finding them. The only interpreter I know of is lying at the bottom of a hole under his own floor.'

'When we first got back here this afternoon, we tried giving her a piece of paper and a brush,' Nimble added, from where he still squatted by the girl. 'I hoped she might be able to copy this message from memory, or a bit of it, but it was hopeless. I don't think she had any idea what to do with them.'

I tried it myself, squatting low like a scribe and pretending to doodle on an imaginary piece of paper resting on my knees. The girl looked fascinated by what I was doing but said nothing.

'That's about all the reaction I got,' Nimble said. 'That's why we were going to take her back to Hare's house – to see if there was anything there she might be able to point out to us. No such luck.'

I stood up. 'Maybe we can try miming it again.' I held up the imaginary paper and then slapped my own chest. 'Hare?' I ventured, while walking around the room trying to look like somebody attempting to hide something. Little Hen watched me in that odd way of hers, staring directly ahead of her while her head turned, following my movements, but she was still silent.

My patience snapped then. Suddenly rounding on the girl, I roared at her: 'Where did Hare put the bloody message, you stupid child?'

'Father!' cried Nimble reproachfully. Little Hen quailed, shrinking away from me and holding her doll tighter than ever.

'Oh, I'm sorry,' I mumbled. 'It's just so sodding frustrating!'

Nimble moved towards her. 'He didn't mean it, Ix Men. He said sorry . . . What's the matter?'

The girl had suddenly begun gabbling at us. I had no idea what she was saying, or what the strange gesture that she kept making meant. She kept putting a thumb and forefinger to each of her eyes and using them to stretch the lids apart, distorting the eyes from their normal ellipses into an odd circular shape.

Eventually she fell silent, dropped her hands and looked at each of us expectantly.

I glanced at my son. 'Any idea what that was all about?'

'None at all.'

Kindly sighed. 'It looks as if we may have to take our chances with the Otomies after all!'

I sat in the courtyard, with my back against the wall of the little dome-shaped sweat bath that was the only luxury the house in Huexotla afforded. It was late afternoon, and I had retreated to this spot as the shadows lengthened around me. It was not a particularly cold day, but I felt the need for the sun's warmth, even as I drew my borrowed cloak more tightly around my shoulders.

I had slept through much of the morning, exhaustion keeping me unconscious until well after noon. When I had finally woken up, it had been to find Little Hen playing silently with her doll, Nimble gone and Kindly lying next to an empty drinking-gourd with his mouth open and emitting noises like a wild sow in heat.

I had kicked him awake. 'Where's he gone?' I demanded.

The old man had stared at me blearily for a long while before mumbling something about Nimble's having gone to Hare's house to have a look around.

'And you let him go?' I protested. 'Why, you old . . .' Rather than wait for some sufficiently imaginative insult to come to mind, I turned towards the doorway. 'I have to get after him.'

'Don't be stupid,' the old man snapped. 'He'll be safe enough – he's the only one of us that neither the Otomies nor Maize Ear's men know, so if there's anyone up there they'll take him for a passer-by. The last thing that lad needs is you barging in and getting you both caught! He said he'd be back before evening. I suggest you rest some more until then. I suspect we're all going to have a busy night!'

Reluctantly I had taken the old man's advice. I should have liked to take a sweat bath, to lie, enveloped in steam, in the dark little room beside me, but there was nobody to stoke up the fire outside it, and so I made do with huddling against walls, pursued by shadows from one corner of the courtyard to another while I waited for my son to return. I could not sleep. Instead, I wasted much of the afternoon reflecting morosely on the events of the last few days and how little I had to show for it all, despite all the effort and terror I and those close to me had undergone. Lily a prisoner, in all likelihood being horribly tortured and almost certain to be executed; the message, whatever it was, whose content might or might not prove to be her lifeline, as elusive as ever; and I, having come to Tetzcoco to flee my deadly enemies, now forced to confront not just them but a whole new set of foes: Rattlesnake, Hunter and their comrades.

'Doesn't look good, does it?'

Kindly's voice jerked me out of my reverie. I had not noticed him emerge from inside the house.

'No.'

He leaned against the wall beside me and slid down it slowly, coming to rest on his bony backside. 'It beats me why you don't just give up and run away.'

'I can't.'

'Why not?'

'I'm a slave, remember?'

He laughed harshly. 'So what? Your mistress isn't going to stop you. If anything happens to her I suppose it becomes up to me. All right, I release you! Go on, bugger off!'

I stared at him. 'What are you talking about? You know I can't do anything like that. What's the matter with you?'

'"Can't" has nothing to do with it,' he pointed out. 'What you mean is "won't." But why not? What's my daughter to you, anyway?'

I looked at the ground. 'She saved my life once. No, twice. And my son's too. We both owe her.'

'Ah, that must be it.'

I looked at him out of the corner of my eye. 'So what about you?' I asked, something cruel in me stirred by my irritation at his questions. 'She's your daughter. Isn't she all you've got left? Why aren't you running all over the city trying to help her, or tearing your hair out and howling with grief instead of sitting there guzzling sacred wine?'

As if I had just reminded him it was there, he pulled the drinking-gourd out from under his arm and offered it to me.

'No, I need to keep a clear head.'

He took a pull at the gourd. 'Me too. Why do you think I need this?' With a smack of his lips he went on: 'In answer to your question, there's not much I can do now but wait. Just like you. I spoke to Obsidian Tongue yesterday, and he told me the trial is set for tomorrow. So we do our business tonight, and then let him do his.'

I wondered whether the old man knew of my argument with the lawyer the previous day. There seemed no point in mentioning it now.

'But as for grief . . .' He sighed heavily. 'Young man, I've seen and done a lot of things over the years – too many.'

'Enough to be hardened to losing your only child?' I asked in a brittle voice.

'No. Enough to know that you can never tell what is going to happen, in spite of what the sorcerers and soothsayers say.' He took another drink. 'Do you know when Lily's birthday is?'

'No,' I said wonderingly, as if this were something I ought to have known.

'Four Wind.'

'Oh,' I said glumly.

The old man gave a cough and a dry chuckle. '"Oh," indeed. I know what you're thinking. An unlucky day, when they execute adulterers and every doorway and smoke hole in the city is stuffed up to keep out evil spirits, yes?'

'It couldn't be much worse,' I acknowledged. Children born on such a bad day sometimes failed to live just because their parents gave up on them, assuming them to be doomed whatever they did.

'But you see, Lily's one of us – a merchant. And for us, Four Wind is a good day. We hold a big feast on Four Wind when we all get blind drunk and brag about our exploits and our wealth. Of course, it's the perfect time to do it, when all those jealous, greedy warriors are cowering indoors, but do you see what I'm saying? One man's inauspicious day is another's festival. Lily's luck may hold yet, you know – but we won't know either way until it's over.' He frowned thoughtfully. 'You know, I do sometimes wonder whether anything the soothsayers tell us about our fates is really worth the breath they expend on it.'

I smiled in spite of myself, thinking that Kindly might equally have cited my own career as Tezcatlipoca's plaything to prove his point.

'Now,' the old man went on, 'let's just suppose we survive meeting these old friends of ours. For a start, we're assuming they've got this message along with the rest of Hare's possessions. How do we get it from them, and what do we do if we can't?'

'I don't know,' I admitted. 'I haven't really got any idea beyond trying to get one of the Otomies on his own and maybe beating it out of him . . . It won't work, will it?'

'Not a chance. Any one of those walking slabs of granite would tear you limb from limb before you could ask him his name. And what do you expect to get out of him, anyway? He's highly unlikely to have this message on him, and as for telling you what it says, well, the chances are none of them can read Nahuatl, let alone Mayan.' He pursed his lips thoughtfully before adding, in a brighter tone, as if the idea had just occurred to him: 'No, I tell you what you need. A spy.'

'A what?'

'A spy. And why not? This city's full of them already – who's going to notice one more? You need someone to get among the Otomies and find out what it is they have got. Someone they don't already know, naturally . . .'

'We can't send Nimble! He's risking his life already, just scouting around the house for us. I wish you'd stopped him from going.'

'You have a better plan?'

'I just don't like it . . . Why don't I just go and look for Mother of Light again?'

'What good will that do? You found her once, and by your own account she didn't say anything useful then. And besides, she's still looking for the message herself, isn't she?'

'I just thought maybe she would have found it by now.'

'Doubt it. What if she has, though? How would you find her again? I gather you more or less stumbled over her before, and it seems that even Maize Ear's spies can't keep track of her for longer than it takes to blink. She and that old man she runs around with, they've got some way of flitting in and out through the palace walls which the King himself doesn't know about. What makes you think you've any chance of finding it?'

I opened my mouth, but the retort would not come. Instead, I looked wistfully towards the interior of the house, where for all I knew Little Hen was still sound asleep.

'I know,' said the old man gently. 'She's a sweet little girl, and I wish she could have told us what we need to know. Maybe she could, if we could only understand her! But she doesn't seem to have any idea what we're on about over this message, does she? It's as if the thing never existed in the first place.'

'I suppose you're right,' I admitted grudgingly. As I stared at the doorway of the house, however, I began to feel something stirring at the edge of my thoughts, an idea I could not quite grasp, like hearing a fragment of speech when the speaker is almost out of earshot. It occurred to me that there was something in what Kindly had just said, perhaps more than the old man himself realized. If I could only work out what it might have been . . .

Then Nimble was back, and my train of thought shattered like ice on a still pond.

Nimble seized upon Kindly's scheme as soon as it was explained to him. 'That's a wonderful idea! I can pretend to be the person they've been dealing with through that market trader all along. I can make out that it was just a casual enquiry, and all I'm interested in is a bargain. If they believe me, I may even be able to buy all the stuff off them without them ever suspecting the truth!'

'They'll be so disappointed!' Kindly chuckled. 'They're obviously hoping to catch either my daughter – no reason why they should know she's been arrested – or Yaotl, or at the very least whoever killed their mate.'

'Only if they fall for it,' I said darkly. 'That captain's nobody's fool and his deputy's smarter than he is. And if they rumble you . . .'

'They won't, Father. I saw a couple of them this afternoon, watching the front of the house.'

'That settles it! They must have seen you. You can't go back!'

'You mean it isn't safe?' he replied innocently.

I fell into the trap. 'Absolutely! It isn't. You're not going near the place. Nobody is, until we've come up with a sensible plan.'

'And how long will that take?' he cried. 'Until the day after tomorrow, when it's too late to matter?'

'Listen, son . . .'

That was when he rounded on me. 'Don't "son" me! How can you talk about being safe when Lily's about to be killed? None of us has been safe since we set foot in Tetzcoco – you, me, Kindly. Can't you see that?'

I stared at him, unable to find my voice. He seemed to have changed before my eyes, his face reddening and swelling with anger, his nostrils flaring, his fists clenched. And I noticed his Tarascan accent had suddenly grown more pronounced.

He stormed on: 'And when are you going to stop treating me like a child? I'm sick of it. You only have to think I might get so much as a scratch and that's it: "Stay here, Nimble. It's not safe, Nimble." I've got along fine so far without you look-ing out for me, you know, and I don't need you telling me what to do now!'

The moment he ran out of breath, I jumped in. 'How dare you!' I spluttered. 'You can't talk to me like that! I ought to shove your face in a fire full of burning chillies for this . . .'

We were squaring up to each other, bristling like two ocelots coming unexpectedly face to face. He leaped to his feet. 'Oh, are you going to try it, then?'

'You're my son!' In my own ears my protest sounded pathetic; Nimble was taller than I and much fitter.

'It took you fifteen years even to admit you *had* a son!'

'Will you two pack it in?'

Kindly had been looking from one to the other of us like a spectator following a ball game, but now he had had enough. As we both turned to him, and an impolite request to mind his own business began to form on my lips, he went on: 'Look, I enjoy a good row as much as anyone, but this isn't getting us anywhere. Nimble, shut up; he's your father. He may not be much good at it, but he's the only one you've got. Yaotl, sorry, but the lad's right. It doesn't matter that the Otomies have seen him: as far as they're concerned he was just following good business practice, sizing them up before he went in. It's a perfectly good plan. Now, can we please get on with it?'

For a moment neither Nimble nor I could think of a reply. We merely glowered sullenly at each other.

'Well?' the old man demanded.

'All right,' I mumbled. 'I still don't like it.'

'I'll be careful.' My son's tone now was conciliatory. 'It's not as if I need to fight anybody. Look, you won't be far away, will you? I couldn't see anyone at the back of the house, so there may be a way in that way if we need it. And no sign of your friends from the palace,' he added, trying to sound encouraging.

'They'll be there,' I predicted gloomily.

The plan, such as it was, was for Nimble to walk into the house through the front doorway and start talking to the Otomies. He was to try to get them to show him everything they had for sale. If he saw anything that might be a message, he was to buy the lot, paying whatever the Otomies asked for it, and get out as quickly as he could.

'Between you and Obsidian Tongue, I shall be lucky if I can afford to eat scum off the surface of the lake after this,' muttered Kindly as he handed Nimble a bag full of goose quills. If

I had not known it already, I could have told from the way they rattled that each quill was stuffed with something. The filling was gold dust, and the amount of wealth in the bag was enough to make me feel giddy just contemplating it.

The old merchant looked at the bag wistfully. 'Are you sure he can't haggle a bit?' he asked me.

'No, he can't,' I said firmly. 'It's too risky. In and out as fast as possible, Nimble, you understand?'

'Where are you going to be?' my son asked.

The plan called for me to hide myself in or near the house, ready to spring to Nimble's aid if he got into trouble. 'In the hole under the chest, I suppose,' I said doubtfully.

'You may want to think again,' Kindly said. 'Hare's body is probably still in there. And I doubt you'll have time to move it.'

'And I don't want to share the hole with it! There wouldn't be room for us both anyway.'

'We'll have to try to hide you at the back of the house somewhere. It's overgrown enough.'

'What about you two?' I asked, looking at Kindly and Little Hen.

'I'll come with you,' the old man said. 'The girl can stay here. I think she's used to being left on her own.'

I stared at him sceptically. 'You want to come?' I had assumed he would be quite happy to be left behind, babysitting the girl. 'Why would you want to do that?'

'You said yourself – Lily's my only daughter. I can't help her by running all over the city, as you put it, but if there's anything I can do, I'll be there.'

13

Nimble did his best to convey to Little Hen where we were going and what we wanted her to do, using hand signals. I could only hope she understood that she was to stay put until one of us returned, but when she looked at him her expression was as inscrutable as ever.

We dropped Kindly off at the bottom of the slope at the back of the house, just around a bend in the stream so that he would not be visible from the courtyard. 'I think this is as close as you dare to get,' I told him. 'Try to stay out of sight, and don't make any noise!'

He grinned at me. 'You forget that I used to do things like this all the time when I was younger! Did I ever tell you about that time in Xoconochco . . .?'

'Not now,' I said firmly.

'Oh, all right. But I promise you, you won't even hear my teeth chattering. Not that I have that many left!'

I looked at the old man curiously. 'You seem in good spirits all of a sudden.'

'Oh, there's nothing like exercise and night air to get the blood flowing through your veins again! And I've got this for company.' He lifted his gourd and shook it so that I could hear the liquid inside. Then he added, in a sober voice: 'It's doing something that matters, do you understand? Risking everything and having everything to gain. Not something I've done much of these past few years.'

'Don't get carried away,' I warned him as I turned to follow Nimble up to the house.

'Good luck!' he hissed back.

My own hiding place was to be a shallow depression right at the back of the house, with the courtyard wall a few hand's breadths away. We found it after scrambling up the bank, keeping our heads down in case anyone should be glancing in our direction. I had been hoping that the Sun, poised just above the mountains beyond the lake, would blind anyone looking westwards, but in the event the house appeared deserted.

Nimble helped me to make my hollow a little deeper, scraping at the soil with his fingers and then with the blade of the Tarascan bronze knife he always carried, his most precious possession. 'When you're in there I'll chuck some weeds and stuff over you. Once it gets a bit darker you'll be invisible.'

I looked up from where I knelt, scrabbling in the dirt alongside my son. 'Funny there's no one about. I know we set the meeting for sunset, but you saw the Otomies earlier, and I'd have thought they'd be keeping an eye on the place. And where are Rattlesnake and his men?'

'I saw the Otomies outside the front. Maybe they were just making sure they had the right house. Why should they bother hanging around any longer than they have to? If you or Lily came here at all, it would be to talk to them. They don't need to do anything except turn up. And Rattlesnake will probably wait for them to arrive so that he can grab all of you.'

'I suppose so.' I looked past Nimble at the courtyard wall. 'Is it me, or is that a bit more broken down than it was?'

He glanced over his shoulder. 'Could be. What of it? It was badly battered in that corner before. Are you going to get in this hole now? I don't think we can dig it any deeper.'

I lay down reluctantly. 'I just wish I could get rid of the feeling that I was being followed all the time.'

'That's just what being in this city for a few days does to
you.'

Within a few moments after Nimble had thrown the last of the
foliage on top of me, I had had enough.

I had seldom been so uncomfortable. Even the cage the
slave-dealers had kept me in, I reflected miserably, might have
been better than where I was now. At least there I had had
room to squat. It did not help that the ends of my fingers were
raw and bloody, the nails torn from scrabbling in the loose soil.

I was cramped, terrified and in need of a piss. As the Sun
began to drop out of sight, I realized that I was going to be bitterly cold as well.

I strained to catch some sound from the house, at the same
time trying to picture what might be happening in there. I
wondered whether my son and the Otomies had found each
other, and, if they had, what might follow. Would the evening
end in a straightforward business transaction, with the captain
and his men congratulating themselves on the price they had
got for their stolen goods and Nimble left with the thing we
had been seeking for days, or in a scene of shrieking carnage as
the Otomies worked out their rage on my son and then on
me, as I rushed vainly to his aid?

I could hear nothing.

I wondered, too, where Rattlesnake, Hunter and the rest of
Maize Ear's men were. Nimble's suggestion that they might
wait for the Otomies to arrive before putting in an appearance
made sense, but I found it odd that we had seen no evidence
of them watching the house. Or were they hiding nearby? I
had found it easy enough to find a place to conceal myself, and
it suddenly occurred to me that they might have as well. I felt

an urge to leap up and look around me, to see whether there were any places where a squad of warriors might be lying low, but resisted it. It was too late now to do anything but wait and hope that, somehow, our plan might succeed in turning up Hare's all-important message, and that the message would say something that might help to save Lily.

As I dwelled on the message, I found myself thinking again about the conversation Kindly and I had had during the afternoon. Once more I had the nagging feeling that had come over me just before Nimble's return to the house in Huexotla, the feeling that I had missed something, something so obvious that Kindly had managed to point it out to me without even realizing it.

Now, away from the old man's chattering, lying in the dark, alone and with nothing to do, I tried repeating to myself everything he had said to me.

I had it in a moment, the solution to the mystery. I did not know what Hare's message was, but all of a sudden I knew where it was, and how it was to be delivered. Then, as if some dam had burst in my head, releasing – not before time – a flood of pent-up understanding, I found I had grasped something else: not only what Mother of Light was going to do with the message when she got it, but how vital it was for us to get it to her, and how we were going to do it.

Cursing myself for a fool, I lurched to my feet, shedding leaves and grass as I clambered out of my hollow towards the courtyard wall. I took a deep breath, meaning to call out to Nimble, to tell him to get out of Hare's house before it was too late. He was in no greater danger than he had been all along, but I now knew that what we were trying to do here was pointless, a waste of time and potentially of all our lives.

I never did call out. Before I could, I heard what I had

been waiting to hear all evening: voices coming from inside
the house. One of them at least was shouting.

I threw myself over the gap in the wall, nearly tumbling headlong over the loose rubble on the other side as it shifted under
me. After setting off a small but noisy avalanche of broken
masonry, I hurtled towards the house. I had no idea what I was
going to do or whether I could do anything at all. I had no real
weapon, only a sharp piece of obsidian in either hand, picked
up from the litter at the back of the house. I had only one
thought: to come to my son's aid even if there was nothing I
could do.

Screaming, I raced through the doorway at the back of the
house's only room.

A painful blow caught one of my shins, snagging my leg,
and I fell headlong. The earth floor slammed into my chin like
a fist. I slid on my belly into the middle of the room, the
obsidian chips flying out of my hands as I fell.

For a moment I lay still, in darkness, confused by the blow,
only dimly aware that there were men standing around me,
and one of them had stopped my charge by the childishly
simple trick of tripping me up.

'Pathetic,' somebody said. The voice was strangely slurred, as
though there were something wrong with the speaker's mouth.
'Stand him up. Let's see if he's who I hope he is!'

A hand seized the knot of my cloak and yanked at it. The
coarse material caught me around the throat, constricting it
and burning the skin as I was hauled upright.

'Who are you, then?' demanded the man with the slurred
voice. 'Cemiquiztli Yaotl? I do hope so. I've waited a long time
and taken a lot of trouble to find you.'

'My son,' I croaked desperately. 'Where is he? What have
you done with him?'

The answer was a blow to my stomach that had me on my knees, retching into the dirt.

Another voice uttered a cry of triumph: 'It's him! It's the Aztec!'

As my heaves and coughing subsided, I looked up at the man who had felled me. His face wore a delighted grin. There was something odd about the way his cloak fell around his shoulders. It took me a moment to realize that this was because he had lost an arm. He held the surviving limb aloft, its muscles bulging, poised as if to strike me again.

I looked quickly about, taking in the scene around me.

A small fire had been lit in the centre of the room, under the smoke hole. It provided just enough light for me to make out the scene around me.

I almost wept with relief when I saw my son. He was standing up just inside the doorway, loosely held by a warrior. The Texcalan stood just above me. A third warrior stood between me and Nimble, leering down at me with a lopsided grin. His one eye and the slab of flesh that was half his face glistened in the firelight.

I looked up towards the one-armed Texcalan. 'Why are you here?' I asked, genuinely mystified. 'What are this lot to you?'

'What do you think?' he rumbled. 'They told me to help bring you in. Said I'd get a flowery death if I did.'

So that was it. The Texcalan and his dead companion had been promised a new life as part of the morning Sun's guard of honour, and rebirth as hummingbirds or butterflies, merely for helping track down a runaway slave. It must have seemed a good deal: all they had to do to have their hearts cut out by the Fire Priest was to tell the Otomies where I was going, and Lily had unwittingly given them that information while they were being untied from the slave-collar.

'Too bad your friend didn't make it,' I said.

Muscles bunched in the Texcalan's arm. 'What do you mean by that?' he demanded, but the captain was speaking before I could answer.

'On your feet.'

I stood up unsteadily. 'Nimble, are you all right? What happened?'

'Who told you to say anything?' the Otomi snapped. 'You talk when we ask you a question, not before. Got it?'

I said nothing. My mouth had suddenly gone dry.

'Right. Now, we were just about to ask the lad here how many more of you there are, but now you're here you can tell us instead. Is that woman, Lily, with you? What about her father?'

I tried to swallow, but my throat had stopped working. I said nothing. I kept my eyes fixed on my son. He seemed unhurt but was very pale.

The captain's grin broadened. 'I knew you wouldn't disappoint me!'

Then he picked up the weapon that had been propped against the wall beside him. Its blades sparkled as he hefted it thoughtfully. I tried not to look at it. It was a hideous tool, not so much a sword as a long, straight club with slivers of obsidian set into it in four viciously sharp rows: a thing designed to crush, maim and shred flesh rather than to kill. In the captain's hands it was an all-too-familiar sight, and I knew he would be only too happy to use it.

'Now, I suppose I ought to ask you again.' He turned and stepped over to my son. Standing just in front of him, he suddenly kicked at Nimble's legs to force them apart and then thrust the club into the space between them. 'Will you tell me where the woman and the old man are or do I turn your boy into a girl? Well?'

'No!' I cried, and tried to step forward. I was held fast. 'All right! I'll tell you, just don't hurt him . . .'

'Father, no!' the boy said, his voice barely audible. 'You mustn't . . .'

'That's enough from you,' the captain hissed. 'I have to take you both back to Lord Feathered in Black, but he didn't say you had to be in one piece!'

'Lily's in prison,' I said. 'In the royal palace in Tetzcoco. And her father . . .'

A scream interrupted me.

It was a short, shrill cry, abruptly cut off as if something had stopped up the throat it came from. It had originated outside the front of the house.

Everyone in the room, even the captain, jumped. The warrior who had been holding Nimble suddenly let go, whirled around and stood in the doorway. 'Cuectli!' he shouted.

Cuectli was the captain's deputy. His name meant 'Fox'. I realized that he must have been left outside, watching the road, and then I guessed what must have happened. Rattlesnake and his men had finally arrived.

'Get away from there, you idiot! Get back in here!' thundered the captain.

He was too late.

The warrior in the doorway shook as if struck and then staggered back, making gagging noises as he fell. There was a dart through his throat.

'The courtyard, quick!' The captain seized Nimble by the arm and threw him forward. Before I could react I had been grabbed as well, the Texcalan's one hand dragging me into the open air with such force that I could barely stay on my feet. As I staggered, completely out of control, he let go of me, plucked at the sword slung over his back and swung it through the air in a graceful arc, accomplishing all this in a single smooth motion.

When I looked past him into the courtyard, a bewildering sight confronted me.

The pile of rubble that had stood against the rear wall had broken down completely, scattering pieces of masonry and slabs of plaster across the ground. In its place stood two armed men: warriors who, I suddenly realized, must have buried themselves under it while they lay in wait for me and the men I was to meet.

'Rattlesnake?' I began wonderingly, but that was as far as I got.

Both of the men in front of me screamed and launched themselves towards us, swords poised high above their heads and blades flashing faintly in the starlight. The Texcalan kicked me hard in the back and leaped over me with his own answering shriek as I fell over.

It was over in a moment, a moment filled with roaring voices, the swish of swords and the crunch of their blades on bone, the dull thud of falling bodies and a warm rain of blood splashing on to me.

More shocking than the clash was the silence that followed it.

I looked up fearfully.

The captain was bending over his foe, using the man's hair to clean the blades of his club. 'Bloody amateurs,' he spat.

The Texcalan stood by the corpse of his own victim, his head darting about like a startled squirrel's in the moment before it bolts. 'Where did they come from? Where are the others?'

I looked around for Nimble. He had been pushed to the ground as well. As he tried to get up, the captain stood on him. 'Don't move! Who are these, Yaotl? Pals of yours?'

'No,' I said truthfully. 'They were Maize Ear's men. They knew about our meeting. They must have set a trap for us.'

The captain gave a contemptuous snort.

The Texcalan said, in a steady but subdued voice: 'We ought to take these two and go. There's no telling how many men are out there.'

His chief rounded on him. 'What do you care? Your death's guaranteed one way or another! I'm telling you, we go nowhere until we find out what happened to Fox! And then we kill the men who did it! All of them, you hear me? As for these – we don't waste any more time with them. You kill Yaotl and I'll do the boy! Now!'

'Wait!' I cried, scrambling desperately to get to my feet. 'You can't! Remember Lord Feathered in Black!'

'Screw him!' roared the captain, raising his sword.

'Look out!' his comrade cried. It was the last sound he ever made. A dart whistled through the air into his chest.

By the time his body hit the ground I was on my feet, throwing myself towards the captain and Nimble, but the captain was not there any more. He had leaped backwards, ducking under a second dart that came near enough to part his hair.

With a snarl, the great warrior stood up, swung the arm holding the club and flung the weapon overarm towards the roof of the house.

The club made a clumsy projectile, but it seemed not to matter. Out of the corner of my eye I saw it spinning end over end as it cleared the top of the house wall, and I heard the sickening soft thump and the agonized shriek of the man on the roof as it struck home. A moment later a dark shape loomed overhead, and the body pitched forward and landed on top of me, smashing me into the dirt and showering me in still more blood.

'Get off!' I cried unreasonably, twisting under the weight of the limp corpse.

The captain was still moving. He crouched and spun like a ball-game player making a difficult return, plucked the dart that had missed him from where it had fallen, jumped to his feet again and hurled the missile with all his might. He had no throwing-stick and no need of one. There was no scream from the rooftop this time, but the Otomi's triumphant cry told me that he had found his target.

'Any more of you bastards out there?' he roared, in a voice that might have been heard in Tlacopan on the far side of the lake.

No answer came out of the night.

Darting over to his dead comrade, he plucked the sword from the Texcalan's limp hand and turned towards Nimble and me. 'You two are going to pay for this!'

I was still struggling with the corpse that lay on top of me. Limp arms and legs seemed to strike out at me as I tried to roll it to one side. To my horror, I saw Nimble standing up but swaying slightly as if stunned, staring through uncomprehending eyes at the warrior bearing down on him.

'Nimble!' I screamed. 'Run!'

His head turned sharply at the sound of my voice. 'Father?'

'Too late!' crowed the Otomi, raising his sword just as I finally kicked myself free of the mass of limp flesh.

Something flew through the air from beyond the broken back wall of the courtyard. It hit the captain on the cheek and clattered to the ground, rolling to a stop by my feet: a stone.

I looked at the wall and the open space beyond it. A face there looked back at me for an instant before vanishing. I gasped: it was a small face, with a grotesquely high forehead and crossed eyes.

The Otomi whirled around with a cry of rage. 'Who threw that? So you didn't all run away!'

He sprang towards the back of the courtyard, his sandals

clapping the ground and his sword swinging as he cleared the
wall in a single bound.

Nimble was still staring at me. I took a step towards him
before I froze, suddenly horror-struck.

I slapped my son on the arm to bring him round. 'We've got
to get after him!' I shouted.

He had a hand pressed to one of his temples. 'Must have hit
my head when I fell,' he muttered. Then he stared at me. 'Get
after him? Why?'

'Because Little Hen's out there!'

His jaw dropped. 'But . . .'

'She must have followed us! Didn't I say I thought we were
being followed? We need her, Nimble! She's the solution to all
of this!'

He looked blankly at me for about a heartbeat, and then my
words seemed to register. We ran together towards the wall,
scrambling over the shattered masonry into the wasteland
behind the house.

I could not see the captain, but I could hear him clearly,
thrashing about lower down on the overgrown bank, bellow-
ing incoherent war cries.

'What's he doing that for?' Nimble asked. 'He's telling Little
Hen exactly where he is!'

'He's out of his mind,' I replied. 'He thinks he's fighting a
battle. An Otomi doesn't sneak up on people; his enemies
usually submit as soon as they realize who they're up against! If
those poor sods back at the house had had any idea what they
were dealing with, they wouldn't have tried anything. Come
on – we have to get down there.'

We picked our way gingerly over the uneven ground.
Beyond the stream and the hillside below us, I could make out
the vast expanse of Lake Tetzcoco, its surface pale against its
dark surroundings, and then I saw something that shocked

me: a massive black shape, human, moving back and forth in front of the lake. The captain was not ten paces away. He was still roaring and wielding his sword.

I reached out to catch Nimble's arm to warn him. 'He can't see us,' I hissed. 'We both go for him at once. Don't try to go for the sword, just get him down! Ready?'

I paused and took a deep breath.

'Now!' I whispered, and without another sound we threw ourselves down the slope.

The Otomi heard nothing above the sound of his own shouting. The first he knew of our presence was when both of us crashed into him with all our combined weight.

It was not enough.

A lesser man would have fallen, bringing himself and his attackers down in a tangle of arms and legs, but not the captain. He staggered but kept his footing, spinning around with a cry of shock and outrage. I fell, thrown aside by his turn and hitting the ground with an impact that jarred my shoulder. Nimble clung on, with his arms around the roaring warrior's neck as the man gyrated this way and that in his efforts to throw him off.

'Nimble!' I cried, clambering to my feet. 'The sword! Watch out for his sword!'

The Otomi's hands were free. I heard the swishing noise the sword made as it swept through the air and my son's scream as it clove his flesh. His grip on the captain's neck failed and he dropped heavily to the ground.

Shouting obscenities, the warrior stood over him with his sword held high in both hands, ready for a last, mortal, chop-ping blow.

Time seemed to stop. The sword seemed to hang in the air, poised there for an age. There was nothing I could do; even as I was urging my legs to throw me between my son and the blades, I knew I could never get there in time.

The captain drew breath, and a terrible silence fell over the hillside.

It was broken by a voice from out of the night: a voice from every Aztec's nightmares.

'Oh, my sons!' It sounded like an old woman speaking: high-pitched, reedy and tremulous, with a husky quality as if the speaker's throat were constricted. 'Oh, my sons! What is to become of you?' It was coming from down the slope, in the direction of the stream.

The effect on the captain was extraordinary. He turned, the sword wavering uncertainly.

'Who's there?' he called. 'Who are you?'

Something was moving below us, near the stream. Whatever it was, it seemed to be picking its way haltingly up the slope towards us, and it was speaking.

'Oh, my children! Oh, the poor warriors, the Eagle Warriors, the Jaguar Warriors! The Otomies – first of all, the Otomies!'

The captain stepped backwards. The sword dangled now at the height of his waist, not threatening anybody. 'I . . . I asked you who you were.'

This man would not quail before any human enemy. He would accept death if it came for him – would welcome it, even, if it was a flowery death on the battlefield or beneath a sacrificial knife. But as with most warriors, the things that haunted the night terrified him beyond reason, and I knew he would have recognized this apparition as the most dreadful of all.

I watched and listened with a curious feeling of detachment. As a priest, I had been trained to confront such terrors and to tell true portents from false ones.

'You know who I am, Captain,' piped the eerie, high-pitched voice.

'Cihuacoatl?' The Otomi whispered the name. Cihuacoatl, the Snake Woman: the most feared of our goddesses, a being so ravenous for human hearts and blood that she was depicted always with gore dripping from her mouth.

'Your captives have nourished me many times. Now it is your turn!'

The sword fell to the ground with a thump. The brave warrior screamed and turned to flee, stumbling blindly up the hill, falling and picking himself up and gibbering helplessly until he was out of earshot.

I felt dizzy. The night sky whirled around me and I fell to my knees.

14

The fire the Otomies had built in Hare's house had all but gone out. I brought it back to life again, feeding it with pieces of the wicker chest for want of any other fuel. I hoped I would not have to burn the whole thing. I had no wish to uncover the merchant's grave again.

Once I had a healthy blaze going, its light revealed the other occupants of the room: Kindly, Nimble and Little Hen. We had dragged the lifeless body of the Otomi into the courtyard to join the dead Texcalan.

Nimble sat close to the fire, silent and trembling, with one leg stretched out before him. Kindly was examining it with the practised eye of a merchant who had seen and treated many wounds in the course of his travels.

'Could be a lot worse. That's a nasty deep cut on your thigh, but it looks clean enough.'

'Good thing you held on to the captain as tightly as you did,' I said. 'It must have been hard for him to get any leverage, hacking away at someone on his back.'

My son grimaced. 'It still hurts!'

'I'll need to wash it and bind it up with something to slow the bleeding,' Kindly said. Standing over my son, he began untying his breechcloth.

Nimble stared at him. 'What are you doing?'

'I told you — I need to wash the wound. Sit still.' The old man aimed a jet of urine over my son's injured leg.

Little Hen giggled. Nimble said reproachfully: 'There's a stream at the bottom of the hill!'

'Sure,' the old man retorted. 'And it's full of shit and turkey heads. Take it from me, if you want clean water, the best place to get it from is your own bladder. You're lucky I drink so much!' He began readjusting his clothes. 'Now, what we really need is some honey to stop the wound going bad, but unfortunately we haven't got any. It should be all right, though, if I can find some clean cloth to dress it with.'

'Our clothes are all filthy,' I said. 'Try tearing a strip off one of the warriors' cloaks outside.'

While Kindly was attending to this, I looked at my son and the girl. He looked ill, weak from shock and loss of blood, but I knew he was young and strong and would recover quickly if he were given a chance. The girl's expression was as impassive as ever, although she kept turning her head towards the remains of the wicker chest, no doubt thinking about what was hidden underneath it. I wondered what thoughts and memories that, in turn, led to. What had Hare done to her, and why had he kept her in that dark, cramped prison?

'Little Hen,' I sighed. Perhaps, I thought, it was just as well she could not speak to us. What horrors would she have to relive as she revealed them? Yet at that moment I simply wanted to tell her that I knew something of how it felt to be shut into a tiny space, without hope, experiencing nothing but cruelty from the people around me.

Kindly came back with a long strip of cloth. 'Only maguey fibre,' he said, 'but it's reasonable quality and it looks clean enough. If we can get you back to our lodgings I'll change it for something better.'

I said: 'I haven't had a chance to thank you for getting rid of
the captain for us. I thought we were dead men.'

He laughed. 'It was easy enough. I knew the brute would
run if he thought the goddess was after him!'

'So what happened?'

'Well, the first thing was when I saw Little Hen coming after
you. She went straight past my hiding place, following the
creek. I don't know whether she'd picked up your trail, but I
think she must have misunderstood what we wanted her to do.
Or maybe she got bored. Anyway, she obviously got the idea
that we were going to Hare's house from our little perform-
ance in the afternoon, and decided to join us.

'I thought I'd better follow her, but of course my eyesight's
not so good and I haven't got her young legs! I'd barely got
going when I heard all this shouting from up the hill. Not a lot
I could do, I thought, but I carried on anyway.'

I turned to Nimble then, to ask what had started the shouting.

'They found my knife. Your former master, old Black
Feathers, must have told them about it. I don't suppose any of
them had seen a bronze knife before. It must have been a dead
giveaway. One of the Otomies took it off me.'

'Here it is,' said Kindly laconically, handing it over. 'Now,
where was I? Oh, yes, at the bottom of the slope, about level
with the house. That's as far as I'd got, when you all came
charging down the hill.'

'Little Hen obviously reached the back of the house at about
the time Rattlesnake's men attacked,' I said. 'It's lucky for us
she joined in when she did. But what gave you the idea of pretending to be Cihuacoatl?'

'I know these warriors. They don't fear anything human,
but the gods scare the shit out of them. It makes sense. War is
a chancy business, isn't it? Some lowlife you wouldn't think

worth spitting on can put a dart through your eye with a lucky shot, or you can miss your footing in a fight and go down, and if it's going to happen then I guess it doesn't matter how valiant or skilful you are. So warriors depend on the gods almost as much as we merchants.'

I understood what he was saying. My brother Lion was a warrior, and as ferocious in battle as any Otomi, but he feared the gods as much as any man I knew.

'That's why our staffs are so important to us,' the old man went on. 'It's like having Yacatecuhtli by your side, always . . . Talking of which, we came here to try to get Hare's property, didn't we? I suppose there's no chance of that, now the Otomies have died or run off?'

I suddenly found myself lost for words. I hesitated. I looked from the old man to my son and back again. I cleared my throat. Eventually I managed to speak.

'Um,' I said.

'What's the matter?' Kindly asked suspiciously. Even Nimble was frowning in puzzlement.

'Er, well, it's like this. We don't need Hare's stuff. The message isn't with it.'

'What?' my son and the old man cried in unison.

'You see, it's like this . . .'

'Are you telling us,' Kindly asked, speaking slowly and in a low voice, 'that all this has been for nothing? We only came here to look for that bloody message!'

'We got rid of the Otomies,' I said defensively.

'But you're saying we never had to meet the Otomies in the first place!' Nimble cried resentfully. 'Look at my leg! If I'd known this was all just for fun . . .'

'I didn't say that!'

'Well, what was it for, then?' demanded Kindly.

'Look, we all thought we were looking for a message . . .'

'We were. We still are.'

'And we were all wrong. All of us.' I hoped to deflect some of their anger by stressing that they had been fooled just as I had. It did not work: by now, Kindly was all but spitting with rage.

'Oh, well, that's just great,' he snarled. 'The one slim hope we had of doing anything for my daughter, and smartarse here suddenly decides it was bollocks all along!'

'Will you just calm down and listen to me?' I asked, exasperated.

'Why, what's next? Don't tell me. You happen to know that none of this matters anyway because the King of Tetzcoco himself is going to come to Lily's rescue and send us all home in his own canoe!'

I looked at him curiously. 'Funny you should say that . . .'

'I wish I had a drink,' the old man muttered disgustedly, and turned his back on me.

I appealed to Nimble. 'Can't you just hear me out? I know I should have worked this out sooner, and I'm sorry, but I didn't!'

My son shifted his injured leg and winced. 'I don't understand what you're saying, but all right.'

I looked at Lily's father. 'He nearly put his finger on it when we were talking this afternoon.' The old man continued to sulk silently. 'He was talking about Little Hen. He said he wished we could understand her, because she could probably tell us everything we wanted to know.'

'We thought that,' Nimble said, 'but she doesn't seem to understand our gestures. I can't seem to get the idea of a message – I mean pictures or writing – across to her, not even by giving her a brush and paper. And as for getting her to show me where it might be, well, it's hopeless! And it's not as if she's stupid.'

'Kindly said more or less the same thing this afternoon. "It's as if the thing never existed in the first place." I think those were his exact words. But, of course, that was it! It never did exist, not on paper, anyway.' I turned towards Little Hen. 'It's in her head!'

Nimble gaped at me. Even Kindly stirred, although he did not look around.

'What were we told about this message? It can only be understood by someone who knows Mayan. And this little girl . . .'

'Can only be understood by somebody who knows Mayan!' Nimble cried suddenly. 'Is that why Hare kept her buried under his house all the time – to keep whatever she knew a secret?' He sounded almost relieved, as if his darker suspicions about how Hare might have used the girl had been shown to be unfounded.

'I wouldn't bet on that being the only reason,' I said sadly. 'But it must have been a very important one. He was dealing with some powerful people, like Maize Ear and Black Flower, neither of whom would have had any scruples about coming and taking what he had from him if he wasn't prepared to sell it to them.'

Kindly finally found his voice again. 'So what? We're no better off than we were before, are we? We still don't know what this message is, and we've no way of finding out.'

'Yes, we have.'

'Oh, you've suddenly learned her dialect, have you? Well, I knew you were a clever bugger, but . . .'

'Oh, shut up!' I snapped, my patience exhausted. 'We know for a fact that there is at least one person in this city who can interpret this message, or have it interpreted, because of what she's prepared to pay for it.'

Nimble grinned suddenly. 'You mean Mother of Light.'

'Who can't be found,' Kindly muttered.

'Oh, yes, she can,' I said.

The old man turned around and stared at me. To my amazement, I saw that his eyes were glistening moistly in the firelight. I had never seen him shed a tear, but perhaps his disappointment and chagrin – the tension and frenzy of the night's work, followed by my declaration that it had all been for nothing, seemingly dashing his last hope for his daughter – had been too much for him at last.

'What did you say?' he whispered hoarsely.

'I said Mother of Light can be found. Easily. I know exactly where to look for her, and I bet when we go there we'll track down that old man she runs around with too.'

'Her father, you mean?'

It felt as though it had been a long time since I had laughed. Now I could not help myself, and once I started I found it impossible to stop, roaring insanely until my sides hurt and my vision went blurry for lack of breath.

'What's so funny?' Kindly asked.

'Oh, excuse me,' I gasped. 'I'm sorry.' I wiped my eyes with a corner of my cloak. 'That old man's no more her father than I am. And he's not as old as he looks, either!'

'So who is he, then?'

I was going to tell them, but my sense of mischief overcame me. Kindly thought I was a clever bugger and a smartarse. Well, I thought, he could wait a little while to find out just how clever I could be.

'You'll see!'

As the eastern sky began to brighten, we went out to survey the courtyard. It was a scene of carnage: an Otomi, a Texcalan and three of Maize Ear's men lay together in a heap, their blood staining the earth around them. I assumed that a sixth body, that of the man the captain had hurled the dart at, still lay on the roof; and it sounded as though Fox had come to grief somewhere outside the front of the house. Seven men killed in a matter of moments.

'We could take their weapons,' my son suggested.

'What for?' I asked. 'I don't know about you, but speaking for myself, if you put a sword in my hand, the only person I'd be likely to injure is me! Besides, it would look a bit odd, a bunch of vagabonds like us running around in Tetzcoco armed like warriors. The last thing we want to be right now is conspicuous!'

Ignoring the Otomies, I turned one of the other bodies over. I felt my teeth clench in something between a grin and a snarl when I saw the face.

'Rattlesnake,' I breathed.

'Recognize him?' Kindly asked.

'Lily's chief tormentor.' I wondered what it meant, finding him here. It seemed too much to hope that the entire gang of torturers who had threatened Lily had died with him. More likely, I thought grimly, he had left her in the care of someone worse than he was, assuming she was still alive.

'Time we were moving.' I looked doubtfully at Nimble's wounded leg. 'Are you sure you're going to be up to this?'

'Walking as far as Tetzcoco?' He sounded mildly offended. 'Of course! I was only a kid when I walked across the mountains from Tzintzuntzan to Mexico, you know.'

He was not so very much more than a child now. I felt a pang as I pictured my son as an Aztec boy, running away from our mortal enemies the Tarascans, only to fall into the clutches of procurers and perverts in the marketplaces of Tenochtitlan. I said nothing, merely clasping his shoulder for a few moments, until the sound of Kindly clearing his throat reminded me where I was and what I was supposed to be doing.

'All right,' I said. 'Nimble, you'd better look after Little Hen. Mind she doesn't wander off – we need her!'

I led the way through the house and along the road towards Tetzcoco.

By the time we found ourselves near the marketplace and the royal palace, the daily crowds had begun to gather. A deep mass of people was pressed against the entrance to the marketplace, each individual eager to get in and get his stall set up and trading as quickly as possible. We skirted around them, thankful that we did not have to fight our way through the mob. I led the way in the direction of our former lodgings.

'Don't worry – as far as the Otomies and Maize Ear's men are concerned, we're long gone!'

'Maybe,' Kindly mumbled grudgingly, 'but I still wish you'd explain this brilliant idea of yours.'

I looked over my shoulder at Nimble and Little Hen. My son smiled wanly back at me, and I consciously slowed my pace, as I had done several times that morning, to match his limping progress. The girl had starting glancing around her nervously as we approached the marketplace but had relaxed visibly once we had passed the entrance. She had her hand in my son's.

'Think about it,' I replied. 'You told me yourself, Mother of Light has some way of flitting in and out through the palace walls that Maize Ear himself doesn't know about. It just occurred to me, back at Hare's house, that you might be exactly right.'

'You mean she and her old man are sorcerers after all,' he groaned. 'In that case, we're wasting our time!'

'No, I don't mean that. Where was I when I saw Mother of Light the second time?'

'The Council of Music,' the old man responded promptly.

'Not quite,' Nimble pointed out. 'I think he said he was in a courtyard near the council's meeting place.'

'Close,' I told him. 'That's where I found her. But where I left her was somewhere different – a little audience room that Maize Ear never uses.'

'So?' asked Kindly.

'So, it was tucked away in a quiet corner of the palace – against an outer wall.'

Nimble's eyes suddenly widened. 'You said the walls were covered with hangings! You think there was a secret doorway behind one of them – in the outer wall!'

'Someone would have noticed a draught,' Kindly said sceptically.

'Maybe nothing so crude as that. I think whatever's there must be covered up, most of the time, by something more than just a featherwork wall-hanging – but yes, that's about it. And the reason Mother of Light can turn up at the Council of Music from time to time and never get caught by Maize Ear's men is that by the time anybody finds out she's there – apart from her own little circle of admirers, who probably aren't all that eager to let on – she's had time to walk a little way into her bolt-hole and vanish without trace.'

Kindly stopped walking and frowned while he tried to make sense of what I was telling him. 'Very well,' he said slowly. 'I see that – I think. But it doesn't tell us where she goes, does it? How come no one's ever seen her coming out on the other side of the wall? And what about that old man – the one you say isn't her father? Where does he disappear off to?'

'I thought about that,' I told him, 'especially about the old man. You remember he ran away from that fight I had with the pedlars who'd been molesting them outside the market-place? His daughter didn't seem at all concerned about his going astray, and looking back on it that seemed odd – shouldn't she have been worried about the guards at the palace entrance picking him up when he went in? Both of them

must have somewhere to go that they can get into whether
they're inside the palace or outside, without anybody else ever
catching them at it. Now, I don't know Tetzcoco at all, but I
can think of one place that would suit their purpose admirably.
And there it is!'

We had almost reached Kindly's and my old lodgings, but
we were not going there. The building I was gesturing towards
stood a little behind them, half hidden by wild plants and neg-
lected bushes and fruit trees, alone, dark and silent.

Kindly let out a long, low breath. 'Ooooh!'

'I don't understand,' Nimble said.

The old man chuckled. 'Your father is a clever bugger, after
all! It's the deserted palace, the one that belonged to Hungry
Child's son, the one they strangled – Prince of Willows!'

The unfortunate young man's residence was as modest and
nondescript as a palace could be. It bore no resemblance to the
sprawling labyrinth that his father and grandfather had occupied, whose upper storey loomed over its roof. It seemed to
cling to the ground, as though trying to hide in the tangled
foliage that surrounded it. What I could see of its stuccoed
walls and the carved and painted friezes that topped them was
not impressive, the whitewash turned a dirty grey, the plaster
cracked and peeling, the paint faded and chipped.

We slunk across the overgrown ground surrounding the
palace, all keeping low to avoid being noticed, and crouched
or squatted by the main entrance.

'Well, we're not going in this way,' observed Kindly in a
whisper. The wide gateway was filled in and piled higher than
a tall man's head with rubble.

'More to the point, neither would Mother of Light,' I said.
'There has to be a way in and out, but it's bound to be well
hidden. We'll have to feel our way around the walls. The back

of this place abuts straight on to the King's palace, so it's only the front and sides we need to bother with. It shouldn't take long.'

I was wrong about that. Leaving Nimble to guard Little Hen, who had come with us this far but could not be made to understand what we were now up to, Kindly and I worked our way twice around the small palace's walls to no avail. The only other entrance we saw was as choked with masonry as the first, and apart from that there was no sign of anything that looked like a doorway or a secret passage. Kindly took to cursing and striking the wall beside him with his staff, sending dust and flakes of plaster through the air, but even that did no good.

'So much for that brilliant idea!' he complained.

'I don't understand it.' I stared at the obstinately blank wall in front of me. 'There has to be a way in. Let's go and talk to Nimble. We must be missing something obvious.'

'Like a big carved glyph saying "Secret Entrance Over Here",' muttered the old man as we wandered back towards our starting point.

Nimble was standing, looking about him with an air of desperation and calling something over and over again. I realized what he was saying, and the awful implications of it broke over me, just at the moment when I saw that he was alone.

'Ix Men! Ix Men!'

'Nimble! What happened?' I cried, breaking into a shambling run.

'She's gone!'

'Well, we can see that,' said Kindly from behind me. 'What happened?'

'I don't know. I only looked away for a moment. She was sitting down just over there, in that little hollow, not doing anything.' He indicated a small depression in the earth, about twenty paces from where we stood by the palace wall. I could see why the girl might have chosen to rest there: although it was surrounded by tall weeds and unkempt bushes, the place itself was as smooth and bare as if it had been swept.

'"A moment"?' Kindly repeated sceptically.

'It was just a glance! I'd just asked her – well, talking to myself, really – which corner of the building you'd be coming around, and when I looked back she'd gone!'

'Did you hear anything?' I asked.

'No.'

I walked over towards the spot he had shown us. I was not worried and only mildly annoyed. I presumed the girl had merely got bored and decided to play tricks on us; there was enough undergrowth around to tempt a bored child into a game of hide-and-seek. After all, I asked myself, what reason could the girl have for running away now? If she had wanted to be free of us, she could simply have wandered off while Nimble, Kindly and I were at Hare's house. It made no sense.

I balanced on the edge of the little depression, calling Little Hen's name softly.

A giggle came back in answer. The voice was high-pitched like a girl's, but it sounded hollow, as though she were in a narrow space.

Nimble and Kindly came up behind me. They were arguing.

'You can't just have looked away. What did she do, turn herself into an ant?'

'I'm telling you I did! She had the time it took to turn my head, no more!'

'Come on, admit it. You went off into those trees to take a leak.'

'I did not!'

'Will you two shut up?' I snapped. 'I'm trying to listen! Oh, it's gone now – I thought I heard her.'

'Where?' Nimble demanded eagerly.

'Try looking down,' Kindly suggested.

I stared at him, and then did as he told me. I saw it immediately: among the bushes, just on the far side of the clear area at my feet, there was a small hole, looking scarcely bigger than what a rabbit might have made.

A little, grinning face stared back at me.

'Little Hen!' I cried joyously. 'How did you get down there?'

'She must have fallen,' my son said, relief plain in his voice. He extended a hand to the girl and she clambered out, shedding earth and weeds on the ground around her.

'But into what?' I got on my hands and knees and inspected the hole. It was a little bigger than it had looked because it was overhung with foliage and a lip of earth, but nobody much larger than Little Hen could have got into it. 'This can't be what we're looking for, can it? It's too small.'

'It doesn't look like it,' my son agreed sadly. He got down on his knees beside me and began poking around in the tangled growth around the edges of the hole. 'Though this is odd – look. Some of these weeds look as if they've been trampled – no, pulled up, rather – they aren't rooted to anything.' He pulled aside a ragged mat of greenery to reveal what looked like a large square of bare earth, but was not.

'This is wood!'

'So are those trees,' Kindly muttered caustically.

'This is more like a plank.'

I hooked my fingers around an edge of the hole and began to pull gently. I felt the ground move under me.

'I think we're kneeling on a trapdoor,' I whispered.

A stranger answered me. A clear, deep male voice, with a touch of asperity in its tone.

'You are. And if you don't get off, it's likely to collapse under your weight!'

I leaped up and twisted to face the newcomer. I knew who
he was, though, even before I took in his appearance, despite
the fact that I had never heard his voice.

He looked a little different from when I had seen him
before, in his guise as Mother of Light's father. He was still an
old man, seemingly, his hair as white and his face as deeply
etched as before, but he no longer stooped. Standing upright
as he surveyed the four of us with bright and baleful eyes, he
was a head taller than I, and the steady hands that now held his
staff up in front of him like a weapon were firm, their strength
evident from their bulging tendons.

'Who are you, then?' Kindly asked coolly.

The tall man did not answer him. Instead he looked at me.
'You must be Yaotl the slave.'

I met his gaze for a moment, but it was too much. His eyes
threatened to sap my will. It was partly their steady, unblinking stare, which gave them superficially an air of authority, but
it was more than that. There was something compelling in
their rich, impenetrable darkness, something redolent of great
pain or grief somehow mastered but never forgotten.

On an impulse I fell to my knees, and then on to my face.
'Oh, lord! My lord! Oh, Great Lord!'

My son and Lily's father stood by, baffled, and Little Hen
laughed, but how else was I to greet the last great King of
Tetzcoco, Hungry Child himself, Lord Nezahualpilli?

15

Hungry Child oversaw the replacement of the foliage that had helped to camouflage his trapdoor. Then he himself opened the contraption.

'It's always been enough to deceive the casual eye,' he remarked ruefully, 'but not to fool a small child, it seems! Unfortunately, we had to leave a hole just big enough to see out of so that we could check there was no one about before we came up. Now, all of you, in you go, and be quick about it!'

'"We"?' Kindly repeated.

'But why?' asked Nimble.

'My lord . . .' I began, but we were all interrupted.

'Go on, before we're seen!'

As I clambered into the hole, I heard Kindly's muffled voice somewhere ahead of me, protesting: 'It's dark! I can't see where I'm going!'

'Just go forward,' Hungry Child told him as he dropped through the hole behind me, letting the trapdoor go at the same time. 'Follow the tunnel. It doesn't branch. Mother of Light will be waiting for us at the other end, although,' he added drily, 'what she'll make of all of you is something I couldn't answer for!'

Afterwards, I realized that our walk through the tunnel must have been short, little more than the distance between the hole Little Hen had found and the palace wall, a distance I had crossed in moments when I was above the ground. It was a different matter stumbling, stooping painfully, through total darkness, with only my fingertips to guide me as they brushed against earth walls and wooden props. I was tempted to turn back, but my way would have been entirely blocked by Hungry Child, who was plainly determined that, having come this far, we were going to finish our journey whether we wanted to or not. Judging by the complaints and curses coming from up ahead, I understood that Nimble and Kindly were no happier with their situation than I was with mine, but Little Hen, who was still just short enough to stand upright, treated the whole affair as a joke, laughing and chattering continually until we all saw a light in the distance and felt the ground under us beginning to rise as we approached the surface. She fell silent only as we emerged, blinking, into the middle of the palace courtyard.

One by one we came out, under Mother of Light's astonished gaze.

Hungry Child was the last to appear. Even before I saw him again I could hear his voice: 'Mother of Light, I think you may know these – well, the scrawny slave at the back, anyway. Isn't he the one we saw outside the marketplace, the fool who got himself into that fight with the pedlars, who came to see you at the palace the next day?'

The woman stood silently in the middle of the courtyard, surveying each of us in turn before reluctantly agreeing with Hungry Child. 'It looks like him,' she conceded. 'I don't know these others. Though the girl . . .'

The former King came to stand by her. 'Ah, yes, the girl.' Leaning forward, he took Little Hen's chin in one hand and tilted it upwards. 'Mayan, of course. So I wonder . . .'

I decided that it was time for me to take a hand before this mysterious man, who had once ruled a large part of the valley and whose powers now I could barely guess at, decided that he had everything he wanted from us. 'My lord, if Mother of Light told you who I am, then she will have told you why I am here, and about the evidence I need to help my mistress. If this girl has what you need, then I ask you . . .'

Hungry Child looked around at me, his eyebrows rising as though he had forgotten I was there and my presence came as a surprise.

'"Ask"?' he repeated. 'What makes you think you're here to ask for things? Now you've brought me the girl. Well done! I'll take her off your hands, and Mother of Light will give you something to eat, and then you can go on your way.'

'But, my lord!' I stammered desperately. 'Don't you understand? I need whatever is in that girl's head! Lily's trial may have started already. We haven't time . . .'

'Oh, I think we have,' the King said coldly. 'I've waited years for this. I have all the time in the World!'

Beside me, Nimble started forward, a protest forming on his lips. I stilled it with a restraining hand, but for a moment could think of nothing to say myself. It was Kindly who spoke for us, more mildly than I would have expected.

'At the very least, you might let us hear what she's got to say.'

Hungry Child looked at him for a moment before responding with a thin smile. 'I might. Very well, then. Let's hear it.'

Mother of Light led the way out of the courtyard, through a portico and into a large, echoing hall. Our heels stirred up clouds of dust that swirled around us before settling at the feet of the statues lining the walls.

'I'm afraid that with just the two of us here, we haven't been able to keep the place up as well as I should have liked,' said Hungry Child. 'All we can offer you is a couple of cold tortillas that Mother of Light bought this morning. We can't have a fire here in case anyone sees the smoke.'

'Father . . .' Mother of Light's face formed a warning frown as we squatted on a few mats in the middle of the floor, the old King among us.

'You needn't call me father now, at least not here. They seem to know who I am.' As the woman's expression softened, Hungry Child looked at me keenly. 'I'd be interested to know how.'

As the woman broke a pair of tortillas in two and shared them out among her four guests, I thought about my answer. Was it worth trying to trade it for a promise of help for Lily? I decided it was not. Hungry Child had been right, I realized, cursing myself for a naive fool: he had as much time as he wanted to learn whatever it was Little Hen had to say, and if I tried to hold out on him he might simply refuse to share it with us, and then we would have nothing at all. 'There were a few clues,' I told him. 'Mother of Light let it drop that there was someone else behind her – it was only a slip of the tongue,' I added hastily, seeing the King's frown and the woman's blush, 'but it was enough. Then you seemed remarkably spry for a man as old as you looked, when you took on those two pedlars and afterwards, when you disappeared in the marketplace.'

Hungry Child gave a wry chuckle. 'I knew I would end up playing a trick like that once too often! But it's so easy to do, when everyone thinks you'll drop dead from shortness of breath if you have to take another step, so they don't bother watching you . . . Go on.'

'Then I worked out how you and Mother of Light were able to come and go without even Maize Ear's spies knowing about it. It's obvious that you sneak in and out quickly, and I'd guess that apart from your occasional sessions among the poets and musicians—' I looked at Mother of Light '—you only do it when you have to and try to be as quick as possible. But that wouldn't be enough. You had to have some secret exit that came out in a place where no one would look – such as this palace. And that meant two things. I knew you must know the royal palace intimately – better than anyone else. And if you were using this place, it meant you were prepared to defy your own edict forbidding anyone from coming here.'

'And who else would dare defy such an order, except the man who gave it?' He sighed. 'You were right, obviously. Very clever! You have tracked us down to this empty palace that belonged to my favourite son – fitting, don't you think, for the man who once ruled all the Acolhuans, and not a few other people too, to have to spend his days surrounded by reminders of his most painful loss?' He glanced at Mother of Light. She returned his look, and I had the feeling that something passed between them then that was beyond my understanding: not just a shared appreciation of his troubles, but something else, a secret. 'So now, as you say, I am reduced to sneaking in and out of my own palace, while Mother of Light snatches what opportunities she can to preserve my songs and poems from withering away entirely. Can you imagine anything worse for a poet than finding his work has died even before he has?'

'It was your choice – my lord.'

Kindly added bluntly, between mouthfuls of tortilla: 'Yes, and while we're on the subject – you're supposed to be dead. Why aren't you?'

Nimble spoke up too. 'I was told you'd died at your retreat in Tetzcotzinco. Someone described your funeral to me.'

Hungry Child shut his eyes. 'Oh, my funeral. Yes. I heard it was magnificent, and about all the slaves and concubines they killed to keep me company in the Land of the Dead. I wish they hadn't, it was such a waste, since I hadn't gone there. Do

you suppose they'll be waiting for me when . . .? Perhaps not.'
He opened his eyes, glanced quickly at Mother of Light again,
and gave a mock grimace. 'But as for why – there were things
I wanted to do that would have been difficult had I still been
King of Tetzcoco. And there was no future in it anyway. If
only Maize Ear and Black Flower realized that, they might stop
squabbling over the throne!'

'What do you mean?' I asked.

He turned those dark, troubled eyes on me and answered
me with a bleak certainty that defied me to doubt him, however much I wanted to.

'I mean our World is dying.'

I heard my son gasp. 'You mean the Sun is coming to an
end?' he cried fearfully. I looked at him in surprise, and then
recalled that, as the youngest, he would have the most to lose
if the present age of the World were to run its course soon.

We believed the World had been created and destroyed four
times. Each succeeding age was named after the birthday of the
Sun that shone upon it. The Sun of our fifth age was called
Four Motion, and prophesied to end in the way that its name
implied: with earthquakes that would shatter the land and
cleanse it of all life.

'No, I don't mean that,' the old King said, but there was
nothing reassuring about his tone. 'The land will remain, but
what will perish is the World of the Aztecs, of the Tepanecs, of
the Acolhuans – everything we know and value. I heard of all
the portents, saw what was in the heavens, looked at the calendars. Something is coming – not this year, or next, but
perhaps a little after that – that will sweep it all away.'

I felt a chill, realizing that I had heard similar things before,
from the lips of another ruler. 'My lord, do you mean the
strangers from beyond the Divine Sea? The pale-skinned men
with beards? Montezuma told me of them. He knows they are

coming. He believes they may be gods, come to call him to account.'

'Montezuma? Ha!' Hungry Child screwed up his face in an expression of disgust at the mention of the Aztec Emperor's name. 'What does he know? Who do you think told him how to interpret the omens to begin with? He fancies himself as a seer, you know, but still he came to me to learn what they meant. And then, when I told him, he wouldn't believe me! Did you know I bet him my kingdom against three turkey hens that I was right?'

'How were you going to know who'd won?' Kindly asked drily.

'We played a ball-game match, so that the gods would tell us through the outcome. Best out of three. I won.' He scowled in mock outrage. 'I never did see those turkeys, though!'

Nimble asked: 'What will they do, these strangers?'

'I don't know,' the King said frankly. 'But there are rumours. There are islands out there, on the Divine Sea, and there are – or were – people living on them. Savages, of course. Occasionally the Mayans tell tales of canoes washed up on their beaches, filled with desperate, terrified refugees. Some of them are diseased, some are wounded, in strange and dreadful ways – bitten by creatures with jaws like giant dogs', or their flesh torn and bones broken by small stones, like slingshots but thrown much, much harder.'

I found it hard to follow what he was saying: I could barely hold in my head this picture of bizarre, alien carnage in a place beyond the edge of the World. But there was one word I seized upon.

"Mayans," you said. This girl is Mayan.' I beckoned to Little Hen. 'Is she what you have been waiting for? Does she have the message you were trying to buy from Hare?'

He leaned a little towards the girl, scrutinizing her through narrowed eyes. 'Maybe,' he said slowly. 'Tell me how she came to be with you.'

I began to relate the story. It took a long time, and Kindly and Nimble did not help; they merely glowered at the King in resentful silence. By the time I had finished, however, Hungry Child knew most of what had happened to us all since the day we had come to Tetzcoco.

At the end I looked at him imploringly. 'My lord, do you understand now why whatever Little Hen has to say is so important to us?'

'I heard as much from Mother of Light,' he replied, before adding indifferently: 'I hope you haven't put too much faith in this little girl, however. What she knows may not be of much help to your mistress.'

I stared at him. 'But Mother of Light said . . .'

He held up a hand to silence me. 'I know. She said it was unlikely to be anything that Maize Ear or Black Flower should be afraid of. And I think she was right, but just remember that my sons may not see it that way.' He smiled at the girl, eliciting a grin in response. 'But let's hear what she has to say before we draw any conclusions about it, shall we?'

Then he began to speak to her.

As I listened to him, to her answering squeal of delight, to her giggle, quickly stifled, and then to the words that came tumbling out of her mouth in response to his, I felt my jaw drop in amazement. Looking about me, I saw my reaction mirrored in my companions' faces. Only Mother of Light seemed unsurprised, watching the old King, her lover, with a look of something like pride.

The conversation went on for a long time. Of course, I understood none of the strange, guttural words, but I could watch and interpret what Hungry Child's face and hands were doing. He spoke slowly and haltingly, frowning in concentration as if he were struggling to recall the phrase he wanted from his memory. He leaned eagerly towards the girl and his hands clenched and unclenched excitedly.

Little Hen seemed to be warming to her topic, whatever it was. She made gestures to accompany her words. There were sharp, stabbing motions, accompanied by joyous cries, that I suspected might be connected with the story of Hare's death. Then a hand waved in Nimble's direction, perhaps to illustrate the tale of her rescue from the marketplace. Finally there were some gestures that I could not interpret. She repeated the curious actions we had observed at the house at Huexotla, at one point tugging at her hair and later pulling on her eyelids to make that by-now-familiar round shape. Then she plucked at her chin, and finally she began rubbing her cheeks and temples, as though scrubbing them vigorously to rid them of some deeply ingrained stain.

Eventually the pace of the conversation began to slacken. There were a few short exchanges of words – final questions from Hungry Child and their answers, I guessed – and both of them fell silent.

There was a long pause. Hungry Child rubbed his chin thoughtfully.

Eventually Nimble asked: 'My lord, how did you learn her language?' Curiosity had overcome his resentment at the King's high-handedness.

'I told you there were things I wanted to do that would be difficult if I were still King. I wanted to know more about the things we were speaking about – the omens, the disaster, whatever it is, that is threatening to overwhelm us all. Not in the hope of averting it – that's impossible. It will come – the portents are clear about that – but perhaps some of us may live through it, and there may be ways to prepare.

'I knew it was to come from the East, from the shores of the

Divine Sea, but that was all. So I set out to learn everything I could about the country around there, both the land and the people – their customs, their politics, even their languages. Before I staged my death I took the precaution of having my dwarfs bring every screenfold book and piece of paper in the royal library concerning that part of the World to this palace, in secret. Of course, I knew they would be sacrificed at my funeral, and so the secret is safe.'

Kindly said: 'So you had yourself taught this girl's language?'

'Among others. Whenever I heard of an envoy or merchant from the East, I would have him questioned. I was able to pick up at least a smattering of some of the dialects from these people. Having a reputation as a man with a thirst for learning meant I could do this without arousing suspicion. What I intended to do, you see, was to go there – that's why I couldn't be King any more. I meant to spend the rest of my years tracking this thing down, and that would have left Tetzcoco leaderless.'

'Why the secrecy?' I asked. 'Why not simply abdicate, or appoint a regent?'

'So that my successor would have the authority to defend his kingdom. The people – in this city and in others – have to know that he rules in his own right, not in the name of another, who is far away and may be dead.' He looked at us significantly, and I understood what he meant: he wanted his Aztec hearers to understand that the person his kingdom most needed defending from was our own Emperor Montezuma, who wanted to strip away its last trappings of independence. 'Sadly, my sons have turned out not to be up to the task.'

'That's your fault,' Kindly said. 'You didn't nominate a successor!'

The King looked startled at the old man's accusation, and his eyes flashed angrily, but he seemed to relent straight away. 'I know,' he said regretfully. 'I thought, after seeing what was to come, that to choose one of my sons to succeed me would be to give him a death sentence. Kings and emperors don't often survive having their rule overturned. I didn't expect things to turn out the way they have . . . but it's too late to change my mind now.'

I was watching Little Hen playing with her maimed doll. She had brought the toy with her all the way from Huexotla, via the skirmish at Hare's house. I wondered just how far they had come together.

'I didn't understand everything she told me,' Hungry Child said, as though he had overheard my thoughts. 'I'm not that familiar with her dialect, and she talks very quickly! I'll need to speak to her again, at greater length, but I picked some of it up. Originally, she came from somewhere called Chactemal, near the coast of the Divine Sea in the East. Very different country from ours; it's low-lying, very hot, overgrown, and it rains almost all year round.'

'I've heard of the place,' Kindly said. 'They grow cocoa there.'

'Now, this little girl, Ix Men – what do you call her?'

'Little Hen,' I supplied.

'Little Hen's father seems to have been some minor chieftain who fell foul of the King. Of course, that's not the way she put it – he was a great ruler, according to her, but, anyway, it does- n't matter. The important thing is that her father was sacrificed, and his household broken up and its members sold into slavery.'

'When would this have been?' Nimble asked curiously.

'She's a bit vague about dates, but perhaps three or four years ago.'

'So she'd have been about seven or eight years old.' My son sighed sympathetically. The events the former King was describing must have represented a common enough occur- rence among barbarians, but no doubt Nimble was thinking of what the little girl must have gone through at the time.

'About that,' Hungry Child said indifferently. 'She seems to have passed through several owners since then. I have the impression that she was a little too wilful for some of them, and she seems to have run off altogether at least once. Why she wasn't sacrificed to one of their gods I don't know, but I suppose she's a fine-looking creature by their standards, and too valuable to waste.'

Nimble was getting restless, fidgeting uncomfortably and biting his lip, and I spoke up on purpose to cut off an outburst that I knew he would quickly have regretted. 'So how did Hare get hold of her?'

'A Mayan merchant took her to Cozumel, a big island just off the coast where there's an Aztec warehouse, and she caught his eye there. After spending so long among the Mayans, I suppose he'd got used to their notions of beauty, but it can't have been long before he realized that what she had to say might be worth money in the right places. So Hare bought her, and soon after that he brought her back here.

'He was a nasty piece of work, this Hare. Very unpleasant tastes.' He raised his eyebrows at my son's troubled expression. 'Well, that isn't a surprise, is it? You must have guessed as much for yourselves. And he went to extraordinary lengths to keep the girl's existence secret. She spent most of the journey from the Mayan country to Tetzcoco in a wicker basket and was only let out at night when no one was looking. Then when she got here Hare rented a house in a quiet suburb, far away from where the merchants usually congregate, and made her hide in a hole he'd dug in the floor.'

Nimble could contain himself no longer. 'Little Hen!' he cried reproachfully. 'How could you let him? Why didn't you run away – you'd done it before!'

'Easy, son,' I said gently. 'I don't suppose Hare was the first. And you know why she didn't run. Where would she have gone, and what would she have done for food? It wasn't like living among her own people. She'd have been alone in a strange city, where no one spoke her language – except Hare, and she'd have been used to him.' I looked at Hungry Child for confirmation.

'True enough. But it seems she did take matters into her own hands eventually, doesn't it? She broke a leg off that doll and used those viper's teeth of hers to turn it into a weapon. I think you've already worked out what happened then. She was babbling too quickly for me to get the details.'

'We think she heard Hare fighting with an intruder, surprised the other man, and then killed Hare when he told her to get back in her hole,' I said.

Hungry Child raised his eyebrows in surprise. 'Quite an achievement! I suppose her blood was up by then.'

'She's not exactly shy of a fight,' I said. 'So we know where she came from.' I looked keenly at Hungry Child. 'But what did she see? What was this message of hers?'

Hungry Child frowned. 'I'm not sure. I think I know – but as I said, I need to talk to her further, and think about what she says in the light of the omens. I think . . . No, I need to be sure.'

Kindly said: 'All right, put it another way. Whatever it is, what is it to Maize Ear and Black Flower? Why have they been prepared to go to such lengths?'

Hungry Child sighed sadly. 'Because they are both foolish, vain young men. You know how careful Hare was to keep the nature of his message a secret – even the manner of its delivery. They both learned through their spies that he had information to sell, and they both wanted it – or, rather, I suppose each of them was determined to see that the other didn't get it.'

So Lily, unknowingly acting as a go-between for the supposedly dead King of Tetzcoco, was to be sacrificed to a petty squabble between two of his sons over something that neither of them truly wanted. 'We have to go,' I said. 'The trial is today, isn't it? We have to get the girl to Obsidian Tongue. It may not be too late.'

Kindly, Nimble and I all began to rise. The King remained in his place, and when Little Hen showed signs of getting up as well, he motioned her to stay where she was.

'My lord,' I said, keeping my voice level, 'the girl!'

'You can't take her,' he said mildly.

'We have to.' I looked at my companions. Lily's father looked grim but determined. Nimble silently produced his knife. 'I'm sorry, but we need her. If it has to be by force . . .'

In one smooth movement Hungry Child stood up and cast his cloak aside. He flexed his muscles deliberately. For a man in his fifties he was in remarkable condition.

'Look, we don't want a fight,' I said uncertainly, 'but we are three against one.'

'Two,' said a voice behind me. I had forgotten about Mother of Light. I whirled to find her confronting me with a hefty flint knife. 'Your son's leg has obviously been hurt already, and I doubt that the old man amounts to much.'

'You don't need the girl,' Hungry Child said. 'She's of no use to you.'

'She's our only witness!' I cried desperately as I turned to face him. 'Without her we can't prove Lily's innocence! If the judges don't know what that message is really about, they'll kill her!'

'They're not going to learn anything about the message from the girl,' he snapped, his patience clearly running low. 'For one thing, how are they going to understand what she's saying?'

I gaped stupidly at him. 'But . . . but they must have, I don't know, interpreters?' I stammered.

'For her particular dialect of Mayan? I very much doubt it. I shouldn't think there's anyone in this city who can understand her at the moment, apart from me.'

'We have to take the chance,' I said. 'It's the only hope we have.'

'Besides, what do you think will happen to the girl once the story of her and Hare comes out? She killed him, remember. A respectable merchant stabbed to death by a slave, and a half-wild barbarian at that. She'll be killed out of hand. I can't let that happen – there's too much I have to learn from her yet.'

'Not really our concern,' growled Kindly. 'You and she will just have to take your chances.'

'No!' cried Nimble, horrified.

'Look, this is my daughter we're talking about!'

'Quiet, both of you!' I cried. My mind was suddenly in turmoil. To have come so close to fulfilling my plan, in spite of all the obstacles that had been put in the way of it, only to have it come apart now was unthinkable. Yet the King's words had got through to me. I pictured Little Hen in one of the palace's huge, echoing halls, staring blankly at the judges on their high-backed chairs as they tried to interrogate her in a language that must sound as much like a baby's babbling to her as hers did to us. Then I imagined the same judges enquiring where this child had come from, and their indignation mounting to murderous wrath as they learned the truth.

'He's right, Kindly,' I said softly. 'We can't take her. It wouldn't do any good.'

He rounded on me. 'What are you talking about? This was all your idea, remember? You brought us here so we could find out what the girl had to say. You said all along that finding Hare's message was Lily's only hope. Now we've got it. It may not be much, but it's all we have. We've got to risk it, Yaotl – there's nothing else we can do!'

For a moment I could only look helplessly at the indignant old man while I tried to think of something to say. Finally I turned to Hungry Child. 'What will happen to the girl now?'

'She can stay here until I've learned what I can from her.'

'But you said you wanted to go to the land of the Mayans,' Nimble reminded the King. 'Are you going to take her with you, or what?'

Hungry Child looked exasperated. 'Of course not! You think I want to be responsible for a child on a journey like that? No, I expect I shall just let her go . . . Or something.'

'You can't leave her alone in this city! She wouldn't last a morning!'

'Maybe not, but that's not my fault. It was Hare who brought her here, not me.'

Then Nimble rounded on me. 'Look what you've done!' he cried. 'It's bad enough if we can't help Lily, but you had to bring the girl here, and now she's going to be abandoned. Have you any idea what they were going to do with her, in the marketplace?'

'All right, all right,' I said wearily, hoping to head off yet another argument. I drew a hand over my eyes and took several deep breaths, forcing myself to think. Then I appealed to Mother of Light.

'Are you just going to let this happen? Lily's going to be executed because we can't convince the court that the message she was trying to get to you was innocent. Even if we can't change that, you might at least try to do something for the girl.'

'But Hungry Child is right,' the woman said slowly. 'You said as much yourself.' She was not looking at me, however. Instead, she had her eyes fixed on the King, and it was only when I intercepted the glance that passed between them that it occurred to me to wonder just why he had kept this one among all his concubines and wives by him since his pretended death. He could not hold her gaze for long.

'I don't know what you expect me to do,' he muttered. 'It's Maize Ear you'd have to convince, you know that. And I can't show myself to him. It would be too dangerous.'

'He wouldn't have the nerve!' Nimble cried. 'You're his father!'

'He doesn't have to believe I am who I am. More to the point, he wouldn't want to believe it. I'd need to convince him of the truth before he set eyes on me. Of course, if we still had Jade Doll's ring, I could have sent him that.'

'How would that have helped?' I asked.

'After she was executed, Hungry Child always wore her ring,' Mother of Light explained.

'It was to remind me of my own stupidity,' the King added, 'in the hope that I wouldn't be taken in so easily again! It was supposed to have been buried with me, but I managed to save it. I know Maize Ear would recognize it if he saw it. But we needed something distinctive to give to Hare as a token, something that was valuable enough to convince him we would be good for whatever price he wanted for the message. That was the point about the ring: there's nothing else in the World like it. Hare wouldn't have known what it was, of course, not being from around here, but he'd realize how valuable it must be. Nobody who did know it could fail to recognize it. But now it's lost.'

'A ring . . .' Kindly murmured. 'This is the first I've heard about it,' he said, looking at me reproachfully.

'Lily swore me to secrecy,' I told him.

'Oh. Um, what did it look like, this ring?'

I glanced at him curiously. He sounded unlike himself all of a sudden. His manner was hesitant, almost diffident, and he kept looking at the floor.

'It was a big greenstone carved like a skull,' Mother of Light said.

'Why do you want to know?' I asked.

His answer was to fumble about in his breechcloth for a moment before producing a large gold ring. It boasted a single jewel: an enormous, flawless greenstone.

The stone was carved in the shape of a skull.

It was a while before anyone was able to say anything. Even the King was speechless. Finally I managed to say, in a weak voice: 'Where did you get that?'

'I found it.'

'What do you mean, you found it? Where?'

'Hare's house. I told you – didn't I? – the first thing you do when you go into a merchant's house is look for the hiding places. I searched a few favourites of mine and Lily's while you and Nimble were skulking about in the bushes behind the courtyard. Sure enough, this thing was pushed into the plaster by the doorframe – hammered in quite firmly, actually. Someone had taken a bit of trouble getting it in there.' Correctly interpreting my look, he added defensively: 'Well, nobody told me it was important! I thought it might help me pay Obsidian Tongue's fee.'

'Why, you stupid, greedy old . . .'

'You should have said! I can't be expected to know everything. What am I, a bloody magician?'

I snatched the ring from him impatiently and turned to Hungry Child. 'My lord, we have your ring. What now?'

'Give me that,' he snapped.

'No.'

He took a step towards me. 'Give it to me, or I will take it from you,' he snarled.

I backed away, conscious of the fact that Mother of Light and her flint knife were very close. Out of the corners of my eyes I saw Nimble tense and Kindly straighten his back as best he could, his swollen knuckles clenched around his staff. Only Little Hen, still playing idly and muttering to herself where she squatted on the floor, seemed oblivious to the sudden change in mood.

It was hopeless, I thought, and then, because I could think of nothing better to do, I put the ring in my mouth.

'If I swallow this,' I mumbled, 'you won't get it back in a hurry!'

The King looked shocked. 'What?'

I repeated my threat. I was not sure whether he was surprised by my action or confused by my indistinct speech.

'You're bluffing,' he declared. 'You can't swallow that, it's too big! You'll choke! Mother of Light . . .'

He was right, of course, and for a terrifying moment I knew I was beaten, because no matter how hard I tried I could not get the thing on to the back of my tongue, never mind down my throat. But then Mother of Light responded.

'No, my lord,' she said suddenly, and I heard a thump as she dropped the knife. 'We can't do this.'

He seemed nonplussed. 'What did you say?'

'Haven't you always said we couldn't skulk around in this empty palace for ever, and the time would come when you had to show yourself? Maybe now's the time. If we can get the ring to Maize Ear, he'll have to acknowledge you for who you are. Then he'll do anything you ask him to, so long as you promise to leave him alone!'

'We'd have to leave Tetzcoco altogether!' he protested.

'But that's what you intended to do all along.'

The King hesitated. He made a curious spectacle, this man who had ruled an empire and still had the air of a monarch, now apparently tongue-tied before a woman. In the end he said, in a small voice: 'What about the girl? I haven't finished with her.'

'Take her with us. I'll look after her.'

I spat the ring out on to my hand. As I reached automatically for an end of my breechcloth to wipe the saliva off it, I said: 'So how about it, my lord? You ask Maize Ear for our lives in return for the ring.'

He looked at me thoughtfully. 'I will need the ring now, though. I have to get it to Maize Ear before I see him. That isn't going to be easy.'

I looked at him suspiciously. Before I could voice my doubts, however, he suddenly dropped on one knee, touched the ground with his fingers and put them to his lips.

'I will eat earth,' he intoned. 'Tlaltecuhtli, Lord of the Earth, will bear witness that I will do as I say. So will the Giver of Life, the Lord of the Near and the Nigh.' He stood up again. 'Will that satisfy you? I will ask my son for your lives, and your mistress's. Of course, I can make no promise about his reply.'

'It will satisfy me . . . my lord,' I said. I held out the hand with the ring in it, ignoring an angry noise from Kindly.

'Thank you.' He looked fondly at the ring as it rested in his hand. 'Of course,' he murmured as though to himself, 'I can't take it myself. Nor can Mother of Light. It has to be someone who isn't known to him or his spies.'

'I'll go,' said Nimble.

The King looked up at him, frowning, as though he suspected a trick.

'Wait a moment,' I said. 'Let's think about this.'

'I've thought about it, Father. Kindly's too old and too slow. Maize Ear's spies know you, and they'll have you in a cage before you get near Tetzcotzinco. I'm the only one who can do it.'

'What about your leg?' I asked dubiously. 'You'd have to go all the way to Tetzcotzinco. Can you manage that?' Nimble's wound looked healthy enough, and very little blood had soaked through his dressing, but it was a long journey. It might take half a day even for someone who was not already limping slightly.

'I'll have to,' the young man said. 'My Lord,' he added, turning to the King, 'I will eat earth too.'

Hungry Child looked at the ring again, seemingly reluctant to part with it again after having it in his hand for so short a time. Then, suddenly, he handed it over.

'It's a simple message you have to convey,' he said. 'You let it be known that the ring's owner will be calling on his son this evening.' He took the ring from me and passed it to my son. 'You'd better go out the way you came in, and mind no one sees you!'

As Nimble vanished into the darkness, Kindly asked: 'What's the quickest way into the palace?'

'Why do you want to know that?' asked Hungry Child.

'Because my daughter's on trial there. The least I can do is go and watch!'

'I don't think you should. It could be dangerous for anyone associated with her.'

'So what? Yaotl here kindly pointed out to me once that she's all I've got left. Besides, most of my wealth has gone on paying that lawyer I found for her. I'd like to know if I'm getting my money's worth.'

'There may be a problem with that,' I warned him.

'What do you mean?'

Shamefacedly, I mumbled my way through an account of my last meeting with Obsidian Tongue, when the lawyer had been so enraged that Hunter had to pull him off me.

Kindly groaned. 'Oh, wonderful! That's the last thing we need! In that case we'd both better get over there now, Yaotl. You're a fast talker, aren't you? Know any law? You may be needed!'

'If you really intend going into the palace,' Hungry Child told us, 'then Mother of Light will show you how. But you ought to think again. There's nothing you can do.'

He was right, of course, and Kindly and I both knew it. But neither of us could stomach the prospect of waiting, sequestered inside this eerily empty palace, with only the ghosts of Prince of Willows and the Lady of Tollan for company, while the old King went about his mysterious business and his son's judges mulled over Lily's fate. And however fervently I hoped we had done enough to save her, I knew that if she was condemned by the court, then there was nothing between her and death except the whim of the young King.

Mother of Light showed us the way into Maize Ear's palace. The arrangement was as ingenious as anyone could have wished for. A short underground passageway led straight into the small room I had seen her in two days before. At its end, a stone slab was set into its roof. As this pivoted above our heads, I realized that the King's own chair was mounted on it. It was just as well, I thought, as Kindly and I clambered up into the room, that Maize Ear spent so much time in Tetzcotzinco.

The passageway outside was empty. I had worried briefly that Rattlesnake's men might have been watching it, since, of course, I had told their chief where I had had my meeting with Mother of Light. It gave me a small feeling of satisfaction to reflect that the fight at Hare's house had probably left them with more pressing things to worry about.

Mother of Light left us there with directions to the hall where we would find the Supreme Legal Council in session.

16

The Supreme Legal Council of the Kingdom of Tetzcoco met in the very heart of the royal palace. It was approached across a paved courtyard large enough to be called a plaza. Looking at the broad square of sky overhead, I could see the summit of a pyramid and a wisp of smoke drifting away from its temple fire. I wondered how many of the people I saw in front of me would glance up at it and see in it, as I did, a reminder that however many clever words might be exchanged in a place like this, it was the arbitrary will of the gods that would prevail in the end. Then I looked at the people more closely and decided that most of them were too wrapped up in their own immediate concerns to trouble themselves about anything beyond simply getting through the rest of the day. Most were commoners, although here and there the tall feathered headdress of a lord or distinguished warrior reared proudly above the mass of otherwise bare heads. Most stood, although a few squatted, perhaps wearied after spending the best part of the morning on their feet waiting for their cases to be called. Some chattered nervously to their neighbours, while others stood apart, staring at the ground in brooding silence.

'These will all be parties to disputes of some kind,' I said to Kindly, recalling what Obsidian Tongue had told me. 'Arguments about slaves, land, status, what kind of cloth your cloak can be made of, that sort of thing. The criminals – the people accused of crimes, I mean – will be in their cages.' I shuddered as I recalled the little box I had last seen Lily in.

'Are they really going to get through this lot today?' the old man asked incredulously.

'They have to. The law is that all cases have to be disposed of in eighty days, and this is the last day. And the day after tomorrow is the first of the Useless Days, remember? The courts can't sit then, and the King has to preside over all appeals and witness sentences being carried out before they begin.'

'And you don't argue during the Useless Days, either, if you know what's good for you,' the old man recalled. 'A bit of a problem if you're trying to hold a trial, I should think.'

'Anyway, many of these people will have had their cases heard before and have come back today for the verdict. And there's more than one court sitting – there are a dozen judges, but they sit in pairs, one lord, one commoner. And two of them preside over the others and report direct to the King.'

'That'll do,' the old man said testily. 'If I want a lecture in law I'll ask Obsidian Tongue. Where is he, anyway?'

I saw one or two people whose dress and demeanour resembled what I had come to associate with lawyers, but not the man we were relying on to defend Lily. 'I don't know. Better find an official and see if we can find out what's happening.'

'I'll try one of the guards over there.'

A broad flight of steps led from the plaza up to the hall where the judges sat. Kindly mounted them to speak briefly to a cudgel-wielding warrior standing at the top of them. I saw him start at the guard's answer, and then he began beckoning me urgently.

'We were almost too late!' he said when I had pushed my

way through the crowd to join him. 'She's in there already.' He paused. 'In the inner room – whatever that means.'

I felt a chill and tried not to shiver in response.

'It's where the most senior judges sit,' I said. 'They try only the gravest of crimes. Like plotting against the King.'

We were ushered through the colonnade that fronted the hall into the largest room I had ever been in. It was a vast, echoing space, its roof held up by rows of square pillars and entire cypress trunks laid flat across the tops of its walls. It was almost as crowded as the plaza outside, but here the people seemed to have more sense of purpose: messengers and officials hurried back and forth; lawyers and their clients exchanged urgent words; grim-faced warriors conducted prisoners to where they were to meet their accusers. It was extraordinarily quiet. The people around me spoke in reverential whispers, and their words seemed to vanish directly into the ceiling.

I barely had time to take any of this in as we were hurried through the room towards a small doorway at its end. It was guarded by two tall warriors whose richly embroidered cotton cloaks and extravagantly plumed headdresses spoke of their military experience. It was not immediately obvious why highly skilled veterans bearing vicious-looking swords were needed for guard duty such as this, which any tall man wielding a cudgel should have been good for, but I guessed they were there to inspire awe. They were scarcely needed: merely to approach that doorway was to feel my stomach churning and my knees turning to water.

'Who are you and what do you want?' one of the guards asked in a bored voice. When you look as frightening as he did, I reflected, you do not need to shout.

'We're here for the trial of Tiger Lily, the merchant's daughter,' I said.

'So?'

I looked at Kindly, who was already beginning to twitch with indignation. 'This man's her father,' I said.

'What's that got to do with it?'

Kindly uttered a curious squawking sound. 'Now look here!' he cried. 'That's my daughter in there. You've got to let me in!'

'No, I haven't,' the warrior said without moving. 'And if you don't watch yourself I'll have you thrown out of the palace altogether.'

The old man's face was turning darker by the moment, and I could see his fists clenching as if he were about to strike somebody. Seeing that this would have done no good at all, I said hastily: 'Look, just tell us this, please. Who is allowed through that door?'

The guard swivelled his huge head in my direction and regarded me coldly for a moment. Then he reeled off a list: 'Court officials, the King, judges, lawyers, witnesses, parties to the dispute. Oh, and prisoners, naturally.' He glanced sideways at Kindly. 'Nothing in the rules about relatives. Now, does any of what I've just said sound like you? Because if it doesn't, you're in the wrong place.'

Without thinking, I blurted out: 'I'm a witness! I was there when she was arrested!'

The man frowned. It was the first change I had seen in his expression. He glanced at his colleague, who spoke for the first time: 'A witness? On whose side?'

'I've got the woman's father with me. Whose side do you think we're on?'

'Well, you never know.' The two men looked at one another again. They looked so much alike that they might have been twins. 'Who's her lawyer?' one of them asked suspiciously.

'Obsidian Tongue,' Kindly growled. 'At least, he'd better be, with all the money I've given him!' He shot me a reproachful look, to remind me of the row I had had with the lawyer the last time I had met him.

'Wait here,' muttered one of the guards. He vanished, while his colleague moved to stand in the middle of the doorway, holding his sword across his chest with one glittering row of obsidian blades pointing suggestively at my neck.

A moment later the first guard was back. He was not alone. Obsidian Tongue almost pushed him out of the way.

'You!' he bawled, staring at me.

Kindly stepped forward. 'Obsidian Tongue! You're here! What's . . .'

The lawyer ignored him. 'You'd better get in here, fast!' he snapped. He reached out as if to grab my cloak and drag me through the doorway by it.

'Not so fast!' snapped the guard. 'Is this man a witness or not?'

The lawyer turned to him, heaved an exasperated sigh and snapped: 'What do you mean, "a witness?" He's the only bloody witness!'

'The only . . .? What are you talking about?' I began, completely confused, but Obsidian Tongue had already turned his back and was heading back into the room. I followed mutely, and the guards stood aside for me, although they had stepped smartly back into their places before Kindly had a chance to move.

'Wait!' he called out plaintively. 'What about me?'

If anybody answered him, I did not hear it. I had already been ushered into the courtroom, and the sights and sounds that surrounded me in there drove any thought of what might be happening outside from my head entirely.

'Where's Lily?' I demanded, the moment Obsidian Tongue and I were through the door.

I got no answer. Before I could say or see anything more, Obsidian Tongue had thrown himself face down on the floor. On the way he plucked with one hand at the hem of my cloak, as though trying to drag me down with him. I took the hint.

'My lords!' he cried into the floor.

There was a brief pause before a clear, perfectly modulated tenor voice, which I thought must belong to one of the judges, sang back: 'Obsidian Tongue! This is most extraordinary behaviour! I do trust you can explain it.'

'Stay on your face until I tell you to get up,' the lawyer hissed at me as an aside. Then, having obviously risen at least as far as his knees, since his speech was no longer muffled, he addressed the judges again.

'My lords, I apologize. I had an urgent message that there had been a development in the case. May I ask for a short adjournment?'

A different, gruffer voice, that of the other judge, answered him. 'If it means we might actually be able to have a trial afterwards, that can only be to the good!'

'Wait, Yolyamanitzin,' said the judge with the tenor voice. I hoped the name 'Just Man' suited his colleague's nature. 'What do you want an adjournment for?'

'My Lord Xayacaxolochatl, I believe I may be able to call a witness on my client's behalf.' The name meant 'Wrinkled Face'.

'Ah, it's about time we had one!' said Just Man cheerfully.

There was another brief pause. I heard whispers, which I assumed were the judges conferring. 'Very well,' Wrinkled Face said. 'We will withdraw for a few moments, no more. We have a lot of business to get through and the Useless Days begin the day after tomorrow.'

'My lords, I am obliged,' said Obsidian Tongue. Then I felt

a kick in my side, just under my ribcage, and he snapped: 'Right, you, on your feet! Time for you to start talking!'

I scrambled upright, looking wildly around me, my lips silently forming Lily's name.

The judges were departing through a small side exit, through which a little light fell, and I guessed there would be a courtyard beyond it for them to take their ease in between sessions. I spared those two dignitaries the briefest of glances, just enough to note the contrast between them. Although both were finely dressed in cotton cloaks that fell to their ankles, one of them, alone, wore a jade labret and a towering headdress whose shimmering plumes displayed the unmistakable blue-green of quetzal tail feathers. The other had a few white heron feathers in his hair, and his earplugs and labret were merely of gold. His costume was finer than most commoners could ever aspire to, but nonetheless that, plainly, was what he was: a commoner whose abilities – probably as a warrior, at least to begin with – had earned him a place alongside his noble colleague.

Obsidian Tongue had told me that the reason nobles and commoners sat together as judges in Tetzcoco's courts was that it ensured impartiality in the many disputes between those who owned the land and those who worked it. I suspected it might just have been the King's way of preventing a powerful subject from getting above himself, by placing a commoner next to him. Here the noble was Wrinkled Face and the commoner was Just Man.

Apart from the few rays of light falling through the judges' doorway, the only illumination in the room came from pine torches mounted on the walls, and a single tall flame from a brazier standing on a dais at the back of the room. This was enough for me to see as much as I needed to. Two high-backed chairs stood, one on either side of the brazier. They were the most splendid-looking items of furniture I had ever seen, richly gilded and encrusted with emeralds that sparkled in the flickering light of the flame between them. They were the Seat of the King and the Seat of the God, the Lord of the Near and the Nigh. On a low pedestal, just to the right of the Seat of the King and within easy reach of a man sitting in it, the naked pate of a skull gleamed whitely. Maize Ear would place his hand on it whenever he pronounced the sentence of death.

Neither of these magnificent, awe-inspiring chairs was occupied now. The chairs the two judges sat in were more humble, plainer affairs of wicker covered in leather. In front of them stood a low table with a single object on it: a wooden spike, its blunt end splintered as if it had been broken off from something, and its point dark with dried blood.

Several men stood in the room and one woman kneeled.

Apart from a few thickset men who were obviously guards, most of those present were similar in appearance to Obsidian Tongue, and I supposed that they were either fellow lawyers of his – including, of course, whoever was presenting the charges against Lily – or officials connected with the court. The function of one such official was obvious from the screenfold book he had placed in front of him, which he was drawing in as he squatted on a reed mat beside one of the judges' seats. In addition, besides having a scribe to record his orders, I knew that every judge had a bailiff to enforce them, a man with functions similar to those my brother carried out in Mexico in the course of his duties as executioner. I was wondering which of the stony-faced men around me might hold that office. I stopped wondering the moment I caught sight of the woman.

What I saw made me gasp in horror.

She kneeled on a reed mat, off to one side, close to the judges' seats. I knew she must be Lily because this was her trial and she was the only woman I could see, but otherwise I would not have recognized her. Her hair fell loose, lank and tangled about her shoulders. Her face was pale and puffy and turned towards the floor, and her eyes were shut, as if she were comatose, or did not care to see what was around her. Then I looked at her fingers.

Her name broke spontaneously from my lips. 'Lily!' I took a step towards her, although she gave no sign of having heard me. Then a sharp tug at my elbow brought me up short.

'You stay here!' snapped Obsidian Tongue.

'But her hands!'

The ends of her fingers were wrapped in bloodstained cloth. From here, it was impossible to see what had been done to them.

'What have they done?' I cried.

'I don't know,' said the lawyer frankly, 'but they're only likely to do worse if you don't come back here and listen to me! We haven't much time.'

I turned and looked at him, noticing for the first time the strain that showed in the shadows under his eyes and his sunken cheeks. He looked as if he had not slept in a while.

'All right,' I said, 'but look, Obsidian Tongue, there's something I want to say first, about me running away and that argument we had the other day, in front of the palace . . .'

'Forget it,' he said stiffly.

I stared at him. 'Forget it? I thought you were going to kill me! I didn't expect to see you here, let alone . . .'

He gave a short, harsh laugh. 'You mean, you thought because I was pissed off with you I wouldn't do my best to defend my client?'

'Well, yes. I mean, that's what Kindly thought too!'

The lawyer looked disgusted. 'You don't understand, do you?' he said. 'I may think the whole lot of you are a heap of worthless Aztec shit, but that doesn't alter the fact that I have been instructed to defend Lily, and that's what I'm here to do. Kindly ought to know that. Why else is he paying me eighty large cloaks?'

I heaved a sigh. 'All right. Sorry, I mean, thanks . . .'

'Now can we get on with this? The judges will be back in a moment. I'd better tell you what's happened so far. Then you'll know why your evidence is so important all of a sudden.'

'Can't I talk to Lily?' I asked, looking longingly in her direction.

He jerked my arm again to get my attention. 'No! Now listen! You know how hopeless this case has been from the beginning.'

'I don't see why,' I said sulkily. 'It's not as if they can prove Lily killed anybody.'

'They don't have to prove she did anything,' the lawyer said with the exasperated air of someone trying to explain why it was impossible to carry water in a wicker basket. 'It's the other way around. Lily has to prove she *didn't* do what she's accused of. Killing's the least of it. I told you that before. Don't forget that if there's any question about the verdict in this sort of case, it'll be for the King to resolve it.'

I knew what he meant. Kings tend not to give the benefit of the doubt to those accused of plotting against them. 'So it's hopeless, then,' I said quietly. 'If they're going to say she was helping to convey secret messages, we can't very well deny it!'

To my surprise, the lawyer smiled. It was a very thin smile, formed of tightly compressed lips curled up almost imperceptibly at the corners, but clearly something I had said amused him.

'Not quite hopeless,' he murmured. 'You see, the prosecution case is in a mess.'

'Why?' I said, surprised. 'They've got Hunter and

Rattlesnake, the men who arrested her, as witnesses. They saw her talking to Mother of Light and found her with that spike. And then, I'm sure . . . Oh . . .' My voice tailed off as I thought about what I was saying.

Rattlesnake and Hunter were, I suddenly recalled, in no position to testify about anything. I knew for certain that one of them was lying cold and lifeless in Hare's courtyard and was fairly sure the other was still on the roof of the merchant's house with a dart sticking out of him.

'The prosecutor said at the start of the hearing that he was going to call those two to give evidence. Not only that – he said he even had a confession, given by the prisoner herself late yesterday.'

I could not help glancing again at Lily's hands. I felt sick, but heard the lawyer in silence.

'But when it came to producing his witnesses – your two warriors, or spies as I suppose they must be, and two others who are supposed to have heard the confession – what do you think happened?'

'Tell me,' I said distantly. I wondered why she did not look up. Did she even know I was there?

'Nothing!' He was chortling now. 'No sign of any of them! So the bailiffs have had to be sent out to look for them, and the judges in the meantime have been giving my opponent a roasting for wasting their time.'

I forced myself to turn my head to look at him. 'What are you saying?' I said. 'There's no case against Lily? Is that it? Is she going to go free?'

He sighed. 'Not quite that simple, I'm afraid. The judges said her confession ought to be put to her, to see what she had to say about it. So it was.'

'And?'

'She repeated it word for word. As if she was talking in her sleep – you know how that sounds, no expression.' He scowled angrily. 'I know perfectly well what's happened here . . .'

'It was tortured out of her,' I said flatly. 'She's like one of those Bathed Slaves the merchants buy to dance and be sacrificed at the Festivals of the Raising of Banners and the Flaying of Men. They give them good food and sacred wine and drill them endlessly – but you can do it just as well with exhaustion, lack of sleep, pain. You can make a person do anything you want. I've seen it done often enough.'

'Naturally,' Obsidian Tongue said drily.

'Didn't you object?' I demanded.

'Of course I did.' He sounded hurt, as if I had asked him if he had had a bath that day. 'But I was told that, since there were no witnesses to the torture, my allegation couldn't be accepted! Unfortunately Lily didn't back me up. She won't say anything except what she was told to say, it seems.'

I groaned. I had tormented myself at the thought of what might have happened to Lily after I had left her in that tiny cage in the dark heart of the palace, but I had imagined nothing like this: Lily with no will of her own. I closed my eyes for a moment, and then reopened them quickly, repelled by what I saw behind their lids.

'What do you want me to do?' I whispered.

'You have to . . . oh, too late! Here come the judges!' Without another word he turned and hurried away.

'But . . .'

'Just do your best, Yaotl.'

Whatever reply I might have made would have been inaudible. With a great cry of 'My lords!', everyone in the courtroom flung themselves on the floor, prostrating themselves before the two men as they walked back through the doorway. Then there was silence, broken only by a faint creaking from the judges' chairs as they settled themselves.

'Now, Obsidian Tongue, can we start?' asked Wrinkled Face as we all resumed our squatting, standing or kneeling postures.

'My lord, yes, thank you. I wish to call one witness.'

Another man, one of those I had taken for lawyers or officials, suddenly leaped to his feet. 'Who is this witness? I don't know anything about him!' he cried indignantly.

'Coayolli, you don't seem to know much more about your own witnesses,' Just Man growled unkindly.

The prosecutor's name meant 'Snake Heart'. Physically he was the opposite of Obsidian Tongue: tall and thin, not to say gaunt, with a wisp of beard at the tip of his angular chin, but his elegant dress and somewhat affected manner were the same. He seemed momentarily lost for a reply to the judge's taunt, but while he was gathering his thoughts Obsidian Tongue said smoothly: 'I was about to tell you, my lords – and my friend, of course – who my witness is. He is the prisoner's slave, Yaotl . . .' He looked at me expectantly.

'. . . Cemiquiztli,' I muttered, reluctantly supplying the other part of my name, the part I always preferred not to share with strangers in case they could use it to work magic on me. It was the date of my birth: One Death.

'We'd better hear him,' said Just Man. His colleague intoned, more formally: 'Step forward, Cemiquiztli Yaotl.'

I looked about me nervously. I had only ever attended one trial before, when I had been arrested for drunkenness in Tenochtitlan many years before. That, from what I recalled through the haze that had surrounded me at the time, had been a much less elaborate affair, even though drunkenness was a capital offence, a crime against the gods. I had been dragged before a judge, the parish policemen who had arrested me had told him what had happened, I had been in no fit state to say anything, and the next thing I had known I was in prison. Evidently they managed things differently in Tetzcoco.

Obsidian Tongue looked at me. 'Your name is Cemiquiztli Yaotl?'

I stared at him. 'You know it is! You just told the judges!'

The lawyer grimaced as if he had just bitten on a broken tooth. A raucous laugh broke from one of the men on the high-backed seats. 'He's putting it to you so the scribe can record it,' Just Man explained.

'Thank you, my lord,' Obsidian Tongue said. He mouthed something obscene at me. 'Now, Yaotl, will you eat earth if what you are going to tell the judges is not the truth?'

'Yes,' I said. The floor was smooth and freshly swept, but all the same I solemnly brushed it with my fingers before putting them to my lips.

'Now tell the judges what you found at Hare's house, on the day the prisoner was arrested.'

I looked at the two men in their chairs, and the scribe scratching away in his book beside them, and tried to work out exactly what it was that Obsidian Tongue wanted me to say. Then I remembered what I had said to Hunter, when I had tried to show him why Lily could not possibly have killed the man whose body we had found in the courtyard, and I stumbled haltingly through an account of that. It took me a while, but nobody interrupted me; apart from my own voice, the only sound in the room was the faint scratching of the scribe's brush.

'So what you're saying is, the victim had been dead for days before you and Lily saw his body,' Obsidian Tongue said.

'Yes,' I said. 'I've no idea who cut his throat.' So much for eating earth, I thought, hoping the gods would forgive my impiety.

'And as far as you know, Lily had not been to the house before?'

The other lawyer jumped up. 'There's no way the witness can answer that!' he protested.

Before Obsidian Tongue could reply, I said: 'Yes, I can! She told me she hadn't!'

'What the prisoner told the witness isn't evidence!'

'Rubbish!' I said. 'She was really worried about going there at all – she told me she didn't want to go on her own. Besides, she was with me practically all the time from the day we arrived in Tetzcoco until she was arrested. If she'd managed to get to Hare's house and back in that time, she must have been bloody . . . Um, sorry . . . very fast.'

'Cemiquiztli Yaotl,' Wrinkled Face said sternly, 'you have not been asked a question! Scribe, please strike what the witness just said from the record.'

Scowling, the man scored the page in front of him with a single pass of his brush. I wondered how he could possibly record what I had been saying in pictures. Perhaps he had drawn a body lying inside a house, with the spike on the floor beside it, and lines of bloodstained footsteps leading away from it.

Obsidian Tongue heaved an audible sigh and then asked me how often I had seen the prisoner between our arrival in Tetzcoco and our visit to the merchant's house.

'But didn't I just tell you that?' I asked, bewildered.

'Please just answer the question,' he said in an imploring tone. I stared at him for a moment, but then I saw Snake Heart smirking over his shoulder, and that made my mind up for me. Meekly, I repeated what I had said before. 'It takes the best part of a morning to get to Hare's house,' I added, 'and Lily didn't look like someone who'd been out on the road all day, even if she had had the time to go there, kill a man and come back. And if she'd had anything to do with what happened to that warrior she'd have been covered in blood, wouldn't she?'

'Just answer the questions,' Obsidian Tongue said heavily. He was smiling, however, and I had the impression that he was not too displeased by what I had said. 'Now,' he continued, 'what did you come to Tetzcoco for?'

'Lily came here to . . .'

Snake Heart was on his feet again. 'The witness wasn't asked what the prisoner was here for!' he cried. 'He was asked why *he* was here!'

'Oh, all right,' I said, before either of the judges could reply. 'I was here to help Lily deliver a message. Some merchant was looking for . . .' I thought furiously, and then suddenly remembered what Kindly had told me on the way to Hare's house, days ago, about his scheme to trick Obsidian Tongue into giving him his money back. 'Looking for someone to take a load of cocoa off his hands. Lily had to put him in touch with a buyer, some woman from the palace – I can't remember her name . . .'

'Mother of Light!' cried Snake Heart triumphantly

'My lords,' Obsidian Tongue protested, 'my friend will have his opportunity to question this witness presently! Until then, I must ask him not to interrupt!'

'Don't interrupt, Snake Heart,' said Just Man in a bored voice. 'However, I have a question. Yaotl, are you really suggesting that the secret messages your mistress apparently confessed to being a party to carrying were all part of some trading venture?'

'Yes, my lord.'

'And the woman at the palace – was she this mysterious Mother of Light, as Snake Heart said?'

'My lord, I don't know why she's thought of as mysterious. She lives in the palace, I think. I saw her here, and in the marketplace. I even saw her in the middle of a crowd of people, reciting poetry to each other.' I looked up at him boldly. 'I don't call that mysterious! Just because the King's spies, or whoever they are, couldn't keep track of her . . .'

'All right,' the judge said, settling back in his seat. 'That's enough about that! Obsidian Tongue, do you have any more questions?'

'No, my lord.' As he squatted, Snake Heart rose to his feet, as though the two men were at opposite ends of a seesaw. The prosecutor glared at me balefully.

'When did you come to Tetzcoco?' he demanded curtly.

I told him. 'It was four days before we went to Hare's house.'

'And the man you found at Hare's house, how long had he been dead?'

Obsidian Tongue jumped to his feet. 'My lords! The witness is not a doctor! How can he be expected to answer that?'

'He already has answered it,' Wrinkled Face reminded him. 'When he was telling us what happened at the merchant's house, in answer to your question. You didn't object at the time. He said . . . Scribe, remind us what he said.'

The man unfolded a page of his book and quoted Obsidian Tongue's words to me: '"The victim had been dead for days."'

Snake Heart asked me: 'How many days?'

'I should think at least three,' I said, frowning.

'It couldn't have been five?'

'I suppose it could. As Obsidian Tongue said, I'm not a doctor.' I caught a look of horror passing across the other lawyer's face, but before it really had time to register, Snake Heart was speaking again.

'So the man may have died before you came to Tetzcoco?'

I was bewildered. 'Yes, of course. So what if he did?'

'Where were you before you came here?'

I sighed. 'In a cage in Tlatelolco, waiting to be sold! Lily bought me the day we came here.'

'Do you know what she was doing before that?'

'Well, no, of course not . . . Oh, now wait a moment!' I began to protest, but it was too late.

The man was grinning at me. 'So she could easily have come here a day or two before she bought you and killed the warrior then, couldn't she?'

'No, she couldn't!'

'How do you know? You've just said you don't know where she was. You don't know she wasn't in Tetzcoco committing murder, do you?'

'I don't know she wasn't in Acolman buying dogs in their marketplace, either!' I snapped. 'What kind of a question is that?'

He smiled blandly in response to my outburst. 'Well, now that we've established that . . .'

'Established what?'

Wrinkled Face said: 'Yaotl, wait until you are asked a question!'

'Thank you, my lord,' said Snake Heart. 'As I was saying, let's deal with this message. You say it was to do with cocoa?'

'That's right.'

'I thought Hare was from the eastern shore of the Divine Sea? They don't grow cocoa there.'

I hesitated before remembering what Kindly and Hungry Child had said to each other. 'They do in one place. It's called Chactemal.'

I was pleased to see him looking momentarily discomfited, but it soon passed. 'Well, I stand corrected. Where is the cocoa?'

'I told you, Chactemal . . .'

'Don't be obtuse!' he snapped. 'I meant the cocoa Hare was trying to sell! Is it at his house? In a warehouse? Well?'

I stared at him. For a moment I felt helpless, and strangely giddy, as if I had suddenly found myself on the edge of a tall cliff and was struggling to keep my balance. 'I don't know where it is . . .' I mumbled as I scrabbled inside my imagination for some answer that would back up my improvised lie.

'Speak up!' both the judges called out simultaneously.

'I . . .' Inspiration suddenly hit me, like a gust of wind blowing me away from the cliff edge and back on to safe ground. Then the words all came out in a rush, tumbling over each other in their hurry to be spoken: 'I don't exactly know where. It's still in the East, and that was the trouble all along, you see, because Hare had bought up so much of the stuff – the year's harvest for the entire province, basically – and then he found he couldn't afford the bearers to fetch it home, so he was trying to sell it where it was to save himself the trouble . . .' I paused for breath, feeling now a little light-headed. A stroke of genius, I told myself modestly, because there was no way the court would be able to check whether my story was true or not, not without sending somebody all the way to the coast to talk to the cocoa growers.

Sure enough, Snake Heart looked nonplussed, but as before he soon recovered. 'So you are suggesting that Mother of Light was prepared to buy a consignment of cocoa, sight unseen?' he said incredulously.

'That's what she told me,' I said.

'Where did she get the money from?'

'She was a King's concubine, I gather. Maybe she saved it up.'

Obsidian Tongue was on his feet again. 'How can this witness be expected to know about the lady's finances?' he asked.

'He has a point,' Just Man said. 'Strike that question from the record.'

Snake Heart looked at me through lowered eyes. 'Perhaps, then, you might care to tell the court what you do know about Mother of Light.'

'Almost nothing,' I said. 'I met her by accident once, and I wanted to speak to her again to find out what this message Hare had for her was all about.'

'You are aware that she's suspected of plotting against the King?'

'No, I'm not. I'm aware that the King's spies seem to have their eye on her, but I've no idea why. It seems to be a crime around here just getting on the wrong side of them.'

'Your mistress admits it, though!' he shouted suddenly. 'She admits she was conspiring with Mother of Light and her father to take messages to Black Flower! She admits that Hare is a spy too, and now he's disappeared . . .'

Obsidian Tongue snapped: 'Is my friend going to ask a question or not?'

But I was speaking before he had finished. To be told of Lily's so-called confession was too much for me. 'What do you mean, she admits it?' I yelled. 'She had it wrung from her by torture! Look at her! She barely knows where she is! Look at her hands! She'd have said anything to you bastards just to make you stop, and you have the fucking nerve to throw her so-called confession in my face . . .' I took a step forward, only to hear a swift footstep behind me and feel my arms pinned roughly behind my back.

'Oh, no, you don't,' rasped the bailiff's voice in my ear.

I stood there, breathing heavily while I watched Snake Heart. He seemed unruffled by my outburst.

'That's all,' he said softly.

Obsidian Tongue was speaking now. 'My lords, I apologize. As you can see, the witness is overwrought . . .'

Just Man muttered something that may have been: 'I'm not surprised!'

'We will confer for a moment,' his colleague said.

As the two put their heads together for a brief, whispered conference, I looked once again at Lily. My heart missed a beat. She was no longer looking at the floor. Now her eyes, swollen and red-rimmed though they were, were fixed directly on me.

It was hard to make out what an expression on her drawn, pain-racked features meant. There were so many lines on her brow already that I could not be sure whether or not I had seen a few more, but I thought she was frowning, as if struggling to remember something. I wondered if it might be my name.

'Obsidian Tongue,' Wrinkled Face called out, but as Lily's lawyer got to his feet he added: 'We don't need to hear anything more from you. Snake Heart!'

Obsidian Tongue squatted again. I caught his eye and saw, to my surprise, that he was smiling. I wondered what this meant. I had thought the judge's dismissal of him somewhat ominous, but he seemed to have taken it differently, as if it were an expression of approval.

'We are troubled,' the judge was saying, 'by the prisoner's confession.'

Snake Heart looked down for a moment, perhaps so as to hide the puzzled frown that crossed his face. When he looked up again, he said: 'My lord, you have already found there was no evidence that she was tortured.'

'Doesn't mean she wasn't, though,' the other judge growled.

His colleague glanced at him and scowled briefly. 'No, we cannot find she was tortured. This court acts in the King's name, and it cannot accuse him or his . . . his agents of anything like that. You know this.'

'Then . . .' began Snake Heart, but the judge had not finished.

'That does not alter the fact that the prisoner has clearly been wounded and is in great pain. What we still have to establish is whether her testimony can be relied on. Perhaps she was deranged by her injuries, however they were caused. Did she know what she was saying? That's what we have to decide. Can you help us with that?'

The lawyer squirmed visibly. He shot a brief glance at the woman, whose eyes were still fixed on me, the way a starving man in the desert might stare at smoke rising from a distant cooking fire. He swallowed. 'My lords, she spoke clearly enough when I cross-examined her . . .'

'What you mean,' Just Man said from his seat, 'is that she repeated faithfully every word you said to her! She might have been talking to anyone. I don't think she even knew who you were.'

'There is evidence besides the confession. She has no alibi for the time before the slave arrived in Tetzcoco, even if you believe what he said about her movements afterwards. And she was found at the scene of the murder!'

There was a long silence. The two judges looked at one another, and then Wrinkled Face said: 'Thank you, Snake Heart. We have made our decision.'

'We have made our decision.'

The judge's words fell on me like a blow. I felt as if I had been stunned. It was as if the room I was in and the people around me, even the bailiff who was still holding me firmly by both arms, had become part of a dream in which time did not pass and the interval between one heartbeat and the next could be measured in years.

When he spoke next, his voice seemed to come from an immensely long distance off, and I had to strain to hear the words, as though my ears were reluctant to take them in.

'The prisoner is accused of the murder of an unknown person at the house of Hare the merchant and of plotting to aid the King's enemy, Black Flower. We have heard the evidence, which has been her own confession and the testimony of her slave. Unfortunately, the prosecutor has been unable to call any witnesses of his own. Moreover, it has been suggested to us that the prisoner's confession was made under duress. We cannot agree with that . . .'

Just Man coughed loudly.

'But we are unhappy about the prisoner's state of mind. On the other hand, these are very serious charges, which cannot be dismissed lightly.'

I found myself wishing that he would get on with it and get it over with, whatever he was going to say. When he did, it was so astonishing that I had to restrain myself from tearing myself free of the bailiff's tight grip and running into the middle of the room to protest. After all I had heard that day it seemed so unfair.

'We cannot decide this case. We are referring the evidence to the King, the Great Chichimec, Maize Ear, Lord of the Acolhuans. He will rule on it tomorrow. Now we will withdraw until the next case is ready.'

And with that, both judges got to their feet, and once more everybody else threw themselves face down on the floor, the bailiff encouraging me to join in by shoving me roughly on to my knees.

Again, there was silence, save only for the sound of the judges' sandalled feet moving across the floor. I gritted my teeth and thought that Lily had been through all this only to be put through it all again the next day. And what more, I wondered, might she have to endure during the intervening night?

A sudden commotion brought me up on to my knees, my head jerking around to follow the noise. The judges had not left yet, but I saw that everybody else in the room was doing the same. Even Lily was looking towards the doorway I had first come through, the first sure sign I had seen that she was aware of anything happening around her.

Someone was shouting, just outside the room. I thought

immediately of Kindly, clamouring to know the outcome of his daughter's trial, but although I thought I had heard the voice somewhere before, it was not his.

Three men burst through the doorway. The bailiffs ran towards them, but stopped with a scraping of sandal-soles against the stucco of the floor as they took in the strangers' appearance. When I realized just what I was looking at, I felt the blood drain from my face.

Two of the three newcomers were new to me. They looked like warriors, with their elaborately piled-up hair and powerful physiques, but they wore short capes whose folds covered their arms, the dress of messengers or envoys. They had been doing something more than delivering a message or a summons today, however. They were sweating and grimy and their capes and skins were soaked and smeared with drying blood.

The third man was propped up between them, his legs trembling as if they had no strength left in them. He had been a warrior too, but he had plainly come off worst in his last fight. His clothes were black with the Precious Water of Life, and some of it at least was his own, if the dart projecting from his left shoulder was anything to go by.

His mouth was slack and his chin flecked with foam. His eyes were wide and staring, and his breathing was a loud, hoarse rattle. He was barely recognizable as Hunter, Rattlesnake's deputy, Maize Ear's spy, who I had thought had been killed on the roof of Hare's house.

'What is the meaning of this?' Wrinkled Face asked, as the two messengers lowered the wounded man gently on to a reed mat. Hunter let out a loud groan.

One of the messengers said: 'My lord, we searched for the missing witnesses, as you told us to. We were directed to the house of the merchant, Hare. When we got there, we found . . .' He seemed suddenly lost for words and turned to his comrade for support.

'A massacre, my lord. A dead man in the street outside the house. Five more in the courtyard. A seventh underneath the house.'

'*Under* the house?' cried Just Man.

'Buried in a pit dug in the floor. He'd been there for a long time, I think – smelled horrible!'

'Dead?' the judge said. 'Dead how? And who's this?'

The other messenger replied. 'We aren't sure about the man in the hole, my lord, but the others looked as if they'd been in a battle. Sword cuts, one with a dart in his throat. And not long ago, because they were still a bit warm and some of the blood was fresh. As for this man, we found him on the ground outside the house.'

'Can he talk?' demanded the judge.

One of the messengers hauled the injured warrior into a sitting position. 'Water,' he croaked.

A gourd was brought and put to the man's lips. He gulped twice and then began to cough, the spittle around his mouth turning slightly pink. Then he groaned again before lifting his head to look around the room.

As his eyes fixed on me, I felt a sudden terror. Instinctively I took a step backwards, only to collide with the bailiff who had held me before.

Hunter's eyes widened even further than before. 'It was him!' he gasped.

'What?' cried the judge, trying to follow the injured man's gaze.

'The slave! It was that slave. He was there. He was . . .'

An ugly gurgling sound broke from the man's lips then, followed by a fountain of blood-streaked liquid as he doubled over, retching and coughing.

'What was that? The slave was there? What was he doing?'

The bailiff's arms encircled me again in a grip as tight as the ropes on my slave-collar had been.

Hunter said nothing. His huddled body twitched violently once, then rolled over silently on to the mat, and it was clear to everyone in the room that he was beyond ever answering another question.

'My lords, it is plain enough! Hunter's testimony could not have been clearer.'

'Too bad I didn't get to cross-examine him,' muttered Obsidian Tongue under his breath.

Snake Heart ignored him. 'That slave—' he all but spat the word out as he gestured towards me '—was at Hare's house this morning, he wounded this poor man, he killed . . .'

'All by himself?' Just Man said sceptically.

'Well, he may have had accomplices, my lord, but . . .'

Obsidian Tongue got heavily to his feet. 'My lords, may I address you?'

Wrinkled Face shot him a look of something like relief. I had the impression that he found Snake Heart's tirade wearying. 'Please do.'

'I merely wish to ask – with the greatest respect, of course – who is on trial here, and for what? I was retained to defend Tiger Lily on charges of murdering an unknown man and of conspiring with the King's enemies. I have no instructions to defend her slave. Now that you have made your decision in my client's case, I have nothing more to do here, and I think I ought to withdraw.'

'Here, wait a moment!' I cried. 'What do you mean, you've no instructions to defend me? I'll give you instructions! Or if you won't take them from me, Lily will . . . Lily, tell him!'

She looked at me dully without speaking.

'That's enough,' Just Man said. 'You'll have your chance to speak presently. Obsidian Tongue, it does seem that the slave would like you to represent him. Do you want to have a private word with him?'

'A very brief one, my lord, thank you.' The lawyer walked over to me, and the bailiff, to afford us the semblance of privacy, relaxed his grip.

'Well?' demanded Obsidian Tongue.

'Get me out of this,' I said.

'Why should I?'

I stared at him. 'What do you mean, why should you? You're Lily's lawyer . . .'

'I was hired to defend her in this case, and if I say so myself, I've done a fine job! But that's nothing to do with you, is it?'

'I can pay you,' I said desperately.

'No, you can't.'

'Well, all right, but Kindly will . . .'

That drew a thin smile from the other man. 'Oh, yes, Kindly. Do you know, that old man tried to swindle me? He tried to talk me into buying into some scheme to grow cocoa in the jungle. As if I was born yesterday! Do you think I don't know where you got that tall story about Hare's message from?'

Then he leaned towards me, putting his face very close to mine, and hissed: 'And then there's the little matter of you persuading me to vouch for you as a lawyer and then running away. Remember that? Remember our little conversation in front of the palace?'

'You said to forget it,' I protested.

He stepped back. 'I just got my memory back!' he declared, and turned on his heel. Aloud, he said to the judges: 'My lords, I will not be representing the slave. May I be excused?'

17

I was to be put in a cage again.

The judges listened indulgently to Snake Heart's accusations against me for a little while before declaring that they had no time to deal with me today and my case, like Lily's, should go before the King the following morning.

As the bailiff seized hold of me once more, I turned to look at Snake Heart.

'What did you do that for?' I demanded. 'You're supposed to be prosecuting Lily. Who told you to start on me?'

The lawyer smiled, the way Obsidian Tongue had smiled at the mention of Kindly's name. 'It can be a risky business, slave, upsetting a lawyer! Now I'm off to share a pipe with my old friend Obsidian Tongue. A risky business!'

'Hold him securely,' warned the noble judge. 'If he really did have a hand in that massacre he must be more dangerous than he looks!'

I was half carried, half dragged from the courtroom through a small side exit and along dimly lit passageways whose many turns might have been designed to baffle the most accurate sense of direction.

'Where are you taking me? Is it the prison?' I was terrified of being sent back to the obscure chamber into which Rattlesnake and Hunter had put me, the distant, dark room where Lily had suffered unspeakably and I had seen a man with crushed fingers.

'You'll find out,' the bailiff grunted. 'Did you really kill all those men? Don't look like you've got it in you to me.'

'I haven't!' I yelled. 'I didn't!'

'No need to shout.'

The passageway opened out into a wider corridor, which had a familiar feel to it. I almost wept with relief as I realized that it led to the part of the palace where Lily had first been held, where ordinary prisoners were kept.

An official met us by the entrance.

'Who's this?' he asked suspiciously.

'New prisoner for you.' The bailiff handed over a piece of stiff bark paper, which crackled as the official took it. 'Here's the judge's order.'

'What happened to the woman? Don't tell me she got off.'

'No, she's on her way back. Both of them to be held until the King decides what to do with them in the morning.'

The other man frowned. 'Oh, no. That won't do. You took one prisoner away; you can't bring two back. I haven't room for them both! Somebody should have checked.'

'Too bad. What do you expect me to do, let this one go?'

I restrained myself from saying that I thought that sounded like a good idea.

The official handed the paper back. 'It's all the same to me what you do with him. Somebody should have checked, that's all. All my cages are full.'

'What about the one we took the woman out of this morning?'

'Well, that one's hers, of course, but . . .'

The bailiff put a hand in the small of my back and shoved me through the doorway. 'Well, there you are, then! Put them both in together. It's only for one night!' With that, he turned and strode away before the other man could utter a protest, just as Lily appeared, under escort, shuffling forward as passively as an old blind woman with her trusted guide.

The official muttered something under his breath before calling out, over his shoulder: 'Mouse! Come here! Two more prisoners, both to go in that empty cage!'

Lily's old jailer appeared to take charge of us. He made a sympathetic tutting noise when he saw Lily and frowned as he scrutinized me. 'Didn't you used to be a lawyer?'

'Briefly,' I said. 'What happened to her?'

He looked at the woman and grimaced. 'I don't know. She was moved out of here a few days ago and only brought back early this morning for the trial. Nobody said anything. It was as if we were to pretend she'd been here all the time. Now come on, I've got to put you both in a cage. It'll be a bit cramped, I'm afraid, but it's only for the night . . .'

I stared at him, bewildered as ever by his manner, more suited to a guesthouse proprietor than a jailer. 'But her hands!' I protested.

'That wasn't done here,' he said firmly. Then, speaking to Lily, he said: 'Will you come with me?'

To my surprise, she looked at him and a half-smile of recognition appeared on her face. 'Mouse,' she said, almost inaudibly.

'Lily!' I cried joyfully. 'You can still talk! For a while I thought they'd cut your tongue out as well as . . . as well as . . .'

She looked at me blankly.

'What's going on?' I asked the jailer, my sudden euphoria turning just as suddenly to despair.

'I don't know, but it happens sometimes. People get used to me while they're in here, I think, and if something like . . . well, if Rattlesnake's men take them, and they come back alive, sometimes they won't talk to anyone else.' He smiled. 'You know, I had a dog once. My parents were fattening it up in a cage for the Festival of Offering Flowers. I used to feed him, and then when it was time to slaughter him I had to do it because he struggled too much if anyone else tried to pick him up. Some of my prisoners, I think they're a bit like that dog. Here we are.'

He helped each of us in turn to climb into the cage, carefully avoiding touching Lily's hands as he guided her over the top of the bars. Then the roof went on, and its stone weights placed, one by one, each with a decisive thud.

'I'll leave you be for a while,' he said.

'Lily?'

She sat with her back against the bars, hunched over as if still trying to fit herself into the tiny box Rattlesnake and Hunter had put her in, although she did not need to. If this was to be our last night on Earth, I thought ruefully, at least they had given us a big cage to spend it in. It was the one that Lily had been in when I had come to see her in my guise as her lawyer, comparatively roomy for one person, cramped, but not excruciatingly so, for two.

'Can you talk to me? Do you know who I am?'

I was dimly aware of movement around me, and sounds: shuffling and grunting noises from the dark figures sleeping or daydreaming in the cages around us. Perhaps, I thought, she had not heard me, and I reached out and touched her shoulder.

She flinched and a violent tremor passed through her.

'Lily,' I groaned, 'where are you? It's me, Yaotl. Your slave, your . . .' I swallowed, suddenly aware that I did not truly know what I might have been to her: a friend, a lover, the man who had tried to save her from Lord Feathered in Black, none of these or all of them? The thought that I might never know filled me with sadness, which was quickly chased away by a sudden dread as I realized what might have happened to her.

She might have lost her soul.

I knew that this could happen. The soul was such a delicate

thing: a terrible shock, or a drunken rage, or even something as superficial as being interrupted in the act of making love could drive it from a man's or a woman's body, and if it were not retrieved quickly then it would be gone for good. But that would need a soul doctor, and plainly there would be none here. I shook the woman again, overcome now by an irrational feeling of despair. Without her soul, her body would die. It might take four years, but Lily would slowly decay from within. Somehow that prospect terrified me more than the likelihood that we would be executed in the morning.

'Lily! It's me!'

She looked at me with dull but not lifeless eyes. Slowly her lips moved. 'Yaotl,' she said flatly.

I moaned with relief. 'You do know me!'

'Yes, of course,' she said in the same monotone.

'Do you know where you are? Do you know what happened to you?'

'In the prison,' she mumbled, and then, as if that were all she could remember, she repeated it.

'Your hands,' I said urgently. 'Did they . . .' It was hard to put into words. 'Did they take your fingertips?'

She looked down at her maimed hands, the bloodstained rags that ended her fingers. I wondered at the fact that they had been bandaged at all, but thought that perhaps that had been for the judges' benefit. 'No,' she said absently. 'Only the nails.'

'Oh, Lily!' This time, when I reached for her, it was not to shake her but to hold her, as though my arms could give her some reassurance that my voice could not. She accepted the embrace passively, as she seemed to do everything else now, neither shrinking from it nor returning it.

'We'll be all right, you know,' I whispered into her tangled hair, whose silver strands seemed to shine even in the gloom of the prison. 'They won't kill us.' Who was I talking to, I wondered even as I formed the words, who was I trying to reassure, her or me? 'The judges didn't believe your confession.'

She replied, in voice I could barely hear even though we were so close together: 'But it was true.'

I pulled away from her a little, just enough to study her face. 'No, no. Look, I know what they did. I know what you had to say, just to make them stop. But it's over now, don't you realize? Rattlesnake and his men – they're dead. The Otomies killed them. They can't hurt you any more, Lily. You don't have to lie any more.'

Then I hugged her again and listened to her repeating what she had said still more softly: 'But it was true. It was too hard to lie; it hurt too much.'

I rocked her gently, whispered soothing words to her, and hoped the obsidian-bladed winds in the Land of the Dead were flaying the naked souls of Rattlesnake and his men, carving strip after strip from whatever remained of their substance until there was nothing left but agony, and I prayed that that would go on for ever.

We must both have slept. It seemed to me that one moment I was cradling the woman in my arms, talking nonsense, and the next I was in the middle of a nightmare, trapped in a dark, airless place with a monster that shrieked and lashed out, striking me with hands and feet, and reeked of blood.

I struggled to free myself, jamming my body against the unyielding bars then trying to defend myself by hitting wildly back.

The shrieks became a long wail, which in turn dissolved into a cascade of desolate sobs.

I knew where I was then, and whom I was with. This time, when I reached for her, she threw herself into my arms, pressing herself against me so that I felt every spasm as it racked her.

'Lily, Lily, Lily!'

'Don't go!' she cried into my chest. 'You mustn't leave me! Please!'

'Not much danger of that, lady,' I murmured as I stroked her hair.

I looked around quickly. It was too dark to see anything, although noises from the other cages told me that some at least of our fellow inmates had been disturbed by Lily's nightmare. I wondered what time it was; had the Sun set, or was he about to rise? This deep within the interior of the palace, I suspected, it might be impossible to hear the trumpets and drums that would signal to the city at large nightfall and morning and other times of the day and night.

I suppressed a moment's panic at the realization that there was no way of knowing how long we had to wait to learn what was to become of us. Then, with a feeling like a swarm of bees waking up in the pit of my stomach, I discovered that we might be about to find out.

I could see something now. The bars of the surrounding cages and the huddled shapes inside them had begun to throw huge wavering shadows across the walls. Someone was approaching with a torch in his hand.

'Something's happening,' I whispered fearfully.

Lily pushed herself free of my clasp, using her palms. They were damp, and I suspected her wounds had opened while her hands were flailing at me in her sleep.

'What?'

'There's someone coming. Surely it can't be time already?'

The torch heralded not one person but several. The little group moved silently towards our cage. Watching the flickering light reflected off their hair, I could see that the men approaching were a mixture. Some were seasoned warriors, but others, who looked more humble, might have been labourers or even slaves.

Leading them all was the official who had reluctantly received us after the trial. Mouse held the torch.

I looked fearfully up at the roof of the cage and listened to the scraping sound of the stone weights being removed.

'What's going on?' I asked.

'You're to see the King,' the official replied. He directed Mouse and one of the newcomers to lift the top off the cage. 'Both of you, straight away. Out you come.'

Two arms reached inside the cage, seeking for Lily. She gave a sharp cry of pain, pressing against me as she shrank from the warrior's touch.

I cringed when I heard it, but started at the response from outside the cage.

'Be careful, you clumsy oaf!' the official barked. 'You'll hurt her! Mind her hands.'

The warrior mumbled something apologetic as he and a colleague gently eased Lily away from me and out of the cage. Baffled, I clambered out unaided to stand facing our visitors, wondering how to frame the question I wanted to ask: what had been in the King's summons to make these men care whether they hurt us or not?

'Can you walk? We've got a litter waiting for you outside. We can bring it in here if we need to.'

'A litter?' I repeated incredulously.

'You've got a long way to go, and the King wants to see you now.'

I looked at Mouse. 'Where are we going? The King's here, in the palace, isn't he?'

'No, he's still in Tetzcotzinco. He doesn't get here until tomorrow.'

'Tomorrow? But surely he has to be here today, to judge the last cases and see to the punishments. Tomorrow's the first of the Useless Days, isn't it?'

Mouse laughed, a strange, high-pitched sound to come from a large man. 'No, that's the day after! What, did you think it was morning?'

'I thought it must be.'

'The Sun hasn't set yet. He soon will, though, so you'd better hurry.'

Lily spoke up for the first time. Looking at the guards surrounding us, she said quietly: 'I can walk.'

We were escorted to a rear gateway, away from the crowds that presumably still thronged the front of the palace. Here, in a narrow lane largely hidden from casual sight by the high walls of two of the houses that abutted the King's residence, we found a litter waiting for us. It was a comparatively plain affair, its canopy fringed with black grackle feathers and its two seats covered with deer hide rather than jaguar skin, but I was not about to complain. I had never travelled in a litter before, and this was not merely because canoes were more useful in Tenochtitlan. Litters represented the kind of luxury that was reserved for lords.

Mouse accompanied us as far as the litter and fussed over Lily as she got into it. 'I knew it!' he was saying. 'I kept telling them they'd better treat you properly. You were obviously more important than you seemed. You won't forget I said that, will you?'

The canopy supported cotton drapes that were unfastened and let fall as soon as Lily and I were seated. Abruptly we were plunged into gloom. I wondered whether this was to prevent us from seeing out or to ensure that no curious passer-by saw who was in the litter. I was still wondering this when I felt the ground lurch away from under me and we were moving.

Lily started. 'Why are they taking us to Tetzcotzinco?' she asked, as if she had only just realized where we were going.

'I don't know.' I fought to suppress a surge of panic. We seemed to be swaying helplessly through the air. My stomach felt as if I had eaten a plateful of bad snails. I decided that I preferred canoes. The open lake could be dangerous, I thought, but at least if you were tossed out of a boat you would have a soft landing.

I wanted to take my mind off the desire to poke my head out between the drapes and be violently sick. Also, there was something encouraging about Lily's innocent question, a sign that she was aware of what was happening around her and beginning to take an interest in it. So I began to explain what little I knew, and ended up relating most of what had befallen me, her father and my son while she had been shut in the prison.

She did not speak until I had finished, and for a while afterwards I wondered whether she had heard me. Then she said, as softly as if to herself: 'So my father had the ring all along . . . But you found the girl, and Mother of Light and the King, Hungry Child?'

'We did, but it doesn't seem to have helped you at all. I'm so sorry, Lily. I thought if we could find the message and make sense of it, we could prove that you weren't any danger to Maize Ear at all, but we couldn't work out what that little girl was on about. Of course, Hungry Child may have got more out of her by now, but I doubt it. I think those gestures she was making must have been some kind of Mayan magic, or something equally incomprehensible.' I recalled the gestures, the stretching of her eyelids, the pulling on her chin, the scrubbing of her face, the handfuls of hair lifted up over the top of her head. It had all had the look of ritual, I told myself. 'Of course, what it certainly wasn't was anything to do with cocoa!'

'Mother of Light wouldn't be interested in cocoa,' the woman confirmed absently.

'No. Mayans, yes, and the things that have been happening in their country lately . . . But as for why we're being taken to Tetzcotzinco, Lily, I wish I knew.' I shuddered involuntarily. I had been summoned before an Emperor on more than one occasion, and it had never been a happy experience. On the other hand, Montezuma had never sent a litter to fetch me. It seemed an odd way for a King to treat someone he was about to punish.

I tried not to think about the possibility that Nimble might have succeeded in his mission, that Maize Ear had seen and recognized his father's jewel and that he had agreed to reprieve us. It was too much to hope for. In all likelihood my son had been caught and driven away from Tetzcotzinco by the guards who, if the rest of Maize Ear's domain was anything to go by, must be swarming around his retreat like wasps around a plate of honey. Besides, if I knew anything about Kings, they did not snatch people from their own prisons and turn them loose merely because they were asked to: far easier and less embarrassing to leave them be and let events take their course.

Perhaps Maize Ear had so many cases to resolve in the morning that he wanted to make an early start. Perhaps the litter was merely the fastest way of getting us to him, and considering the state his minions had left Lily in, I thought angrily, that was entirely possible, as she might not have managed the walk. Perhaps there was a line of litters snaking its way out of Tetzcoco, and we were simply in the middle of it.

The reminder of how the woman had suffered settled over me like a cloud darker than the space within the drapes. I remembered how I had felt in the cage, terrified that her soul might have fled, bitterly sad that I might never learn what I represented in her eyes. Now, I knew, there was nothing to be done, but I needed to speak to her, to try to draw out whatever might be left.

'Lily,' I began awkwardly, 'I don't know whether we're going to live through this, but . . .'

She interrupted me suddenly. 'No one lives for ever on Earth.'

Sensing there was more to come, I waited, with the breath stopped in my throat.

'That's what I kept telling myself, you know, while I was in that little cage, while they were pulling my nails out and asking me about the man in Hare's house and Mother of Light. It won't be for ever, no one lives for ever on Earth. I must have . . . I must have got confused. I started saying that Hare wouldn't have lived for ever, as if that excused what happened. Then I had to tell them, didn't I? I didn't want to, for her sake – I thought they'd go looking for her – but it was so hard to lie about everything . . .' Her words rambled to a stop and a stifled, choking sob.

'What are you talking about?' I asked. 'What was it hard to lie about?'

'Killing Hare.'

'But you didn't kill him. Lily, listen, it's me, Yaotl. Yaotl, your slave, your . . . whatever. You're safe with me. It's over, do you understand? You don't have to lie any more.'

'I didn't lie,' she insisted in a whisper.

'All right,' I said helplessly, appalled to think that the shock of what had happened to her had really convinced her that she had killed a man. 'That's enough, Lily. Don't say another word.'

She was silent again after that, and her breathing became quiet and slow.

At some point we must have joined a highway, because the litter's violent plunging and jerking had become a steady rhythmic rocking that was not unpleasant. In spite of my fear,

I was so tired that I found myself drifting off to sleep. I tried to fight it at first, but then gave up. Dozing could hardly make my situation any worse.

I found myself in a confused dream in which Little Hen was on trial for murder and being cross-examined by Snake Heart. He kept asking her whether she could prove that she had not been at Hare's house on the day the warrior we had found there was killed. But, of course, she was unable to answer him because she could not understand a word he was saying, and there was nobody to translate. All she did, in response to his repeated, ill-tempered questions, was make her familiar gestures: stretching her eyelids, pulling her chin, scrubbing her face, tugging at her hair.

Then I was awake, leaping to my feet, or rather trying to and striking my head on the canopy. I felt myself topple over and clutched wildly at the drapes, clinging to them for a moment before they gave way with a loud ripping sound and I was tumbling headlong out of the litter.

It was not a long fall and what was left of the cotton slowed me a little. I crashed to the earth with a yell, but it was cry of triumph more than pain, because I knew what my dream meant, and what it meant was the solution to the mysteries that had dogged me ever since I came to Tetzcoco. Suddenly I knew what Little Hen's message had been and why it was so important. And I now knew that we had all been wrong about who had killed Hare and his uninvited guest.

The merchant's killer had been the last person I would have suspected, but I was quite sure. I felt a bleak certainty about it that washed away all pleasure at my own cleverness like a shower of icy water.

18

'What's your game?' the warrior in charge of our escort demanded, as the bearers set the litter down beside me.

'Sorry,' I mumbled. 'I fell.'

'I can see that. Well, if you're that keen to get out and walk, you may as well. We're just about there.'

I scrambled to my feet and looked about me.

The Sun had set, and a grey twilight had descended over the mountains in the West, fading to a starry blackness in the East. A couple of torches lit up the litter and the men around it and glinted off the smooth surface of the well-made and clean-swept road we stood on. There were no other torches or signs of traffic on the road, which seemed to disprove my notion that we might be part of a convoy of prisoners.

Up ahead, vaguely discernible against the eastern sky, loomed a tall, conical shape, its outline like that of a pyramid, but a pyramid studded with rocks and trees and little flickering lights on its sides that might be torches, and here and there a pale spot that daylight might have revealed as a whitewashed wall.

I had never seen the place, but I had heard enough about it to know it for what it was: the hill of Tetzcotzinco, where the Kings of Tetzcoco had their retreat.

'You're to go up alone,' the chief of our escort told me as he helped Lily to her feet. He walked with us to the foot of the hill, leaving his men standing around the litter, some of them no doubt anxiously wondering who would have to answer for the damage I had done to it. Two guards stepped forward at our approach, but when they recognized our escort by the light of his torch they instantly turned their backs. Somebody must have instructed them in advance to take no notice of us.

'There are five hundred and twenty steps,' the chief warned us. 'Will the woman make it?' Once again I noted this odd concern for our welfare.

'Yes,' I said. Whatever we were getting into, I wanted it over with. 'I'll help her. She'll be all right.'

Without another word he turned and walked back towards his men.

I turned to Lily. 'Come on. We can take it slowly. I think they'll wait for us.'

'They?'

I smiled, although it was probably too dark for her to see my expression. 'That's right. The King and . . . whoever else is up there.' And who would that be, I wondered? Hungry Child and Mother of Light, or men with cudgels or ropes, ready to dispatch both of us the moment their ruler gave the word?

'I think,' I said cautiously, 'that we may have some explaining to do.'

I heard her catch her breath. 'I can't lie any more, Yaotl. I haven't the strength left for that.'

It was the first time since the trial that I had heard her use my name with any sense that she recognized it. On impulse, I stepped towards her and took her upper arm in my hand, keeping well away from her fingers. 'Don't worry,' I assured her. 'If any lies have to be told, leave them to me. I'm probably better at it than you are.'

As we began to climb I felt curiously light-headed. For all I knew our return down these smooth, broad steps might be like that of sacrificial victims down the stairway of a pyramid, our lifeless bodies rolling limply all the way to the bottom, but now it seemed not to matter. For most of my life I had ignored or defied my fate. To surrender to it now was a relief. And the place we were in was like something out of a beautiful dream.

The steps wound their way upwards among broad terraces. Out of the twilight on either side of us loomed the deeper shadows cast by groves of oak and cypress, with statues in some pale stone such as marble or porphyry lurking wanly in their midst. Past the trees we found ourselves walking through a shrubbery, with a little brook trickling softly among the roots. I wondered where the source of the water was, and found out when we had gone a little further, because we found ourselves on the edge of a pond, a large, regular basin hewn out of the rock of the hillside. There was a statue in the middle of it, and a building – a large house, or a small palace – behind it.

'It's magnificent,' I breathed. 'Too bad we came up so late. What would it look like in daylight?'

The Moon was up, however, and I could see enough by its light to get a sense of what lay around me. The little palace gleamed, I realized, as if its walls had been polished.

'Is that the King?' Lily asked nervously.

I looked at the statue in the middle of the pond more closely. 'No. It looks like a jaguar, but with wings . . .'

'I didn't mean that. I meant that man on the other side of the water.'

I stepped back in surprise, to find one of my feet waving in midair as I missed the step I had been standing on. I began to topple backwards, but my cry of alarm was cut off by a gasp of astonishment as Lily hooked an arm around one of mine to stop me falling. We tottered together on the edge of the step until I managed to regain my footing.

'Thank you,' I said. 'What man?'

She disengaged herself. 'Look.'

A lone dark figure stood in front of the house. I had taken him for another statue, but then I saw that he must be an uncommonly realistic one, for the cotton of his long, elegant cloak billowed gracefully as no stone could, and the long, curling feathers of his tall headdress shone like real plumes and rustled gently in the light breeze. And would a statue, I wondered, wear real jade in its lip and ears?

I swallowed. The stranger did indeed look like a king, but why would he meet us here, and where was his retinue?

Where was my son?

I gulped. 'My-my lord,' I stammered. I dropped to my knees.

The stranger laughed, but there was no mockery in it. 'Not here, Yaotl, not now. Once, yes. But I promised my son I would do nothing to disturb his rule, and it would distress him to see me offered obeisance. Besides, I've no use for it any more!'

As I got up, Hungry Child began walking around the edge of the pond. 'You weren't wholly wrong about the statue, though. If you look in the creature's mouth you can see a little figure of my father. He always said it was the only good likeness of him ever made!'

I looked into the beast's jaws again, but it was not light enough to make out much more than a hint of a tiny carving.

'How did you get here?' I asked. 'And what happened to Nimble and the jewel? And why are you dressed like that?'

'I grew up on this hill. It became mine when my father died, when I was eight years old, and by then I knew every rock and tree on it.' He sighed regretfully. 'I missed it, and I will miss it when I finally leave, but still . . . it wasn't hard to creep up here unseen, while your son was distracting the guards with my ring.'

'Distracting the guards?' I echoed, suddenly outraged. 'You mean, you used him to create a diversion while you . . . Where is he?' At the thought of Nimble's being caught and interrogated by Maize Ear's guards, all the fear I had lost for my own safety came back in the form of terror for his. I stepped towards the former King, with my arm raised, momentarily unable to master my anger.

Hungry Child took no notice of my gesture. 'Your son is with mine,' he said softly. 'Waiting for us at the top of the hill.'

I dropped my arm, breathing heavily. I watched him suspiciously as he resumed, speaking as if I had never interrupted him. 'As for the costume,' he said, plucking at the rich cotton, 'I suppose it may be vanity, but I thought that when I presented myself to Maize Ear I had better come dressed as a King. I did not want him to be in any doubt that I was who I said I was.'

Then he turned to the woman. 'I'm so sorry. You must be Lily.'

'Yes,' she said. 'I've come to tell you . . .'

I interrupted her smoothly. 'Maize Ear sent for us both, but I expect you know that.'

'Of course. I told him to.'

I shot him a curious glance. 'Did you find out what Little Hen's message meant?'

'Some of it, yes. There's still a lot I have to find out. I'm looking forward to practising my Mayan!'

'I figured it out myself,' I told him, unable to stop my voice swelling a little out of pride.

The jewel at the King's lip sparkled as he formed his all-but-invisible smile. 'I had a feeling you might. Well done! Madam, you made a fine investment when you bought this slave! Now, shall we go up and tell my son what we've discovered?'

*

We climbed past more lushly planted terraces, past whispering streams and waterfalls cascading noisily over boulders, past the still pools they splashed into and tumbled out of. From time to time I glimpsed, looking sideways through the trees or down on to a lower level, an expanse of water, like the pond where we had found Hungry Child only larger, and I saw clearly now what I had caught sight of, looking at the hill from the ground: the houses, palaces and little temples with thatched roofs that dotted its slopes.

Nowhere did we see another person. There must have been a vast staff of retainers and many guards, but like the men who had so conspicuously ignored Lily and me at the bottom of the hill, they had obviously been told to have nothing to do with us.

Lily stumbled on the stairs near the summit. Hungry Child and I both seized her arms to save her from falling, and I noticed from her shallow, quick breathing that she was almost exhausted.

'Nearly there now,' I whispered encouragingly.

'When we get there, my son's physicians will look at those fingers,' Hungry Child said.

'Thank you,' Lily managed between gritted teeth.

'Why would he do this for us?' I asked, curiosity overcoming my manners.

'Because you've brought both of us what we want, one way and another,' Hungry Child said mysteriously. 'And besides, you extracted a promise from me, if you remember, and I have kept my word.'

'I'll be all right when I get my breath back,' the woman muttered, moving her arms weakly as if trying to shake us off. I nearly laughed aloud, for it was the sort of impatient gesture I would have expected Lily to make. I dared to hope that her soul had not strayed after all.

'A little further,' Hungry Child told her. 'I assure you, it will be worth the climb.'

And so it was.

'Water,' Hungry Child mused. 'Such a precious thing, in a land that's parched for most of the year, and the rains can't be trusted to fall when they're due. Is it any wonder my father wanted to surround himself with it?'

I stared at the scene in front me, speechless. Beside me, I could feel Lily trembling, but I could not tell whether it was from fatigue or awe.

A sheet of water lay spread before us, gleaming in the moonlight: a man-made lake, dug out of the rock like the ponds we had already passed. This one, however, was at the very summit of the hill, with the ground on each side falling away, and Hungry Coyote had built his palace in the very middle of it, on an island rimmed with great spreading cedars that almost hid the building nestling among them now and would shade it in summer. I realized that they must have been here before either palace or lake were dreamed of, and perhaps they accounted for the choice of location. When I looked East, though, I could see another possible reason. The whole of the valley of Mexico lay stretched out beneath us, with the vast expanse of Lake Tetzcoco in its centre.

The Emperor of Mexico might rule the World, but he had nothing like this: a prospect that reduced his own city to a small dark smudge in the middle of the pale, moonlit waters.

'It looks magnificent, doesn't it?' Hungry Child said softly as he led us over a broad causeway towards the cedar trees and the colonnaded walls of the palace.

'Yes,' I said simply. It was more than magnificent, it was entrancing, and I found myself craning my neck to look around me and straining to catch the tiny splashes as ripples on the water caught the sides of the causeway.

'Well, the winter rains have left it fairly full. Come the end of the dry season, half the water will be gone, all the pretty streams and waterfalls you saw will have disappeared and the place will be buzzing with mosquitoes. But the view down the hill will still be good.'

The wry comment shook me out of my reverie. I looked ahead, and for the first time since meeting Hungry Child I saw strangers, a little knot of people among the tall dark trees, some watching us, others gazing raptly out over the valley.

It was all I could do not to break into a run as I approached and began to realize that some of them were not strangers at all.

The King of Tetzcoco sat in a high-backed chair that had been positioned to let him look out over the valley, although he seemed too deep in thought to be merely contemplating the view. He leaned forward, with one elbow on his knee and his chin resting on his hand, and when the dappled moonlight falling between the branches overhead shifted to his face it looked as if his eyes were shut.

The King had been the last person I had noticed. As we walked towards the trees, I had spied, with mounting disbelief and delight, not merely my son but also Lily's father, Mother of Light and, squatting close by Maize Ear's throne as casually as if he had been her uncle, Little Hen. None of them looked as if they had been harmed in any way. In fact, Kindly seemed to be bored, from the way he kept shuffling his feet.

I wanted to smile and laugh and call out to my son, but I had appeared before an Emperor before and I knew what I had to do. Stopping well short of the King on his seat, I threw myself upon the immaculately swept ground, crying: 'Oh, lord! My lord! Oh, Great lord!'

There was silence for a moment. Then the King spoke, in a soft, clear voice that was like a younger version of his uncle Montezuma's.

'You have expended breath to come here,' he said formally. 'You are weary; you are hungry. You must rest and have some food.'

I got to my knees and risked a look around. To my surprise, Hungry Child had rendered his son the same obeisance I had, and his feathers fell forward over his face as he began to rise. Lily, however, had remained standing. Her wounded hands would have made prostrating herself exquisitely painful, and from the way she was swaying she was now so tired that she might not have been able to get to her feet again.

Evidently the King noticed her condition as well, for as his servants appeared with cups and jugs and platefuls of delicacies, little intricately shaped tamales with sweet and savoury fillings, he called for a chair. While Lily was being lowered gently into it, I munched on one of the snacks and studied Maize Ear slyly through the corner of my eye.

He was a young man, a little over twenty. He had been on the throne less than three years, but in that time he had seen more trouble than many of his elders. There were plenty in his kingdom who still mourned the days when Tetzcoco had been the chief power on this side of the valley and resented the Aztecs and our invincible city on the lake. They resented him, because he was half-Aztec and they thought he was his uncle's puppet. He had had to cede many of his richest provinces to his brother in the North, knowing that Black Flower would not be happy until he had the throne as well. Now, on top of all that, he had discovered that the last King, his father, whose body he had seen burned with all the pomp and sacrifices due to him, had not died at all but had been living within shouting distance of his own palace.

None of this showed in the young man's face. The eyes he fixed on Hungry Child were clear and steady, and there was no sign of tension under his smooth skin or in the hands resting on his lap.

'I sent for the woman and the slave, Father,' he said simply. 'And the old man also – he was picked up outside the court.'

Hungry Child replied: 'Thank you, my lord.'

'You will have something for me.'

Hungry Child looked sideways at me. 'I believe the slave does, my lord.'

I looked from one to the other of them, suddenly conscious that I might have crumbs on my chin. 'My lord – er, lords? – I'm not sure . . .'

'Tell him about the message, Yaotl!' Hungry Child hissed. 'What Little Hen was trying to tell us!'

The King added: 'My father has been able to tell us something of the little girl's past. But there was one thing he was unsure about, and it may be the most important detail of all. He seems to think that you may be able to help.' He leaned forward. 'Don't forget how much blood has been spilled over this already!'

I understood him. He was reminding me how important what I was about to tell him might be, perhaps, in his eyes, important enough to be worth all the lives that had been lost over it. I might have taken his words as a threat, but instead I heard them as a warning of what might happen if I was wrong. I could not be sure, but I felt that the King was giving me an opportunity to change my mind and plead ignorance, rather than lead him into an error that might cost still more lives. It did not matter, because I was sure, and the more I thought about it, the more convinced I was that the King was right – what I had to say was probably the most important thing he would ever hear.

'I don't know anything about Little Hen's past, or where she comes from, except that it's somewhere in the East,' I said. 'I couldn't understand a word of what she was saying. Your father – er, Lord Hungry Child – would have to tell you about that. But she wasn't just speaking to us. She made some gestures, when Kindly and Nimble and I were trying to talk to her, and again when we were in Prince of Willows' palace. I don't know whether you've seen them.'

'No,' the King said.

'Perhaps I can get her to . . . No, may I ask my son? She trusts him more than she does me.'

At a gesture from the King, Nimble stepped forward. I smiled weakly at him, and he at me, before he turned to the girl. Squatting in front of her, he spoke her name and then began gesticulating, as we had seen her do, pausing to allow her to follow him. She got the idea straight away, and then ran through the whole sequence on her own. She pulled on her eyelids to make that by-now-familiar round shape. Then she plucked at her chin, and finally she began rubbing her cheeks and temples, as though scrubbing them vigorously to rid them of some deeply ingrained stain.

As I watched the girl repeating her actions, I said: 'My lord, many people lately have seen and heard portents, and you will have heard the rumours from the East. Now, this little girl comes from the East, and I think she is confirming some of what we have been told and what your uncle himself once saw in a vision, when strangers riding on beasts like deer appeared to him in a bird's head.

'When she rubs at her face like that, she is pretending to wash the colour out of her skin. She is showing you a man with a pale face, a long beard and round eyes.'

Maize Ear closed his eyes and sighed as if in despair. Then he said: 'It is as my father thought. You are right, Yaotl. We have heard the rumours. And you know, perhaps, what else has been said about these strangers: that they came in canoes the size of pyramids, and that where they have landed, on the islands far out in the midst of the Divine Sea, they have brought war and disease and slavery.'

'I have heard this, my lord,' I confirmed. 'I heard it from your uncle himself. Lord Montezuma is convinced that they are on their way to call him to account for his conduct, maybe even to supplant him. He thinks one of them may be Quetzalcoatl, the ancient Toltec King.'

'One of them may be, or he may not,' mused the young man on the seat.

His father took up the story. 'I don't think Little Hen knows anything of that. But this is what I was able to gather from what she told me. The man she is describing is her former master. She was a slave in his household, grinding maize. He is a warrior, a general serving the King of Chactemal. When Little Hen's father died, the King gave her to him as part of his share of the spoils from his household. He then sold her to a slave-dealer, who took her to Cozumel and sold her on to Hare. But the important thing, for us, is where her first master came from.

'He was in a giant canoe that was wrecked a long way off the coast. He and some companions got into a smaller boat and paddled until they reached land. Apparently most of them died for lack of food on the way.'

'Surely not,' I said, astonished into speaking out of turn, in spite of the King's presence. How could a boat go so far that a man could starve before reaching the shore?

'That's what the girl was told. Most of the survivors were sacrificed, but this man – her former master – and another lived. She doesn't know what became of the other. Still, you see why Hare thought that what she had to say might be valuable, and why he was right?'

'The rumours are true,' said Maize Ear. 'Pale strangers with beards, coming across the sea . . . but from where?'

'Somewhere far away. Apparently he occasionally used to mutter to himself in his own language, and it was like nothing Little Hen or anyone else had ever heard. And he still speaks her Mayan with a thick accent, although,' he added with a wry smile, 'not as thick as mine!'

'If my uncle learns about this . . .' muttered Maize Ear, half to himself. Then, speaking aloud, he voiced the question that all of us wanted to ask: 'So is this man, who was the girl's master, a man or a god?'

I stared in awe at Little Hen. What manner of being had she been made to serve after her father had died?

'A man,' Hungry Child assured us. 'I told you, this pale stranger at least is merely a general in King Na Chan Can's army. He married one of the King's daughters and has three children by her.'

Then I heard Lily's voice, for the first time since we had come here. She groaned.

I looked around in alarm as she said, seemingly to no one in particular: 'So that was her message. And she ran away! If only she hadn't run away!'

'What's she talking about?' demanded Maize Ear.

I looked at Lily, and then in turn at everyone else gathered around me: at Nimble, still conversing in gestures with Little Hen, at Hungry Child, at Kindly, who had stopped fidgeting and was now watching me intently, and finally at the King.

I opened my mouth to speak, but no words would come out. I was ready with the lie: ready to tell the King how Hare had found a Texcalan warrior in his house, how they had fought, how Little Hen had come to Hare's aid and then slain him as he finished the warrior off. Then I looked at Little Hen, quite oblivious to everything going on around her, and finally I looked at Lily, and saw that the appeal in her eyes was not for another of my lies but for the truth, whatever it cost.

'Yaotl . . .' Lily said.

I interrupted her. 'It's all right. The truth won't hurt anybody now.' I wanted to believe it. 'You'll have to help me, but you won't need to tell any lies.'

The King concurred softly. 'It would be good to have the truth. It has been in short supply in Tetzcoco lately.'

'My lord,' I responded, 'a lot of men have died in or near the house Hare rented in your domain. There's no mystery about most of them, though.' I gave a brief account of the fight of the previous night, when the King's own agents had surprised the Otomies and been massacred by them. His concerned frown deepened to one of consternation when I told him who the captain's men were and where they had come from, but he said nothing.

'But there were two that remained a mystery. You know that when Lily and I went there the first time, we found a dead warrior. And Hare himself had been killed and hidden underneath the house.'

'I have the report of your mistress's trial,' he confirmed.

Suddenly Kindly interrupted. He had never been any respecter of persons. 'I thought we'd worked out that Little Hen and Hare killed the Texcalan and then she killed Hare,' he said, 'or something of the sort, at least. Are you saying that isn't right?'

A look of irritation crossed the King's face, but he did not speak. He looked to me to provide an answer.

'Yes, I am,' I said. 'At the time it seemed the only explanation, because it fitted what we knew, or what we thought we knew. Hare had been wounded by a wooden spike, which we were pretty sure Little Hen had made out of one of her doll's legs. We thought she must have heard Hare and the Texcalan warrior fighting and popped up out of her hole to surprise the Texcalan. Then Hare finished him off with a blade, but Little Hen took the chance to rid herself of the merchant. That's what we thought, and, of course, we put on that little act for Little Hen to see if we were right.'

Nimble looked up from where he had been squatting by the young girl. 'There was something about it Little Hen didn't like,' he reminded me. 'Remember how she kept pulling her hair and shouting at us, and how she pressed that doll into your hands?'

I glanced anxiously at the King to see whether this interruption had annoyed him as much as the previous one, but he was looking at me intently, as if he was content to treat Nimble and Kindly as part of a spectacle being performed before him and was eagerly awaiting my response.

'My son's right,' I said. 'She seemed happy enough with our attempt to reconstruct what had happened, but there was obviously some detail that wasn't quite right, something to do with Hare finding the Texcalan and fighting him, and with how that spike ended up in Hare's back. She kept making this gesture, pulling her hair, and we couldn't understand what she was going on about, although I saw her make the same gesture when she was talking to Lord Hungry Child.'

The former King said: 'This was when she was babbling about what happened to her after she came to Tetzcoco. All I could get then was that it had something to do with a woman, but I couldn't really follow it.'

I heard a sharply indrawn breath from Lily. I turned to her and smiled reassuringly. Then I went on: 'Yes, it had something to do with a woman. A woman with her hair bound up with the ends standing over her forehead, like horns. Which, of course, is just what the girl was trying to show us.'

It was a style worn by most conventional, respectable Aztec

women, the style Lily usually favoured, although at the moment her hair hung untidily over her shoulders.

I hesitated before continuing, speaking to Lily herself in a gentler tone: 'I didn't think of it before your trial. After all, I thought you'd never been to Hare's house before, and it was true what I said to Snake Heart – you didn't have the opportunity to go there after we'd got to Tetzcoco, while I was laid up in that guesthouse. But then Snake Heart asked me if I could prove you hadn't been to the house before we came here. Of course, I couldn't – because you *had* been there! That was what Little Hen was trying to tell us. And no wonder – why should she have gone to Hare's aid when he'd been keeping her in that hole for who knows how long? You, though, were another matter.'

Lily looked down and said nothing.

'Wait a moment!' cried her father. 'You're seriously trying to tell us my daughter took on that Texcalan warrior by herself?' It was hard to say whether he was outraged at my accusation or impressed by Lily's courage. 'It's ridiculous!'

Lily cried: 'No, that isn't true! I didn't know the Texcalan had even been at Hare's house before Yaotl and I went there and found him dead!'

Maize Ear frowned at me. 'So what are you saying?'

'What Lily says is right,' I confirmed. 'The mistake we've all been making is to assume that Hare and the Texcalan were killed at the same time. But they weren't. I think Rattlesnake and Hunter, or some crony of theirs, found the Texcalan at the house and killed him themselves. I'd guess they went there hoping to surprise Lily, discovered that the place had been ransacked and murdered him because they mistook him for a thief and he was in their way.'

'But what was he doing there in the first place?' demanded Kindly.

'Waiting for Lily and me, of course. Ironic, isn't it? He was there for the same reason his murderers were — albeit they were only after Lily, of course, since they didn't know anything about me. But that's how I know he wasn't killed at the same time as Hare. He can't have been. The Texcalans and the Otomies didn't overhear Lily saying we were going to Hare's house until after Hare was dead.' I looked expectantly at Lily.

'It's true,' she said quietly. She kept her eyes fixed on the ground in front of her. 'I killed the merchant. I stabbed him in the back with that wooden spike.'

There was a long silence. The King broke it eventually. 'Are you going to tell us why?' he asked mildly.

'Yaotl was right: I had been to Hare's house before. It was on Eleven Wind.' A quick calculation told me that had been the day before my auction. 'I hadn't arranged to meet him there — to be honest, I was hoping to find him out, so that I could have a look around. I wasn't planning to steal anything,' she added hastily, 'but you've got to remember I had no idea what his message said. I thought if I could find it and find out what it said in advance, it might give me an advantage. At least I would be able to tell Mother of Light what she was buying.'

'So what happened?' I asked.

'He wasn't there. There wasn't much in the house, just a few odds and ends, a sleeping mat and so on, and the big wicker chest. So I had a look in it. And — well, one thing led to another. I took a few things out of it to look at them and soon I had practically everything on the floor.' She took a deep breath, but nothing more came, as though she were reluctant to go on.

Maize Ear cleared his throat loudly.

'I'm sorry,' Lily whispered. 'It's difficult . . . That was when Hare came back, while I was looking at his things, trying to work out whether any of them looked like a message or not.

I didn't hear him. He came up behind me. He . . . There was a struggle. He got me on the floor. I kept screaming at him to stop. I was only looking, I had Mother of Light's ring, but I don't think he heard me. He'd been drinking. I could smell it on his breath. He was holding me down with one hand – he was stronger than he looked – and pulling at his breechcloth with the other.'

Out of the corner of my eye I could see Lily's father looking sick.

'Then all of a sudden there was someone else in the room.'

'Little Hen,' I suggested.

'She must have pushed the box out of the way. She started screaming. She threw herself at Hare, waving this sharp piece of wood. He heard her in time, though, and he managed to get off me and knock the spike out of her hands. Then he . . .' She took a deep breath which turned into a sob.

'Go on,' said Maize Ear grimly.

'I didn't have any choice! He was hitting her, while I was still on the floor, and then he had his hands around her neck. He was mad; he'd have killed her. So I picked up the spike and stabbed him. It was all I could do.'

She was crying now, shaking violently, with tears streaming uncontrollably down her cheeks, and even while my head was whirling with the facts of her story, the things I had begun dimly to guess at now playing themselves out vividly in my imagination, I thought that at last she had been able to speak about this. Some people carried such terrible secrets inside them throughout their lives, letting them gnaw away at them until they were close to death, when they could at last unburden themselves to the priests of Tlazolteotl, the Filth Goddess. I was relieved that perhaps this would not be Lily's fate.

I felt an urge to put an arm around her and whisper some words of comfort, but to my astonishment her father got there first. It was the first time I had ever seen the old man show her the faintest sign of affection, but now he held her against him and crooned softly to her as he might have done when she was a little girl: 'Never mind, love. Never mind. Have a good cry.' Then, in a voice that was more like what I was used to from him, he muttered: 'It's not as if anyone gives a toss about Hare anyway!'

'Let me see if I can guess what happened next,' Hungry Child said. 'You and the girl buried Hare under his chest. What happened to my ring?'

As Lily seemed beyond speech at the moment, I answered for her. 'I think the girl just ran off, through the back of the house, because there was just one set of bloody footprints in the courtyard. Lily buried Hare by herself. Little Hen wouldn't have been any help with that, anyway. As for the ring – Kindly found it hidden in the wall, by the doorpost. Lily took her time wedging it firmly in there, because for the moment she wasn't sure what to do with it, and Hare's empty house seemed the safest place in which to hide it. Remember she was planning to come back the next day, by which time, I guess, she'd have arranged to get it back to Mother of Light. She wouldn't have wanted to risk getting caught wandering around in the city with it. She didn't realize it would be five days before she could return or that anyone else would be taking such an interest in the house.'

The King, who had been staring at me open-mouthed, suddenly laughed. It was a wry chuckle, not like the high-pitched giggle that people said was how his uncle expressed amusement, and it reminded me that he was descended from Hungry Child's father as well as Montezuma's. 'Well done! You sound as though you were there at the time.'

I allowed myself a thin smile. 'My lord, I at least have an alibi! But it was the ring that convinced me eventually. When

I was there with her, Lily didn't have time to hide the ring properly before Rattlesnake and Hunter found her. She could only have done it during a previous visit to the house. But she told me she'd never been there before!'

Lily lifted her head from her father's shoulder and turned her tear-stained face towards me. 'I couldn't tell you the truth,' she said huskily. 'Before we went to Hare's house I thought I could just get the ring and no one would know what had happened. Afterwards, we were never alone.'

The King sat in thoughtful silence, his eyes shining in the moonlight as he looked at each of us in turn.

Kindly said, in a voice that sounded more than ever like a very old man's: 'She was trying to protect herself and the child. Can that be a crime?'

I felt sick. I had no idea what the law of Tetzcoco might have to say about the matter, but if it was the same as in Tenochtitlan then a master would not be allowed to ill-treat a slave, but an occasional beating probably would not count. However, to intervene, in the way Lily had, would surely be murder. As for trying to protect herself, I could imagine Snake Heart demanding harshly why she had not simply run away.

'Interesting,' Maize Ear said slowly.

'My lord . . .' I began, but he held up a hand to silence me.

'The old man has overlooked something. The merchant's body was not found until this afternoon. Lily has not been charged with his murder. I have not been asked to determine whether she did it or not. I can't very well convict Lily of a crime she hasn't been accused of!'

I felt my jaw drop. I was too amazed even to feel relieved, and I listened to the rest of his speech in breathless silence.

'Now, I do have to decide what to do about the charges that *have* been referred to me – against both of you, slave, you and your mistress,' he added severely.

I swallowed nervously as a gesture from Maize Ear drew a servant, bearing a piece of paper, to his side.

'My judges have left it to me to rule on the charges against Tiger Lily,' he said formally, 'that she murdered an unknown man at a house occupied by Hare, the merchant, and that she plotted against me by passing secret messages. And there is the matter of her slave, Yaotl, accused of carrying out or participating in the killing of . . . seven?—' he looked at me quizzically over the paper '—seven men at the same house, last night.'

Then, in a gesture that was far from formal, he seized the tough bark paper in both hands and tore it in half with a single violent jerk.

As the two pieces drifted to the ground, I heard him mutter contemptuously: 'Lawyers!'

Lord Maize Ear sat silently in his high-backed chair and stared out over the lake shining far below in the distance and at the dark, irregular blot in its centre.

The rest of us were too shocked to say anything. Only Little Hen and Lily could be heard, the one singing quietly to herself, the other still weeping, but more calmly now than before.

In the end it was the King's father who broke the silence.

'My lord, what will you do with the child?'

At first, his son seemed not to have heard him, and when he responded he seemed to be answering another question entirely.

'I don't know how it got like this, Father. I wanted to rule as you did, and my grandfather, Lord Hungry Coyote. I wanted to be remembered as a law-maker and a poet and a warrior . . .'

'You were unfortunate in your choice of uncle,' Hungry Child said bluntly.

'I was that! But I grew up down there. What else could I have done? If only Black Flower . . .'

'Montezuma should have known better than to try to place you on the throne. This isn't Mexico. The people don't treat the King as if he were the next best thing to a god, and the chances always were that they'd rebel if they didn't accept him. So you and he ended up with half a kingdom.'

'And that half full of spies and torturers who do whatever they want in my name, but on my uncle's orders.'

I felt a sudden chill, realizing what that meant: Rattlesnake and Hunter and their sinister comrades had seen themselves all along not as their own King's men but as Montezuma's.

'As for the child – I suppose I should send her to Tenochtitlan, shouldn't I? With a full report of everything she has said, for my uncle's soothsayers and sorcerers to pore over.'

Little Hen played with her doll and sang to herself, blissfully unaware that her fate was being discussed. I felt a pang of dread on her behalf, and out of the corner of my eye I saw my son tense.

'Your uncle would put her in a cage,' Hungry Child said coldly. 'Or more likely, have her killed out of hand to prevent word of what she has seen getting out and causing still more panic. And I haven't yet learned all she has to tell me.'

'He watches the sky every night, as if he expects the stars to tell him that the year after next will not be One Reed, the year of Quetzalcoatl . . .' The King paused as though making up his mind.

'You are going to the lands of the Mayans, aren't you? Take her with you, then. Take her home.'

19

Lily shrieked, and then she swore. Her language had always been more colourful than was quite seemly in a respectable Aztec woman.

'You're supposed to be a fucking doctor! I've seen the bodies of sacrificial victims treated better than this!'

Watching her have the dressings on her fingers changed was, I had learned, a hazardous pastime. She was apt to lash out at anyone nearby, including me, so I had left her and the doctor in a courtyard while I came out to sit at the front of the secluded little villa Maize Ear had installed us in.

There was a small pond, little more really than a large basin lined with pink porphyry, in front of it, and I watched a pair of ducks descend to take a drink before flapping clumsily into the air again.

'A bit early for them to be courting, isn't it?' I said.

'Is that another thing you shouldn't do in the Useless Days?' Nimble asked.

I grinned. 'Besides arguing, you mean?' I replied as another tirade came from within the house.

'Lily's not arguing,' Kindly said knowingly. 'She's complaining. A very different thing, especially for women!' His expression changed abruptly as the doctor appeared. He had the look of a man who had a narrow escape from death. His cloak and the black pitch that covered his face were spotted

with blood, as though he had been in a fight with a wild
animal.

'How's the patient?' I asked.

'She'll live,' the man grunted.

'Will the nails grow back?' Kindly demanded anxiously.

The doctor sighed. 'You asked me that yesterday and the day
before. It's too early to be sure. All I can say is that there's no
reason why not – the flesh isn't too inflamed, which is more
than can be said for the lady's temper!'

I looked up at him as he left, the hem of his black cloak bil-
lowing at his heels, and caught sight of another person coming
along the path towards us.

I stood up. 'Who's this?' I asked, suddenly feeling nervous.
If the newcomer was who I thought she was then it was time
to say something I had been putting off ever since the evening
at the summit of the hill, a few days before, when the King and
his son had made their pact: Lily's and my life, in return for
Hungry Child's promise to leave the realm the moment the
Useless Days were over, and never return.

'Mother of Light,' said Kindly.

I took it upon myself to greet her as I thought fitting for a
royal concubine. 'Lady,' I said formally, 'you have expended
breath to come here. You are weary; you are hungry. Please,
rest and have something . . .' I suddenly found myself lost for
words as I caught sight of her hand.

A great greenstone in the shape of a skull adorned it.

'Thank you,' she said, clearly amused. 'It's all right – I've
eaten.'

'You off, then?' enquired Kindly casually.

'Tomorrow,' she confirmed, 'before sunrise. Maize Ear is
very anxious to have his kingdom back again!'

I drew breath to speak and let it out again. Then I tried once
more, this time managing to get as far as saying the lady's name.

She looked at me curiously. 'What is it?'

Forcing the words out one by one, I said: 'Take my son with you.'

Nimble almost fell into the pond. 'What?' he spluttered. 'Father, have you gone mad? I'm not going . . .'

Mother of Light looked at him and then at me. 'Why?' she asked.

'He could be useful on your long journey. He's tough and resourceful, and Little Hen trusts him. He and Hungry Child could . . .'

'Bugger useful!' my son cried. He was almost in tears. 'What are you talking about? I'm staying here! I can't leave you!'

I sighed. 'You're not staying here,' I said patiently. 'For one thing, Maize Ear isn't going to let us be his guests for ever. He gave us this place until Lily was better, remember? But he doesn't want us in his kingdom any longer than we have to be. And that's my point – as long as you and I and Kindly and Lily are here, Lord Feathered in Black is going to keep coming after us. Not to mention the captain!'

'So let's all go!'

Mother of Light frowned. 'The boy, yes,' she said. 'Hungry Child may well agree, especially if he can help look after the girl. But . . .'

Clearly she balked at the prospect of dragging the four of us along with her and Hungry Child, but Kindly set her mind at rest. 'Can't,' he said. 'I'm too old to uproot myself now and go trekking over mountains and through jungles, and Lily's simply not up to it yet.'

'But you, Father . . .'

I groaned. I had agonized over this choice for days, tossing and turning on my sleeping mat every night, and staring at my reflection in the little pond for half a day as if I expected it to speak to me and tell me what to do. Even now, I could not convince myself that the decision I had made was the right one.

'Nimble, I'm an Aztec. For good or ill, I belong down there, in that anthill in the middle of the lake. My family's there. I may have to face old Black Feathers one day, for their sake. Your uncle Lion can protect them for now, but that could change – he could get himself killed in battle, or the Chief Minister could find some way of having him turned out of office. If that happens, I've got to be there. Can't you see that?'

'I'm an Aztec too,' the lad said sullenly.

'Only by birth. You were brought up Tarascan. You've got no reason to be here, or in Tenochtitlan, apart from me. You can make a new life among the Mayans. But if you stay here, then sooner or later Lord Feathered in Black or the captain will find you.'

'But . . .'

'Look, once things are settled here, I'll come and find you,' I said. 'I promise. I will eat earth!' I made the ritual gesture, touching the ground and my mouth with my fingertips. 'But until then . . . Nimble, I'm sorry. I'm needed here.'

And that at least was the truth, I told myself, as I glanced over my shoulder at the villa where Lily was recovering from her ordeal. Lying to Nimble had been almost as hard to bear as the thought of separation, but how could I tell him what it was that really held me here, when I only half understood it myself?

'So you're sending me away, then.'

Just in time, before I could say 'yes' I recognized the challenge in his statement. He was asking me if I was giving him an order. If I were, perhaps he would obey it; but I saw, in that moment, what that one short word would cost us both.

With my eyes on his strained, tear-stained face, which was

half distraught and half defiant, I said: 'Nimble, I can't send you anywhere. You know that, and so do I. But I'm asking you, for both our sakes. Go where you can be safe, where you don't have to hide all the time. Please.'

There was a long silence. Then, at last, I heard the lad's choked voice mumble brokenly: 'If that's what you want, Father, then I'll do it.' He stood up, looked briefly at me and Mother of Light and then turned on his heel. 'I'm going in to say goodbye to Lily,' he said shortly over his shoulder.

'He resents you for making him leave you,' the woman observed.

'He'll come round,' Kindly said roughly, 'and his father's right: he'll be much safer where you're going. He's a useful lad.'

'I meant what I said, you know,' I said to no one in particular. 'I'll come after him when I can.' I turned to Mother of Light. 'Don't let him forget it.'

She regarded me shrewdly for a few moments. 'You'll have to look for us in the jungle,' she reminded me. 'But you're talented that way, aren't you? You found me and Hungry Child, and the meaning of Little Hen's message, and you knew what had happened at Hare's house.'

'That's enough,' muttered Kindly darkly. 'It'll go to his head.'

The woman hesitated, looking away, surveying the countryside spread out below the hill of Tetzcotzinco as though something down there had caught her attention. When she turned back towards me, it was with the air of having made a decision.

'I can think of one mystery you haven't solved, though.'

'What?' I asked.

She stood up. 'What became of the Lady of Tollan?'

For a moment I stared mutely at her, uncomprehending.

The word formed only slowly on my lips, so slowly that I was barely aware I had uttered it: 'You?'

Then I understood.

Mother of Light: the concubine of whom no record existed, yet who was the only one Hungry Child had kept by him, concealed in a house kept empty for her by his edict; the favourite of a King whose own death was only the second he had faked, the first being her execution; the talented poetess.

Speechless, I could only gape stupidly at her. It was Kindly who spoke up, in his usual blunt fashion. 'Well, that explains something.'

'What?' I asked as the woman looked at him curiously.

'Why Hungry Child keeps you around. Aren't you like that palace you were living in, and the ring you're wearing – a reminder of how he let himself be taken in?'

I was horrified, imagining the woman would strike him across the face or, worse, go running to Maize Ear and demand that we all be killed immediately, but to my surprise she did neither.

'Oh, I don't think so,' she said softly. She smiled. 'I think after all these years I've a pretty good idea why I'm still with him.'

I found my voice. 'When I saw you in Maize Ear's palace, you told me not to believe everything I heard. So what really happened between you and Prince of Willows? Why didn't Hungry Child have you killed as well?'

'Because he knew there was nothing to it! The young man was a fine poet, but everything he composed was on conventional themes – in praise of the gods, the fragility of life and so on. I used to encourage him, and I suppose he was flattered by the attention. I was very young, you see – but there really was nothing more to it than that.' She sighed. 'Some informer in Prince of Willows' household started circulating rumours about what was in his poems. It was hard to deny them because, of course, there's no way of setting the words of a poem down exactly. The informer was probably an Aztec spy, of course. The King had to act before it became a scandal, but he wouldn't sit in judgement on his own son because he didn't want to appear biased. It never occurred to him that your Emperor Montezuma might have his own interest in what happened to his son. He can be strangely naive. But after his son died he came to me and told me that no more innocent blood was going to be shed on account of his own stupidity.'

We all sat in thoughtful silence for a few moments. I reflected on the odd character of the former King, whose reputation for wisdom and scrupulous fairness seemed belied by his inability to understand people. Perhaps that was what happened if you grew up in a palace.

Kindly broke the silence again. 'So you re-created yourself as Mother of Light? Weren't you afraid someone would recognize you?'

'No. Kindly, I stayed hidden in that empty palace for such a long time – from the time Prince of Willows was killed to the day of his father's funeral. More than ten years! Can you imagine that? By the time I started to come out again, scarcely anyone would have remembered what I'd looked like as a girl.'

'And those who did would mostly have been palace servants,' Kindly interjected sardonically, 'so I suppose a number of potential witnesses were conveniently sacrificed at the King's funeral!'

'You were alone in that palace all that time?' I asked wonderingly.

'Hungry Child came when he could – and, yes, I'm sure it was out of remorse as much as love to begin with, but not in the end. It didn't matter. Without him and the books he brought and the poems we composed and learned together, I'd probably have gone mad.' She looked at me, her expression suddenly earnest, as though it was particularly important that I should understand what she was about to say next: perhaps it represented the last chance for her royal lover to explain himself to his people before he left them for good. 'He's a strange man, in some ways, and I know others find him cold and forbidding, but they don't understand what he's trying to do. He's seen something, Yaotl – something in the movements of the stars and in the calendar, some omen. His father saw it too, and they both reached the same conclusion. There is some power beyond the Thirteen Heavens, older and stronger than any of the gods we recognize. Hungry Coyote and Hungry Child worshipped it as the Lord of the Near and the Nigh, but that wasn't the same as understanding it. Maybe no human ever can understand it, but Hungry Child will never stop trying. He thinks the pale men that appeared in the East – men like Little Hen's old master – may be closer to this thing than we are. That's the real reason we have to go – do you see that?'

I had no answer. It was beyond me. I could cope with the gods I knew, at least to the extent of ignoring them when I could and trying to placate them when I could not, but trying to understand them was quite another matter. I was starting to feel that life here on Earth was more than mysterious enough, without needing to probe beyond the Thirteen Heavens.

Eventually, with a sigh, Mother of Light turned and began walking slowly towards the house.

'I'm going to see Lily,' she said. 'And I have to speak to your son about the journey. Are you coming in too?'

Afterword

Aztec Lawyers?

Much of the inspiration for *City of Spies* came from an excellent book by Jerome Offner, *Law and Politics in Aztec Texcoco* (Cambridge University Press, 1983).* Offner brings together all the sources dealing with the Tetzcocan legal system and shows how elaborate it was. He also discusses briefly the question whether this system included lawyers.

Unfortunately there is no definitive answer to this; as with so many details of Aztec life, there simply is not enough information to say with certainty one way or the other. True, Book X of the Florentine Codex contains descriptions of 'the Attorney' (*Tepantlato*) and 'the Solicitor' (*Tlacihuitiani*); but as Offner concedes, these have 'a decidedly post-conquest ring to them', and probably represent practitioners in the busy courts of colonial New Spain.

That does not mean there were no lawyers in Mexico before the conquest, however; merely that we have no evidence as to what they may have been like. I used to be a lawyer, and I can easily imagine how expert advocates and

---

*Offner prefers an alternative name for Tetcoco. Incidentally, this is probably the place at which to point out that, of course, 'inspiration' is not the same as 'guidance' and any mistakes made or liberties taken are solely my responsibility.

advisers might have thrived in a legal system as complex as Tetzcoco's. In fact, the system might well not have been able to function without them. As Obsidian Tongue points out, there were four distinct courts in the city, each responsible for trying offences or resolving disputes concerning different things and classes of person. The potential for technical arguments over which court had jurisdiction over what must have been considerable. This might not have mattered in a state where the ruler's whim was enough to settle any dispute, regardless of the law, but – remarkably for a culture teetering on the edge of the Bronze Age – Tetzcoco does not appear to have been that kind of place.

Obsidian Tongue, Snake Heart and the rather formally constituted profession they represent are therefore necessarily a blend of fact and imagination. The institutions and the physical descriptions of the courts are broadly as I understand them to have been, from my no doubt imperfect interpretation of the sources and allowing for a certain amount of simplification. The procedure is, of course, entirely invented, since naturally we have no transcripts of an Aztec trial. I hope it rings true enough, though. Besides, I've always enjoyed lawyer jokes!